Åke Edwardson is one of Scandinavia's most successful crime writers. He has won numerous awards, including the Swedish Academy of Crime Writers' Award three times. His Erik Winter series has been published in twelve countries.

Praise for *Sun and Shadow* by Åke Edwardson

"Åke Edwardson is a three-time winner of the Swedish Academy of Crime Writers' Award and it's easy to see why. He weaves a rich, psychologically satisfying tale. His writing is nuanced and literary, and his characters are deep and fascinating. The recurring themes of sun and shadow, light and dark, good and evil, are elegantly interwoven within the narrative. . . . Readers looking for a gritty, well-paced, thoughtful thriller will appreciate Edwardson's masterful novel."
—*I Love A Mystery*

"Edwardson, winner of three Crime Writers' awards from the Swedish Academy, has penned a solid procedural neatly balancing the professional and personal lives of Winter and co."
—*Kirkus Reviews*

"Mystery fans on this side of the Atlantic can be grateful that the travails of Erik Winter, the youngest chief inspector in Sweden, are now available in English. . . . This dark police procedural is a top-notch work, suspenseful to the very end, with appealing characters."
—*Library Journal* (starred review)

Åke Edwardson

SUN and SHADOW

An Erik Winter Novel

Translated from the Swedish
by Laurie Thompson

Penguin Books

PENGUIN BOOKS

Published by the Penguin Group

Penguin Group (USA) Inc., 375 Hudson Street, New York, New York 10014, U.S.A.

Penguin Group (Canada), 90 Eglinton Avenue East, Suite 700, Toronto,
Ontario, Canada M4P 2Y3 (a division of Pearson Penguin Canada Inc.)

Penguin Books Ltd, 80 Strand, London WC2R 0RL, England

Penguin Ireland, 25 St Stephen's Green, Dublin 2, Ireland (a division of Penguin Books Ltd)

Penguin Group (Australia), 250 Camberwell Road, Camberwell,
Victoria 3124, Australia (a division of Pearson Australia Group Pty Ltd)

Penguin Books India Pvt Ltd, 11 Community Centre, Panchsheel Park, New Delhi – 110 017, India

Penguin Group (NZ), cnr Airborne and Rosedale Roads, Albany,
Auckland 1310, New Zealand (a division of Pearson New Zealand Ltd)

Penguin Books (South Africa) (Pty) Ltd, 24 Sturdee Avenue,
Rosebank, Johannesburg 2196, South Africa

Penguin Books Ltd, Registered Offices:
80 Strand, London WC2R 0RL, England

First published in the United States of America by Viking Penguin,
a member of Penguin Group (USA) Inc. 2005
Published in Penguin Books 2006

10 9 8 7 6 5 4 3 2 1

Originally published in Swedish as *Sol och skugga* by Norstedts Forlag, Stockholm.

Grateful acknowledgment is made for permission to reprint excerpts from the following copyrighted works: "Lime Tree Arbour" by Nick Cave. Reprinted by permission of Nick Cave and Mute Song Limited. "Back in Your Arms" by Bruce Springsteen. Copyright © 1998 Bruce Springsteen. Reprinted by permission. International copyright secured. All rights reserved. "Happy" by Bruce Springsteen. Copyright © 1998 Bruce Springsteen. Reprinted by permission. International copyright secured. All rights reserved. "The Price You Pay" by Bruce Springsteen. Copyright © 1980 Bruce Springsteen. Reprinted by permission. International copyright secured. All rights reserved.

PUBLISHER'S NOTE
This is a work of fiction. Names, characters, places, and incidents either are the product of the author's imagination or are used fictitiously, and any resemblance to actual persons, living or dead, business establishments, events, or locales is entirely coincidental.

THE LIBRARY OF CONGRESS HAS CATALOGED THE HARDCOVER EDITION AS FOLLOWS:
Edwardson, Åke, —
   [Sol och skugga. English]
   Sun and shadow / Åke Edwardson.
      p.   cm.
   ISBN 0-670-03415-0 (hc.)
   ISBN 0 14 30.3718 8 (pbk.)
   I. Title.
PT9876.15.D93S6513 2005
839.73'74—dc22 2004061157

Printed in the United States of America   Set in Dante   Designed by Francesca Belanger
Map by Reg Piggott   Photograph by Connie Wellnitz, Digital Vision Ltd.

For Rita

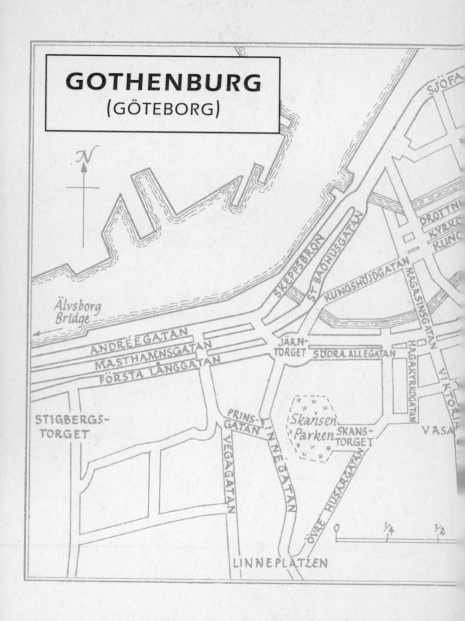

GOTHENBURG
(GÖTEBORG)

N

Älvsborg Bridge

SJÖFA

DROTTNI

KYRKG

KUNG

SKEPPSBRON

ST BADHUSGATAN

KUNGSHÖJDGATAN

MAGASINSGATAN

ANDRÉEGATAN

MASTHAMNSGATAN

FÖRSTA LÅNGGATAN

JÄRN-TORGET

SÖDRA ALLÉGATAN

HAGAKYRKOGATAN

VIKTORIA

STIGBERGS-TORGET

PRINS-GATAN

VEGAGATAN

LINNÉGATAN

Skansen Parken

SKANS-TORGET

ÖVRE HUSARGATAN

VASA

¼   ½

LINNÉPLATZEN

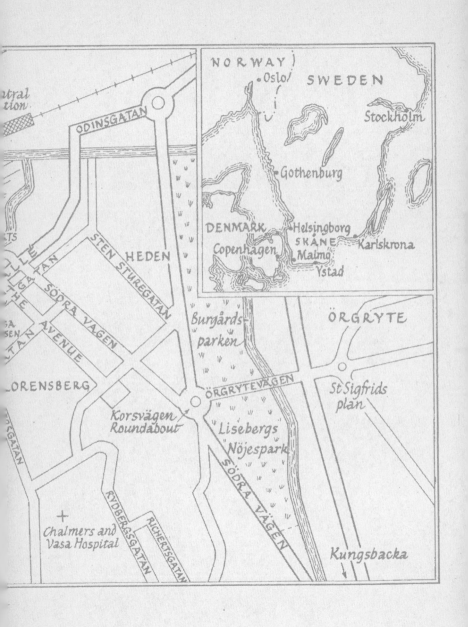

NORWAY

SWEDEN

• Oslo

Stockholm

• Gothenburg

DENMARK
Copenhagen

• Helsingborg
SKÅNE
Malmö
Ystad

Karlskrona

ntral
tion

ODINSGATAN

STEN STUREGATAN

HEDEN

Burgårds-
parken

ÖRGRYTE

LE TAN

SÖDRA VÄGEN

THE

ALTAN AVENUE

ÖRGRYTEVÄGEN

St Sigfrids
plän

LORENSBERG

Korsvägen
Roundabout

Lisebergs
Nöjespark

GATAN

RYDBERGSGATAN

RICHERTSGATAN

SÖDRA VÄGEN

✝
Chalmers and
Vasa Hospital

Kungsbacka

SEPTEMBER

1

It had started raining. Simon Morelius adjusted the radio. No instructions from HQ for five minutes. It was nearly ten, and everything was quiet. Two women crossed the road and one turned to look at the police car and smiled. Greger Bartram raised his hand in greeting.

"Twenty-seven and good-looking," he said. "And she thinks the same about me."

"She was smiling at me, not you," Morelius said.

"She looked me straight in the eye," Bartram said.

The lights changed and Bartram drove on to the roundabout at Korsvägen.

"Yeah, and found there was nobody home," Morelius said.

"Ha, ha."

"She looked you in the eye and found nobody home. Just a middle-aged cop at the wheel of a squad car and then—"

A woman's voice on the radio. "Nine-one-twenty. Nine-one-twenty, come." A mumbled response from somewhere or other. Then the woman's voice again. "There's somebody lying outside Focus at the Liseberg amusement park, drunk or ill, with a crowd of kids standing around."

They heard the patrol who'd responded to the call.

"Roger. We're in Prinsgatan and will head for Focus."

Morelius reached for the microphone:

"Eleven-ten here. We're closer, we're in Korsvägen and will deal with it."

"Okay, eleven-ten."

The patrol car from the Lorensberg police district left the round-about and drove up to the shopping center. A group of youths were huddled together in the car park. As the police pulled up, one of them ran over to the door that Bartram had just opened.

"It was me who called," said a girl who looked no more than sixteen. She was waving her mobile phone as if it might confirm what she'd just said. Her hair was straight and shiny, molded to her head by the rain. Big, scared eyes. She smelled of alcohol and tobacco. Arms flailing. "She's lying over here. Maria's lying over here, but she's better now."

"I'll call an ambulance," Bartram said.

Morelius went with the girl to the group of youngsters. They were gathered in a semicircle around a girl who was slowly getting to her feet. As Morelius came up to her she staggered and he reached out an arm to grab hold of her. She weighed nothing. She looked like the twin of the girl they'd been talking to, but her eyes were miles away. Certainly nobody at home here, thought Morelius.

She stank of alcohol and vomit. Morelius could feel the sticky mess under his shoes. Be careful not to slip. Seconds later the girl was staring at the police officer, her eyes suddenly focused.

"I want to go home," she said.

"What have you taken?" Morelius asked.

"No-nothing," she said. "Just a couple of beers."

"A couple of beers, eh?" Morelius eyed the group of friends. "What has she got inside her? This is important. If you know, speak up now, and I mean RIGHT NOW, DAMMIT." They looked frightened.

"It's like she said," a boy in a woolly hat and a tracksuit top piped up. "A couple of beers . . . and some liquor."

"Liquor? What liquor? Who's got the bottle?"

They looked at one another.

"THE BOTTLE," Morelius said.

The boy in the woolly hat put his hand inside his baggy top and produced a bottle. Bartram held it up in the glow from one of the street-lights.

"There's no label," he said.

"Er . . . no."

"What is it?" asked Bartram, as they all heard the sirens from an approaching ambulance. "What kind of piss is this? Is it moonshine?"

"Yes . . . I think so," said the boy. "I bought it off a friend." He looked as if he were about to burst into tears. "He said it was completely okay."

"Well, it's not okay," Morelius said. "He could feel the girl's weight increase on his arm. She was about to pass out again. "Where's that damn ambulance?"

They were in the ER waiting room. The girl had been taken for treatment. Twenty minutes later a doctor appeared. Morelius could see from his face that she was all right.

A young boy was shuffling nervously in the waiting room. Morelius recognized him. Maybe he'd been one of those outside Focus. How had he got here?

"Alcohol in a young body, well . . . not a good combination."

"How is she?"

"Not too bad, under the circumstances. She'll have to stay here overnight, though."

"So the stuff she drank was . . . okay?" Bartram asked.

The doctor gave him an odd look. "You mean the moonshine? Is that ever okay?"

"You know what I mean, for fuck's sake."

The doctor eyed him up and down.

"There's no need to lose your temper," he said. He stroked his hand over his white coat as if to brush off Bartram's outburst. "No need at all."

"I'm sorry," Bartram said. "It's just that we care about the girl. Some of us police officers are like that."

"We just want to know if she's . . . done any other damage to herself, apart from the usual, whether the stuff was more dangerous than liquor normally is," Morelius said.

The doctor looked at them doubtfully, as if he thought they were putting him on.

"Everything seems to be normal at the moment," he said. "But we leave nothing to chance here. Has her family been contacted, by the way?"

"Yes," Morelius said. "Her mom should be here any moment."

"Well . . . in that case," said the doctor, starting to leave.

"Thank you, Doctor," Bartram said.

They watched the doctor disappear through the swinging doors. "Arrogant bastard," Bartram said.

"He no doubt thinks the same about you."

Bartram muttered something inaudible and looked at his colleague. It was shortly after eleven and Morelius's face seemed speckled in the bright light of the waiting room.

"So she's the vicar's daughter, is she? Are you sure? Hanne Östergaard, who heals our suffering souls."

"There's no need to be sarcastic." Morelius had the girl's purse in his hand. He'd examined her ID card. "Maria Östergaard. An address in Örgryte. Our police chaplain is called Hanne Östergaard and lives in Örgryte. And she has a daughter called Maria."

"How do you know all that?"

"Does it matter?"

"No, no."

"I'm not a hundred percent certain." A woman hurried in through the door. "Now I'm certain," said Morelius, and went over to Hanne.

"Where's Maria?" she asked. "Where is she, Simon?"

"She's still in the treatment room, or whatever it's called," Morelius said. "But everything seems to be all right."

"All right? Everything seems to be all right?" Hanne looked as if she were close to hysterics. "Is there anybody here who can show me where to go?" A nurse had just come in through the swinging doors and the police officers watched as Hanne half-ran into the corridor leading to the treatment room.

The boy who'd been hovering in the background followed her. He glanced over his shoulder, then disappeared into the corridor.

"You were right, dammit," Bartram said. "And you're on first-name terms."

Morelius didn't answer.

"Not even vicars are spared," Bartram said.

"From what?"

"From shattering events involving their nearest and dearest. You don't have any children, to my knowledge."

"No. But it looks as though this business is going to have a happy ending."

"Thanks to us."

"Maybe. A young kid has too much to drink and throws up. She'd probably have come around after a while and her friends would have helped her to get home. Happens all the time. Hasn't it happened to you?"

"Me? Not that I remember."

"That doesn't mean a thing."

"Let's go," Bartram said.

They drove toward the center of town, past Chalmers and Vasa Hospital. The rain had gotten worse. Streetlights seemed fainter now, as if wrapped up in the night. Bartram stopped at a red light. Two women crossed the street but neither turned to look at the patrol car and smile. Morelius adjusted the radio. They listened in to the spasmodic calls. A bewildered old pensioner who'd been reported missing in Änggården a few hours ago had turned up again. A heated discussion taking place in an apartment in Kortedala had calmed down by the time their colleagues arrived. A drunk leaning against a stationary tram in Brunnsparken had fallen over when it moved off. Could that be classified as a traffic accident? Bartram thought to himself.

Morelius was thinking about Hanne Östergaard and the conversation he'd had with her a couple of weeks ago. Bartram hadn't asked any more questions, and he was grateful for that.

Erik Winter turned off the light and left his office. It had stopped raining. He cycled home through Heden, giving way to somebody in Vasagatan who seemed to assume there was nobody else in the road. Water splashed all over his trousers, probably other crap as well. It was too dark to see. He had thought of stopping in at the covered market, but decided to pass. His mobile rang. He stopped and took it out of the inside pocket of his raincoat.

"I can't make up my mind about the sofa," Angela said when he answered. "I just had to get some advice without delay."

"I hope you're not lifting anything?"

"No, of course not."

"I think you should bring it with you if you can't make up your mind. I've got loads of room, after all."

"But where would we put it?"

"Can't this wait until tonight?"

"I wanted to be as well prepared as possible."

"Hmm."

"It's a big decision, this."

"I know."

"Have you really thought it through? Maybe we should buy a house . . ."

"Come on, Angela."

"All right, all right. It's just that everything's so bewildering. Everything."

Maybe that's the right word, Winter thought, brushing some drops of rain off his shoulder. Bewildering. For the first time in his adult life he was about to start living with somebody else. He and Angela had been conducting an affair for years, but now they were going to live together. He had the feeling that she was the driving force behind the decision. No, that wasn't fair. He would have to accept some of the responsibility as well.

There was no alternative. Either they would live together or . . . it would be over. But they'd gone beyond that now. He wouldn't dare to call it off. The loneliness would be too great, no doubt about it. It would make things worse. Lonely into the new millennium. New Year's Eve: a disc in the CD player and a glass of something. That would be it. Bleak prospects lit up by all the fireworks.

Soon there would be only three months left before the year 2000.

And he was going to be forty, and before long not the youngest detective chief inspector in Sweden anymore.

Winter got back on his bike.

"See you at eight," Angela said, and he switched off his phone.

It was night in the apartment, no lights burning anymore. A standard lamp had been on all day, but the bulb had gone. As dawn broke, autumn sidled in through the venetian blinds and a roller blind in the bedroom let in patches of light.

The fridge was humming away. There were wineglasses on the kitchen table, and an empty wine bottle. On the work surface next to the cooker was an oblong dish with some dried-up lumps of tagliatelle. Next to it was a pan with the dregs of some mushroom sauce. The sauce had turned black. Three slices of tomato were slowly decomposing on a wooden chopping board.

Three dinner plates were in the dishwasher, with some side plates and more glasses, cutlery, another saucepan.

The tap was dripping; it needed a new washer. The sound could be heard throughout the apartment, day and night, but the couple on the living room sofa didn't hear a thing.

Items of clothing were strewn around them and traced a line from the kitchen and through the hall to the living room: men's socks, a couple of pairs of trousers, a pair of stockings, a skimpy sweater. Near the sofa were a blouse, a shirt, some underwear. The sounds of the night drifted in through the window. Trams. A few cars. A sudden gust of wind. A laugh from somebody on the way home from a restaurant.

The man and woman were naked. They were holding hands. They were turned toward each other. There was something odd about their heads.

Was that right? Was that how it should be? Was that the image? He tried to conjure it up, tried to envisage it.

He was in the kitchen. He walked through the hall. The clothes were on the floor. He put his hand over his eyes as he approached the sofa. Then he looked. Nobody there. He looked again and there they were, facing each other. Her face was so familiar.

Their heads. Their HEADS.

He rubbed his eyes. Now he could hear the street noise as he opened the car door. He could feel the rain on his face as he got out of the car and stood in the street in front of the building.

He wished he could put the clock back. The people strolling down the street didn't know, they knew nothing. Nothing. They didn't know they were living in paradise.

 OCTOBER

2

Winter stood in the hall without switching on the light. Angela would be home in an hour, if not sooner.

How long had he been living here? Ten years? Was it really ten years? Something like that. How many women had he brought back to his apartment during all that time? He preferred not to think about it. He could hold up both hands and count his fingers: that would probably be enough.

He walked through the rooms illuminated by the light from the city streets. He smiled. Soon he'd have to wade through piles of underwear in the hall. A stocking draped over the back of the sofa. He knew Angela. You need a bit of untidiness in your life, she'd said. You'll bring chaos, he'd said. About time, was her reply.

What if she says no in the end? he'd thought not very long ago. Grown tired of him?

The trams came and went in Vasaplatsen down below. The wall opposite the big window in the living room was white in the evening glow. Just to the side was the shiny red dot on the CD player. Winter went over to it and took out the Springsteen box he'd been sent at great expense last autumn by his London friend, DCI Steve MacDonald. He'd done it so that Winter would be impressed by how much the postage had cost and listen as seriously as he could. Winter liked jazz and MacDonald accepted that, but he'd damn well see to it that Winter got a decent education in all the good things he'd missed during his sheltered youth, growing up with John Coltrane.

The strange thing was that he listened to even more jazz now that he'd started listening to rock as well, and he could hear different nuances in Coltrane, a new dark side. To his surprise he'd also discovered things he liked in simple rock. Perhaps that was just it. The simplicity.

As you grow older you search for simplicity. I'm getting older. I'll soon be forty. That's old, relatively speaking. Maybe I'm not a simple person, but I can learn, still. Or perhaps I've always been a simple soul. Angela has noticed that. That's why she's picked me out of ten thousand others.

He put the fourth disc into the CD player and selected the tenth track, his favorite all this last month, or at least ever since the decision was made. The decision. *I'm happy with you in my arms, I'm happy with you in my heart, happy when I taste your kiss, I'm happy in love like this.* The simple life. Angela had understood. Maybe he would find happiness.

The ballad oozed through the room as he got undressed, *happy, baby, come the dark,* and suddenly he was in the shower thinking of nothing. He could hear the music through the water, and then the sound of a key as Angela let herself in.

Lars Bergenhem drove over Älvsborg Bridge. The car was rocking in the wind. He was off duty, and when he came to the tunnel he wondered what the hell he was doing there. In the tunnel. In the car. He could be sitting at home, watching his two-year-old daughter as she slept. That's what he used to do. Ada would sleep, and he would watch. He could be watching Martina cleaning up the kitchen after Ada's evening meal. He could be doing the cleaning up himself.

It had started the way it always did. A word neither of them understood. After Ada had fallen asleep it was so quiet that he didn't have the strength to try to find words that wouldn't make everything worse. He was used to investigations, but this was too much for him. He was a detective, but he wasn't a detective of love. Didn't that come from some song or other? "Detective of love?" Elvis Costello? "Watching the Detectives."

He turned northward when he came to Frölunda Torg, heading back. A drive he'd done before, but not for a long time.

Everything had been fine. The apprehension inside him had long since died away. Had it come back? Was it his fault? Was it to do with him or Martina? Those words that neither of them wanted to understand. Where did they come from? It was like a headache.

His townhouse looked cozy when he got out of the car. Cozy. There were more lights on than necessary.

Martina was in the kitchen with a cup of tea. She'd been crying and he felt guilty. He had to say something.

"Is Ada asleep?"

"Yes."

"Good."

"What is?"

"That she's asleep. Ada."

"What are you talking about? You just march out of the house and drive off, then come back home as if nothing had happened."

"What did happen?"

"And you need to ask?"

"Was it me who started it?"

She didn't answer. Her head was bowed but he knew she was crying again. He could do one of two things. Either say something sensible or go out to the car and drive over the bridge again.

"Martina . . ."

She raised her head and looked at him.

"We're both tired," he said.

"Tired? Is that it? We should be merry and bright and be thinking about Christmas that's just around the corner. Ada has started talk . . ." She let her head sink down toward the table again.

He was searching for words. The wall clock was ticking louder than before.

"Is it going to be like this until I go back on duty?" he said.

She muttered something.

"I beg your pardon?"

"Not everything is about you going back on duty again," she said. "Does everything have to be calm and quiet so that you have enough strength to work as a detective?"

"You know what I mean."

"I won't know anything at all soon."

He stood up and went to Ada's room and watched the girl sleeping with her thumb in her mouth. She didn't make a sound. He bent down over her face and listened for her breathing, and heard a faint peep as she breathed in through her nose.

They had let things calm down as far as was possible. He was drinking coffee in the living room and Martina came in from the kitchen.

"Winter and Angela are going to live together," he said.

"Why do you call him Winter when his name's Erik? People don't refer to us as Bergenhem and Martina, do they?"

"No, of course not, but people just usually call him Winter."

"It's not so personal that way, is that it? Does that make it easier? Is that what it's all about?"

"I . . . I really don't know."

Martina had met Angela for the first time nearly two years earlier, just before Ada was born. It had been pretty dramatic. Bergenhem had been badly injured and had disappeared and Winter had asked Angela to go with Martina in the ambulance while he searched for his colleague.

"I hope it turns out well," she said as he sat, lost in thought. "I think it will."

"What?"

"The move. Moving in together. Erik and Angela. I hope it goes well."

"Yes."

"Where are they going to live?"

"I haven't asked. But I . . . well, I suppose the obvious place is his apartment. It's bigger than hers."

"How do you know?"

He looked at her. She was smiling now.

"I don't know, to tell you the truth," he said. "It's funny. I just took it for granted."

"Perhaps they'll buy a house."

"I can't imagine Winter in a house."

"Why not?"

"I don't know. . . . He seems part of the city somehow. High-rise buildings, squares, taxis."

"I don't think so. He'll buy an old house in Långedrag and fill it with his family."

"That sounds like Utopia."

"It will soon be the year 2000," she said. "Anything can happen."

Not quite anything, he thought. Some things mustn't happen. It would be best if everything stays as it is, as it is just now.

"There might be a moving-in party," she said. "When's it happening?"

"What?"

"Them moving in together, into wherever it is they're going to live?"

"Before Christmas, I think."

"Good. I'm happy for them."

3

Angela arrived before eight. Her hair was down and gleamed in the light from the staircase following her in through the open door. Perhaps she had a new expression in her eyes, something he hadn't previously noticed: a conviction that there was a future for them despite everything. But there was something else as well. The other thing. It appeared as a different sort of light in her eyes, as if the strong lamps on the staircase had shone through the back of her head and given them a special glow.

She pulled off her boots and dirty water splashed onto the parquet floor. Winter saw, but made no comment. Angela knew that he had noticed. She raised both hands over her head.

"It won't happen again," she said.

"What won't?"

"I saw you looking."

"And?"

"You were thinking at that moment: what the hell is going to happen, what will my floor look like once she's moved in."

"Hmm."

"It's something you'll have to work on," she said.

"Meanwhile I suppose I'd better go around to your place with muddy shoes and wander around the apartment with them on and jump up onto the bed and the armchairs. Get it out of me, as it were."

"As I said. Work on it."

He took her hand and they went into the kitchen. There was a smell of coffee and warm bread. On the table was a tub of butter, Västerbotten cheese, radishes, coarse liver pâté, cornichons.

"A banquet," she said.

"Rustic and simple. But elegant even so."

"You mean the liver pâté?"

"That's the rustic bit. Here comes the elegance," Winter said, going to the work surface and fetching a glass dish.

"What is it?" she asked, going to the table. "Ah. Pickled herring. When did you find the time to make this? I assume you made it yourself?"

"Don't insult me."

"When did you find the time?"

"In the early hours of yesterday. Just before two in the morning. And now it's perfect."

"Now it's perfect," she repeated. "All that's missing is the schnapps, but we're not allowed to have any of that, are we?"

"*You* are not allowed to have any of that," he said. "I could indulge, but I'll display my sympathy for your situation. For tonight, at least."

"It's quite usual for men to show their sympathy for their women in a situation like this."

"Really?"

"Some of them even put on weight."

"You can count me out on that score."

Morelius felt stiff. He'd felt stiff before setting out for work, and it hadn't gone away as a result of the routine workout before the upcoming night shift.

Afterward he sat on the bench in front of his locker, massaging his neck and looking at the pictures of naked women taped to the inside of Bartram's locker door. They were fairly innocent pictures, cut out of some 1960s men's magazine. Not the kind of thing that got printed nowadays. Bartram lived in the past. He sometimes claimed the pictures were of his wife, but he didn't have a wife.

They were now in the last week of the six-week rotation. That meant an extra night shift this Friday followed by two more over the weekend. It was the last Friday of the month, payday. He knew that people were already out celebrating the fact that their pockets were full. It was just eight o'clock and the station was closed.

"A touch of a stiff neck, is it?" Bartram asked, who was fiddling with his pistol, checking the mechanism with an ease born of long experience. His SIG-Sauer still had the original wooden butt. Bartram sometimes went on about losing the Walther, which he considered a better weapon for the job, but not today. He was calm and serious, ready for the coming night and the coming weekend.

"It's just a bit stiff," Morelius said.

"Watch out for drafts."

"I will."

"You'd better stay indoors tonight."

"Why?"

"Drafts. There's a nasty wind blowing through Gothenburg tonight."

"Bullshit. It'll be a routine shift."

"It's payday today, Simon."

Morelius and Bartram were walking down the Avenue. Some preferred to walk it alone, and Morelius had been one of those; but the last six months had been different. Being on his own no longer felt like liberation as far as he was concerned. He'd been well and truly scared on several occasions. Had seen things that terrified him.

On one occasion he'd come face-to-face with death in the Gnistäng Tunnel when a young couple drove straight into the wall. He'd been in the following car and seen everything. Like in a film. Real, but somehow unreal. The Mazda in front of him had swerved left and crashed into the wall with a noise of shattering glass and twisting metal. He wasn't even on duty, he'd just been driving around for fun, as he some-times did when he was off duty. He'd managed to pull off an emer-gency stop, then leaped from his car and raced over to the wreck where the girl was hanging with . . . with . . . He'd gotten violently sick, right in front of her, like your ordinary . . . and then he'd tried to phone, but even as he was punching in the number he could hear sirens as his col-leagues and an ambulance converged on the scene.

He thought about that now, as they passed the park for the second time. Beautiful people glittered on the other side of the windows, in bars, in restaurants. Women. Bartram turned to admire the sights to the left.

"Watch out for that stiff neck."

"Ha, ha."

"Maybe it would be worth it."

"The trick is to compensate by looking in the other direction as well."

Morelius looked in the other direction, over the Avenue. A gang of kids was approaching from Götaplatsen. One of twenty or so that were tempted to gather in the center of town on a Friday night. The Avenue became an odd mixture of middle-aged elegance, desperate thirty-year-old crises, and desperate fifteen-year-old crises.

Those who were most drunk tried to make contact, to provoke. The gang pushed their smallest member to the front, waited, then at-tacked. Bartram looked to his right now too.

"I recognize her."

"Eh?"

"That blonde girl over there, in the gang. Nearest to us. She's the vicar's daughter."

"Yes. Maria Östergaard."

"She recovered pretty quickly."

"That was a week ago. And I said at the time that it wasn't all that serious."

"But she's out on the town, even so. What does our vicar have to say about that?"

"Why not ask her? Here she comes."

It was true. Hanne Östergaard was hurrying toward them, practically running, crossing over the Avenue from the theater, and the two police officers watched her march up to the gang of youths. She grabbed hold of her fair-haired daughter.

"Come home with me this minute!"

"You can't tell me what to do."

"I asked you to stay at home tonight."

"You always want me to stay at home." She tried to pull her arm away. "Let go of me!" She looked at her friends.

"I just want you to come home with me," Hanne said. She had let go of her daughter's sleeve. "I'm worried stiff by all this. What if it happens again?"

"Nothing's going to happen," the girl said. "I haven't even had a beer." She breathed in her mother's face. "Can you smell beer? Well, can you?"

Hanne had started crying. "Please, Maria, I just want you to come home with me now. I get so . . . so terribly worried."

"There's nothing to be worried about, Mom. I'm with my friends. I'll be home by one, as I said."

Hanne looked at the girl, at the group of teenagers, then over the street at the two police officers. She made a move as if she were about to run over to them, ask them to arrest the girl and take her home to the house in Örgryte.

Please don't come over here, Morelius thought. Though if it gets much worse we'll have to go and sort it out. He heard a shout. "NO!" He watched the girl turn on her heel and start running down the Avenue. The gang hesitated. One youth suddenly started running after her. It looked like the kid who'd been lurking in the background at the ER. The group moved off, seeming to be pulled along the wide pavement, away from the woman who was left standing there on her own.

"Do you often think about what it'll be like, being a father?"

The question took him by surprise. It was like interrogating a suspect. Taken by surprise. No time to think.

"Of course."

"I don't believe you."

"How on earth could I fib about that? It'll be the most important event of my life, along with my own birth." He looked at her. Hair combed back. A slight swelling of the stomach. "That, and when I met you."

"Good answer. But I think you're already starting to worry about all the bad things that could happen."

"That's where you're wrong, Angela. I'm an optimist, as you know."

She burst out laughing.

"About this, anyway," he said.

"I think you're already starting to think what it will be like when . . . when our child is a teenager roaming around the Avenue with a gang."

"Come off it."

"I'm right, though, aren't I? That's what'll happen."

"There won't be any Avenue by then."

"No parade street in Gothenburg anymore? Is that the optimist talking?"

Winter's mobile rang on the bedside table. It was 12:03 A.M. The few people who had his mobile number rang on police business, apart from Angela, but she was lying in bed beside him, still soft and red, with three small beads of sweat on her forehead.

His mother was the only other person it could be. It's either murder or Mother, Winter thought, without smiling. He scrambled over to the other side of the bed and answered.

"Erik! Thank God you answered." His mother was out of breath, as if she'd just run up two or three hills in Nueva Andalucía. Winter could hear crackling over the line from the Costa del Sol.

"What's the matter, Mom?"

"It's your dad, again. This time it's serious, Erik."

Winter recalled the last time, last year. His father had been taken into the Marbella hospital with a suspected heart attack, but it was in fact myocarditis. Winter had considered flying down to Spain, but it turned out not to be necessary.

He hadn't seen his father since his parents had more or less fled Sweden, taking their money with them. He hadn't wanted to see him last year and he didn't want to do so now either, if it could be avoided.

"Is it myocarditis again?"

"Oh, Erik. He's had a heart attack. Just a couple of hours ago. I'm phoning from the hospital. He's in intensive care, Erik. ERIK? Can you hear me?"

"I'm here, Mother."

"He's dying, Erik."

Winter closed his eyes, took a deep breath. Keep calm. Calm.

"Is he conscious."

"What . . . no, he's unconscious. They've just operated on him."

"They've operated on him?"

"That's what I said. He's undergone a long operation. Cleaned out his ducts, I think."

Angela had pulled the sheet up to her chin and sat up in bed. She looked at him, a serious expression on her face. She gathered what had happened.

"Have you spoken to Lotta?" he asked. His sister was a doctor. Angela was also a doctor, but she couldn't speak Spanish. His mother spoke a bit of Spanish, but he wasn't sure whether she understood what people said to her. She was best at wines and spirits. Even if the doctor spoke in English to her, she would be too upset to listen properly. Even if the doctor spoke Swedish.

"I phoned you first, Erik."

"Has the doctor said *anything?*"

"Only that he's still under the anesthetic." She was sobbing into his ear. "What if he doesn't come round, Erik?"

Winter closed his eyes, saw himself in the car on the way to the airport, in an airplane seat. A blue sky over the clouds. He glanced at his hand. It was shaking. Perhaps these are his last hours, he thought.

"I'll take the first flight."

"Will there be . . . will there be any seats? Flights are nearly always full at . . . at this time of year."

"I'll fix that."

Angela looked at him. She had heard it all. He would fix that. He would be aboard that aircraft at seven o'clock, or whenever it left. Some other passenger would have to lean against his golf bag and wait for another flight before he could lower his handicap on the Costa del Sol.

4

He had locked the apartment door behind him when he came in. Or left the others in the room and did it later, before they'd started, he wasn't sure. Anybody trying to get out would lose a few valuable seconds.

He had eaten, he couldn't remember what. He hadn't thought about what he was putting into his mouth. She had laughed, once or twice. He, the other one, hadn't. As if he sensed it . . .

As if he knew who *he* was. Why *he* was there.

Here I am, he thought, sitting. Now I'm speaking. I'm saying words that don't mean a thing. I don't know if they're listening either.

He could hear the music inside his head. It started soft, got louder, then faded away, got louder again, then softer. It was like being at home, listening, or in the car, but he rarely did it in the car. He didn't want to drive into a tunnel wall.

He was listening, that was before it started. Or maybe it started *with* him listening. He had tried to avoid listening and that had worked for a while but now it was impossible. And it didn't matter now, now that he was sitting here. He looked around the kitchen. They'd asked if he wanted to sit in the kitchen and he'd shrugged. Then we'll move into the living room later, she'd said in a tone of voice that had made him feel cold inside his head as the music got first louder, then softer. He wondered if they saw that, if they'd eventually get around to hearing it, the very moment before it happened.

The guitars were screeching inside his head. The vocals screeched, rattled, hissed through the music that wouldn't leave his head: *lying in the black field, memories start to move into my mind, visions of the red room, my bloodied face, her bloodied head.*

Visions of the red room. He closed his eyes. He grew more excited. She noticed that and smiled. She had no idea. The man seemed to be fidgeting but gradually started to fade away, to turn into a shadow. When he looked at her she too started turning into a shadow. It was time.

She spoke.

"What?"

"Hello! Anybody home?"

"What . . . yes . . ."

"You look miles away."

"No . . . I'm here."

"You were moving your head as if you were listening to something. Inside your head."

"Yes."

"Can we listen too?" she said with a grin. The other man didn't laugh. He looked straight at him, as if he could see them sitting there, playing inside his head. "What's it sound like?" she asked, getting up and walking around to him and leaning against his ear. He could feel her weight and the strong smell of alcohol on her breath. They'd been drinking before he arrived. He hadn't touched a drop. Not then and not now. "I can't hear anything," she said, leaning more heavily against him; then she kissed him. He could feel her inside his mouth. He didn't move. "What's the matter with you?" she said. "Aren't you feeling excited?" She turned to the other man. "He doesn't seem to be very excited. I thought he was a swinger."

The other man said nothing. He was still scrutinizing him. Maybe it didn't mean anything.

She left the kitchen. When she returned there was music coming from another room. He didn't want to look at her. He could see a bit of her exposed skin.

"What do you think of that?" she asked.

"Eh? What?"

"The music," she said. "The music! I thought we could all listen to something!"

He tried to listen but no sound could penetrate the metal screeching inside his head.

She shouted something, started wiggling in a sort of dance.

She dragged the other man to his feet, kissed him. Glanced over toward him. She started unbuttoning the other man's shirt and put his hand on her left breast. Moved in time with the music. Laughed again.

"Elton John!" she yelled. "It's swinging!"

He suddenly felt sick and at the same time extremely aroused. They were both looking at him. The other man nodded, had his hand inside her blouse.

They took two or three dance steps in front of him.

He stood up.

5

Winter collected his case from the carousel, passed through customs and out to where his hired car was waiting. He took off his jacket and settled behind the wheel. The car had been parked in the shade behind the terminal building. As the plane approached, Málaga had announced itself as gray cliffs climbing skyward from burned earth fifty thousand feet below. A semicircle embracing a calm sea. It was ninety degrees in the shade. The heat was reluctant to release Andalusia from its grip. He'd never been here before.

He felt tired, and his head was pounding. He started the engine. He felt sad, and his emotion seemed to be exaggerated by the heat. As if the heat were an omen.

Winter unfolded the map of the Costa del Sol he'd been given by the car rental firm and checked his route to Marbella. It seemed straightforward. The E15 all the way. The motorway was reputed to be the most dangerous in the world, but he reflected that the media had suggested the same thing for other roads as well, as he reversed out of his parking space.

He drove westward and switched on the radio. A Spaniard was singing a version of "My Way" in lisping Castilian. That was followed by a flamenco set for orchestra: it sounded cheerful but out of tune to

Winter's ear. The flamenco gave way to a Mexican rhumba with ten thousand trumpets. Then the Spaniard came back with "The Green, Green Grass of Home."

The grass bordering the road was dry and almost colorless.

He drove through the suburbs. The high-rise blocks looked black in the shade. The concrete façades were dotted with colorful washing hanging on balconies. The wasteland between the clusters of houses seemed to be deserted, apart from small groups of feral dogs chasing one another through piles of trash. No sign of any people now that it was siesta time.

He steered well clear of a truck that overtook him on a bend. The driver was sitting back, smoking, his elbow resting on the window frame. A woman in the passenger seat was playing with a couple of toddlers in the seat in the back, and the children waved to Winter. He waved back, then wiped his face. He was very hot. The air-conditioning didn't work ("The very best, *señor!*") and the slipstream was insufficient to cool him.

To the left he could see what must be Torremolinos, or "Torrie," as his mother had called it, the way the English do: a series of concrete blocks halfway to heaven and halfway out into the sea. It could be a paradise or a living hell, depending on whom you asked. Winter didn't ask, and had no intention of staying: he devoted no further thought to Torrie, regarding it as no more than a wall built along the shore, and drove on to the hospital.

Four miles outside Marbella, Winter noticed the Hospital Costa del Sol to the right, colored white and green. He turned off at the Hotel Los Monteros, followed a road running parallel to the highway, and then came around to the hospital. He parked close to a bus stop and followed the signs to the ENTRADA PRINCIPAL. The grass was green and the flowers red. A circle of pines had been planted around the gigantic building: cactus, bougainvillea. Flowers tumbling from balconies.

Broad steps led up to the entrance, which looked like a black hole. Winter took a deep breath, ran his hand through his closely cropped hair, and went in.

. . . . .

Morelius left Bartram standing outside the Park Lane Hotel and crossed over the Avenue to Hanne Östergaard, who was still rooted to the spot. She didn't see him until he was next to her. "You can't stand here, Hanne."

She looked at him.

"It's not out-of-bounds, is it?" she said, and he thought he heard a dry laugh. She raised her head and looked for the youngsters, but they could no longer be seen among the mass of people. "This little drama seems to have attracted an audience. At least you were in the right place at the right time," she said, looking straight at him. "Again." Then she laid her hand on his arm. "Forgive me, Simon."

"Nothing to forgive," he said. "Can we give you a lift home?"

"No, thank you, I have the car parked at Heden . . . Assuming it hasn't been stolen." She looked down Berzeliigatan. "According to one of your younger colleagues who I speak to occasionally, all cars parked at Heden get stolen sooner or later."

"That's probably true."

"Maybe I will need your help, then."

"I can go there with you and take a look," Morelius said.

"Aren't you on duty? You're in uniform. Shouldn't you be on patrol?"

"This is duty."

"All right," she said, and started walking. Morelius signaled to Bartram, who waved back and continued toward Götaplatsen.

"All this makes you giddy," said Hanne, staring fixedly ahead. "Chasing your child all over town." She turned to Morelius. "I even start using words I've never used before. Like 'giddy.'"

Morelius said nothing.

"It started out of the blue," she said. "I never thought I would have to put up with this kind of thing. Never. Huh! Talk about being naive."

Morelius didn't comment. He knew that she lived alone with her daughter, but he didn't want to say that it couldn't be easy in those circumstances, or any of the other silly things people say.

"I suppose it's a sort of emancipation," she said. "And if your mom's a vicar the emancipation is all the more hotheaded. More marked." She looked at Morelius again as they crossed over the Avenue and waited for the lights to change at Södra Vägen. "Do you think that's what it is, Simon?"

"I really don't know," he said, staring straight ahead. "I'm not the right person to ask about things like that." He could feel the sweat breaking out under his cap. He hoped she wouldn't see it. Sweat trickling down his face.

"Why not?" They crossed the road and aimed for the farthest corner of the car park. "Surely you can have an opinion on it. Why not?"

"I don't have any children."

"So much the better." That dry laugh again. "No, I must stop this." She halted and looked around. "I'm not quite sure where I left it. The car, that is." She looked again. "I didn't think about it. Then."

"What does it look like?"

"It's a Volvo. One of the early models. It's about ten or eleven years old."

"License plate number?"

She looked around again. "Do you know, I can't remember. This is ridiculous."

"It's pretty common," Morelius said. "Forgetting your car's license plate number."

"Especially when you're under stress, is that right?"

"Yes." He scanned the surrounding cars. Volvos everywhere.

"There it is, over there." She pointed and set off toward it. "The one with the empty space at the side of it. To the right."

The car was very dirty. He could see that from thirty feet away.

"We wouldn't have been able to read the license plate number in any case."

"That's what happens when you keep putting things off," Hanne said. "But it's not good, when you think of rust and whatnot."

"No."

"It doesn't seem to matter just at the moment."

They had reached the car. Hanne unlocked it and sat down behind the wheel.

"Anyway . . . thank you," she said.

"It's a pleasure."

She was staring straight ahead with the car keys in her hand, then turned to look at Morelius, who was leaning toward the car. She started the engine.

"And I always thought we had such a good relationship," she said, but Morelius didn't catch every word.

6

When Winter arrived at Room 1108 his father was awake. He approached the bed. It was a difficult moment. Winter had trouble swallowing. His father held out a hand. Winter took it. The hand felt warm and firm, as with a healthy man, but Winter could feel bone and sinew. He tried to say something, but his father got in first.

"Good of you to come, Erik."

"Of course I came." Winter could see that his father was in pain. Moving his hand had been awkward. "Take it easy now." Winter squeezed the hand gently. "That's the main thing."

"It's the only . . . possible thing." Bengt Winter looked at his son. "This wasn't exactly how I'd planned to greet you when you finally got yourself down here to the sun."

"That doesn't matter. Hurry up and get well and then you can greet me as planned later."

"You can . . . you can bet your life I will. Oh sh—, can you move this pillow up a bit?"

Winter pulled up one of the pillows behind his father's head. He noticed a pungent smell, and something more. It took him a second to recall his father's aftershave. When he did, his headache returned. The sadness of the situation stuck in him like a lump of stone.

He fluffed up the pillow a little.

"That's fine," his father said.

"Are you sure?"

"It's perfect," his mother said. She was sitting on a chair next to the bed. Winter didn't want to look at her.

"How was the journey?" his father asked.

"Everything went well."

"Which airline did you use?"

"Some charter company. I forget what they're called."

"That's not like you."

"Hmm."

"It was short notice. But they found a seat for you even so?"

"Yes."

"I bet some golfer or other had to wait for a few more hours, was that it?"

"I don't know."

"Serves him right. There are too many of 'em down here nowadays. They ought to have something better to do." He looked up at Winter. "Look what happens. One minute you're out on the golf course and the next you're lying here."

"Yes, it's not good."

"It's an extremely dangerous sport."

"You'll soon be back."

"On the golf course?"

"Yes. And . . . everywhere else too."

"I wouldn't put a hell of a lot of money on that. This feels like the big one."

"Hmm."

"It feels like . . ." Winter couldn't hear what came next. His father's speech became slurred. Winter waited, but no more words came. His father's eyelids drooped, shot up again, drooped once more. Winter realized that he was still holding his father's hand when it lost strength and sank down.

"He needs to rest again," his mother said, who had stood up and come to the bed. "He was so pleased that you'd come." She gave Winter a hug. "He was quite excited when he heard you were here."

"Hmm."

"He woke up about a quarter of an hour before you came back."

"He seems to be pretty . . . strong, despite everything," Winter said, looking down at his unconscious father. Could he hear what they were saying? Did it matter? "Everything will turn out all right."

"That was a lovely conversation you had," his mother said.

It was a careful conversation, Winter thought. No risks taken. It went in big circles around a big fucking hole.

He could hear the hum from the air-conditioning. It was the first time he'd noticed it. Maybe his nervousness was fading. Next time he would ask a few questions, and maybe get a few answers.

They'd gone into the living room. She had turned on the video and bodies were writhing. . . . The only light in the room was the blue glow from the television screen, the shadows flitting around the walls like living beings.

The sound was rising and falling. He couldn't stand it. He wanted to march up to the television set and switch it off, but he couldn't interrupt her ritual. He was sure she was the one who'd decided what was going to happen.

"Why are you standing there? Come and sit down here. With us."

She beckoned from the sofa in front of the television where they were both sitting. The other man had his hand inside her blouse. On the table in front of them were glasses and bottles. He hadn't touched a drop, but the pair on the sofa were well oiled.

He closed his eyes and it was like another time, when he'd come home and caught her on a sofa just like this one. He shouldn't have been there. They had been surprised. He'd turned on his heel and left.

It wasn't the first time this sort of thing had happened.

It was something to do with him. He'd thought it was to do with *them*, but he was beginning to realize that it was something inside himself.

He was trying to crack it. He was there now.

"Don't laugh," he said. "Please don't laugh."

They both looked at him. Their faces were patchy in the blue light. They looked as if their foreheads were tattooed.

"We haven't laughed," she said. "Nobody laughs here."

"Please don't laugh at me."

"What the hell's the matter with you?" said the other man, half-rising from the sofa.

"Nothing."

"I think you've come to the wrong place."

The other man stood up and started toward him. She stayed where she was, glass in hand, her body following the movements of those on the television screen.

"I've brought some music with me."

"Eh?"

"I've brought some music we could play."

"Music?" The other man was still standing by the sofa, and pointed to the television screen. "We already have something going on here. Or didn't you notice?"

"Have you got a cassette player? This is something else." He'd already seen the stereo system over to the right, various pieces of equipment stacked on top of each other in a tall, black shelving unit. He walked over to it, taking the cassette out of his breast pocket. For a fleeting moment he saw another face in his mind's eye, like a hovering head. He recognized it. He knew that it meant something. Now the head was gone. It hadn't had a body. The song was already echoing in his brain, he didn't know if it was coming from his throat, if the others could hear it as well. His own head was spinning, floating toward theirs, everything was merging. He saw the face once again. Then the real music started.

Dusk would soon be falling, but it was still hot. Winter drove into Marbella. A flamenco singer gave vent to her pain over the car radio. Winter turned up the sound and rolled the window down. There was a smell of gasoline and sea. When he parked on a side street off the promenade, there was a smell of grilled octopus and eggs fried in oil. His back felt sweaty as he got out of the car and locked the doors.

The hotel was in the Avenida Duque de Ahumeda, near the beach. Winter had to wait a quarter of an hour in the foyer, then took the elevator up to the twelfth floor with his bag. He wanted to see the room before checking in. That was his usual routine.

The door lock was hanging loose. The suite comprised two rooms and a kitchen. The window facing the balcony was ajar, and the wind was making the awning flap. It was ragged, faded by the sun and the salt air. A loose strip of the awning was slapping against the window. Winter investigated further and saw that the balcony faced east with a view of another hotel. He looked around the large living room. The furniture in imitation leather had once been white.

He went to the bathroom. There was a trail of rust underneath the bath taps. There were bits of soap in the washbasin. He examined himself in the mirror. He had lost weight in the last five hours, turned paler.

He shared the elevator down with a couple in their forties who tried to avoid eye contact with the man of their own age. They had a five-day tan and were dressed for dinner.

"I don't like that room," Winter said to the man at the desk, handing back the key. Why do I always end up in situations like this? he wondered.

"What's wrong with it?"

"I don't want the room. Do you have anything else? Lower down?"

"But what's wrong with it?"

"I DON'T WANT THAT FUCKING ROOM," Winter said. "It's out of order."

"What isn't working?" the man asked, his eyes darkening.

"Nothing's working. Things are broken. The bathroom's dirty. Do you have another room?"

"No. We're fully booked."

"For how long?"

"For another month."

"Can you recommend another hotel near here?"

Winter had seen the hotel next door, but hadn't been tempted. He was tired and hot and sweaty and miserable. He wanted a nice room and a shower and a glass of whisky and a little time to think things over.

"No," the man said.

"A smaller hotel, perhaps. A more modest establishment."

"No idea," the man said, turning away. He has every right, Winter thought, It's not his fault. I could have been more polite.

"Do you have a town guide that lists the hotels here?"

"What am I going to do with that room?" the man said, avoiding the question. He eyed Winter up and down like a hostile barrister. "I'm stuck now with an empty room."

"Board it up," Winter said, and marched out, trailing his case behind him.

He was lucky. When he'd driven into town earlier that day, he'd noticed a sign attached to a wall. It couldn't be more than a hundred yards away.

He drove back a short stretch of the Avenida de Severo Ochoa and found the sign on the corner of a little side street that was for pedestrians only. He parked and walked down the Calle Luna, which was filled with afternoon shadow. About a half block along, on the right, was the Hostal La Luna, behind a glass door at the back of its own patio. Winter could see that each room had a little balcony.

There had been a last-minute cancellation, and he took a look at the room, which was very Spanish and quiet and clean, with a refrigerator and a bathroom.

He had a shower, then drank his whisky naked in the semidarkness. The elderly couple who ran the establishment were chatting quietly down on the walled patio. Marble floor and whitewashed walls.

They couldn't speak English, not a single word, but the man had assessed Winter's state and served him a chilled San Miguel on the table in the shade of a parasol, even before Winter had checked in for an indefinite stay.

The whisky circled around his mouth and slid into his brain. His head cleared somewhat. The room had an unfamiliar smell to it, as if it had been scrubbed with sea salt and southern spices. The twin beds were of timeless Latin design, medieval in style. Between them was an image of the Madonna, praying for him and his father. That was what occurred to him when he first saw the picture in his simple room. It was the only item of decoration.

This is the way to live.

He reached for his mobile. It was nearly seven and the sun was much weaker now. The door to the patio was ajar, and the wooden venetian blinds were half up in the glassless window opening, protected by a black wrought-iron grille.

"Angela here."

"It's Erik."

"Hi! Where are you?"

"In my room. But not the hotel whose number you have."

"So you moved," and he knew she was smiling.

"Of course."

"How's your father?"

"They've moved him out of intensive care. Is that a good sign?"

"I suppose it must be."

"Suppose? You're the doctor." He hoped he didn't sound as if he were complaining.

"I don't have access to his chart, Erik." She paused. "Did you speak to him?"

"Yes."

"And?"

"He seems pretty . . . well, strong."

"That sounds encouraging."

"Yes."

"What was it like, seeing him again?"

"As if we'd been chatting only last week."

"Sure?"

"Depends what you mean. We spoke about safe subjects."

"Everything takes time. He has to get better first."

"Hmm."

"Are you tired?"

"Not so tired that I can't indulge in a glass of duty-free whisky. What about you?"

"We're fine."

He took her "we" as a greeting from the new family: Angela and her ever-enlarging stomach.

"Take it easy at work."

"I always do. The mergers have resulted in much better working conditions, as you know."

"I know."

"You are a genius."

"Stop it, Angela. Give your stomach a hug from me instead."

"What are you doing tonight?"

"I'll find somewhere for a bite to eat, then drive back to the hospital."

"With whisky in your blood?"

"It stays in my brain. And, anyway, this is a different country."

7

He could see the lights of ships plying the jet-black sea. The heat wafted into the car as he drove to the hospital. The eastern suburbs of Marbella were quieter now, with fewer cars in the streets. The streetlights, too far apart, helped to soften the darkness.

Winter had eaten a seafood meal in a modest bar near Hostal La Luna. Five men almost hidden by a cloud of smoke in front of a television set in the corner had been shouting and making obscene gestures at the footballers. Football spectators were the same the whole world over.

His father was awake again. His mother was on the chair, which she had moved closer to the bed.

"I'm going down to the cafeteria for a coffee," she said when Winter arrived. "Can I get you anything?"

"Nothing for me, thank you."

"You can bring me a Tanqueray and tonic," his father said.

His mother smiled, and left. Winter sat down on the chair.

"I can hear that you're fighting fit," he said.

"It's T and T time now," his father said, who was lying with his head turned toward the window. "A little something cold and uplifting before dinner."

"Isn't it a bit late?" Winter said, pointing at his watch, which said nine o'clock.

His father started coughing, and Winter waited. There was a clanking noise as a trolley passed by in the corridor. A woman's voice asking something in Spanish, and a reply from a man. A snatch of guitar music. His father coughed again.

"We've adapted to Spanish customs." He cleared his throat tentatively, as if to ease the pain of talking. "Do you see the outline of that mountaintop over there?"

"Yes."

"It's the Sierra Blanca. The White Mountain. A lovely name, don't you think? I can see the same peak from our house. Funny, eh?"

"I don't know about that. The mountain dominates the whole area, you could say."

His father seemed to be pondering what he'd just said. He looked at his son. "I could have landed in a different room. Facing the other way. There's a meaning behind this."

"What, exactly?"

"That I'm here, in this room. That I can see the mountain peak. The same damn peak. It's as if I were meant to see it from here too. This is my new home. I've moved into here now, and I'm never going to move out."

"Of course you will."

"Alive, Erik. I mean move out alive."

"You seem better already. Keep going on as you are now."

"I'm serious, Erik."

"What does the doctor say?"

"Alcorta? He makes typical Spanish gestures that could mean anything at all."

"Isn't that what all doctors do?"

"Not like they do in Spain. Does Angela do it? How is she, by the way?"

"She's fine."

"And you're going to be a father, Erik. Good Lord! I hope he gives me the strength to hang on long enough to see the miracle."

"You'll soon be back at home. Then you can study the mountain peak from the other side again."

. . . . .

Morelius spent the first two hours or so of his evening shift working at the front desk. An officer who used to work on the beat would soon take over, hold the fort.

He was one of the worn-out, older officers who had been given desk jobs as a result of the latest reorganization. They'd done their duty and now just concentrated on keeping their noses clean. Lots of officers here had lost their drive like that. But this old officer was a very bitter man. Some people were born to take a top job, but those who reached retirement age and still hadn't got one became bitter.

Time to go out on patrol now. Bartram strapped on his holster. He hadn't lost his drive. He might seem worn out at times, or angry—but there were other reasons for that.

The control room had saved some interesting assignments they didn't want to give to the day-shift patrols that were just about to go off duty. Many were break-ins that were more than met the eye. Like this one. A caretaker had noticed that somebody had broken into the basement of an apartment building in Rickertsgatan, over at Johanneberg. They set off in a patrol car, three of them: Morelius and Bartram plus Bo Vejehag, who really had lost his drive and couldn't wait for his retirement day after thirty years of hard work on behalf of the general public.

The apartment buildings around Viktor Rydbergsgatan were often targeted for burglaries. Large, substantial buildings, wealthy inhabitants away in their holiday homes.

They pulled up outside the one that had just been broken into, and were met by the caretaker, who was evidently working overtime, or had stayed behind because he was fed up with all the burglaries, one after another, in his basements.

"Fuck this shitty weather," Vejehag said, getting out of the car and turning up his jacket collar in an attempt to seal out the wind and the rain.

"There were some young thugs running up and down the stairs and then they went down into the basement," the caretaker said.

"Did you see them?" Vejehag asked.

"No. But one of the tenants did."

"When was that?"

"Just now."

"Just now? We received the message hours ago."

"That was then. Now they've come back again. I've only just called, and you've turned up here like greased lightning."

"The message has just come over the radio," shouted Bartram from the car, and responded to control: "We're there already."

"Has anything been stolen?" Vejehag asked.

"A few small items earlier this afternoon from one of the cellars. I don't know about this time."

"Which basement was it?"

"Do you mean now? Or this afternoon?"

"I mean now."

"Down there," said the caretaker, pointing to the nearest flight of stairs. The property was in need of a coat of paint. A gang of kids were standing fifty yards away, watching the police officers.

"We'd better go and take a look," said Vejehag. Morelius got out of the car and followed him into the building.

Bartram stayed in the car, waiting for messages. He looked up at the sky: it was a dirty, grayish blue, streetlights mixed with dusk.

Winter looked at the sky over the mountains. It was lit up from the left by the city lights, but had turned darker, made a deeper color by what might have been rain clouds. The wind was getting up, rustling through the palms on the other side of the graveled courtyard.

"How's work going?" His father's voice sounded distant. "I've read about some of your cases in the Gothenburg papers we have sent out."

"I try to do my best."

"That seems to be more than good enough, as far as I can make out."

"Hmm. I don't know about that."

"I could never work out what happened to that young woman who was murdered last year. The one you found in the lake at Delsjön."

"Helene."

"Was that her name?"

"Yes. What was unclear?"

"What happened to the child."

"She was okay."

"But she'd disappeared."

"Not really. She was . . . being looked after. Protected."

His father didn't ask any further. Winter listened to the sick man's labored breathing, like a weak pair of bellows. He thought about his work. He'd never had any doubts about what he did . . . or even thought that he did much at all, really. Or was it just the challenge that interested him? Might he just as well be doing something else? That thought had suddenly entered his head, in the car as he was driving to the hospital. It was a worrying thought. It could be constricting.

"I think I'll have a nap," his father said.

"I'll be sitting here."

"Shouldn't you go back to your room and get some sleep? It was a long journey."

"I'll get some rest here, on the chair."

He could hear the patter of rain on the window, gentle at first but growing louder.

"It's raining," his father mumbled. "That'll please a lot of people."

Bartram was daydreaming when the door to the basement stairs was flung open and two youths came racing out and ran off to the left.

Bartram leaped out of the car, shot over the flowerbed, and tackled one of them with a kick on the shin.

The other boy disappeared down the next flight of stairs. Bartram looked down at his captive squirming on the ground, glanced around, then slammed his foot down on the youth's back.

"Ouch! You bast—"

"Shut up."

"Take your foot off—"

"*Shut up*, I said."

Vejehag and Morelius emerged from the basement and ran over to Bartram and the boy.

"What happened down there?" Bartram asked.

"We caught 'em red-handed," Vejehag said.

"That's bullshit! *I* caught 'em red-handed," said Bartram, pressing his foot down harder on the kid's back.

"That's enough of that," Vejehag said. "Where's the other one?"

"Ran down the basement stairs over there," Bartram said, pointing.

"Get up," Vejehag said to the boy, gesturing to Bartram to take his foot away.

A patrol car was approaching.

"This bunch is from the emergency call-out squad," Morelius said.

"Have you been yakking over the radio?" asked Vejehag, glaring at Bartram.

"Of course I haven't, goddam it!"

The car drew up alongside them. The driver's window was wound down and a very young face appeared—the officer looked about twenty-five.

"What's going on, Granddad?"

"We've lost a nightshirt and a nightcap and thought we might find them in the basement here."

"Ha, ha."

"And what are you lot doing here?" Vejehag said.

"Who's that?" asked the constable in the patrol car, nodding toward the youth slumped between Bartram and Morelius.

"It's my young brother," Vejehag said, and at that very moment the door behind them flew open and out charged the other youth. Bartram let go and raced after the second kid and tackled him after only ten yards. The constable's jaw dropped. Somebody said something inside the car, but it was impossible to see anything through the tinted windows. There was some faint applause.

The young constable looked at Vejehag.

"Another brother of yours?"

"We're gathering the family together for a party. It'll soon be Christmas."

"Ha, ha."

Bartram strolled up with the boy in handcuffs.

"Nice bit of work," the constable said.

"Look and learn," Vejehag said.

"Are there any more?"

"Eh?"

"If there are any more assembling for your party, you might need a bit of backup. I mean, all that violent resistance."

"We're not expecting any more violent resistance."

"Oh no?"

"We normally capture the villains verbally."

"Eh?"

"We try to talk to people. Even villains. We don't expect violent resistance when we're at work."

"I can see that."

Vejehag pretended not to hear. "If anybody thinks that violent resistance plays a significant part in our work, maybe they ought to think again about their choice of profession."

"Be seeing you, Granddad," said the young constable, and the car moved off. The buildings that comprise Rickertsgatan were reflected in its windows.

"What a bunch," Vejehag said. "Six officers who can't bear the thought of being parted from the other. Hiding behind tinted glass." He looked at Morelius. "There's something perverse about that, don't you think?"

"Could be."

"There's something perverse about the whole idea of special call-out units," Vejehag said. "They should be sent on Swedish-language courses instead of all that goddam macho nonsense. We talk every day, but it's pretty rare that the Gothenburg police force gets to storm a Boeing 757. Even so, that bunch practices it every few days."

"We sometimes catch villains using methods other than words," Bartram said.

"Yes. Now, let's see if we can get these boys somewhere warm and cozy."

·　·　·　·　·　·

Maria Östergaard felt cold. She'd been in such a rush to get away from home that she'd forgotten her gloves. Her hands felt like lumps of ice only a couple of minutes after they'd left the café.

"Where should we go?" Patrik said.

"I wanted to stay where we were," answered Maria.

"I didn't like the people in there. Can't we go back to your place?"

"Mom's impossible, completely around the bend. Why can't we go back to your place?"

"Dad's impossible, completely around the bend," said Patrik, with no trace of a smile.

There wasn't a soul to be seen in Vasagatan. Trams clattered over Vasaplatsen. A woman got off the tram that had approached along Aschebergsgatan and disappeared into one of the apartment buildings. As she opened the front door her face was lit up by the light from the entrance hall and the streetlamps.

"I recognize her," Maria said. "That woman going in through the door over there."

"Oh, yeah? What about it?"

"She's pretty."

"What about it?"

"She lives with that guy who's a detective, a cop. Mom works for the police every other week, that's how I know of him."

"You mean the police have vicars?"

"Evidently. I think his name's Winter. That detective. Cool name, don't you think?"

"Hmm."

They walked across Vasaplatsen.

A squad car came down Aschebergsgatan from Johanneberg. Morelius was driving.

"I recognize those kids over there," he said. "Those two, next to that stand."

"I recognize the girl at least," Bartram said. "Small world."

"Winter lives over there, to the left, incidentally," Morelius said. "The star of the force. That entrance there," he said, gesturing with his hand as they drove past the building.

"How do you know?" asked Vejehag.

"I drove him home one night."

"Winter?" said Bartram. "Oh, right. So that's where he lives?"

8

When Winter got up, the square of sky he could see through his bathroom window was gray. When he went out the door, the same thing applied to the whole horizon. But it was warm. He was wearing a short-sleeved silk shirt, cool linen trousers, and sandals with no socks.

He passed the landlord and landlady, whose kitchen was next to the front door; they seemed to spend all day under the parasol, or under the sheet of canvas that had been stretched over half the patio when Winter arrived yesterday. Yesterday. Hadn't it been longer than that?

As he passed by, the woman said something to him. She held up a finger, as if issuing a warning. He thought he had heard the word *chicas*. Yes, she had said *"No chicas"* and pointed to his room at the other end of the house, then added what sounded like *"en la habitación."* Her man smiled, perhaps in embarrassment. After a few seconds the penny dropped, and Winter made a dismissive gesture. No, of course not. He wouldn't bring any women back to his room.

Winter turned right into Calle Luna and then left into Calle del Sol before coming to a little square. He continued to the open Plaza Puente de Málaga and found a café in the corner to the left: GASPAR. PANADERÍA AND CAFETERÍA. He sat outside at the only empty table. It was eight-thirty. He was surrounded on all sides by Spaniards, men and women. They were drinking coffee with milk in tall glasses and eating small bread rolls with butter and jam, or just olive oil and salt. A waiter came, and Winter managed to order *café con leche* and *pan* with *confitura*. *"Mantequilla?"* the waiter asked, and Winter nodded without knowing what it meant. Butter, perhaps?

His coffee was duly served and was very good, strong espresso with hot milk. The bread arrived and was also hot. *Mantequilla* was indeed butter. He prepared his breakfast sandwiches while the Spaniards on all sides coughed their way into the new day between deeply savored drags on their cigarettes. A man at the next table turned away and started coughing something awful. Another one joined in. It was like sitting through breakfast in a sanatorium. When the man at the next table had cleared what remained of his lungs, he signaled to the white-clad waiter as if to a nurse, and the waiter disappeared into the café before reemerging with what Winter assumed was a glass of water. But as the waiter passed he could smell gin. A glass of gin to start the morning. Why not? Winter smiled, finished his breakfast and lit a Corps cigarillo. Now everybody at the Gaspar café was smoking. The smoke drifted up toward the sky, which was gray, still. There was a different kind of stillness today, compared with yesterday, a silence that he hadn't noticed then. He couldn't work out where the sun was, which seemed almost an impossibility in a place like this.

Winter checked his watch and ordered another coffee. He still hadn't finished his cigarillo. A young woman was walking from table to table, handing out leaflets. She came to Winter and he automatically held out his hand. She gave him a leaflet, her eyes fixed on his cigarillo. The message was from Centro Cristiano Exodus. He read it. It urged him to say NO! to *heroina, cocaina, alcohol, tabaco, condenación, juegos de azar, Éxtasis,* and SÍ! to *el amor, la sinceridad, la paz, el perdón, la paciencia, la libertad, la vida* . . .

He stubbed out his cigarillo, paid his bill, and checked his watch again. An Andalusian dog wandered over the road, chasing shadows. Winter thought about his father. He felt a drop of rain. The sky had turned a deeper shade of stone. The mountains beyond the *avenida* were an extension of the sky and hence whiter now than they had been before. Everything looked different. The buildings no longer reflected any light, which made people's skin seem luminous. The rain was getting heavier, and Winter could picture his father in his hospital bed. The holiday season on the Costa del Sol was coming to an end, and Winter tried to avoid seeing symbolism in what was happening now, here and in the room at the Hospital Costa del Sol.

He crossed over the wide Avenida des Ramón y Cajal and continued as far as the promenade. Another Andalusian dog wandered over the paving stones, stopped outside a café, and listened to the flamenco music being played with the treble turned up. It cocked its leg against a wall.

The sea flowed into the sky, just like the mountains in the north. The feeling that the holiday season was over was stronger down here by the beach. Winter took off his sandals and walked to the water's edge. A beach guard was carrying parasols. A café was open, its curtains flapping in the breeze. Winter could feel the wind now, and what seemed almost like a blast of cold. Sand was being whipped up as the wind strengthened. The song coming from the café was suddenly audible on the beach below. Winter thought about his child, and how the winter was creeping up on all sides. He thought about Angela, and suddenly longed to phone her; but he knew that she would be at work.

For people living down here the promise of winter must be a kind of hope, he thought. A mixture of desire and longing. Maybe people living here would now be able to be themselves, instead of constantly putting on a show.

He felt a warmer gust of wind and looked up. The clouds were breaking. Half of the sky was blue. It had opened up on the far horizon, over Africa. The sea was changing color, as if it were being lit from underneath.

Now the sun was visible, and seemed to be racing at breakneck speed through the remains of clouds resembling flakes of snow. Winter thought about the cold weather back home in Sweden: it would soon be upon them. Once again he thought about his child.

He could feel the heat on his head. As the sun returned he could appreciate its incredible strength even more clearly thanks to the preceding chill. The sudden surge of light made him feel strangely elated, as if he were starting to hope that the holiday season was back, that the sun had returned for good. He tried to avoid seeing symbolism in that as well. The sun is life, but it is also death.

As he stood there more and more people arrived to slump down on a *hamaca* and adjust the *sombrilla* to shield them from the sun. One man was building a sand sculpture about ten feet tall, representing a sphinx and a pyramid. This is the same sand as they have in Africa, Winter thought, blown here over the Mediterranean.

A street musician sat down on a chair a couple of feet away from Winter, put on his sandals, and launched into the first of the day's flamenco songs: *Adiós Graaaanaaaada, Graanaada Míiía.* Winter dropped a few pesetas into the guitar case and went back to his car.

When he arrived at Room 1108 he found it empty. His stomach turned over.

Why the hell hadn't she phoned? She took the mobile with her wherever she went, after all.

He went into the corridor and said his father's name to the woman who hadn't been standing there when he arrived, and she pointed to the exit and said: *"Cuidados Intensivos,"* with an appropriately worried expression on her face. Calm down, Winter thought. This is only what you expected when you came here yesterday.

He found his mother in the corridor outside the ward.

"I haven't had a chance to phone," she said.

"How is he?"

"Stable, they say. He's stable now."

"What happened?"

"He had breathing problems. And his pulse."

"What do the doctors say?"

"Dr. Alcorta wants to wait a bit before forming an opinion."

"This fucking Alcorta! Where is he? I want to talk to him."

"He's operating."

"On Dad?"

"No. Another patient."

"Where is Dad?"

"He's asleep. I can take you to him."

They went into the intensive care ward. Everything was white and clean. There were no windows here looking out onto a graveled courtyard and dusty palm trees swaying in the wind. But there was a window with a view of the room where Winter could see his father in a bed surrounded by tubes and machines. He looked as if he were part of a medical research project.

"We're not allowed to go in now," his mother said.

"No." He looked at her. In this intense light she appeared as ill as his father, possibly even worse, as her thin face was incapable of hiding anything. Winter could smell the smoke clinging to her dress and thought about the leaflet he still had in his pocket. *La vida. Paciencia.* Life and patience, in that order.

"How long is he going to have to stay here?"

"I don't know, Erik."

"How long have you been here now without a break? Three days? Four? Can't you go back to the house? I'll stay with him today and tonight."

"Not now, Erik."

"I think you need to get away from here for a while. Just a few hours, if you prefer that. You can take my rented car."

"I don't think I'm fit to drive just now."

"Take a taxi, for Chr—"

She looked at him. Her eyes more red than white.

"Maybe I should, I suppose. Just for a bit."

"I'll stay here," Winter said. "Go on, off you go."

Bartram and Morelius were back at the station with a double portion of sweet-and-sour chicken from Ming's down the road. They sat in the coffee room, halfheartedly watching a crime film on the box.

"That could have been us," said Bartram, nodding at the television.

"The detectives, you mean?"

"They could have been us. The problem solvers. Think of all those women they get as perks."

"We solve enough problems as it is. For ladies as well."

"You know what I'm getting at."

"I'm afraid so."

"Meaning what?"

"I'm not sure I have the strength to listen."

Bartram said nothing, just poured more chili and soy sauces over the rice. The film had finished and was followed by a commercial for diapers. A baby was rolling around on a blanket and was then lifted up by his smiling mother.

"What a nice mom," Bartram said.

"As long as the cameras are there, at least."

"A nice mom," Bartram said again. He chewed, swallowed, and poured on some more soy sauce.

"Your rice is black now," Morelius said. "Black rice."

"A nice lady," Bartram said. "A nice lady. A nice mom."

Morelius tried not to listen, to concentrate on something else. The wall. The next commercial. The wall again. The last greasy lump of chicken. Bartram kept on and on.

"Nice . . . lady," Bartram said.

"Put a sock in it now."

"What's the matter?"

"Put a sock in it."

"But for Chrissakes . . . What have I said?"

"PUT A GODDAM SOCK IN IT!" screamed Morelius, standing up and walking over to the sink, where he threw his foil tray into the bin. He wished he could have stuffed Bartram inside at the same time.

Morelius hurried out of the room, into the bathroom, and sat down on the seat. Images were flashing through his head. Bits of conversation intruded, movements, faded, there again. The conversation he'd had with Hanne . . . when was that? Weeks ago? Two weeks? It had been a mistake to go to her. It was only a few of the young cops who went to see the vicar, and then only when . . . when . . .

"I can't stop thinking about it," he'd said.

"It takes time," Hanne Östergaard had said.

"I have to be patient, is that it?"

"That's not the word I would use."

"I try not to think about it, but sometimes it's too . . . hard."

"Is there nobody you can . . . talk to about . . . your experiences?"

"No. You mean, am I living with somebody? No."

"What about your colleagues?"

Morelius thought about Bartram and Vejehag. Neither had been with him at the time. They wouldn't understand. The others? The ones who arrived on the scene later? No. They'd been too late.

"No," he said again. "I was with a new recruit and he was useless after no more than a minute. Just leaned against the car and threw . . . didn't feel well." He looked at her. "I don't know why I didn't do the same."

"We all react in different ways," she'd said.

"I had a job to do," was his reply.

He really did have a job to do.

They'd arrived at the scene just a couple of minutes after the crash. It was another occasion, not the one in the tunnel.

Glass and metal thrown fifty yards in all directions. Sleet, early for the time of year. Slippery road surface. His colleague had stood on a foot as he got out of the car. Just one foot. In a shoe. Rendered him totally incapable of anything. He'd radioed in and could hear the ambulances and fire engines in the distance even before he'd finished the call.

Somebody might have been screaming from inside the pile of twisted metal on the highway. Screaming louder and louder. Louder than the ambulances that still hadn't arrived. Where the hell were the ambulances? This was their job. He couldn't do anything, but he'd rushed over to the screams to see if he could help. Then he couldn't hear them anymore.

The nearest car had been hit head-on and the driver thrown out. Possibly across the road and behind the protective barrier. Morelius couldn't see any bodies in the wreck.

Next to it was a smaller car wedged between the others and it had been sliced in two. There was no roof. Two people sat in the front seats.

That was the image. That was the image he couldn't stop thinking about. He kept waking up in the middle of the night with a freight train plowing through his brain and he was still dreaming about the bodies in that sliced-through car.

He told Hanne all about it. Tried to.

At first he wasn't sure what he was seeing. He'd moved closer, but from behind, to see why they were lean . . . why they were leaning so strangely. A man and a woman. You could see that from behind because one was wearing a jacket and the other a short-sleeved dress. It had been warm in the car, so they hadn't needed coats.

He stood at the side of the car and saw that neither of them had a head. He couldn't stop himself from looking, and then he saw . . . the man's head was in the woman's lap.

Morelius had heard the ambulances, and the voices of the doctors and the paramedics and all the other thousands of rescue workers swarming around the scene of the accident. He was frozen to the spot, as if welded to the chassis, glued to the tarmac.

He closed his eyes again and heard the knocking on the door.

"Are you okay, Morelius?" Bartram was standing outside. "We ought to be on our way now."

He flushed the toilet.

"Yes, I'm coming."

"I'll be in the car."

9

When Winter arrived at the intensive care ward, he found his father's bed empty. His mother wasn't there either.

"What the hell has happened?" he asked a male nurse who came over to him.

"Your father is operating," the man said.

That was a pretty rapid recovery, Winter thought. His father was back on his feet and working as a surgeon.

"Where's the doctor?" asked Winter. *"A . . . dónde está? Dr. Alcorta?"*

"He is operating."

"My father? Is he operating on my father?"

The man nodded. Somebody came in through the door. Winter turned around.

"I tried to phone you but I couldn't get through," his mother said.

"I was stuck behind a damned crane truck for miles. It was impossible to hear a thing."

"He took a sudden turn for the worse. Again."

"Oh God. What is it this time?"

"I don't know. Oh, Erik," she said and burst into tears. He went over to her and gave her a hug.

"I've brought your things." He didn't know what else to say. "In the bag here."

"Dr. Alcorta will come and talk to us when he's finished."

"When will that be?"

"I've no idea, Erik. I know no more than you do."

"Does he know any more? Alcorta?" She looked at him. "I'm sorry. I'm just . . . frustrated by all this uncertainty."

"You must be used to waiting, Erik. Being patient. No . . . I suppose . . . this business is something quite different."

He thought about what she'd just said. Did he have the patience to wait, in his job as a detective? That was what it was all about, but he never felt he had the placid temperament to just wait for something to be solved. His impatience always got the upper hand. Sometimes that turned out badly, but most often it had proved to be no bad thing. His impatience had pushed investigations forward. An opening always appeared, but now he wasn't sure, not this time. There was nothing he could do. He couldn't even arrange a conversation with Dr. Alcorta.

This business is something quite different, his mother had said.

"Shall we go and have a coffee?" he suggested. "Downstairs."

"Maybe that's a good idea." She said something in Spanish to a male nurse, and nodded at his brief reply. "They'll call us immediately if anything happens. But we'll only be gone for ten minutes, in any case."

10

Angela closed the door behind her and tried to take off her raincoat without dripping water onto the parquet floor in the hall. Her face was wet, and despite sprinting from the tram to the front door, her hair had gotten wet as well.

What a day! Patients lying on gurneys in the corridors. No time for anybody. One visitor had called her "mysterious," as he'd been trying to contact her for two days, or was it three? I've been here all the time, working, she told him, but he seemed skeptical. She had been furious, but hadn't shown it. Of course. She was tired, and felt sick again.

She kicked off her boots and went to the kitchen. Rain pattered on the windows. The scarcely audible swish of trams in the square down below. Her new home. The big apartment building in Vasaplatsen.

It hadn't been completely straightforward. She still had her apartment at Kungshöjd. She smiled. Erik would come home and she'd tell him she wanted to keep her apartment. He might well believe her. At times she felt he was prepared to agree to anything. But at others nothing escaped his critical attention, not the slightest detail.

No. They would be better off here, to start with, at least, when the baby . . . She stopped her train of thought for a moment, didn't want to think about it too much until . . . until they'd had a bit more time. Until I've settled in, she thought. Until we're living together. I don't really live here yet. I just come back here after work because it feels better. In order to get used to living here.

She made a cup of tea, sat at the kitchen table, and listened to the rain outside. She stood up, went to the living room, and came back when Springsteen had already been singing for half a minute about the price you pay for what you do. Angela stroked her stomach. The price for what you do. She smiled again. *You make up your mind, you choose the chance you take.* Springsteen was carrying the whole of human vulnerability on his shoulders. Erik had started listening to Springsteen. Only the melancholy songs, of course. But even so. It wasn't only for her sake. Things were always happening to people who accepted that they kept on growing. Coltrane was still there, but he'd had to give way. Erik now knew two names from the history of modern music. The Clash and Bruce Springsteen. That should keep him going for a while. They had acquired something else in common, she thought, stroking her stomach again.

Am I afraid? No. Is he afraid? Perhaps. Will he admit it? He's saying more and more. He'll be forty in a few months, and he's learning to talk. That's early for most men.

The refrigerator was humming, but was almost empty. She stood in the light it cast with the door open. The twilight in the room had thickened into darkness. She had thought there was some cheese left, but there wasn't even enough margarine to last until morning. She had a sudden craving for anchovies. She'd read and heard about such cravings, but never experienced them herself. Anchovies had nothing to do with foul weather, but they could have something to do with her pregnancy. Just like veal headcheese coated with chocolate and other old wives' tales. Spaghetti with cola sauce.

Anchovies. Cheese. Margarine. Maybe the latest *Femina*. She'd canceled her postal subscription before moving, but now she missed not finding it in the mailbox, neither here nor at ho—No, not at home. She'd have her furniture there for a few more weeks, but that was all.

Clean break.

But what a pain, she was now longing for *Femina* almost as much as for a tin of anchovies, all yummy and caramelized by the grains of salt. She looked out of the window with rain streaming down it. The streetlights were on but had difficulty in piercing the darkness. She sighed, could hear herself doing it. Closed the refrigerator door, went into the hall, put on her boots and raincoat. The umbrella was just as elusive now as it had been this morning.

The elevator was down below, so she took the stairs. Her footsteps echoed in the stairwell, a deeper sound than the ones she'd been used to every day at ho—At Kungshöjd.

She walked along Vasagatan to the little supermarket. The rain had eased off, with just a little moisture dripping from gutters. She moved closer to the curb and heard an engine behind her, one of several. But after a minute the same vehicle was still there, and she turned around and saw a police car driving slowly a few paces behind her. She resumed walking, but the car continued crawling along at the same speed. She turned to look again and tried to see who was driving, but she could only make out a dark silhouette behind the wheel.

Were they on the lookout for somebody or something? Why was the car going so slowly, following her? Suddenly the driver flashed his headlights, turned left, and drove back toward Vasaplatsen. She looked around to see if there were any more police cars in the vicinity, but couldn't see any.

She went into the shop and bought the items on her list. Then paused at the tobacco counter, bought her magazine, and took the opportunity to snap up a packet of cola sweets, while she was there.

Spaghetti tasting of cola. The myth was about to become reality.

It had started raining again, so it didn't matter which part of the pavement she walked on. The shopping bag was heavier than she'd expected, especially when she changed hands to punch in the door code for the main entrance. She could see a police car again in the corner of her left eye. It was coming up from Aschebergsgatan now; it passed over the crossroads and slowed down as it approached her. She kept her hand on the keypad. The car drove slowly past but she still couldn't see the driver's face, as he had lowered the sun visor. She watched the car drive away and noticed the taillights blink like two red eyes. At the end of the block, it turned and disappeared.

She got in the elevator. There were evidently a lot of police cars out this evening. Or was it the same car? A raid on some shady premises in Vasastan. Where the dregs of Gothenburg live. Social dropouts. Desperadoes. Chief inspectors. Doctors. Mad widows with fortunes acquired in mysterious circumstances. There was one of those on the same floor as Erik. Very old, but she doesn't fool me, Erik had once said when they'd greeted her as she got out of the elevator. Sometimes you can hear noises from her apartment that sound like some kind of mass. Did you see her nails? No? Not surprising because she doesn't have any. But what she does have is lots of strange visitors.

She'd actually shuddered at the time. She thought about that as she stepped out of the elevator and saw Mrs. Malmer's dark-painted door.

Rosemary's Baby. The thought came from nowhere. She was Rosemary, and had moved in, for good. Erik started making late-night visits to old Mrs. Malmer and she would start hearing rhythmic murmuring through the wall. One morning Erik would have a Band-Aid on his shoulder. Somebody would die a tragic death at his workplace. The chief of police. Erik would be promoted into his job. She would be introduced to Mrs. Malmer's eccentric but very gentlemanly old friend and he would introduce her in turn to a new gynecologist, which could lead . . .

She'd opened the door to the apartment and the phone was ringing. She put down the shopping bag, kicked off her boots and took a couple of paces to the bureau in the hall where the telephone was.

"Hello?" She could hear her heavy breathing.

"Have you been running up the stairs?"

"Hi, Erik!"

"Is it good for you to run up the stairs? Or have you started doing gymnastics?"

"I took the elevator."

"That can be strenuous."

"Yes. I start imagining all the horrible things that might be going on in this building."

"Old Mrs. Malmer?"

"Why mention her by name?" she asked, noting the tone of suspicion in her own voice. Good Lord!

"That was silly of me. I don't want to scare you—"

"Stop now and tell me about your father. It sounds as if you've been able to relax a bit."

"Maybe. He was critical again for a while and they did something new to his blood vessels, adjusted something. He's resting now in the recovery ward."

"Have you managed to talk to the doctors yet?"

"Are you kidding? You ought to know better than anybody how impossible that is. The world over."

She thought about the complaints that had been directed at her earlier that day. About her never being there.

"Don't be too hard on us," she said.

"Dad isn't complaining, and that's the main thing," he said. "How are things otherwise?"

"I had the classic longing for anchovies and rushed out into the rain and was shadowed by your colleagues."

"Shadowed? By the crime unit? They can't have been all that discreet, then."

"What are you saying? Is it something that you're behind?"

"Eh? I don't understand what you're talking about."

"Being shadowed. By the crime unit."

"Do you really feel you're being shadowed by the crime unit?"

"I didn't say that."

"You said precisely that just now."

"I said I was being shadowed by your colleagues. I meant the police."

She could hear the sigh all the way from the Costa del Sol.

"Let's start again from the beginning," he said. "Tell me again. I'll listen and I won't say a word."

"I went out shopping and a police car followed me. Slowly. All the way. When I stopped to see if that really was what it was doing it flashed its headlights and turned off down a side street."

Winter said nothing.

"When I came back and was about to go through the main door a police car appeared again and drove slowly past, in the same way," Angela went on. "And after it had passed, it flashed its lights again. The taillights this time."

"Was that all?"

"Yes. For God's sake, I expect they were keeping somewhere under observation, or whatever you say. It must have been a coincidence. I said it mainly as a joke."

"Ha, ha."

"Yes, funny, wasn't it?"

"Did you get the license plate number? Or numbers if there were two cars?"

"Of course. I noted everything down right away on the inside of my eyelid." She laughed. "I'm afraid not. I didn't go to police academy."

"Well . . . I don't know what to say."

"Forget it. It was a coincidence, of course. Always assuming that you haven't . . . haven't put somebody on to keeping a discreet watch on me, to make sure I'm all right while you're away."

"It doesn't seem to be all that discreet."

"Well, have you?"

"Are you joking?"

"I'm not sure."

"I don't have the power to do anything like that. Not yet, at least."

"But soon, perhaps?"

"What do you mean?"

"If something happens to your boss? The chief of police. What's his name?"

"Birgersson. What are you talking about, Angela?"

"Nothing." She laughed again. "I'm just talking in my sleep, as it were. Or in my daydreams." Not a sound from the Costa del Sol. "Hello? Are you still there, Erik?"

"This is a very odd conversation."

"It's my fault. I'm sorry. I still feel an outsider in this building, even though I've been here so often for so many years. But it's different now. And I suppose it's really to do with me wanting you back at home again. As quickly as possible. As soon as your dad's better."

"We must keep hoping."

"It might take time."

"If he has any time left."

"It sounds as if he has."

"Now you'd better fix those anchovies."

"I suppose you get a lot of that kind of thing down there."

"I haven't tried any yet."

"No tapas?"

"There hasn't been any . . . time. I stayed at the hospital last night."

"What was it like?"

"Better than being somewhere else. Anyway, make sure you get some salt down you, so that you don't think so much about ghosts."

"Mrs. Malmer?"

"Police cars."

"I've bought some cola sweets as well."

"Eat them with mashed anchovies and Parmesan cheese."

"I've made a note of that," Angela said.

The car drove around the town center, then returned to Vasaplatsen. The driver was listening to the emergency call-outs. A traffic jam near the Tingstad Tunnel. A mugging in Kortedala. Somebody who ran away from a tram in Majorna without paying.

He parked at the newspaper stand and bought a paper, any paper. Maybe he'd read it, or just leave it on one of the seats. Maybe he'd just drop it in the trash bin.

Lights were on in most of the apartments. He knew which block, but not which apartment. It would be easy to check the names on the intercom on the front door, but what would be the point of that? He asked himself that question as he got back into the car and fastened his seat belt. What-would-be-the-point-of-that? He had a question but no answer. When he knew why he was going to go up to that door and check the address and the floor, he would also know the answer to several other questions. Things that had happened. That were going to happen. Going-to-happen.

Had he flashed his lights? If he had, there would have been a point. It would have been a start. He looked down at the newspaper on his knee. He didn't know which one it was: *Göteborgs Tidningen* or *Expressen* or *Aftonbladet,* only that there would be things in it, and in the others, that he could have told them about himself, but they hadn't asked and it was the same as it always was because nobody ever asked him anything, anything with a POINT to it, but that was all over now, ALL OVER NOW. He squeezed his hand around the newspaper and tugged at it, and afterward, after a minute, or a year, while he was still sitting in front of the newspaper stand, he looked down again and saw that he had torn the paper in two.

11

Winter was up before eight. The strip of sky he could see through the bathroom window at La Luna was blue today. There was a smell of sun outside already, tinged with the soft soap that Salvador, the landlord, had been using to scrub the patio. Winter could hear blows from a hammer, and a woman's voice.

He could feel the heat seeping into his room through the wrought-iron grille in the window. This could become the hottest day since he'd arrived. Salvador pointed up at the sky and rolled his eyes as Winter walked past. Summer was hanging on.

He had coffee at Gaspar's café and smoked a Corps. He was already a familiar face to the staff and to the lung patient, who was at his usual table coughing his way through the morning at Plaza Puente de Málaga, and calmed down briefly when the waiter brought him his glass of gin. The man nodded politely at Winter as he raised his glass.

Winter felt stiff. He would soon be driving out to the hospital again, but decided on a brisk walk first, to stretch his legs. He drained his coffee, stubbed out his cigarillo, and paid his bill. Before leaving he made a quick call to his mother, who was sitting by his father's bed in the recovery room. No change.

He consulted his tourist map of town. He could walk up the hill to the bus station and back. About an hour, he thought. The exercise would do him good.

Calle de las Peñuelas ran north from the plaza, and he followed it for a few hundred yards before turning left at Calle San Antonio, which the map suggested would wind its way gently up the hillside toward the mountains.

After only a block or so he found himself in a very different Marbella, not at all like the residential area in which he was staying. Here were bars and shops for the locals; women lined up outside their front doors, men in cafés, children on the way to and from school. *Heladeía, panaderías, carnecerías.* The smell of fresh meat outside butchers' shops.

A young girl with a loaf under her arm. Sun and shadow already playing games despite the early hour. He passed by the enormous Caja Ahorros Ronda, Bar Pepe Duña, Colegio Público García Lorca over the road, voices from schoolchildren at playtime. A newsstand at the crossroads with a large sign advertising *Sur,* the local newspaper.

He continued northward and came to the main road, Avenida Arias de Velasco, glanced at his map and turned left.

He soon passed the police station on his left, Comisaria de Policía Nacional. It was small, built of gray marble, with some of the walls made entirely of glass; there were wide steps leading up to the entrance, where two notices indicated: OFICINA DE DENUNCIAS and PASAPORTES EXTRANJEROS. He felt sorry for his colleagues. There must be a lot to do in Marbella, especially during the holiday season. Pickpockets. Lost passports. More pickpockets. Winter had no time for pickpockets, almost as little as he had for the poor devils who couldn't manage to protect themselves from them.

The Mafia. Rumor had it that Marbella had become a favorite center for organized crime. He recalled reading something to that effect in some report or other. Tax exiles and the Mafia. Villas in the mountains. Tapas at Paseo Marítimo in the evenings, where deals were done.

Two colleagues in uniform came down the steps from the police station and Winter automatically nodded to them as they passed him, crossed the street and went into the Bar del Enfrente on the other side. A late-morning glass of gin to bolster their strength. Winter felt thirsty and wanted a beer, but continued up the steps. One of the police officers left the bar and went into a motorcycle showroom.

Winter had reached the plateau by now. He took the footbridge over the highway and turned left toward the bus station. He turned around to gaze down at the town below, with the sea and the horizon in the distance. No sign of any clouds. It had been worth the walk. He could see for miles, as far as Nueva Andalucía, and to the east, in the far distance, was the outline of what might well be the Hospital Costa del Sol.

He was closer to the mountains. He could see them through the glass doors of the bus station, and went inside. A crowd of people came surging out, forcing their way past him and down the steps. He could smell sweat and sun lotion, an elbow poked into his ribs and he tried to dodge out of the way.

Half a minute later all was calm again, and Winter was inside the building. He got his bearings and went in to a large cafeteria where he ordered a coffee and a small bottle of mineral water. He put his hand into the inside pocket of his linen jacket and . . . and . . . what the he—. He tried his other inside pocket: also empty. His hand slid straight through, meeting no resistance. What the HELL? The man behind the counter was waiting to be paid, and seemed to see the panic in Winter's eyes. He pointed at Winter, at his jacket. Winter raised his left arm and examined the side of the jacket. A neat cut had been made through all the layers of cloth and through to his inside pocket where his wallet had been. HIS WALLET. What had been in it? Ten thousand pesetas, perhaps. Addresses. Driver's license. Credit card—oh, shit! His credit cards, Visa, MasterCard. He took out his mobile phone, dialed, and waited impatiently for an answer.

"Angela here."

"It's Erik. I hoped you wouldn't have left already. I've just been robbed and I don't have the number I need to block my credit cards. First Card, or Nordbanken, and the Savings Bank."

"Were you mugged? Are you hurt?"

"No, no. It was a pickpocket. But I can tell you the details later. Can you ring them? I think the phone numbers are on the bulletin board in the hall. Over the bureau, yes, I'm sure. Two cards. No, just phone them. They have all the details. What? It was just now, less than five minutes ago. Seven o'clock, maybe. I'm on a hillside some way above Marbella and the bastard will have to make his way down to an ATM in town. If we can stop them now he won't have time."

"I'll fix it."

"Phone me back when you've done it."

He switched off and turned to the man behind the counter, who had been following the conversation. Winter still hadn't touched his coffee, or the water.

"*Un ladrón, eh?*"

Winter didn't understand what he meant, but made a gesture in response.

"*Ha robado la cartera, eh?*" He pointed at Winter's sleeve. "*La cartera. Hijo de puta.*" He shook his head, as if regretting the existence of all the world's riffraff. "*Hijo de puta.*"

"Yes," Winter said. "The sonofabitch stole my wallet." He looked at the cup of coffee. Steam was still rising from it. He'd have loved to take a sip, but he couldn't pay for it.

"*Sírvase,*" said the man, gesturing sympathetically toward the cup. "Please. It's on the house."

She laughed at him. It was like the first time . . . when it had all started. She, the other one, and he . . . they'd both laughed.

She'd accused him of not being a real man. Just look at yourself, she'd said.

Now he did exactly what he wanted to do in this room, which had turned completely white in his eyes. He hardly noticed them as he walked over to the stereo and switched on the cassette that the other one had switched off with a curse only seconds after he'd started it.

"Do-not-switch-off-that-music," he said.

"You're out of your fucking mind."

"Do-not-switch-it-off."

"We want you to get out."

"Just fuck off," she said. "We don't want you here."

"I-am-staying-here," he said, turning the sound up and starting to react to the bass, to the guitars. The room was white. He closed his eyes tightly. He had stopped seeing. There was no darkness. He felt something hit his stomach, like a punch, or a kick, but he didn't open his eyes. The white was still out there. He didn't want to see it. The music was everywhere, WOAHWAOHWHÄÄWHOAWHÄÄWHO, he felt another blow and somebody was pulling his hair and he opened his eyes. The other guy hit him again, knocking him to the floor. This cretin was trying to get to the music, but *he* was in charge now. *He* was in charge. If he lay still and allowed him to turn off the music it would all be over, but that was impossible. *He* was in charge now. The real man. He stood up, opened his eyes and peered at them through the whiteness, and he no longer knew if it was quiet. He heard nothing as he grabbed hold of her, felt nothing, nothing as he groped after him as well, after his body. The white glow was still there, but at a distance now, as if waiting. He grabbed at her again, at him again.

A long time.

He was shaking like a dog. The music was still on when it was over. He'd done everything and toward the end he'd had all the help—the courage—he'd lacked earlier. He was still there in the white glow. He could hear the words, one after another, nobody else could make out any words in the blare of the music, the-blood-is-sacrificed-in-my-face.

Angela rang after five minutes.

"All done."

"Good."

"So, what now?"

"I'll borrow money from Mom today. But you could phone the bank and ask them to send me some money to arrive tomorrow."

"Where to?"

"To one of the banks in town. I'll call in at the first one I come to and ask if they can receive transfers. Actually, I can phone my bank myself if you can give me the number now."

"Okay. That was . . . pretty bad luck."

"It was badly handled by me. That shouldn't happen."

"Every cloud has a silver lining. You'll learn to have a bit of sympathy with the victims from now on."

"Hmm."

"You'll have to report this to the police."

"Oh, please."

"Of course you must, Erik. You can't come back home and contact your insurers and all that without having reported the incident to the police on the spot. Do I have to spell that out for you, of all people?"

"No."

"Maybe the thief will pocket the credit cards and send all the rest to the police."

"Maybe Santa lives at the North Pole."

"I'm serious, Erik."

"Okay, okay. I'll report it to the police. At least I know where the police station is."

"Good. Worse things have happened, Erik."

"I know, Angela. I know."

He walked around the bus station, investigating the waste bins and the dusty bushes, but the thief hadn't thrown away the wallet.

Winter was still feeling furious, but Angela was right. There were people worse off than he was.

The gray marble walls of the police station had turned white when the sun started shining on them. He went up the steps and turned left to the Oficina de Denuncias, and tried to explain his problem to a uniformed officer at a desk. The man held up a hand, and used his other to point to a door. It was closed, but the sign, white on blue, said: INTERPRETER'S OFFICE.

Winter sat down. After a few minutes the door opened and a couple who could well have been Swedes came out. The police officer beckoned to Winter.

Inside was a woman at a desk. She was busy filling in a form, looked up and indicated to Winter that he should take a seat on the chair in front of her desk. She looked twenty-five, possibly thirty, years of age. Dark, close-cropped hair; but when she looked at him he noticed that her eyes were blue. She didn't seem to be wearing any makeup. An attractive woman. Wearing a loose-fitting dress, and her skin tone was unusually light for a Spaniard.

He told her briefly what had happened. She listened with interest, which surprised him.

"Please fill in this form. I'll be back in just a moment," she said.

She handed him a form headed *"Diligencia,"* and he started filling in personal data and a summary of what had happened. He hesitated at the word *"Profesió,"* but decided to tell the truth.

She came back and read quickly through the document.

"Do you still have your passport?"

"It looks like it. Otherwise I wouldn't have been able to fill in the passport number, would I?" He'd sounded aggressive. He regretted his words. But she didn't react at all.

"So, you are a chief inspector?" He thought he could detect a trace of a smile, but couldn't be certain.

"Detective chief inspector," he said.

"Aren't you a bit on the young side for that?"

"You think so? I'm in my fifties."

"In that case you have lied about your age on this form."

"I was only joking." Winter could feel something inside his head, a sudden weak rush of blood. She looked at him again. "You also seem to be on the young side for an . . . interpreter," he said. Oh, come on! I hope I'm not sitting here flirting.

She smiled and stood up. She was tall, taller than he had expected.

"I apologize for all the criminals we have here on the south coast." She pointed at the door. "If you'd like to wait outside I'll pass on this form to a police officer who'll enter the information into the computer. You'll be called in to him shortly."

"Is that everything?" Winter said.

"I can't think of anything else."

He stood up. There was a sign by the door with three names under a heading that presumably meant "Police Interpreters." Two men's names and a woman's: Alicia. She noticed that he was scrutinizing the sign.

"Yes, my name's Alicia."

"Erik."

"I know," she said with a smile, indicating the form she had in her hand.

He waited outside. A constable emerged and ushered him into a room looking out over the main road. It was the man Winter had seen earlier that morning going into the bar, and later into the motorcycle showroom.

"I apologize for the problems, Chief Inspector."

"It was my own fault."

The man said nothing. Perhaps he wondered how on earth I could have been such an idiot, something I was asking myself as well.

"They are getting more and more bold."

"That's the way it is."

"But we mustn't give up, must we?"

"Of course not."

"Where would the world be if the police were to give up?" wondered the officer, but Winter decided not to enter into that philosophical debate just now. The officer spoke excellent English. Their discussion could have been very involved. "When the police give up, the world is doomed."

"Do you need any more information?"

"I beg your pardon? Er, no. I'll just finish filling this in."

The man wrote in silence, much more slowly than he had spoken. He needed to concentrate hard. Winter had no intention of disturbing him. He might take it amiss.

"There. It's done. Could you sign here, please? Both copies."

Winter duly signed and got to his feet, one of the copies safely in his pocket.

"Be careful out there, Chief Inspector," said the police officer, and Winter searched for a trace of irony; but the man's face was a complete blank. "It's a jungle."

As he passed by the front desk, Alicia emerged from her office carrying more forms: Winter could see another tourist in the chair in front of her desk.

"Good-bye, Inspector Erik," she said, giving him a winning smile.

He thought briefly about her as he walked down the hill. He was behind the wheel of his car and ready to drive to the hospital before he remembered that he needed to stop in at the bank.

12

Maria and Patrik were wandering around the center of town. It was chill-ier now. A northerly wind. Maria plunged her hands into her pockets.

"Didn't you bring any gloves?"

"I thought I had put them in my pocket."

"It's cold."

"That's better than rain, though."

"Have you got any cigarettes?" she asked, stopping outside McDon-ald's. The big stores in the Nordstan shopping center were closed, but the doors into the warmth were still open.

"I'm trying to stop."

"Stop? You've only just started."

"I don't like it."

"Who does?" she said, going into the shopping center. They walked under a blast of warm air. A group of adults followed them in. They all seemed to be laughing. Maria could smell booze and perfume and af-tershave. The group stopped outside King Creole, then went in just as Maria and Patrik were passing.

"Dance band," he said with a laugh.

"At least they have somewhere to go."

"I'd prefer to stay outside."

"Even so."

Groups of people were dotted around the square outside Femman. Two police officers strolled across to where a street musician was play-ing the guitar. He didn't stop playing just because they were standing over him. He started to sing. One of the officers, the older one, seemed to be swaying in time to the music. The singer increased his volume.

"He sounds as if he's in pain," Patrik said.

"It's meant to sound like that," Maria said. "It's something from Spain. Flamingo, they call it."

"Flamenco. It's called Flamenco."

"I didn't think you knew about stuff like that."

"But it sounds as if he's hurt himself."

"Just imagine being able to fly off there."

"A last-minute package to the Canary Islands."

"Have you been there?"

"We were all there, the whole family . . . before Mom moved out."

"What was it like?"

"When Mom moved out? Just let it drop."

"I meant the Canary Islands."

Patrik paused, listening to the musician, who had launched into a new tune that sounded identical to the previous one.

He could tell her about a swimming pool and how he'd dived from a little stone ledge where there was a palm tree and the pool was just one story below the balcony of the apartment they'd stayed in. His little sister had had water wings and his mom had walked beside her in the blue water, laughing. He'd been diving and swimming all day long and in the afternoons they'd played bingo. He'd been swimming after dark as well, and demonstrated a new dive to his parents as they'd sat at a poolside table with his sister. Watch this, he'd shouted, and they'd clapped. It was nearly as hot in the evenings as during the day, but back home in Sweden there was snow everywhere. He'd held his father's hand.

But there was no little sister, no mom, no trip to the Canary Islands, no swimming pool, no palm tree, no bingo. Had never been. He used to dream, sometimes, dream aloud. Maria knew nothing about that. She could visit whatever islands she wanted.

"There was nothing special about the Canary Islands," he said.

Morelius was standing outside Harley's, waiting for Bartram, who'd gone inside to chat with the owner. Morelius stamped his feet. It had turned colder, and felt much chillier and drier after only a couple of hours.

"It'll take place tomorrow," said Bartram as he came out. "They're not thinking of changing it."

"Okay."

"Maybe that's just as well."

"Does it matter when the Harley-Davidson club have their party?"

"I suppose not."

"Same high jinks no matter when."

"Pretty girls, though," Bartram said. "They always have some top-class babe with 'em."

"Don't you include them among the members?"

"They're hangers-on," said Bartram. "Attractive hangers-on." He stamped his feet. "I wouldn't mind an HD chick to warm me up right now."

"You don't say."

"Get her inside all this leather." He stroked his leather jacket. "Get down to the basics. Get what I mean, Simon? The basics."

"Oh, shut up."

"Now what's the matter?"

"I'm fed up with your chatter."

"Relax a bit, for God's sake! It's a . . ." But Bartram shut up as he saw two young people approaching along the Avenue. They were only six feet away now. "Ah, some old friends! Good evening."

"Good evening," Patrik said.

"So you're out walking again," Morelius said.

"It's a free country," said Maria.

"Of course it is," said Bartram. "Aren't you cold?"

"No," said Maria, but Morelius could see her red nose and earlobes and her bare hands stuck into her pockets.

"Are you on your way home?"

"Whose home?"

"Suit yourselves," Morelius said. "We're just about to pick up a car and could give you a lift."

"The night is yet young," Patrik said. He'd heard that somewhere and thought it sucked so much, he just wanted to say it. Morelius looked at Bartram but made no comment.

"It is indeed," said Bartram. "Have you something special in mind?"

"We'd thought of going to a pub," said Maria.

"You're too young for that."

"Exactly. That's just it."

"What do you mean?"

"There's nowhere we can get into."

"You don't want to be sitting around in pubs."

"I'm not just talking about pubs. I'm talking about places. Anywhere. Any place where young people can get in and hang out."

"Hang out?"

"Hang out. With other people."

"Okay," Morelius said.

"But it's no good," Patrik said. "There isn't anywhere."

"I'm with you on that," Morelius said.

"What are you going to do on New Year's Eve?" asked Bartram.

"What?"

"The night of the century. Of the millennium. Will we be seeing you up at Skansen?"

"Eh?"

"Won't you be there? We'll be there."

"You mean you'll be working on New Year's Eve?"

"Of course. Both Morelius and I are on duty then, and we'll be up at Skansen when the big moment comes."

"Jesus Christ! Working on New Year's Eve!"

"Why not? Half of Gothenburg will be up on that hillside, in any case. The younger half, at least. And we'll be getting paid for being there." He turned to Morelius. "We're in luck, aren't we, Simon?"

"We certainly are."

Patrik looked at Maria and shook his head.

"We'd better get going," he said.

"Go home and get warm," Morelius said.

"It's a free country," Patrik said. He enjoyed saying that, because it sucked.

Bergenhem had finished his late shift but hadn't gone straight home. Instead he'd driven southward and played the fourth CD from Springsteen's *Tracks, happy with you in my arms, happy with you in my heart.* Last night Martina had whispered something and stroked his arm, but he'd pretended to be asleep. She'd turned away, and he really did fall asleep in the end. He'd tried not to think.

The bay glimmered over to the right as he drove through Askim. He kept on straight ahead. Traffic was lighter as the city started to peter out. Lower, richer. The detached houses twinkled like oases as he drove past, tires singing. The last of the buses pulled up at stops that seemed deserted in the darkness, *happy, darling, come the dark, happy when I taste your kiss, I'm happy in a love like this,* and Bergenhem listened as he drove. It was like listening to a language he didn't understand but nevertheless could follow every word.

He thought about his child. He thought about his wife. He took the Billdal slip road and followed the minor roads as far as the sea, parked, and got out of the car. The lights from a fishing boat bobbed up and down around the islands in the southern archipelago. All around him were the outlines of beached sailing boats. More lights twinkled out to sea, and in the distance was a broader light that could well have been the midnight ferry to Fredrikshavn.

Before long its crossing would be labeled a New Year's cruise. A new millennium greeted in international waters, Bergenhem thought. Water. He squatted down and dipped his hand into the water: it felt like a glove of ice. I'm in deep water, he thought. I really must sort this out.

Back on the main road he noticed a patrol car parked at a bus stop. The driver was standing beside his car. Bergenhem couldn't see anybody else in the car as he drove past. In his rearview mirror he could see the officer gazing out over the houses and treetops. Maybe he had a cigarette in his hand. We all need a break now and then, Bergenhem thought. He had the impression at first that he recognized his colleague, but he wasn't sure now. One thing was clear: it wasn't somebody from the Frölunda station.

There was a sudden hard pattering on his windshield: hail, which soon turned into snow, the first of the winter. Almost November. Springsteen was still singing: *and honey I just wanna be back in your arms, back in your arms again.* Bergenhem drove home and crept down between the cold sheets. Martina was asleep and he pretended to be as well.

. . . . .

Winter's head lolled onto his shoulder and he woke from his doze with a start.

"Go and lie down on the guest bed," his mother said.

"I'm all right."

"He's resting now."

Winter looked at his father's face, which had lost what had remained of the color it had possessed when he first saw him in the hospital. That was three days ago, or was it four?

How is he still managing to breathe? Winter went up to the bed. His father's head was turned toward the window, but his eyes were closed. The outline of the mountain peaks was sketched against the sky. An airplane was descending toward Málaga. Winter thought of Sweden, and as he did so the mobile phone rang in his pocket. He strode quickly out into the corridor and answered.

"How's it going?"

"Not good, I'm afraid. Worse."

"I'll try to get there tomorrow." His sister coughed, wheezed. She tried to say something, then tried again. "It was only one hundred and two this morning."

"You ought to be in the hospital. High temperatures like that are dangerous, Doctor."

"It's a da . . . , a da . . ."

"I beg your pardon? I can't hear what you're saying, Lotta."

"It's a damn nuisance to be suffering from the flu of the century—no, the flu of the damn millennium—when Dad's in the state he's in."

Winter didn't know what to say. The blue light coming from the corridor was faint, but, even so, brighter than that in his father's room. It was reminiscent of a tunnel of ice.

"Your temperature's bound to go down," he said, and could hear two nurses talking softly to each other at the office desk, where the light was different, warmer.

"I think I'll take some pills that will knock me out," she said. "Make or break."

"You know best."

"The hell I do. But I'm not the important one now." She started coughing, rasping, gasping for breath. She tried to say something, but coughed once more. "I might manage to say a few words to Mom."

"I'll get her," Winter said, going back into the room and handing the telephone to his mother.

His father mumbled something and turned his head, and Winter could see that he was awake.

NOVEMBER

13

The bank, Unicaja, had eventually received the money, two minutes before closing time, following three calls by Winter to his bank in Sweden: reference number, account number, Swift code. The bank did not accept payments in Spanish currency: Winter had no alternative but to pay the exchange fees.

He missed the feeling of having a plastic card in his hand. The notes were new and stiff in the inside pocket of his jacket. He paused as he emerged from the bank and took stock, determined to avoid crowds of people.

Another month, but it was still just as hot. That morning Salvador, his host at La Luna, had thrust his arms out wide and said something about *el cielo azul*. The blue sky, constantly hovering over the people who were desperate for some cooler weather.

Winter stood outside the bank in the main street, Avenida Ricardo Soriano. He felt hungry, more so than at any time since he'd arrived here. He turned right and bumped into Alicia. She was alone. Perhaps it was she who stopped and spoke to him.

"Have you sorted out your financial problems, Chief Inspector?"

"I've just picked up the money from Sweden," he said, pointing at the bank window.

"That's good."

"It makes things easier."

"*Sí.*"

"Now I can afford to have lunch."

She checked her watch, but made no move to leave.

"Don't let me keep you," Winter said.

"I've just finished my shift," she said.

"I see." Winter shuffled uneasily. "I'd better have lunch before I drive out to the hospital."

"Have you injured yourself as well, Chief Inspector?"

"Please call me Erik. No, my father is seriously ill. That's why I'm here."

"I'm sorry to hear that." She looked as if she meant it. She was wearing a skirt today, black, and a brown blouse that seemed to be keeping the heat at bay, despite its color. Winter had noticed that Spanish women seemed to survive the heat better than the men, who appeared to bluster their way through the day. The women dealt with it rather more elegantly. "I hope everything turns out for the best." She seemed to be thinking about something, turned to look in the direction she'd come from, then turned back to face him. "Did you have anywhere particular in mind for lunch?"

"No . . . I suppose I'll head in that direction. That way leads to the Old Town, doesn't it? I haven't seen much of Marbella yet. The town itself, I mean."

Alicia looked at her watch again.

"Anyway . . . there we are," said Winter, making as if to leave.

"There's a good little restaurant a few minutes down the road. I can show you it, if you like."

"Have you had lunch yourself yet?"

"No, not yet. But I usually just gulp down a sandwich when I get a moment."

"I'll be happy to treat you if you'd be so kind as to show me this place you mentioned," Winter said.

It was in the Calle Tetuán and was called Sol y Sombra, specializing in fish and seafood. There were a few tables outside under parasols, and a large room that gave the impression of being cool, with white tablecloths and open windows facing the little pedestrian plaza.

"What do you think?" Alicia asked.

Winter noted a large glass counter with fish, prawns, and lan-goustines on ice. Behind the counter was a proud-looking man with shiny black hair and a white shirt. A party of locals was sitting around one of the inside tables. A couple outside had just been served a bottle of white wine, now covered in condensation. It seemed to be hot everywhere, despite the parasols.

"This looks ideal. I'd like to sit inside. What do you think?"

"Okay."

They sat down and the man from behind the counter came with the menu and a jug of water.

"I'd be grateful if you did the ordering," Winter said.

"Are you very hungry?"

"Very."

"Appetizer and main course?"

"Sounds good . . . maybe something to pick at first."

"Wine?"

"A glass, perhaps."

Alicia ordered, and they were served with a carafe of wine, a basket of rye bread, and a few large, green olives. Winter poured the wine, which tasted of sun and soil.

"Do you work as an interpreter full time?"

"Just now I do. I'm actually a grammar school teacher, but . . . well, I got a bit fed up last year, and this is how it turned out."

"Do you live here?"

"In Marbella, you mean? No, if only. But then somebody who's just been robbed probably wouldn't see it that way."

"Apart from that it seems to be . . . a pleasant-enough town. Not all that many tourists. But it's hardly high season."

"It's pretty good in the high season as well. Unlike where I live, Tor-remolinos."

"Oh, Torremolinos."

"Do you know it?"

"Everybody the world over must have heard of Torremolinos, surely? But I've never actually been there. Only seen it from a distance."

"That's the best way," said Alicia. "That's what everybody says, unfortunately."

"Is it really as bad as that?"

"Worse. Maybe not the part where I live, but on the whole . . . Some people call it Terrible Torrie, and that's a good name—although most of the awfulness is their fault."

"Yes, I hear it's very popular with the English."

"The tattooed and shaven members of the population, that is. They're escorted from the airport by the Guardia Civil and taken to their hotels in armored cars."

Winter laughed, and coughed as some wine went down the wrong way. Alicia smiled.

"And that's only the start of their vacation," she said.

"And you live in the middle of all that?"

"As I said, it's not so bad where I live, overlooking an old fishing village called La Carihuela, a couple of miles outside the town. You can walk along the beach from there to Torrie. If you dare."

"But you work here."

"The police station is nicer here," she said, taking a sip of wine. "The . . . clientele as well," she added, looking at Winter and smiling again.

"My head's more or less clean-shaven," he said.

"But I don't see the half-gallon glass of beer and a portion of fish and chips on the table in front of you," Alicia said.

"What's this?" Winter asked, indicating the two large plates the waiter had just put down on the table between them.

"Fish and chips," said Alicia with a laugh. "But you'll get something else in a minute or two."

Morelius looked hard at his deep-fried prawns, but they seemed to have taken root in the foil container: he threw them in the trash bin. Everyone on television was going on and on about the millennium. Nobody had ever heard that word until a year ago.

If your work gets under your skin so much that you need to talk to a priest, you can't be suitable for the job. You have to have a tem-

perament that can cope with it. A surgeon at a cancer clinic can't demand counseling after he's been operating and perhaps speaking to a
patient.

You simply barge your way through. Barge-your-way-through,
Morelius thought.

"Penny for your thoughts," said Bartram.

"Why? What do you mean?"

"You seemed so damned preoccupied."

"I was thinking about the Gamlestaden Motorcycle Club, which'll
be having their Christmas party at Harley's soon."

"Hmm, that's something worth thinking about."

"I'll miss it this year."

"You know the date?"

"I checked."

"The special call-out boys will sort that out. They'll surround the
place with five squad cars."

Some people can cope with policing the streets, others can't, Morelius thought. I'm going to cope. I have so far, haven't I? Haven't I? I've
been out there in the night.

"The girl who worked in the cloakroom at the Park Hotel died yesterday. Did you know that?"

"Eh? No. I knew she was in a bad way."

"Her boyfriend seems to be about to follow her."

"Really?"

"Do you think she took it herself?"

"The GHB, you mean? I wouldn't like to say."

"She wasn't the type."

"None of them ever is."

"She was pretty."

Winter said good-bye when they emerged into the Calle Tetuán.

"Perhaps we'll meet again," Alicia said. "You know where I am . . .
if you feel hungry again and need some advice." She looked at him.
"Or if you run into any more trouble." She gave him her business card.
Winter put it in his pocket.

"Can I give you a lift if you're heading east? I have a car down by the bank."

"No thanks, I have a few things to see to and then I'll take a bus. I hope everything turns out okay with your father."

Winter nodded and they went their separate ways. He walked back to the *avenida*. The car was hot inside and out, and he could feel the sweat trickling down his back even before he'd sat down. His mobile rang.

"I can't make it," said his sister. He could hear her coughing again. "Tomorrow, though. For sure."

"I'm on my way to the hospital again."

"Is he still awake? Is he with it, I mean?"

"We had a little chat last night, in any case."

"That's good," she croaked.

"I don't know. He was trying to make a sort of farewell speech, but I wouldn't let him."

The wall surface was rough, like the trunk of a tree. Had he found the paintbrush somewhere in the flat? Or had he taken it with him? He was calm enough now to ask questions, but he couldn't answer them.

There. He'd finished.

They followed his every movement. Him and her. He didn't approach them. They just had to sit there, and he'd drawn up the blinds so that it wasn't so dark inside. It wasn't quiet in there either. It-wasn't-quiet-in-there-either. The music was on auto-reverse. The light from outside shone onto the other guy's head as he kept an eye on everything from the sofa. Nothing moved. He was pleased that nothing moved. It had been harder with her, but now she was still as well, watching him. Nobody was laughing anymore. Who was in charge now? Who was making the decisions now?

He'd shown them.

He'd show *him* now, make him understand.

He switched off the music, but that was not good. He switched it on again, but lowered the volume and looked around. He could leave now.

14

Angela woke up before midnight with the feeling that something was about to happen. Something she didn't want to think about.

In the no-man's-land between sleep and waking she had seen the images one after another, like slides projected onto the big, bare bedroom wall.

She got out of bed and put on her robe, her heart pounding. She sat at the kitchen table with a glass of milk. Everything was quiet in the street outside. Somebody flushed a toilet in an apartment upstairs. She considered switching on the radio, but decided not to. Mustn't get too wide awake. She sat with her hand over her stomach. Mustn't plan too far ahead.

The swishing noise in the pipes stopped. Still no late-night tram outside, no voices in the darkness, which smelled of snow. She could smell it when she opened the window and breathed in deeply. A premonition of winter, and she closed the window, put the glass in the sink, and went back through the hall. The hiss clattered up, stopped on the landing, and she could hear the door opening and shutting and the sound of gravel scraping against the stone floor. She paused in the hall. Why am I standing here? I want to hear those footsteps go in through a door. Mrs. Malmer's door.

Good grief.

Some more scraping footsteps. They sounded as if they were outside her door, just outside the door. Angela suddenly found herself incapable of moving. Everything was concentrated on listening for those footsteps.

I shouldn't sleep here when Erik's away.

This is ridiculous.

A rasping, grinding sound again. Footsteps again; moving away. She could hear the hundred-year-old elevator rattling its way back up, and the soft clatter as it came to a halt in the corridor outside. The clinking of the sliding steel door followed by a little click and the sound of the cage heading back down again.

Angela stood behind the door. She peered out through the peephole and could see the landing in a grotesque wide-angled perspective, but there was no sign of anybody outside. The light was still on. She opened the door, and immediately outside were some grains of black gravel, and a shallow pool of water glittering in the light.

That could be from me, she thought. It takes some time for water to evaporate in the stairwell when there's a constant cold draft coming from below. Persecution mania. I'll be wandering around checking for pools of water and grains of gravel all over the building next. She gave a little snort and closed the door.

The alarm clock on the bedside table said twelve-fifteen. She'd have to be up again in six hours, ready for the hospital corridors. The lumps of plaster that had fallen out of the green examination-room walls. Did they always have to be green? Doors with the paint peeling off. Patients must lose hope as they sit waiting and see how the hospital is slowly falling apart. If they couldn't repair a wall, how the hell could they heal a body that had—

The telephone rang. Angela gave a start. It rang again, seemed to be moving across the table. It'll be Erik, she thought as she lifted the receiver. It's happened.

"Yes? Angela here."

Not a word, just the sound of static.

"Hello? Erik?"

A rustling. Another sound that she couldn't identify. Was that a voice in the background? Perhaps, very faint. Calls were finding it difficult to make their way across Europe tonight.

"I can't hear anything. Maybe you should redial? Can you hear me? I can't hear you."

Now she could hear the echo of voices, but that was normal: fragments of conversation from anywhere in the world could be picked up by different lines and transformed into a sort of Esperanto. It could be any language at all, a conversation on a mountain peak millions of miles away.

Now she could hear breathing. That wasn't from a distant mountain peak. It sounded nearby.

"Hello? Is anybody there?"

Breathing again, clear, intentional. It had taken over from the distant babble.

She suddenly felt scared to death. She wanted the babble to return. That had been reassuring. She thought about the images she'd seen in her mind's eye. The footsteps, the images again, the pool of water . . .

More breathing.

"Say something! I can hear that there's somebody there." She made her voice sound as threatening as she could, but it came over as tiny, frightened. "Who is it?" And then she thought she could hear something else, something more . . . and she dropped the receiver. It hit the edge of the table and fell to the floor and lay there, the earpiece pointing upward. She stared at it for a few seconds, then lifted it up.

It was silent now. The silence was broken by a click, then came the familiar dial tone.

For Chrissakes, Angela! Keep calm. There are idiots who dial a wrong number but can't bring themselves to admit it. There are also madmen who ring numbers haphazardly in the hope of somebody answering.

But she wanted to talk to Erik, hear his voice, be reassured.

His mobile was switched off. She left a message. What was going on? He promised he would never switch it off while he was away.

She looked at the receiver in her hand. Should she leave it off for the rest of the night? That would be stupid. Erik might need to phone. No doubt there was some temporary fault affecting his mobile. She dialed his number again.

"Erik here."

"Why the hell don't you answer the phone?"

"Eh? What are you talking about?"

"You haven't been answering. Your phone was switched off."

He looked at it, as if half-expecting to see some fault or other.

"When was this?"

"Just now. A couple of minutes ago."

"Really? Well, it's working okay now."

"I can hear that, for God's sake."

"What's the matter, Angela?" He looked at his watch. Nearly one. "You seem . . ."

"Somebody's trying to phone me here."

"What do you mean?"

She explained.

"That's happened to me," he said. "I expect it happens to everybody at some time or other."

"That makes me feel a lot better."

"But I don't like what you're saying. Was this the first time?"

"I've never experienced anything like this before. Never in *my* apartment."

"So you mean that it has to do with my apartment, is that it?"

"No, Erik. For God's sake, I don't know what I'm saying. I expect it was just somebody who dialed a wrong number and didn't want to own up."

"Hmm."

"I'm overreacting. I just wanted to hear your voice. Now I can hear a tram outside. I feel calm again now."

"You can call me whenever you want."

"How's your father today?"

"So-so. I'm at the hospital now, but I'll probably go back to my hotel before long."

"Have you spoken to your dad's doctor yet? Al—Whatever his name is?"

"Alcorta. Of course not. He's a ghost. In a white coat."

He slept badly for a few hours. The refrigerator in his basic room was noisier than it had been before. No, no, it was the same as ever. All the noises were the same. The woman in one of the next-door houses bawled her husband into life before six, and a quarter of an hour later Winter heard muffled hammer blows. So, it was the carpenter.

He had emptied his pockets onto the table next to the wardrobe.

Her business card was illuminated by the morning light shining in from the patio.

Winter shook his head and went for a shower.

The table next to his at Gaspar's was empty. Winter missed his breakfast companion with the hacking cough. The waiter arrived with coffee and *tostadas* even though Winter hadn't ordered. He saw how Winter was looking at the neighboring table and made the sign of the cross. Winter lit a Corps after breakfast and watched the smoke drifting up into the sky. The sun was clawing its way up behind the mountain.

Lotta Winter arrived by taxi just as he was getting out of his rented car in the hospital car park. She looked pale and had a hacking cough, though it was nothing compared with that of his former breakfast companion.

"A decent flight, I hope?"

"No. I was sitting next to a drunk."

"That's a charter flight for you."

"I see you haven't been in the sun much."

"Let's go in," he proposed.

"If we dare."

"He's awake. Mom called not long ago."

"She phoned me as well. In the taxi."

"He's back in the nursing ward."

"How many times is this?"

"Does it matter?"

"I think I'll cross my fingers," she said as they climbed the steps and entered the cool gloom of the entrance hall.

Their mother was waiting for them in the corridor. A short man in a white coat came up to them and held out his hand. Lotta shook it and looked at her brother.

"*Soy Pablo Alcorta. Médico.*"

"*Soy Lotta Winter. Médico también, pero ahora hija de Bengt Winter.*"

"Ah."

She's been here for three whole minutes and has already met Alcorta, thought Winter, holding out his hand. Maybe I'm the ghost around here.

Bergenhem collected Ada from nursery school and walked around the block with her. She was fascinated by everything. He tried to settle her into the car, but all she did was scream.

It had been impossible yesterday to get her into the child seat in the car, and he'd driven home from the Co-op with her on his knee, behind the steering wheel. Luckily none of his colleagues had stopped the car.

Martina had been quiet all morning, almost as quiet as he had.

She'd gone to work now, and he'd felt as if he'd been liberated when he came back to the empty house. Ada was laughing at something in her own private world. He looked at her, and felt ashamed of what he was thinking. It started to snow.

He prepared a bowl of mashed apricots for her and made coffee for himself. He scanned the front page of the newspaper and tried to read while Ada was eating. He adjusted her bib, and let her splash milk and mashed apricot all over the table.

He put the paper to one side, without remembering anything of what he'd read. He felt stiff all over after an uneventful night spent in the car outside a building in Hisingen. Waiting and waiting, then going home. Martina had already delivered Ada to nursery school by then. An empty house, a feeling of liberation. What a stupid expression! Liberation from what?

He was driving his own car. It wasn't yet noon. He'd tried to get a good night's sleep, but that was ages ago. He stopped to make a few purchases. He'd no idea what when he went into the shop. The owner nodded to him, as if he were a regular.

There was something lying on the counter. Had he bought it? Should he buy it? He turned away and left the shop. He had it in his hand. Nobody shouted after him. He looked back, and the owner waved to him. Of course. He knew where he was now.

Of course. It was here.

He looked around as he came out. Nobody there.

He went back and waited outside the shop, looking in another direction.

15

When evening came, the family was assembled in the intensive care ward. Dr. Alcorta had decided to move his Swedish patient there an hour ago. The umpteenth move, Winter thought.

It was a different room, with a window facing west. Winter found it hard to tear his eyes away from the mountain. He thought about the white house in Nueva Andalucía. His father was also looking out the window, possibly at the white mountain. The mountain was a stage and the sky was the backdrop. All the blueness was draining into the backdrop, turning black.

"What's that smell coming from outside?" asked his father, turning his head to look at his family, who were sitting in a semicircle in front of the bed. "It struck me just now that I can smell something different in here." He needed some help with a tube that had been placed in his nose and was pressing against his chin. Lotta stood up and adjusted it. "That's not why," he said when she sat down again. "It wasn't the tube."

"There's a smell of sun and pine needles," Lotta said. "Coniferous forest. Pine trees."

"Pine needles? You think so."

"Yes."

"In that case it's just like home," he said, turning his head toward the window and the mountain again. Nobody spoke for a while. Suddenly his father coughed and it sounded as if he were clearing his throat. A spasm ran through his left arm. He looked as if he wanted to sit up. A nurse hurried over to the bed and shouted something in Spanish. Winter looked at a screen that was evidently showing his father's heartbeat, and the white line leveled out with a metallic clang. Winter could see his mother and sister sit up and stare at him. People in white came rushing in and crowded around the bed.

When Winter finally had his conversation with Dr. Alcorta it was too late, and not much of a conversation. He still felt in shock. His mother had been calmer than he'd expected. She had been prepared, at least to some extent. His sister seemed to have frozen into herself, on one of the green chairs in the dayroom. "I should have stayed at home," she had just said, but she wasn't aware of what she was saying.

"It wasn't possible to do anything this last time," Alcorta had said.

"No. I understand."

"I am sorry."

"Yes. Thank you."

"What happens now?"

They were in the cafeteria. It smelled of oil and fish. A group of doctors and nurses was having dinner by one of the windows facing south. Winter was drinking strong coffee. His mother and sister hadn't touched their cups.

"What do we do now?" Lotta repeated her question.

"The hospital has an arrangement with an undertaker in town," said her mother. "In Marbella."

"I haven't thought about it at all," Lotta said, "but you think Dad should be buried out here, do you?"

"That's what he wanted. It's a long time since he first mentioned it."

"What do you think?"

She shrugged.

"It was what he wanted. And . . . what I want as well."

She looked at her children.

"This is our home, after all."

"Are you going to stay on out here?"

"I don't know, Lotta. I mean, I have my . . . my friends out here, some of them. I don't know."

"Will the undertaker take care of everything?" Winter asked.

"Yes. As soon as Dr. Alcorta has confirmed the . . . cause of death and all that sort of thing. The undertaker will look after all that needs to be done with the authorities. The court. In Spain the formalities have to be approved by the court."

Her children nodded.

"Let's go back up to your father now," she said.

Winter was walking along the Ricardo Soriano. It was evening again. He went into the *cervecería* Monte Carlo and ordered a glass of draft beer at the bar. The place was full of men watching a football match on a large screen. Real Madrid versus Valladolid. He drank his beer and felt comfortable among all the shouting. There were no women inside the bar. They were sitting at tables on the pavement outside, waiting for the match to end and the evening to begin.

He crossed the road and entered the maze of alleys in the Old Town. The Plaza de la Iglesia was teeming with people—men, women, and children. Everybody was shouting and applauding, and Winter saw a newly married couple emerge from the Nuestra Señora de la Encarnación. The church towered high above everybody and everything, shutting out the sky. The couple walked slowly past him over the cobbles. Two children clapped enthusiastically. The bride was pretty, radiant. Three young men in tails whistled, and the groom acknowledged his ex-cronies. Consider yourselves dismissed.

Two statues standing side by side both had heads missing. The couple walked past the statues, looked at each other, then disappeared, swallowed up by the crowd.

In Orange Tree Square many people were already sitting in the cafés under the orange trees, with carafes of sangría in front of them. Winter could hear people speaking Norwegian, Swedish, and German. A black man in a white suit with beads in his hair was playing "Lili Marlene" on an accordion. Winter hurried past the cafés and continued westward to the Plaza Victoria. He sat down on a bench opposite a tapas bar.

His father was in a mortuary at a cemetery called Cementerio Virgen del Carmen. One of three in Marbella.

"The old cemetery doesn't have a mortuary," his mother had said the previous day, in a tone of voice more appropriate to a discussion of a holiday apartment. It was a defense mechanism, of course. He was glad that she was able to do that. "San Bernabé has a lovely location, but Virgen del Carmen is just as pretty. It's in a pine wood to the north of town. Not very far from the other one, in fact."

Winter had nodded. His mother wiped away a tear, but her voice was calm, determined.

"We never picked a spot, but we've actually been there and taken a look. Your father and I."

"Good."

"There's a little chapel there as well."

"Hmm."

"That's where the funeral will be. A Swedish clergyman, of course. The Protestants used to be allowed to conduct funerals in the old church in Marbella, but I don't think the Catholic priests approved of that."

"So it will be at the cemetery."

"The day after tomorrow. I was informed half an hour ago."

"That was . . . quick."

"Oh, I don't know."

He stood up and retraced his steps eastward through alleys and little squares lined with restaurants. In one of the cobbled squares he noticed the Bar Altamirano, where all the outside tables were occupied by customers eating deep-fried fish and shellfish. As he passed, he thought he could see Alicia among a group of people at one of the tables, her hand half-raised in greeting.

He hurried into an alley at the other side of the square without looking around.

When he arrived back at his room, he saw her business card lying on the table.

He took a cold shower and drank a glass of whisky. Lotta phoned from the house in Nueva Andalucía.

"Mom doesn't feel up to going into town tonight."

"No. I can understand that. What about you?"

"To tell you the truth, I feel absolutely shattered."

"I'll drive out to you tomorrow morning."

"Yes, I think that would be better."

He sat in the dark in his boxer shorts, finished his whisky, and tried to establish if he could hear anything inside his head. Then he got dressed again and went back to the Plaza Altamirano.

The cemetery was at the Carretera a Ojen, a respectable distance away from the new commercial complex La Cañada.

All that was left of his father was in the urn. That's all that's left of him, Winter thought.

The sun was directly overhead. They could almost touch the mountain peak. The cemetery was very close to the white mountain. A long way down below, the horizon formed a semicircle. The sea was dead calm.

There was a smell of sun and pine needles outside the chapel, and the scent accompanied them inside. He didn't know many of those present. Some had flown in from Sweden on the same flight as Angela. Old friends. Angela had seemed composed when he met her at the airport not far from Málaga.

The grave was overlooked by the mountain. Angela held his hand. A man he'd never seen before sang a hymn in Swedish, and another one in Spanish.

They assembled for coffee afterward at a café in Puerto Banús, close to the beach.

"This is your father's favorite café," his mother said.

"What's that statue over there?" Winter indicated the angel on a high pedestal, looking out to sea.

"Un Canto de la Libertad."

"I beg your pardon?"

"It's supposed to symbolize a hymn to freedom." She pointed to the statue about a hundred yards away. "It's your father's favorite statue." Winter thought he could see a trace of a smile on his mother's face.

He was feeling a little better now. He had avoided thinking about several things, but felt that it would be easier to do so now, for a while at least. Maybe it was that trace of a smile that helped. Maybe he would allow himself to think those thoughts before long.

He wanted to make a gesture, to do something. Angela was looking at him. Lotta was gazing out to sea, watching a sailing boat heading for the horizon.

"Let's go home and have a drink," he said. "Tanqueray and tonic. That's Dad's favorite."

16

The mobile phone rang in Winter's breast pocket. He thought he'd switched it off. It was Bertil Ringmar. The elderly DCI sounded more subdued than usual.

"I just wanted to send you greetings . . . today of all days."

"Thank you, Bertil."

"We're all thinking about you here."

"Thank you."

"Er . . . I don't really know what else to say."

"How are things at your end?"

"Quieter than usual."

"So my absence has had a calming effect on Gothenburg crime."

"It's a bit more boring as well."

"Maybe I should keep out of the way in future."

"You don't really mean that, surely?"

"No."

"When are you coming home?"

"My flight is tomorrow morning. I'll see you the day after tomorrow."

"We'll hold the fort, as they say. Await the new millennium with bated breath."

"Everybody's getting on with it, in other words."

"Bergenhem's taken a few days off, on health grounds."

"What's wrong?"

"He's out of sorts. I don't know exactly what's wrong with him. He has a headache he can't shake off. And he's worrying about something."

"Has he said anything?"

"No . . . but there's something bothering him. I'm not a psychologist, but there's something there."

"Has he talked to anybody—someone who could help him?"

"I don't know, Erik, but I assume he must have, now that he's off sick."

"Yes, seems likely."

"Maybe it's all the excitement as the millennium approaches. They say it can affect people in all kinds of ways. Seriously as well."

"Really."

"I can't say I've thought much about it."

"No."

"How are you reacting to it?"

"I haven't got around to thinking about that yet."

"Shouldn't you stay in tonight? You have an exam tomorrow, after all."

"I've done the work for that."

"When?"

"At school."

"Don't you want me to test you on it?"

"No."

"Maria, please. Can't you stay in tonight?"

"I have to go now. They're waiting for me."

"Who is? Who's waiting for you?"

"Patrik and the others."

"Can't you ask them to come here instead?" Hanne asked and immediately felt foolish. Would they really want her to serve them sponge cake and lemonade?

"They've already been here."

"We've moved the VCR into your room," said Hanne, feeling foolish again the moment she'd said it.

"Bye, Mom." Maria closed the door behind her. Hanne heard her daughter's footsteps on the steps and on the path outside. The snow was already packed so hard that it sounded like somebody bouncing on a trampoline. Winter in November, and it might well have come to stay, although you never knew. It could be fifty degrees over Christmas.

Hanne went back to the kitchen table and her newspaper and her reading glasses. She tried to spin out the time and avoided getting down to her Sunday sermon until the last minute.

If only the Christmas spirit would hurry up and arrive. They ought to go away, as far away as possible. . . . Two weeks in the Canary Islands.

It would be best if they didn't come back. A house in some southern country. All those Swedish expats. There was lots of work for a vicar. Several Swedish clergy were working on the Costa del Sol. She thought about Erik Winter. Yesterday, when she'd been at the police station, somebody had told her that his father had died. She could hear a tram approaching from Saint Sigfrids Plan. It sounded as if it were plowing its way through the snow. Maria might be on it. She thought about Winter again, his father. Maria's father hadn't been around since she was a baby. Had that sowed the seeds of the harvest she now was reaping? What am I saying, she wondered. "Whatsoever a man soweth, that shall he also reap."

And now the girl was a teenager. She saw her home as a potential prison, as they all do at that age—a part of growing up.

I'd better write that sermon now.

Málaga looked as it had done before. Nothing had changed of the city or the sea since he last saw them from the air.

The plane banked, and all he could see was sky. The coast was no longer visible behind them. The flight attendants started trundling their trolleys down the center aisle, and passengers ordered their drinks. Angela was feeling sick. Nothing unusual in the circumstances, she'd said, but she'd rather it wasn't in an airplane.

He tried to read, but couldn't concentrate. He avoided alcohol and ordered mineral water instead, like Angela. He didn't touch his sandwich.

They passed through a pocket of turbulence that caused the aircraft to shudder once or twice.

"That actually helped," Angela said. "I feel better now."

"You look better too."

"I can see the coast."

"Which coast?"

"Denmark, I think."

Half an hour later the plane began its descent. Winter glimpsed Gothenburg through the clouds before they were swallowed up by them. The buildings were gray, but the ground was white.

The snow was about four inches deep at the side of the runway at Landvetter.

It smelled like a different country as they left the terminal building and made their way to the long-term car park. He could feel the cold through his thin coat. There were a lot of people milling around, but fewer than he'd been used to for some time. Coming back home was always like that. A lot of noise, but even so it was quieter than when he'd been away.

They didn't speak much in the car. Angela intended to say something in the elevator, but didn't.

"Is it Saturday we'll be moving in the last of your things?" Winter asked.

17

Patrik waited for the snow plow to pass. There wasn't enough snow for that, surely? No doubt they'd been told off again. The local authority. Whenever it snowed in Gothenburg the local authority was always told off for not getting the plows out to clear it soon enough. So here they were already, cruising around town even though there was barely enough snow to turn the streets white. Patrik checked his watch, then pulled his sleeve down over his freezing hand. His gloves were at home, doing an excellent job on the shelf in the hall, ha, ha.

He unloaded Beck from his Walkman, replaced it with *Boy with the Arab Strap* and sauntered over Aschebergsgatan while the music washed away the city sounds. That was good. He sometimes had more cassettes with him than newspapers, but they were all his own choices and it helped to keep changing, often. It made time pass more quickly. The sounds of the city were transformed into something else. Not that there were so many of them. The first trams. A few taxis, some of them apparently being driven by madmen. Drunken men and women yelling for taxis, especially on Friday and Saturday evenings.

And sounds like now, the snow plow attachment scraping against the tarmac, vibrations shuddering their way through the road surface until they caught up with him, then continuing up his legs and taking possession of his whole body.

He removed The Boy and replaced it with Gomez. Music was his life. He was a millennium ahead of everybody else. He was before his time. People listened to Eminem. Even some people he knew. Or used to know. Previously known people. He could feel himself making a face when he listened to Eminem. He felt provoked by Eminem. He had seen a television interview with Eminem devoid of intelligence and conducted by a couple of girls. Maria had been watching and he could see that she liked it, so he'd gone to his room and put on "Walking into Clarksdale" at top volume. That was wicked stuff. *That* was a millennium ahead of its time. Page and Plant, who would soon be sixty and still way ahead of everybody else, who hadn't a clue and started laughing when he played them. It was almost the same with Morrissey, but not quite as bad.

The electronic lock on the front door wasn't working properly, as usual. He had to key in the code twice. There was a smell of old age in the stairwell and he started to feel tired, as there were so many stairs left to climb before he'd delivered all the newspapers. He always started to think along those lines when he'd got this far. He was on the third floor. For the last few days he'd paused here and asked himself what seemed amiss. He switched off his Walkman now and took away the earphones.

It was several days ago, when he was about to push the newspaper through the mail slot. He thought back to that occasion, again. Some newspapers had landed on end and were blocking the slot. He'd had to push quite hard and he'd heard the music coming from inside the apartment. It was five in the morning, just like now. There were no lights on in the apartment, but he'd heard the music. Listening to metal at five in the morning! Death metal, eh! Or black. Somebody was sitting there, listening to metal, but whoever it was didn't read his newspapers, nor did he open his mail.

It said VALKER on the door. Nothing else. Valker. He couldn't even get the newspaper through the slot anymore. He squatted down and could see the darkness inside the apartment and hear the music as usual. But there was something else now—you couldn't miss it, couldn't avoid it. A smell that was worse than . . . he didn't know, worse than . . . he couldn't think of anything worse, but he could smell it and had been able to smell it for several days now and not only in the morning. He'd felt obliged to go back several times and check. Hell's bells, he had to admit it. He was curious. Maria had been with him the day before.

"Can you smell it?"

"Yes, phew!"

"What is it?"

"I don't know."

"Do you know what I think it is?"

"Maybe."

"What, then?"

"Somebody . . . inside there."

"Right."

"Somebody dead."

"It could be."

"And still listening to . . . to that stuff."

"Well . . . it could be part of the point. Listening to it. I mean, they don't call it death metal for nothing."

"Ha, ha."

"It seems to be on repeat. Or auto-reverse. It's playing all the time."

"Doesn't it drive the neighbors crazy?"

"There are thick walls, floors, and ceilings in this building. What do you think we should do?"

"I don't know. Is that noise really music?"

"Yes."

"Can you call that music? It's so . . . repulsive."

"You'd never believe how many people in Gothenburg listen to that crap."

"Such as whoever lives in this apartment. What exactly is it? I mean, you know everything. Even about stuff you can't stand."

"I'm not sure. Quite a lot of stuff sounds like that. Could be . . ."

A man walked past, and they moved away from the door. He had no idea what was going on. He looked at them over his shoulder. Patrik started walking downstairs and Maria followed him.

"You've been here lots of times, haven't you?" Maria asked. "I mean, you've noticed it. You'd better report it. I think you should."

He stood in front of the door, thinking over what she had said. He was forced to put the newspaper on the floor outside the door, just as he'd done yesterday. It couldn't go on like this. He thought again about what to do. The smell seemed stronger than before. It seemed to be everywhere, just like the music that was seeping through the thick walls. Odd that the neighbors weren't up in arms about it.

He left the newspaper on the floor and delivered to the rest of the apartments, then checked to see if the list of residents' names by the front door gave any information about a caretaker.

He went back out into the street. It was just as dark, but there were more passengers in the trams now. He was behind schedule, but that wasn't surprising. He'd lost interest in his Walkman, left it in his pocket and continued toward Vasaplatsen. He went into the apartment building that he and Maria had been looking at before, the one where that detective lived, with his girlfriend. He ought to know that if anybody did, delivering newspapers every day all week long. He'd told Maria, or reminded her about it.

It was the same sort of big, black building as the other one. There was the same kind of echo when the elevator clattered its way up.

· · · · · ·

The call was passed from the central control to the Lorensberg station, on to the constable who dealt with incoming calls, and from him to the duty officer. He listened, asked a few questions, and made a note.

It was Friday evening. Another half-hour and it would be eight o'clock, when the station closed to the general public.

The duty officer checked his rotation list and went out to the front desk, where the constable was talking to a woman who had just come in from the street. He waited. The woman left, taking a form with her. He had seen her there before. A dog was waiting outside, wrapped up in God only knows what. It barked a welcome as she opened the door. The duty officer turned to his younger colleague.

"Send Morelius to me as soon as he comes back from the gym. Bartram as well. I need to see them urgently."

A quarter of an hour later they were in the car driving west toward Aschebergsgatan. The caretaker was waiting for them outside. He was elderly, gray-haired. His last year in the job, and now this had happened.

"The third floor," he said. "The elevator isn't working, I'm afraid. I've phoned the repair—"

"Was it you who called the police?" asked Morelius, cutting him short.

"Well, yes. I suppose so."

"What do you mean?"

"I'd thought of calling sooner . . . thought there was something odd going on . . . and then I phoned and reported it." He was breathing heavily. "Here it is, anyway."

"Hmm." Morelius eyed the newspapers piled up on the floor; one was sticking out of the letter box. "Have you rung the bell?"

"Yes. Several times these last few days." He gestured toward the door. "But nobody answered."

"Who lives here?" Morelius looked at the nameplate. "Valker. Somebody living on their own? A single tenant?"

"It's a couple—at least, I think it is. You can never be sure nowadays. . . . But I've seen two people. A man and a woman."

Morelius rang the bell. They could hear some sort of music coming from inside the apartment. He rang again, but there was no answer. He looked at Bartram and then bent down and opened the mail slot.

"Oh, damn!"

"I've smelled it as well," the caretaker said.

"What's wrong?" Bartram wondered.

"Smell for yourself," said Morelius, moving out of the way.

"Just say what it is," Bartram said.

"It's impossible to describe," said Morelius, looking at the caretaker again.

"I don't know," he said.

"There's a noise coming from inside. What is it?"

"I don't know what it is either. But it's been going for ages now."

"Ages?"

"Evidently. According to the newspaper boy, at least. And I suppose I've heard it myself as well, when I've been here wondering . . . wondering what's going on. But one's reluctant to interfere."

"Open the door," Morelius said.

"Shouldn't we wait?" Bartram asked.

"What for?" Morelius turned to the caretaker. "Come on, open up."

Morelius looked at the door. He had no feelings just now. It could be any door at all. Any people at all. The light on the landing was very bright. It didn't worry him.

The man fumbled with a bunch of keys, picked one out, put it in the lock and turned.

Winter had mashed the anchovies and mixed in olive oil and garlic when the telephone rang, piercing Charlie Haden's bass.

"I'll get it," said Angela, on her way through the hall from the bathroom.

She came back into the kitchen.

"It's for you. I'll hang up the receiver in the hall."

Winter picked up the phone.

· · · · · ·

There were two cars parked outside the apartment building. Winter could see them the moment he stepped outside the entrance door of his own building. They were only a few yards away.

Walking distance from the scene of the crime. You could have mixed feelings about that. He rubbed his chin and could smell garlic and anchovies. It felt as if crime had intruded onto his home ground, his home.

There was a young constable he didn't recognize in the entrance hall. Cars braked behind him as he went in through the front door, and he knew there would soon be lots of people in there. Outside as well.

Welcome home, Chief Inspector.

He went up the stairs.

"Hello, Winter."

"It's you, is it, Bartram? Long time no see."

"We took the emergency call."

"Who's that?" asked Winter, gesturing toward the elderly man leaning against a wall.

"The caretaker."

"He looks in a bad way. Get him to the station and I'll have a word with him later."

"Okay."

"Who's inside the apartment?"

"Morelius. Simon Morelius. We were the first. And now you."

Winter went in through the open door. He had to step over a pile of mail and newspapers. The hall was dark, long and narrow, not unlike his own. There was no sign of a light on anywhere. He knew that these officers were experienced enough not to touch the walls and switches.

The stench was awful, but he'd tried to prepare himself for that, and it helped. He breathed it for a couple of seconds, then took out a handkerchief and pressed it over his nose and mouth.

Music was thundering through all the rooms. He couldn't be sure where it was coming from. The volume wasn't all that high, but it was very intrusive even so.

It sounded like something from another world. He'd never heard anything like it. I've lived a sheltered life, he thought.

The guitar was grinding like a mill wheel, as did the bass, the drums . . . Winter was reminded of a concrete mixer. Suddenly: a voice, hardly human, a high falsetto hissing noise. No discernible words. The drummer seemed to be having an epileptic fit.

The music was coming from a room directly ahead of him. A door at the far end of the hall stood open. Light from the street was coming in through the large windows. A figure was visible in the doorway, outlined against the lighter room behind him, motionless. Winter could see the silhouette of a police officer, his uniform, his weapon. He didn't seem to have heard Winter approaching, but ought to have done so despite the music.

He hadn't seen Morelius for ages. He was younger than Winter, but not all that much.

The music stopped and Winter approached the room. The outline moved, then turned back toward the room again without speaking. The music surged, louder now, more intense. It seemed to get louder as Winter advanced. When he reached the door, the figure that had now become a man in uniform moved out of the way. Winter nodded. He could smell the stench through his handkerchief now as he stepped into the room.

The singer wasn't hissing any longer, he was screeching at top volume. The stereo equipment was on the left, glowing red and yellow. Next to it was a sofa, and on the sofa sat a couple who didn't appear to be wearing any clothes. Their bodies were crisscrossed with shadows and light and something else. Winter realized what it was.

Their faces were turned toward the door, toward the police officers who were looking at them. Winter had a sudden feeling of disgust, of wanting to be sick.

It was always the same. He was violating these people now, when they were defenseless.

He took a step forward. There was a dark wreath around their necks, like a jagged necklace. He took another step forward and looked into their faces and the feeling of sickness was suddenly more than a vague feeling. He turned back to the door.

"There's something written on the wall as well," said the police officer, pointing to the right at the far end of the room.

18

The room quickly filled up. Winter had sat alone in his office for ten minutes, watching the snow falling outside. Somebody had put a vase of flowers on the table, but there was no card accompanying it. As he was about to leave for the meeting, there was a knock on the door and Ringmar came in. He'd been home to get some pills to ease his tonsillitis. He had looked far from well when he turned up at the apartment, taken one look at the dead bodies, started coughing, and gone back into the hall.

"You ought to be in bed," said Winter.

"Yes."

"Do you have a temperature?"

"Yes."

"Go home."

"After the meeting."

"We can't risk you infecting all of us, Bertil. The bottom line is that I don't want you here."

"Erik . . ."

"If you really have to work, take the photographs and all the rest of the stuff and do some thinking as you lie in bed, if it's possible to think with the infection you've got."

"All right, all right." Ringmar was in the middle of the office now. "This is a fine welcome-home for you." He looked at Winter, who had retreated behind his desk. "What a goddam mess!"

They went to the meeting. Winter started by summarizing what they knew. The photographs were passed around.

He hasn't got much of a tan, thought Aneta Djanali. That wasn't why he went to Spain. Aneta Djanali didn't have much of a tan herself, although she was very black. She was born in Gothenburg, to parents who had had to leave the troubled African nation of Burkina Faso for political reasons. But "leave" was not quite accurate; they had fled for their lives.

When Aneta became a police officer, her father had mixed feelings, having had his tough experiences with the police of Ouagadougou. His daughter kept telling him it was different here, though sometimes she wasn't so sure.

Fredrik Halders listened to what Winter had to say. He looked at the photograph in his hand. How are we going to approach this? What shall we tell people?

"What are we going to tell people about this?" he said, holding up the photograph. "How much detail should we . . . reveal?"

"What do you mean?" asked Sara Helander, who was sitting two chairs away from Halders.

"What's happened to them," Halders said. "How much should we say about what they look like?"

"We have a couple who have been murdered in their apartment, that's what we'll say," said Winter. "There's no reason why we should give any more information at this stage."

"Is there ever?" Djanali said, but Winter ignored the question.

"Christian and Louise Valker," said Winter. "Married for four years. He was forty-two, she was thirty-seven. No children. Christian Valker worked as a computer salesman—hardware—and Louise Valker worked part-time as a hairdresser." He glanced at his notes. "They had been living in the apartment in Aschebergsgatan for two and a half years, roughly. Tenancy rights. High rent." We might well have seen each other in Vasaplatsen. At the supermarket, in the street, in the garage, perhaps. The garage was big, hundreds of square yards, under all the apartment buildings. We'd better check if they rented a garage space. "They had previously lived in Lunden, two rooms and kitchen, sublet. Before that, Christian lived on his own in an apartment in Kålltorp. Louise moved to Gothenburg seventeen years ago from Kungsbacka and started work at a hair salon in Mölndalsvägen. She lived in Ran-nebergen then, on her own. Neither had been married before. No criminal record either. Not in Sweden, at least. We'll check with Interpol. No relatives in Gothenburg, as far as we know. Christian Valker grew up in Västerås, Louise in Kungsbacka."

"He came to Gothenburg to seek his fortune," muttered Halders to Djanali, who was sitting next to him.

"Shut up, Fredrik," she said.

Winter signaled to the probationer in charge of the slide projector. The lights were turned off. It was dark enough outside not to draw the curtains.

"You can see for yourselves the wounds on their bodies. Here and here. Any one of the blows could have killed them. They were made with extreme force."

"A serrated blade," Halders said.

"We don't know that for certain," Ringmar croaked.

"He obviously sawed them," said Halders. "He must be hellish strong."

Helander closed her eyes momentarily. She had never seen anything like it. She heard a familiar noise behind her, and somebody jumped up and ran out of the room. The young officer had knocked some chairs over when he had thrown up. Winter could smell it from where he was standing.

Ringmar had been standing at the side of the room, watching the bodies glittering on the slides. It made him think of somebody slinking into a cinema showing pornographic films and staring, transfixed. Like a compulsion. But this was worse. These bodies were exposed for all to see. Looking at them seemed obscene.

The murderer knew we'd be standing here, looking at the fruits of his labor, Ringmar thought as the smell of vomit wafted as far as his corner. All this is a stage setting. It's a message.

There was another picture on the screen now. The same scene, but from another angle, closer. Winter had approached the screen and raised his hand toward the bodies, but it seemed to Ringmar that he was hesitating. Winter thinks like me. He also feels a sort of shame.

Winter said something, but Ringmar couldn't hear what it was. He felt as if he had cotton wool between his ears, as if his infection had got worse during the time he'd spent in this room. Someone turned the lights on.

"And this is what we heard when we entered the room," said Winter, switching on a tape recorder. Music filled the room, louder than Winter had intended and he lowered the volume. It seemed to get louder again of its own accord when the song started. Song? thought Winter. This is something new for me.

The crime unit officers listened, and looked at each other. Somebody grinned, somebody else put their hands over their ears. Winter could see no sign of recognition; none of the younger officers raised a hand. He switched it off.

"Damn," Halders said.

"You're saying that's what they had on?" Djanali asked.

"Yes. According to the caretaker there's been music coming from the apartment for some time."

"That particular music?" asked Möllerström, the registrar.

"He says he's not an expert," said Winter drily, "but it sounded very like that."

"What the hell is it?" asked Halders.

"I've no idea," said Winter. "That's why I'm playing it for you now. Does anybody know?"

Nobody responded. After a few seconds Winter saw a hand go up. One of the younger officers. Setter. Johan Setter.

"Johan?"

"Er . . . are you asking for the name of the band? The band that's performing the stuff?"

"I'm asking what it *is*. If anybody can tell me what band it is, then bingo. But, well . . . I haven't a clue about this."

"Well . . . it's some kind of trash metal," said Setter. "Not really my thing, but it's metal all right. Death metal, I'd say. Or black metal."

"Death metal?" Winter said, gaping at Setter, who looked unsure of himself. "Death metal?"

Somebody giggled.

"An appropriate name," Halders said.

"What on earth is death metal?" asked Ringmar.

"You've just heard it," Halders said. "Quite a beat to it."

"Zip it, Fredrik," muttered Djanali.

"It's pretty popular," Setter said. "Well . . . more popular than you might think."

"Popular with whom?" asked Halders. "The Swedish Nazis? The Liberals?"

"Popular with the Valkers?" Möllerström wondered.

"We don't know," said Winter, looking at Halders. "We haven't got around to examining the CD collection in the apartment yet."

"So it wasn't a record?" Helander asked.

"No, an unmarked cassette tape. BASF. CE Two Chrome Extra. Ninety minutes."

"Fingerprints?"

"The forensic boys are busy with that now. What you've just heard was a copy we had made."

"Did they have a lot of cassettes?" Halders asked.

"Apparently none at all," said Winter. "At least, we haven't found any yet."

"Where's Bergenhem?" asked Halders. "Lars listens to all kinds of peculiar shit."

"He's off sick," Ringmar said.

"Send this crap to his place for him to listen to."

"Will do," Ringmar said.

"It could be a message, then," said Djanali. "A message to us. Or am I jumping to conclusions?"

"You could be right," Winter said. "At least the murderer left the tape running."

"For how long?" one of the younger officers asked.

"How the hell could we know?" Halders said. "If we knew that we'd have won half the battle."

"So this is the music the caretaker heard, is that right?" asked Helander.

"We don't know," Winter said. "But I know what you're getting at.

If we can get him to remember when he first heard it, we might be on to something."

"How long have they been dead?" Djanali asked. "Have we heard from the pathologist?"

"Could be fourteen days," Winter said. "Could be longer."

"Oh, hell," said Halders.

"Can a tape run for as long as that?" Möllerström asked. "Can it keep going on repeat for two weeks?"

"Evidently."

"It's called auto-reverse," Halders said, looking at Möllerström. "When the tape comes to the end it turns around and goes back to the beginning. It keeps going back and forth until it's switched off. Or the tape breaks."

"There is another possibility, though."

Ringmar nodded. He was standing next to Winter now.

"What's that?" Setter asked.

"That the gentleman responsible sneaked back a week or so after the murder and put some music on to improve the atmosphere," Halders said. Somebody giggled again.

"So what are we going to do with this?" Helander asked.

"Well, it's been suggested that Bergenhem should listen to the cassette, and that thought had occurred to me as well," said Winter. "But we'll have to check with anybody who might be able to help us with this. Record shops, including ones that sell secondhand stuff. Bands here in Gothenburg. If this music is so popular, somebody must recognize it. Recording studios. Check with rock critics working for newspapers, radio, television." He looked around those present. "Johan. Can you look after that? You'll get some help. Take the cassette around to Bergenhem's place, then see where you go from there."

Setter nodded.

"There's one more thing," said Winter, signaling to the rookie. A new picture appeared on the screen. It showed the wall in the room where the two dead victims had been sitting. There was something on the wall. Everybody could read it, the letters were a couple of feet tall and covered a large part of the wall:

 ALL

"And that was there when you got to the apartment?" Djanali asked.

"Yes. We're waiting to hear how long it's been there."

"As long as that couple have been sitting on the sofa," Halders said. Winter made no comment.

"A message," Djanali said. "That's not exactly a wild guess."

"Is it red paint?" Halders asked.

"No."

"'Wall,'" said Ringmar. "Is the murderer trying to tell us that he's writing on a wall?"

"Assuming it was the murderer," Winter said. "But this doesn't look as if it's a single word. I don't quite get it. A circle around the *W*. What does that indicate? A gap between the *W* and *all*."

"All," said Ringmar. "It could mean he took all of them."

"All two?"

"All who come after."

"Pack it in, Bertil. Go home to bed now."

"Are we all going to be off sick? All?"

"Bergenhem will be back tomorrow."

"Have you spoken to him?"

"Half an hour ago."

"Had Setter been with the tape?"

"Yes. Not Bergenhem's cup of tea," he said.

"Okay. Anyway, this is another message for us, as well as the music. He's trying to tell us something."

"Does he want to be caught?" asked Winter.

"Or is he playing with us?"

"It took a lot of time to write . . . to prepare this. To fix . . . the paint. He had to go backward and forward."

"He used a paintbrush."

"Yes."

"Did he have a paintbrush with him?"

"He? You're saying 'he' all the time."

"Do you think it's a she?"

"No."

"The question is whether he had a paintbrush with him."

"One of the questions," Winter said. "Another is: where is it now?"

"I hate this kind of thing," Ringmar said. "Riddles."

"Isn't that what we're always dealing with?"

"Riddles within riddles, then. I hate it. It makes me upset. It makes me angry. So angry that I can feel my infection dissipating."

Winter was alone in the apartment in Aschebergsgatan. He had gone back.

The smell was still there in the room. The pictures he recalled from that morning, the real thing he'd seen first, then the photographs. I saw it live, he thought. I saw death live and I heard the sound track. What am I thinking about? The sound track?

The sofa was empty now, stained. The roar from the music seemed still to be there. The text on the wall was lit up by the sun coming in through the window. The clouds had cleared as Winter walked across the street, and now the bright light was streaming in through the window and the shaky letters seemed to be starker, more powerful. Winter stared at the circle around the W. What did it mean?

How can you classify degrees of lunacy?

Is it as simple as that?

Or is this a sick act by a sane man?

I've only seen one thing before that comes anywhere near matching this. But I never thought I'd have to encounter such human brutality again.

He could see the bodies in his mind's eye, each on a chair of its own. Was that three years ago now?

But it's continuing.

Water was running along a pipe somewhere in the building. It was a noise he recognized. This building was similar to the one he lived in: a stone block built in the old-fashioned way. He might have been standing in his own apartment. He suddenly thought of Angela.

Angela and her stomach, which had now become a part of him as well. That's how it was.

This apartment even had the same layout as his own. He hadn't thought of that when he first entered it yesterday evening, he'd been concentrating on other things. But he could see it now. The rooms radiated from the hall and kitchen, the big living room, where he was standing, the bedroom next to it, another room. A toilet and a separate bathroom.

The forensic officers were working their way through every little thing, but he wanted some time in the apartment to himself. Go and get yourselves a cup of coffee, boys. Give me half an hour.

There were clothes everywhere. It had started in the kitchen and finished on the sofa. When had they started getting undressed? In the kitchen? Why? Had the clothes been put where they were afterward? It should be possible to establish that. Was there a pattern to it? Was there another accursed message? Another riddle? He thought of Ringmar, and his sudden cure.

All the blood was in the living room. Nothing in the hall, or in the kitchen. There didn't seem to have been any blood left in the bodies. Christian and Louise Valker. At least her eyes had been closed.

They had been sitting in the kitchen. Winter couldn't know, but he was sure the dried-up drops of wine in the glasses and the dregs in the bottle were from *then*. He vaguely recognized the label, from the glass-covered shelves at the System liquor store on the Avenue. One of the cheaper Spanish brands.

19

Angela came home late to an apartment in darkness. She switched on the hall light and took off her coat and boots. She could hear music coming from the living room. Guitars. Somebody singing in a loud voice, almost shouting.

"Anybody there?!"

No answer. She tried again.

"I'm in here."

She went to the living room and found Winter in the leather easy chair next to the window. The room was in shadow. He was only an outline.

"You're sitting in the dark."

"I like it like this."

The guitars became more hectic, faster. The song was a screech.

"Are you thinking about . . . your dad?"

"Yes. Among other things."

"Does the music help?"

"I don't know. Perhaps. I bought the disc in a shop in Marbella."

"It's . . . interesting." She listened to the singer, who was now completely drowning out the acoustic guitars. "There seems to be a lot of hurt in flamenco."

"Hurt and heart. Romero. He's called Rafael Romero. An old man."

"You can hear that he's had a life."

Winter stood up and crossed the room to embrace her. He stroked her cheeks and kissed the tip of her nose and her mouth.

"What sort of a day have you had?"

"I haven't felt sick so much as the day wore on. It was worst at the beginning. Apart from that it was the usual running around from patient to patient, ward to ward. I apologize when I get to the patients later than I should, but I suspect I'm the only one who does." She caressed his arm. "What about you? How was work?"

"We have our double murder to keep us occupied," he said, going to the CD player and turning down the volume. "But don't ask me about details."

"Wouldn't dream of it."

The phone rang. Winter automatically checked his watch. Eleven-fifteen. He picked up the receiver.

"Winter." No reply. "Hello?" He could hear a crackling noise on the line. He gestured to Angela that she should turn off the music. "Hello? Who is it?" He could hear distant voices flitting through space.

Thought he could pick up a few words of Spanish. There was a click, and the line went dead. Winter held the receiver at arm's length, looked hard at it, then replaced it.

"Who was it?"

"Nobody," Winter said. "At least, nobody prepared to say anything." He looked at Angela, who was still standing by the CD player. "Didn't you say that somebody rang once before but didn't say anything?"

"Was it him again?"

Winter shrugged and held his arms out wide.

"It was him," she said. "What the hell's going on?"

"Sit down," Winter said, pulling the other easy chair to the window. He switched on a desk lamp. That felt better. "Sit here, Angela."

"This is scary," she said, sitting down. "Can't the call be traced?"

"That's not as easy as a lot of people think. But nine times out of ten it's somebody dialing a wrong number and being too shy to admit it. Or they are surprised when somebody they don't know answers. Then the shock passes and they hang up."

"You're used to receiving calls like this, are you?"

"It happens now and then."

"And you're trying to convince me that it has nothing to do with . . . your work?"

"Meaning what?"

"You come up against God only knows what strange people. Maybe they're trying to frighten you. Get their own back."

"Stop exaggerating."

"But that could be it, couldn't it?"

"I don't know, Angela. There have been a few calls like this, but I don't know who made them because he never says a word."

She gave him a skeptical look.

"Now that I think about it, I wonder if it was a mistake moving in here," she said.

"Stop exaggerating. I think everybody's had calls like this."

"Not me. And I certainly haven't brought Mr. Creep here with me, if that's what you think."

"No, no."

"What kind of haunted house is this that you live in, Erik?" She thought of the neighbors, could see the stairwell in her mind's eye. The stark, unpleasant light when she emerged from the lift. When she came home tonight she'd had a momentary urge to creep up to Mrs. Malmer's door and listen. The memory almost made her smile. Was it something to do with her pregnancy? Anonymous phone calls. Mrs. Malmer's midnight masses. She was smiling now. She could see that Erik had noticed. She felt silly, embarrassed. A wrong number. Nothing to worry about. Even so . . .

Winter was still in the easy chair. The lower part of his face was illuminated by the desk lamp. His chin was covered with a day's growth of stubble. He hadn't changed since coming home from work, although he had taken off his jacket and tie. The shirt from Harvey & Hudson was unbuttoned at the neck, its discreet stripes almost invisible in the gloom.

She felt worried about him, about what had happened to him. She knew that he was struggling with his memories, the relationship with his father that had drifted away. He was trying to cope with it by not speaking about it, but that was not the right way of approaching it. He needed to talk to somebody, perhaps just occasionally. She could see that his chin had dropped slightly, as if he'd fallen asleep in the chair once the music had finished.

He's intelligent, he understands. But it's a big step from understanding to actually coping. Coming to terms with his memories. But keeping quiet doesn't help. Nor does throwing yourself all out into a new and horrific investigation. It might provide an odd kind of comfort for a brief while, but only for a brief while.

"I can see you've got me under the microscope," he said, raising his chin so that almost all of his face was in shadow.

"I thought you were asleep."

"I'm resting. I feel better now and am ready for another eighteen hours of work."

"But you must have something to eat."

"It's the middle of the night."

"Something suitable for the night, then. Did you have anything at all this evening?"

"Coffee. A cheese roll."

"I could make you a Paris sandwich, but I'll fry some ham with the egg instead of a burger."

"A Paris sandwich! Do they still exist? Is the term still in dictionaries nowadays? I haven't had one of those for at least thirty years."

"Then it's about time you did. It's one of my late-night specialities."

"There are still things about you that I don't know, Angela." He slid down out of the easy chair, crawled over to her, and crouched with his head on her knee. She stroked his head, but her fingers found little purchase thanks to his close-cropped hair. "Dark late-night secrets," he said. "Yes. Yes! I can't wait to try it, this Paris sandwich."

As they ate, he avoided thinking about his father and those last days in Marbella. He almost managed it, but for a split second he could see Alicia in front of him, the table at Altamirano, her surprise, and possibly pleasure, to see him standing there. Her friend had managed to find a spare chair and he sat down. Food was served. They'd been waiting for the food, too long according to Alicia, and she'd looked at him as if expecting him to answer a question he hadn't heard her ask. He had drunk wine and the black iron balconies on the far side of the little square had seemed closer, as if carried down by the bougainvillea. He could feel the sweat on his brow.

"What do you think?"

Angela was looking at him, and nodded toward his plate.

"Fantastic," he said, cutting another piece of the bread, egg, and ham.

"Yes, it's pretty good, isn't it?"

"And yet it's so simple."

"It's like you say. Fantastic."

"And so quick. It's only just turned midnight," he said, checking his watch. At that moment, the telephone rang.

Patrik and Maria could see the white street through the café window. It was unusual for snow to remain in the city center, on the few occasions there was any. Patrik was waiting for the idiots to put up the Christmas decorations in the streets and the shop windows. A Merry Christmas in November, as it were. Why bother to wait? Celebrate Christmas Eve on November 24. Why not? Santa Claus is coming to town.

"Imagine it happening only just around the corner," said Maria, taking a drink of her hot chocolate. Smoke was rising from her cigarette lying in the ashtray. Smoke was rising from thirty million cigarettes lying in ashtrays in there, and when they went outside he'd be able to smell smoke in his clothes and right through to his brain. He didn't like it. There was no need to smoke just because everybody else was doing it.

"A bit farther than that," he said. "But more or less just around the corner."

"And that you were the one who discovered it."

"That old caretaker guy had noticed it as well."

"Why didn't he do something about it, then?" she said, taking a puff of her cigarette. "Why didn't he report it sooner?"

"How should I know? He's an old guy. Old guys are cowards."

She laughed, replaced her cigarette in the ashtray, and took another drink of her hot chocolate. What a mixture. If she'd been drinking *espresso* he could have understood it, but not a cigarette and chocolate. He was drinking *espresso*. Double *espresso*. It tasted awful. You didn't get much either.

"What do you think they saw when they went in?" she asked.

"No, idea."

"It must have been awful."

"A dead married couple," he said. "There's only one thing worse than that."

"What?"

"A live married couple."

She grinned, but noticed that he wasn't even smiling. Maybe it wasn't a joke. She knew what he'd been through, was still going through. She reached for his hand, brushed against her cigarette and burned herself.

"Ouch!"

"That's what happens when you mess around with that crap."

She stroked her finger and blew on it.

"It hurts."

"About time you stopped."

"I've only just started."

"I think they saw something worse than a Wes Craven," he said.

"What do you mean?"

"Halloween. I think it was Halloween in that apartment, sort of."

"Explain."

"Come on, Ria. For once I've been following this in the newspapers. I mean, you could say that I'm an interested party. I checked to see what the police had to say about what they found inside there. What had happened. Are you with me?"

"No."

"It says nothing at all about it. About what had happened, sort of. I think that's fishy."

"Take it easy. They never tell you all that much, do they?"

"Do you read the papers regularly?"

"I read about the TV programs. What's on in town."

"Don't you see what I'm getting at?"

"Are you saying that they're keeping quiet because there was something extra horrific inside there?"

"Yes. That's the way I see it. Less is more." He drank the last drops of his cold *espresso* and made a face.

"That's smart."

"What?"

"A smart way of putting it. Less is more."

"There's another thing."

"And?"

"I think I might know what kind of music they were playing in there."

20

They were three cars behind and Morelius saw the Volvo jump a red light.

"We can get him under the bridge," Bartram said.

They pulled out and passed the cars that had stopped at the red light and waved to the Volvo driver to stop next to the Shell gas station. They walked toward the car, one on each side, and the driver, who was alone, rolled down his mud-covered window as Morelius approached. They were about the same age.

"Can I see your driver's license, please?"

The man took his wallet out of his inside pocket and produced his license from a collection of other plastic cards. He was wearing a thick polo-necked shirt and a thin jacket. Glasses, his thinning hair combed back. He seemed nervous, but it would have been odd if he hadn't been. Morelius couldn't smell any alcohol.

"You were a bit ahead of yourself back there."

"I know."

"You're supposed to stop at a red light."

"I know, I know. I thought I could make it before it changed from yellow." He looked up at Morelius. "You can usually make it on yellow."

"That depends," said Morelius. "Were you in a hurry?"

"I'm late picking up the kids from nursery school. Very late, in fact. They actually phoned me to ask where I was." He looked at Morelius again, but he wasn't playing for sympathy. "They even phoned," he said again.

Morelius thought he saw Bartram struggling to suppress a giggle.

"It's true," the man said. "It's in Fräntorp," he said, as if that confirmed everything. "I can call them," he said, pointing to his mobile phone in its holder on the dashboard.

"That won't be necessary," Morelius said. "But make sure it doesn't happen again."

The man took his driver's license and stared at it, as if expecting it to turn into an arrest warrant any moment.

"Er . . . you mean there won't be anything?"

"What do you mean, anything?"

"Fine, or points docked, or whatever."

"Is that what you want?"

"Er . . . no."

"Be more careful in future," Morelius said, and walked back to the patrol car. Bartram was already inside. Morelius heard the man start his engine and drive off.

"He was lucky to get stopped by officers who weren't on traffic duty," said Bartram. "They have to think about their success rates."

The law and order boys had to think about everything, Morelius thought. Drugs, traffic offenses, robbery and burglary, violent assault. All-arounders. Double murders.

"We drive around town and see that bastard who mugged that woman and beat her up so badly that she was off work for three years, and he was in prison for a month. Does anybody expect us to take twelve hundred kronor off a guy who's rushing to pick up his kids from nursery school?"

"Not today, in any case," Morelius said.

"I let a shoplifter go the other day," Bartram said.

"Eh?"

"I took it upon myself to let a shoplifter go, without reporting him."

"You don't say."

"You can't always throw your weight around. Show who's boss."

There was a crackling from the radio: "Eleven-ten. Come in eleven-ten."

"We're at the roundabout just north of Central Station," Bartram said.

"We've just had a call from a mobile phone at Kungsportsplatsen. They're holding somebody who's stabbed a passenger in a tram, and they're trying to restrain him, over."

"Roger," said Bartram, and Morelius switched on the lights and siren.

"They're at the stop for northbound traffic. Did you get that? Over."

"Yep, roger," Bartram said, and they raced past Brunnsparken and turned left.

Winter wrote down the message: W ALL. Drew a circle around the first letter. What was the point of sitting here, doing this? Riddles like this took time that could be spent on other riddles, but he was fascinated by the message, gave it a higher priority than it might have deserved. No obvious answer. One word? Several? Or was the murderer just being facetious, pointing out that there was a wall there? Did "wall" have a symbolic significance? Was it something to do with the music? Was "wall" a frequent symbol in this kind of music? Setter had come up with a new suggestion regarding the genre: black metal. Not death metal. Black metal. Even worse.

He looked at the word once more, wrote it again, drew another circle. All? Had he killed all? Were all going to die? He'd already been thinking about that. Why was there a circle round the *W*? Is that what we should be thinking about? What begins with *W*?

He got up and went to the mirror over the sink. The slight tan he'd brought back from the Costa del Sol had gone, replaced by the usual bluish hue typical of winter. Winter. Winter started with *W*. He pressed his right hand lightly against his cheek. Winter. A bit early for paranoid thoughts.

The investigation had only just begun, but it didn't seem like that. He felt as if it had started the moment he'd boarded the plane for Málaga. That's when the tale started.

W. Double-U. Double murder.

The telephone rang, and he thought about the phone ringing at home with nobody speaking at the other end. He'd answered last night just before Angela made him his Paris sandwich, but there was nobody there. Not even any breathing this time, just the tone signaling an open line. Maybe he should change his number and go unlisted.

He went to his desk and answered.

"Hello, it's Lotta. I bet I'm disturbing something important, but I wondered whether you and Angela would like to come around for dinner tomorrow evening? It's Friday tomorrow."

"I'll ask her."

"What about you yourself?"

"Well, I suppose I can come."

"I'm overwhelmed by your enthusiasm."

"Assuming nothing more happens, nothing new."

"I read about it. A couple in Vasastan."

"That's where they lived, yes."

"Only a few doors away from you, if I'm not mistaken."

"Don't remind me. And, above all, don't remind Angela."

"I'll try not to. Mom has just called, by the way."

"How is she?"

"She seems to be coping okay. Better than I'd expected, to be honest."

"What's she doing?"

"She seems to have become a bit more sociable. She's meeting some of their friends down there more often than she used to."

"That's good."

"She's coming home for Christmas."

"Is that what she said?"

"As good as."

"I'd better buy some Tanqueray."

He noted the ensuing pause and knew what was coming next. He'd also wondered when he should mention it.

"I dreamed about Dad last night," she said. "He was emerging from a clump of trees. It was summer. Bright sunshine, you know."

"On his own?"

"I don't know. I woke up then, I think. Incidentally, he was younger . . . more or less like we are now. I remember noting that from his face. Isn't that odd?"

"I don't know. It's not so odd to have been dreaming about him. I . . . I think about him as well. I've had that kind of dream."

•   •   •   •   •

The madman with the knife had calmed down by the time they got there. So much, in fact, that he was lying on the ground. Morelius bent down to examine him.

"He's not dead, is he?"

Morelius looked up at Bartram.

"Coma, I think. He's on GHB."

"Here comes the ambulance."

"I said they should send an ambulance too," said a young man with a mobile in his hand.

"Was it you who reported the incident? Okay, what happened?"

"He started stabbing at random, then focused on one person when we stopped here. I ran after him and tackled him."

"And then?"

"He tried to get up, but there were several of us holding him down."

"Where's the knife?"

"He dropped it. It's over there," he said, pointing toward the pavement. Morelius could see the knife on the road midway between where they were and the pavement.

"Was anybody hurt? In the tram or out here in the street?"

"No. Apart from him."

"Who was he after?"

They moved out of the way when the ambulance team arrived with a stretcher and gave the man a quick examination. He was still lying there with no signs of life.

"GHB, probably," Morelius said.

The man was lifted onto the stretcher and carried to the ambulance. Morelius turned to the hero and repeated his question.

"He was after somebody in particular, is that right?"

"I don't know. It looked that way, but he's, well, he's as high as a kite, so . . ."

"So he wasn't after anybody in particular?"

"I really don't know."

Winter had gone to get a cup of coffee, and returned. It was snowing again. It wasn't December yet, but winter had set in. Several inches of snow, and he had no doubt they would still be there over the holiday period. The new era. He breathed deeply in, then out, then in again.

This was something new. He lost concentration, regained it, then lost it again. He thought about his father, about Angela, about their child, about his mother, about his sister, about the case again, about the telephone that kept ringing, about Angela again. About Alicia.

Möllerström came with some new photographs. Winter had asked to see all of them. They were taken from every conceivable angle.

From the front all that could be seen was the jagged necklace. The same was true from the side. That applied to both of them.

But you could see from the back, if you knew. They didn't quite fit, the balance wasn't right. Considerable strength had been needed to do this, Pia Fröberg had said. She was a pathologist who knew what she was talking about. Even she had paled at the thought.

But the bottom line was the lack of balance.

There were no fingerprints apart from their own. We checked especially around the eyes, Lars Beier had said. The deputy chief of the forensic division had looked pretty sick himself, and surprised. As if they'd been presented with something unreal.

The puzzle was the same as always: why? Why had he done it?

Winter tried to examine all the photographs one more time. The worst was the photo of her face in profile. The body leaning against a big, fat cushion.

They were holding hands, a grip welded by death. Afterward, the pathologist had said. The fingers had been intertwined after death.

He switched on the tape again as he scrutinized the pictures. The guitars as loud as possible. Incredibly fast. It was mainly the drums, furiously beating. The base drum, bang-bang-bang-bang. The voice was hissing, like a disembodied spirit. A witch. Were they words he could hear?

"Even somebody who's used to it—a fan, that is—can hardly ever work out the words."

Johan Setter was sitting opposite Winter. His leather jacket was scuffed with age. Setter's brow was wrinkled in thought.

"I went to Madhouse in Drottninggatan, but they couldn't help much. They listened to the tape, but they weren't able to make any specific comments."

"Specific comments? What do you mean by that?"

"The bottom line is that they didn't have a clue. Even so, it's one of the best shops in Gothenburg for metal music. The girl did say that it was more like black metal, rather than death metal. Not that there's much of a difference. That made it more difficult, she said."

"What is the difference?"

"With regard to the music, the tempo is quicker with black metal. The singing is shriller. Deeper in death metal. As if it were coming from the back of the throat."

"With regard to what else, then?"

"Eh?"

"With regard to the music, you said. What else? The words?"

"Oh, yes. The text in black metal is evidently more . . . er . . . mythological. Sort of Viking Romanticism and that sort of crap. A dose of Satanism."

"Satanism?"

"Well, evidently some of the fans get inspired—more than when they're listening to death metal."

"Inspired by the words?"

"Apparently so."

"How the hell is that possible when they can't hear what's being said?"

"You need to have the text," said Setter. "They always supply that."

"So this is more intellectual than it first appears," said Winter.

Setter hoped to see that he was smiling, but he wasn't.

"So, we need to have the words for this stuff," Winter said, gesturing toward the cassette that Setter had put on the desk in front of him. "And that will also mean that we'll know who's playing. And singing. Or hissing, rather."

"I thought it would be dead easy," said Setter. "Straightforward. But they were sort of surprised that they didn't recognize it. The people at Madhouse said that all the tapes sounded the same."

"Couldn't they say if it was Swedish or foreign?"

"Not even that. It's not going to be easy."

"Who said it had to be easy?" Winter recognized that he was being a pain. "But you've eliminated one thing at least." A good word, that. Eliminated. "It's not death metal."

"I bought all the magazines and fanzines they had on display," said Setter, bending down and producing a little pile from his shoulder bag, putting them on the desk. "I haven't gotten around to going through them yet."

Winter picked out some of them. *Necrologium—the 9th Book of Blasphemy.* He'd missed the previous eight. *Combichrist. Fear. Reinforced.* He hesitated when he saw the title of the next one: *Amputation Magazine.*

21

The picture was on the kitchen table. He picked it up and looked at it. Who had done that? Who could do anything like that? Put up your hand, whoever did it. Come on, hands up!

He put up his right hand, and held the Polaroid photo in his left, as he was left-handed. That's what you do, isn't it? Why should he do it any differently? Hold the photo in his right hand? He shook his head, and wondered what to do with the picture. He couldn't make up his mind. As usual.

But he had made up his mind, hadn't he?

He lowered his right hand and pinned the photo to the wall using a thumbtack with a black head. He took a close look at it. They were looking back at him, but something wasn't right. The guy on the sofa seemed to be about to nod, but evidently he'd prevented his head from falling forward at the last minute. That was cleverly done. The same applied to her. C-l-e-v-e-r.

He was crying now. Apart from that it was quiet everywhere. Quiet. Snow quieted everything down. He was crying, and could hear his own misery. He knew there was somebody listening, but that devil hadn't put in an appearance yet.

He didn't want it to be quiet. He went to the record player and chose an LP, put it on, and hummed along with the music—*the old hometown looks the same, as I step down from the train*—now *that* was real music, he'd had the feeling that *she* would like it when he played Tom for her the first time, but she'd laughed at him. Not like later, when she did that terrible thing to him. "Switch it off." She'd laughed. "It reminds me of home. For God's sake, ha ha ha, switch it off before it kills me."

She'd looked through his records, and laughed even more.

"Is this what you listen to? Oh no, I don't think I can survive this." Ha ha ha. H-a h-a h-a.

Almost like when it happened. He ought to have realized.

"What's the matter?" his father had asked on one occasion. "There's something the matter with you." The next time he went home he hadn't said anything at all, because there was nothing more for him to say, was there? Never again.

The sun came out and the whole room was lit up. The photograph melted into the light. Burned up. I can forget it now, he thought.

Fredrik Halders and Aneta Djanali went to Hair.

"Unisex," Halders said. Young men and women cut the hair of young men and women. Halders had put all that behind him. He eyed his crew cut in the mirrors on every side. Nothing for an artist of hirsute inclinations to exploit, but at least he still owned his own skull.

"Do you patronize places like this?" he asked.

"Eh?"

"Do you come to places like this to get your Afro curls straightened out?"

"Shut up," Djanali said to Halders, via one of the mirrors.

They were an odd couple. It wasn't the first time she'd made that observation.

"What can I do for you?" asked a woman in her thirties who emerged from a room on the left and stationed herself behind the counter and the cash register where they were standing. She was very tall, not far short of six feet, wearing a black blouse and a black skirt.

Her hair was parted, an apparently simple style. Halders breathed in all the pleasant perfumes and listened to the music from the local radio station. He felt out of place, and no doubt all the others present felt that he was out of place as well. Come on, get a grip. You are with Aneta. You have to show her what you can do. Screw all the fags.

"We'd like to ask you a few questions about Louise Valker," said Djanali, producing her ID card. "We're from the crime unit." The woman nodded, poker-faced. "Are you the owner of this establishment?"

"Yes. My name is Irma Fletcher." She looked at the doorway she'd just come through. "Perhaps we could go to my office."

Once there, they sat around an oblong table with a glass surface. There were several glossy magazines strewn over it. All Halders could see on the covers were female heads; he closed his eyes, then looked at the walls, where he found a number of black-and-white fashion posters depicting women in clothes that had been torn to shreds. They looked as if they'd been splattered with blood. One woman was lying on the floor, her eyes staring. In the background was a man in an overcoat and hat carrying a machine gun. Halders looked at the outline and guessed that it was a dummy Uzi.

"What the hell is that?" said Halders, gesturing toward the wall.

"What do you mean?"

"What's that? Have you been swiping pictures from the forensic lab? Photos from a murder scene?"

The woman looked at the wall and started to blush. She'll soon be so hot that her makeup will melt, thought Djanali. "Oh, I thought we'd taken them down. I suppose it's been overlooked. They've been hanging there for a while and then, well, after a while people only see the wall." Her face was still scarlet. "But they are very unsuitable."

"What are they?" Halders insisted.

"Er . . . well . . . they are a series of new fashion photographs." She looked at the wall again. "We've had quite a few like that this autumn."

"Is this the fashion for the new millennium?" Djanali wondered.

"A rush of blood to the head," Halders said. "Brave New World."

Irma Fletcher looked as if she were shouldering the shame of the whole planet. She leaped to her feet, pulled down all three of the posters, crumpled them up, and stuffed them into a wastepaper basket next to the door. Then she sat down again.

"As far as we can make out, Louise Valker hasn't been working here for the last couple of months?" Aneta Djanali was checking her notes.

"No. She worked sort of seasonally. I mean, she came to help out when we needed her. No regular pattern to it, in fact."

"It sounds a bit shady."

"That's what I meant when I said 'no regular pattern.' But that seemed to be how she wanted it."

"That's how she wanted it?"

"I offered her a part-time job with regular hours a year or so ago, but she turned it down."

"Turned it down? That must be unusual."

Irma Fletcher shrugged.

"She didn't elaborate, and I didn't ask her."

"Was she any good?"

"Yes. She was competent enough. Maybe not too keen to learn anything new. But, there again, I suppose she wasn't exactly a youngster anymore. I don't know. And I'd rather not speculate."

"Did she socialize with any of the other hairdressers here?"

"Not as far as I know. Feel free to ask them, but I don't think so."

"So she kept to herself."

"We all work hard here, and you could say that we all keep to ourselves. Some of them have their own chairs, and they're running their own business under my umbrella. And then everybody goes home when we close up shop."

"Did you get to know her at all?"

"No, not really. We once had a coffee together at the café next door—that was when I offered her the job. I think that was the only time."

"Can you tell us anything about her? What she was like?"

"She liked men."

"Excuse me?"

"I had the impression that she was very interested in men. A bit of a flirt, you might say. That's something you tend to notice."

· · · · · ·

"Christian was a good salesman. What a tragedy."

It was afternoon. They were sitting in an office with a view over Gothenburg—apart from Halders, who preferred to stand.

Comec's open-plan office was on the twelfth floor. People were leaning over computers and conducting conversations. They're talking over the computers' heads, thought Halders. I'd better stop thinking along those lines.

Comec's head of sales and personnel was sitting in front of them, looking serious at one moment and cheerful the next. He keeps forgetting himself, Djanali thought.

It was early afternoon on Friday, and all the men were casually dressed in checked shirts, T-shirts under comfortable tweed, polo shirts. The few women Halders could see were dressed normally. Maybe the occasional one in jeans. The sales boss was dressed in a black T-shirt under a black single-breasted jacket, boots, black jeans.

Casual Friday, Djanali thought. When Comec becomes Comic.

"In what way was he good?" Halders asked.

"Knew what he was doing. Conscientious. Got results."

"Why didn't you miss him, then?"

"Excuse me?"

"He was absent for ten days. Why didn't you miss him?"

"In the first place that's not how we work here," said the man, crossing his legs. "We don't keep a daily check on our workforce in that way. They are highly qualified people who take care of themselves."

Highly qualified, my ass, Halders thought. The only thing . . .

"And in the second place, Christian had taken a week's vacation around that time. I didn't know about it until later."

"But that was only a week."

"As I said, our staff take care of themselves. Perhaps he hadn't booked anything for the days before and after his vacation. I haven't checked that. Yet." He looked at Halders, perhaps somewhat arrogantly. Halders wasn't sure, and couldn't be bothered to find out.

"Did you know Christian?"

"Excuse me?"

"Did you know him socially? Did you mix in your private lives?"

"No. Maybe the occasional beer with the guys," he said, and looked at Djanali. "With the team, I mean."

"Okay. Anything else?" asked Halders.

"What do you mean?"

"Can you tell us anything about his personality? Did he ever talk about his friends? Or his wife? Anything at all apart from Comec?"

"Only the usual."

"What's the usual?" Djanali asked.

"You know, girls, that sort of thing."

They took the number-four tram to Hagen. Angela had been surprised when he suggested it.

"I thought you never went by tram."

"I am tonight."

"Why?"

What could he say? That he wanted to see the town in the same way as most people see it? Huh. He simply didn't want to take a taxi, or to drive himself. He also wanted to walk a bit.

"I feel like walking. Let's walk as far as the Avenue and take the tram from there. Are you ready?"

"Surely you can see that I'm not ready," she said from the bathroom.

"Okay. I'll wait."

She brushed her hair and put a bit of gloss on her lips. She looked in the mirror and opened her eyes wide. The light in the bathroom wasn't good. She had bags under her eyes in there. They weren't there when she looked in a mirror at the hospital. She made a face at the mirror. It's not the light. You want a house. Your apartment days should be over. A house by the sea.

Winter had gone to the living room and was standing by the window. Coltrane was playing with Red Garland. "Soft Lights and Sweet Music."

The city was wrapped in gauze. Soft light shone out through the bandages. Lights blinked on top of high buildings. Gothenburg had acquired a different topography in recent years. It was reaching up to the sky. Airplanes cruised between its arms on their way down.

He looked down. Down there. Somewhere. How many times have I stood here and thought: the answer is down there, the solution. The man I'm going to meet is down there somewhere, perhaps he's walking past at this very moment. He's walking through the park. Now he's passing the obelisk. I've done that as well. I've kept meeting him.

"Ready," Angela said from the hall. The music came to an end at the same moment, and it was the last track. He switched it off and left the room.

As they were waiting for the elevator an elderly man came out of Mrs. Malmer's flat and closed the door carefully behind him. He hesitated when he noticed them, but nodded and stood alongside them to wait. He was tall, graying hair, moles on his face.

"Who was that?" she asked when they left the building and started walking toward the Avenue. The stranger had disappeared in the opposite direction.

"Never seen him before."

"Hmm."

"What's the matter?"

"Nothing."

There were a lot of people waiting at bus and tram stops in Vasaplatsen. Their breath came out of their mouths like smoke. Angela could feel the cold through her coat and wished she was wearing a hat. Her ears were freezing cold already. Twenty degrees, and it was still only November. Perhaps it will be up to fifty on Christmas Eve.

"There's a colleague of yours there," she said.

"Where?"

"In the police car on the other side."

"Yes, I can see it."

"It's not moving."

"Well . . ."

"Can you see what it is?"

"What do you mean?"

"Where it comes from."

"The district? I suppose it ought to be from Lorensberg. Why?"

"Noth—"

"Now I remember. We can . . ."

The car started moving and passed by them. Winter waved at it.

"Simon Morelius," he said.

"Was that the driver? Do you know him?"

"Only by sight."

The tram was full when they eventually got on, and they stood in the middle, holding on to the straps. Angela was standing with her legs apart so as not to lose her balance, and seemed to be protecting her stomach. Not such a bright idea after all, Erik, he thought.

A lot of passengers got off at Kungsportsplatsen and Angela was able to sit down. It was quiet where they were, but somebody was muttering away and occasionally shouting threats at the back. Everybody looked the other way. Several drunks came on board at Brunnsparken. Winter had to move.

After two more stops the seat next to Angela became vacant. There was a smell of smoke and alcohol in the tram, and sweat from the fat man in front. Some teenage girls were staring at Winter. A black man was playing something on his Walkman that was making him jerk his head from side to side. At Järntorget a group of young men got on. They were all wearing black leather jackets covered in names and symbols. A devil, two witches. An ax dripping with blood. There was a clanking noise from the shopping bags full of beer cans when they put them on the floor, which was covered in black slush. A teenage couple three rows ahead of them kept turning around, apparently to look at him, or at Angela. There was something vaguely familiar about the girl. He looked out the window. A police car overtook them as they approached Stigberget. The long arm of the law again, he thought.

Lotta Winter welcomed them in a cloud of garlic and herbs.

"Where are the girls?" asked Winter.

"It's Friday night. Eight o'clock. They won't stay at home anymore, not even for you, Erik. Let me give you both a hug!" She embraced them. "You're FREEZING!"

"They'll be back before eleven, won't they? The girls?"

"Grow up."

"He'll find out eventually," Angela said.

"What can I get you to drink?" Lotta asked.

"I'll have some wine, please. Angela will just have water."

"Have you spoken to Mom?"

"Yes."

"How was she?"

"Still says she's coming for Christmas."

"How was she otherwise, did you think?"

"As you said, she seems to be . . . strong. Let's hope she can keep it up."

Let's hope she can, for all our sakes, thought Lotta, as she poured the drinks.

22

Hanne Östergaard was shoveling snow. Her spade scraping over the stone paving, through the snow drifts. The garden was covered in white.

The trees are sticking up like the skeletons they now are, she thought, and could feel the sweat under her woolly hat.

Several neighbors were also out snow-shoveling this Saturday morning, using fancy types of "spade" that still didn't seem to be much good. Gothenburg isn't inside the Arctic Circle. Nobody expected the snow to last for very long.

Three houses down the road a man was busy putting winter tires on his car. She looked toward her own garage as the side door opened and Maria appeared in wool sweater and a six-foot scarf, but with no hat or gloves. She was carrying a broom, and now sat astride it and jumped three paces.

"I thought I'd do a bit of flying," she said.

"Wrong time of year, love."

"Exactly. Swedish witches appear at Easter. So you believe in witches, do you?"

I believe in everything evil, thought Hanne, but it was only a fleeting reaction.

"I believe in what I see before me," she said instead. "Sometimes, at least."

Maria looked put out, for a couple of seconds. Then she looked up again.

"I thought I would give you a hand." She cleared a strip of the path with one sweep of the broom. "Get rid of the remainder."

"That's terrific."

Maria brushed away. Suddenly, she was a child again. Hanne Östegaard saw the little girl in her face, and was overcome with love and affection when Maria looked up and smiled. Her attempt to ask for forgiveness. Hanne was determined to swallow it, hook, line, and sinker. She's only a child.

Patrik appeared and walked along the newly cleared drive sporting a thick and gigantic knitted hat that was big enough to accommodate Maria as well.

"Patrik, hello." She held out her hand. "Long time no see."

"Hello! I thought I'd pay you a visit. About time I ventured into the sticks." He looked around. "Virgin white out here."

"That's one way of putting it."

"Virgin white. Most of it's already gone in town."

"What would you say to a cup of hot chocolate?"

"Well, what do you say?" said Maria, looking at Patrik.

"I'd love it. I'm freezing. There was something wrong with the heating in the tram."

She'd made cheese rolls and two mugs of hot chocolate, with another on the way.

"Do you know what it is yet?" asked Maria, barely audible with her mouth full.

"I was playing it over in my mind last night, but I was so damn . . . so tired," he said, looking at Hanne, the vicar.

"It's all right."

"Did you listen to the disc I lent you?" he asked.

"Not on your life. You put it into my bag without my knowing." She took another bite. "I don't like that kind of stuff."

"What don't you like?" Hanne asked. "I'm curious."

"Hard rock."

"Death metal," Patrik said. "Black metal."

"Eh?"

"Not Ria's thing. Too heavy."

"What is it? A sort of punk?"

Patrik roared with laughter. "Metal punk, in that case," he said, and Hanne noticed he had finished his chocolate. She went to the stove to heat up some more milk.

"Patrik knows everything about music," Maria said. "And about stuff that doesn't deserve to be called music as well."

"And you're saying that this, er, metal is in that category?"

"It's not music as far as I'm concerned, Mom."

"But you can't just . . . sweep it under the carpet," Patrik said.

"But what does it sound like?" asked Hanne, who had returned to the table with the hot milk. "I'm getting curious again."

"All right," Maria said. "Hang on a minute."

"We're not going anywhere," said Patrik.

Maria left the kitchen, and a minute or so later some kind of music could be heard coming from the living room. Hanne looked at Patrik when somebody started hissing like a madman against a background of what sounded like a plane crash.

"Black metal," Patrik said.

Maria came back.

"The idea is that it should sound like a witch singing," Patrik said.

"I'll go and get my broom," Maria said.

It was Patrik's fourth mug. They had finally gotten around to telling Hanne about his suspicions about the apartment, and the phone call he'd made to the caretaker.

"Haven't the police spoken to you as well?" asked Hanne.

"No."

"That's odd."

Patrik put down his mug for the last time. He shrugged.

"Suits me and I don't suppose it matters. They were informed, after all. I can't tell them any more than the old guy will have."

"That's usually something for the police to decide."

"Come on, Mom. You've spent too much time at the police station."

"I bet the old guy wants to grab all the credit for himself," Patrik said. "Maybe he thought he'd get a reward." He looked at Hanne. "Maybe there *was* a reward, in fact." He looked at Maria. "Maybe I made a big mistake."

"I think you ought to get in touch with whoever it is handling the investigation," Hanne said. "The crime unit."

"It's the man you know," Maria said. "He works for the crime unit, doesn't he?"

"Erik? Erik Winter? I don't know if he's involved in that particular case, but I suppose he may well be."

"It was him," said Maria, looking at Patrik.

"What do you mean?" Hanne Östergaard looked at her daughter.

"We saw him on the tram last night," Maria said. "He was with his girlfriend or wife or whatever she is."

"Angela."

"They were on the same tram as us. We went to Stigbergstorget."

"What were you going to do there?" Hanne asked. She was aware that her voice was suddenly suspicious.

"Oh, Mom! It was eight o'clock, or thereabouts, and Bengans was open late."

"On a Friday?"

"Yes," Patrik said. "It was a special release promotion. Ultramario played some tracks from their latest disc."

"That explains everything then," said Hanne, and tried to smile. Maria looked angrily out of the window where the sun was glinting on the snow in the back garden.

Neither Patrik nor Maria spoke.

"So you saw Erik Winter? I didn't know he ever used the tram."

"It was definitely him," said Maria. "And we've seen the lady going into the building where he lives."

You two get all over Gothenburg, it seems, Hanne thought, but she kept it to herself.

Patrik had also been looking out the window. The sun was bright now, lighting up the snow. Like a lamp. He thought about the bluish-yellow light on the stairs, the newspapers, that hellish music pounding out when he opened the flap of the mail slot.

But there was something else as well.

There was something else.

The thought had been there in the back of his mind, or rather the memory had. Something he'd seen a few weeks ago, or whenever it was.

It had grown stronger. The memory. It had something to do with when he'd been thinking about what kind of music it was. It couldn't be more than a guess and presumably not even that. But . . . the other thing. He could see it again as he stared out at the sun on the snow, twinkling like stars in a white sky. It was there when he said thank-you for the chocolate and went into Maria's room. She was already there and had switched off the music, which he was pleased about.

He sat on the bed and looked out at the garden again. There was a greenhouse in the shade. He gazed at it. It seemed to help him sort through what was in his mind. The greenhouse that the sun hadn't reached. There was something there in his mind. Not quite enough light. It was . . .

"Have you seen something?" Maria asked. "Is there something mysterious in the greenhouse?"

He didn't answer.

"Say something, Patrik. I don't like it when you're like this. It's bad enough as it is." She looked out, then turned back to Patrik. "All the horrible things that have happened."

"There was somebody there . . . then," he said.

"What, there was somebody in the greenhouse?"

"No, no." He turned to look at her. "The stairs. The apartment building. When I came with the newspapers one of the mornings."

"And . . . ?"

"People come and go even in the early mornings. But not very often. I haven't seen many people at that time."

"I see. It's all clear now. Clear as mud."

"Listen, Ria. When I was going to walk up the stairs there was somebody who got on the elevator on an upper floor and started to come down. It must have been a couple of weeks ago, ten days, maybe."

"You mean *those* stairs. *That* building."

"Yes, obviously. I don't usually take the elevator but I had a bit of a temperature or something and so I thought I would that day. That's probably why I can vaguely remember it. But the elevator wasn't there . . . so I started walking up, and then I heard it start moving from two floors up or so. I've been thinking, and I reckon it could well have been *that* floor. Maybe."

"What makes you think that?"

"I dunno, I suppose you get used to staircases. You listen to things. I stood on the stairs, not far up, and waited for the elevator to come down."

"And?"

"Somebody got out, then went out of the front door. A man."

"Did he see you?"

"Nope. I was a few steps up and he didn't turn around."

"What did he look like?"

"He didn't turn around, as I said."

"But was he old or young, or what?"

"I'm not sure. He didn't seem to be all that old. But when he went through the front door I think I saw a little bit of his face. His profile."

"You're a scream, you really are."

"It's not the first time I've seen people in the early morning."

"What made you think about this particular thing? Why now?"

"I don't know, maybe it's the time . . . no . . . it occurred to me that . . . it might have been the music. That something was coming from the door."

"This is awful. Terrible. You might have seen . . ."

"Let's keep it quiet."

"What Mom said is even more important now, Patrik. You have to go to the police."

"Eh?"

"You must. You must, you must." She'd picked up a pillow and was hitting him on the shoulder with it. "You must testify, you must testify!"

"Give it up, Ria."

She dropped the pillow onto the bed.

"There might be tons of important things they want to ask you about."

"Such as?"

"Are you stupid? Such as what he was wearing, for instance." She'd picked up the pillow again, was holding it, thinking. "Do you remember what he was wearing?"

"He had on an overcoat."

"Long? Short? Black? Brown? Beige?"

"Dark . . . is this a cross-examination?" But Maria wasn't smiling. "There was . . . there's something else as well. I'm trying to remember what it is. . . . It's been at the back of my mind. It was something he had on . . . under the overcoat, that I saw. But I can't remember what it was."

"You mean something you recognized?"

"I'm not sure. Yes, could be. Something that . . . seemed familiar. But I can't put my finger on it."

23

The letter was third in the pile. The return address said "Dirección General de la Policía," but Winter had no doubt about who had written it. He put the white envelope to one side. It was burning the light-colored wood of his desk in protest at the intrusion of his private life into the workplace. The Spanish police stamp was a symbol for the borderline between life and work: dangerous, shifting. The scorch marks on his desk were much the same as those made by Alicia's business card on the dark table in his room at La Luna.

.   .   .   .   .

They had drunk another glass of wine—or was he the only one who had done so? His despair had intensified when he heard some people walking past in the Plaza Altamirano, speaking Swedish. The older man's voice reminded him of his father. Alicia had understood. Just then, at that moment, he had sensed that she understood.

Hours later he had seen the sea from the window in a house overlooking the ocean. He had no idea of the name of the street, or how to get there. A dog had barked down below, then all was quiet. There was nobody else around.

Some hours later he had woken up in his room at La Luna, and could no longer remember. It had been morning. He'd taken a shower and driven to the airport.

Bergenhem knocked on the door and entered. Winter was holding the envelope in his hand.

Bergenhem looked thinner. He didn't look at Winter to start with. He remained standing.

"You wanted me?"

"Sit down, Lars, please."

Bergenhem sat down and ran his hand over his brow. His hair looked damp.

"I'm a bit late. Somebody had skidded off the road just after the bridge."

"Nobody is ever prepared for winter."

"Then again, we hardly ever have one."

"How are things in general, Lars?" Winter kept his voice down.

"Fine. I took Ada to nursery school."

"Have you managed to get . . . a bit of rest?"

"I certainly have. I only needed a few days."

"A week. Is there anything that we can talk about?"

"Meaning what?"

"Is something getting too much for you? Something to do with work?"

"Of course not."

Winter took a deep breath and considered his next move. He leaned forward.

"Listen, Lars. I know that some of the things we do here are . . . pretty difficult to put up with. We get bad memories. It's hard to shake off some of the things we go through. And you have been subjected to worse things than a lot of others. No, not subjected to. That's not a good way of putting it. You've had to . . . survive things."

"It was my fault after all," Bergenhem said.

"Stop it."

"But it was."

"I said STOP IT." Winter lowered his voice again. "What I'm saying is that we have to try to work as a team, and give it our best shot. Our best shot. Do you feel that you—"

"For God's sake, Erik, I've been at home for a few days to get a bit of rest, and it sounds as if you're trying to get me put away in a home. A mental home."

"Did I say that?"

"No, but . . ."

Bergenhem seemed to have fixed his gaze on a spot over Winter's head.

"Look at me, Lars." He did. "What I wanted to say is that you are perfectly normal. You're a human being. But if a person feels . . . if you feel that things are getting to be too much, it's best to face up to it."

"What do you know?"

"I beg your pardon?"

Bergenhem had risen to his feet.

"You don't know the whole damn story," he said. Winter could see his lower lip trembling slightly. Bergenhem started to sit down, but remained standing. "Just think if you'd—" he said, then sat down. Winter waited. Bergenhem looked up. "For Christ's sake, Erik, I'm sorry. I know of course . . . your dad."

"Maybe I said too much myself." Winter reached out to grasp Bergenhem by the arm. "I'd just like you to know that you're welcome to talk to me . . . about what's on your mind. I'll try to listen. And I won't call in any psychologists."

Bergenhem breathed out. It sounded as if he'd spent the last half-hour collecting air.

"It's just that there are a few little problems at home."

"Hmm."

"That's the kind of thing you have to sort out yourself."

Work and private life, thought Winter, glancing at the letter lying on the desk between them. That's the kind of thing you have to sort out yourself. This is work. Private life is this evening. Tonight. He'd meant to ask Bergenhem about other things. About children. What it was like.

Some other time.

"Johan called in on you," he said instead.

"Setter? Yes, he did."

"But it wasn't your thing?"

"Death metal? No thank you."

"Or black metal. There seems to be a difference."

"I'm not at all sure that I want to know what it is," said Bergenhem, smiling for the first time.

"It might be necessary to know in this particular case," Winter said. "Setter said this morning that there's a distributor in Gothenburg who specializes in the genre, or genres. They have a couple of record companies as well. If they don't know what this is, then nobody will, according to Setter."

"Has he been there?"

"No. I thought you and I might pay them a visit."

Their premises were in Kyrkogatan. Church Street—an appropriate name, Winter thought as they walked up the stairs. Posters with infernal and Satanist motifs covered the walls.

The poster to the left of the door of Desdemona Productions featured a naked woman at prayer: Fuck Me Jesus. Something new from the group Marduk. There was more: the rocking Dildos, Driller Killer, the Unkinds, Ritual Carnage. Necromantia. Dellamorte. Order from Chaos. Angelcorpse.

Winter paused and considered the name. Angelcorpse. They were proudly presenting a new disc: *Exterminate.*

A man with long black hair and wearing a colorful T-shirt opened after the third ring. The T-shirt was black with a bright yellow sun setting behind mountains and a burning cross hovering above. The message was etched into space: Eternal Death.

Makes you feel at home, thought Bergenhem. Or rather, at work.

"Well?"

"Rickard Nordberg?"

"Yes. Are you Wester? The detective?" He eyed Bergenhem up and down. "Two murder hunters from the crime unit?"

"Winter, and this is Bergenhem. May we come in?" Winter could hear music coming from inside, guitars, drums. The singer was screeching in unspeakable horror. Death patrols were executing victims nonstop.

Rickard Nordberg ushered them in.

The place was a loft. Computers, paper, stereos, some guitars in one corner. CD covers wherever you looked, posters. The loft was light and clean, daylight poured in through skylights, a bright blue visible through all of them. Rickard Nordberg sat down at one of the desks. Winter noted that they were about the same age. Nordberg's hair was waist-length, graying, thin at the temples. He was wearing tight black jeans and boots with chains. He lit a cigarette. Seemed content with life. On the wall behind him was a poster for his own record company, Dead Sun, on which somebody's innards were being cut out. Nordberg was partially obscuring an armful of intestines. When he flicked the ash off his cigarette, Winter noted next to the ashtray a photograph of two little girls. Next to it was a card in a frame: "To the nicest dad in the world." To the right of the frame was a pile of CDs. Winter read the title of the top one: *Tortura Insomnae.*

"There's a lot of death around here," said Bergenhem, surveying the room.

"Well, yes. That's my job." Winter noticed the gleam in Nordberg's eye. "I suspect the topic isn't all that unfamiliar to you gentlemen either?" He spoke with a refined Gothenburg accent.

"Have you brought the tape with you?" Nordberg asked. He gestured with his hand and a man similarly dressed and of more or less the same age came up to introduce himself. Winter handed over the cassette, and Nordberg inserted it into a cassette player. The music started to play, and Winter was transported back to the room in Aschebergsgatan.

Nordberg and his colleague listened attentively.

"Low budget," Nordberg said after ten seconds.

His colleague shook his head.

"I've never heard this before. Must be American. It's not Norwegian, in any case."

"Norwegian?"

"They're biggest when it comes to black metal," Nordberg said.

"So this is black metal?" Winter asked.

"No doubt about it."

"How can you tell?"

"The drive, the speed. Just listen. A drum roll on every beat. At least."

"And the vocals," his colleague said. "Pretty high-pitched." They listened to the screeching that had long since passed the limits of falsetto. "This is GOOD."

"I don't agree," Nordberg said.

"Why is it good?" asked Bergenhem, turning to the colleague.

"It's straightforward and unpretentious. Straight to the point. Influenced by the early eighties."

"Is it early eighties?" asked Winter.

"No way. Sounds as if it was made a couple of years ago. Rubbish production. A touch of Bathory, but it's not them."

"Why isn't it good?" asked Winter, turning to Nordberg.

"It's too uniform. Nothing that stands out. I prefer something with more of a tune." He stopped the tape and started a CD. More guitars strumming away at full speed, drums everywhere. Vocals from the crypt. "Can you hear it? That's what I mean."

Bergenhem looked at Winter.

"I can hear the tune," Winter said. "A touch of The Clash."

Nordberg gave him an odd look.

"Funny you should say that, they've said themselves that they owe a lot to The Clash."

"*London Calling,*" said Winter.

"Sweden is very big in black metal," Nordberg said.

"How big?" Bergenhem asked.

"Depends what you're comparing it with. But it has its niche market. Let's say that a big-name Swedish band sells five thousand CDs. There are a few that do better, such as giant companies like Music for Nations, Dimmu Borgir from Norway, and Cradle of Filth from England. There we're talking about a hundred and fifty thousand."

"Black metal?"

"Black metal."

"Who listens to it?"

"Well, mainly young guys. Almost exclusively young guys. Ordinary people."

Ordinary people, Winter thought. The nicest people in the world.

"Where does . . . Satanism fit in?" he asked.

"That's the basis of black metal," Nordberg's colleague said. "But it's more Devil worship."

"What's the difference?"

"Devil worshippers like the Devil, but they jettison all the rest," Nordberg said in his posh accent. "But I'm no expert. Nor a worshipper, actually."

"And this is music for Devil worshippers," said Winter, indicating the CD player. A new track had started, just as intense as the first one.

"Not necessarily," said Nordberg's colleague. "Not many of the people who listen to this stuff are really Devil worshippers, or Satanists. It's more the packaging that counts."

"Packaging?"

"The style just as much as the music. People want to look like KISS, but in spades."

"Sverker knows all there is to know about KISS," said Nordberg with a smile. "By the way, I haven't gotten around to introducing you. Crime unit, Sverker. Sverker, crime unit." He stopped waving his hand about. "Sverker works for a record company. Depression. Mainly metal punk. Knows all there is to know about punk. Just like you do," said Nordberg, nodding at Winter. "He's collared a few new bands only today."

"Slaktmask and Skitsystem," said Sverker modestly. "And Arse-destroyer."

"But neither of you recognizes the music on this cassette?" Winter said.

"Let's do this," Nordberg said. "We'll post a sound file on the Net with one of the tracks from the cassette. I can say that I've discovered an unknown band from somewhere or other and I'm curious to know who they are."

"Which is the truth anyway," said Sverker, stroking back his long, wispy hair.

"Great idea," said Winter.

"He has thousands of addresses all over the world," Sverker said. "Radio stations, record companies, private customers."

"Excellent. When can you do it?"

"As soon as we finish work. Whether we get a response is another matter, of course."

Winter went back to the apartment one final time. Everything was the same as before. The stains were no bigger, no smaller. The music still seemed to hang in the room. Black metal. Fresh in his memory from the airy loft that was Desdemona Productions.

The forensic team had finished. What needed to be analyzed was already in the laboratories, in marked containers. The apartment would be cleaned up and restored to pristine condition. New tenants would move in. I'll have some new neighbors, he thought.

He waited for the elevator that never came. Probably somebody hadn't closed the door properly. He walked down the stairs, at which point the elevator started moving down. It passed by, but whoever was in it had already left the building by the time Winter reached the ground floor. The stiff front door was slowly closing.

It was windy, but a clear evening. Winter noted the back of a man walking down the street. Perhaps the person who had taken the elevator. Winter turned left. The sky was a dull blue in the direction of Nordstan. He poked his scarf inside his overcoat and fastened a few more buttons.

There were four crisp rolls left at the baker's. He hoped Angela was home by now. He wanted to say something to . . . them. He could lie down next to her stomach and tell them a happy story.

A woman with a stroller passed by as he left the baker's. He stepped to one side. He had a sudden desire to take a look at the baby. He caught up with the woman.

He apologized to her and she stopped.

"Do you mind if I take a look at the baby?" he asked.

"Eh?"

She seemed more surprised than scared.

"I'd just like to take a look at your baby." He felt like an absolute fool, but he didn't care. "I'm going to have a child myself soon. For the first time." The stroller was colorless in the neon light. "I'm going to be a father," he said.

24

They traced back the lives of Christian and Louise Valker. They had requested all available data from colleagues in Västerås and Kungsbacka, but the couple had committed no recorded crimes. The church, the state, and the local authorities supplied what information they had, but so far nothing useful had emerged.

"Was it somebody they knew?" wondered Ringmar. They were sitting in his office after the morning meeting. Djanali and Halders were there as well.

"Well, he didn't break in," Winter said. "He might have stolen a key or had a copy made, but it clearly wasn't a surprise visit."

"No," said Ringmar. "Not in that sense. They'd eaten, after all. And drunk."

"Two bottles of wine," Winter said.

"And harder stuff. Beier says there were traces of gin and tonic in their glasses."

"Does Beier know what brand it was?" said Halders.

Winter thought of Tanqueray. Might as well buy the Christmas bottle now, before Mom gets here.

Ringmar looked at Halders.

"Hmm. Are you suggesting that knowing the brand might help us?"

"If the murderer had brought the gin to the party, yes. If he always drinks Gordon's, for instance, and somebody at the System shop in the Avenue remembers somebody who always buys Gordon's . . . well . . ."

"He'd have to have bought it by the crate for anybody to remember. Every week. That sounds a bit far-fetched, Fredrik," Djanali said.

"I'll see what Beier has to say," Winter said. "Every little detail can be significant."

"What else do we know?" Djanali asked nobody in particular. "What have we established about this couple?"

"That they didn't exactly have a wide circle of friends," Halders said. "Not many who cared whether they were alive or dead."

"There were some messages on their answering machine," Ringmar said.

"Trygg-Hansa," Halders said. "Some guff about pensions. That's the only link some people have with the real world nowadays: insurance companies trying to flog pensions to keep you going when you're so stricken with arthritis that you can barely move." He thought of suggesting that they were obviously wasting their time with this couple, but he didn't.

"Two other calls as well," Ringmar said, who had waited patiently until Halders finished his rant.

"We talked to them," said Halders. "Those others. Last night."

"There's something that doesn't add up," said Djanali.

"What do you mean?" Winter asked.

"It's true," Halders said. "There was something . . . odd."

"It wasn't clear to us why they'd been to see the Valkers."

"Hang on," Winter said. "One thing at a time. Who went to see whom and in what order?"

"All right. A couple more or less the same age as the Valkers, Per and Erika Elfvegren—they live in Järnbrott. Similar to the Valkers in several ways. No kids, same age, similar appearance . . ." She glanced up at the others as if to say: the way they looked *before* . . . "We went to see them yesterday, after five. She'd only phoned them to find out what was going on, as she put it."

"How well did they know one another?" Ringmar asked.

"That's exactly it—they were pretty vague on that score. They'd met at some dance restaurant or other, they said, but they couldn't remember where. They'd had dinner at the Valkers' once, and the Valkers had paid a return visit." Djanali looked at Halders. "We had the impression that it was a very superficial relationship."

"They didn't have a clue about what happened to the Valkers," said Halders.

"Did they have an alibi for when the murder took place?" asked Winter. They now had an approximate time and date from Pia.

"They were both at home," Halders said, "and the only witness is their television set."

"Hmm."

"What is it that doesn't add up?" said Ringmar to Djanali. "You said before that there was something that didn't add up."

"Yes . . . it was their attitude, somehow. They were so . . . detached, or knew so little about the Valkers. But at the same time they were scared stiff."

"Is that really so odd?" Ringmar said. "Their friends have been murdered."

"Yes, fair enough. But it's obvious that they're hiding something. Something they don't want to talk about." She looked up. "You know how it is. You can see that there's something there that a person knows you want to know, but he or she doesn't want to say what it is."

"That's exactly right," Halders said, nodding in the direction of Djanali. "I couldn't have put it better myself."

"And it was just the same with the other couple," Djanali said. "It really was."

"Which other couple?" asked Winter. "You mean the other message on the answering machine?"

"Yes. These . . ." She consulted her notebook. "Martell. Bengt and Siv Martell."

Bengt and Siv, Winter thought. The same names as my parents.

"No connection with the cognac," Halders said.

"I just knew you were going to say that," Djanali said.

"What was odd about them?" Ringmar asked, who was becoming somewhat irritated. "They live in . . . Mölndal, if I remember rightly."

"Yes. You could say that they are a carbon copy of the other two. The same type. The same answers. The same superficial acquaintance."

"We were with them last night," Halders said. "But there are one or two differences. For a start, the Elfvegrens are childless, but Siv Martell is divorced and has a couple of teenaged children. They live with their father, and he lives in Malmö." Halders looked at Djanali. "Even I could see that she found it hard to say anything about the children. It was . . . painful."

"No shared custody?" asked Winter.

"She hadn't seen them for several years."

"What about the other difference?" Ringmar asked.

"Well, the Elfvegrens were a bit frightened," said Halders, "but the Martells were scared shitless, and not of us."

"It was even more obvious that they were hiding something," Djanali said. "I don't know if it has anything to do with the murder."

"Alibi?" asked Winter.

"Perhaps," Halders said. "Meals at two restaurants and a few more . . . 'meetings,' as they put it. We can check them out. Haven't gotten around to it yet."

"They're hiding something," Djanali said.

"I'll have a chat with all of them," Winter said. "Starting with the Martells."

"I recommend that you see them in their home territory," said Halders. "They seemed to be uncomfortable in their own home."

"Coming back to the Valkers, you said at the meeting that they'd both acquired a bit of a reputation at work." Ringmar was addressing Djanali.

"I don't think I said 'reputation.' But there were hints. Nobody wanted to go into detail."

"But neither of them had anything against a little flirting?" said Ringmar.

"You could say that. I suppose the husband had more of a reputation. Well, how should I put it? He saw other women, but I think she was just a bit of a flirt."

"So there could well be other couples," said Winter. "Let's start with the Elfvegrens and the Martells. Or, rather, take another look at them."

Winter read his notes. The others had left. He played the black metal cassette at low volume, but the screeching of the "singer" was just as penetrating. The phone rang.

"Winter."

"Sacrament."

"I beg your pardon?"

"Rickard Nordberg here. We've found the band. It's called Sacrament. Canadian. Sverker wasn't far off the mark."

"Are you certain?"

"I think so. We've received several responses. Twenty or so, I think. They all say it's Sacrament. I've never heard of them. Nor has Sverker."

"Sacrament," Winter said. Baptism, or Holy Communion, he thought.

"Some of the responses have given the name of the song, and of the disc," said Nordberg. "I posted the first track as an MP three file, and it's evidently called 'Evil God.' The CD's called *Daughter of* . . . hang on a minute . . . *Daughter of Habakkuk*, or however you pronounce it."

"Habakkuk? What's that?"

"No idea. If you force me to guess I'd say it's a fantasy name for a devil."

"Habakkuk's Daughter," Winter said.

"Perhaps she's nice," Nordberg said, bursting into laughter. "We placed ourselves at the mercy of the Net and got ninety-eight hits on Sacrament. Then we dove deeper into the morass, and found that Sacrament comes from Edmonton and that they've made another CD as well as Hab . . . well, whatever. And a promo as well."

"That's very well done," said Winter.

"Well, another forty-seven hundred twenty-one visitors think so," said Nordberg. "Sacrament's home page has had forty-seven hundred twenty-one hits so far. That fits in with what we said when you were here, more or less. Statistics suggest that they have an audience of five thousand fans, give or take."

"You don't have a list of names, I suppose?"

"Eh? Ha, ha."

"What do you think we should do now?" Just for once I'll listen to what the experts have to say, he thought.

"Well . . . I suppose we could try to get a copy of *Daughter* direct from Canada. Or we could check with other distributors, now that we have the name of the band. See which shops have stocked the disc. Or if it's been puffed in the fanzines. That would cut out the record shops. I'm inclined to think that the fanzines are the best bet in this case. But it'll be a hell of a job. The problem is that the disc came out in 1996, but so much has been published since then that it might as well have been 1896." Nordberg gave a snort. "Judging by the sound quality, it could even have been from then!"

"Can you help me with this case?" Winter asked.

"Okay. I have to say that I'm getting quite curious myself. Just a minute . . . Sverker wants to say something."

Winter waited. Heard distant voices on the telephone. Then Nordberg returned: "Well, let's be honest, we get lots of promotional CDs every year, and we farm a lot of them out to our friends or whatever, but we do save a few, or, rather, we dump them in the attic archive. It's expanded beyond our wildest dreams. There's a possibility that the disc is up there. I mean, it's highly probable that we've had the disc here at one time or another."

"Do you have time to check your archives?"

"No."

"Okay. I'll send a colleague."

It was evening. Winter walked home through Heden. It was still cold, clear. A dozen or so men were playing football on one of the gravel pitches, with much shouting and dull thuds as the ball was kicked. Football in November? Why not? In England the season has barely gotten off the ground by then. Somebody shouted. He turned and saw that the ball was rolling toward him. He side-footed it back to them. Far from finished yet.

He thought about Steve, a colleague in London. Steve was obstinate about what records he listened to. Winter had sent him some jazz, but had been forced to accept that it was a waste of time. I'm more impressionable than he is. People who listen to classic rock are conservative.

They hadn't spoken to each other for months. Winter had considered dashing over to London briefly before Christmas, but now he wasn't sure. Go by all means, Angela had said. If it's possible.

Why shouldn't it be possible? The baby wasn't due until the beginning of April. The first one, Angela had insisted, and she wasn't joking. London was tempting. London calling. It had been a long time.

Winter heard more dull thuds behind him, followed by whoops and cheers: somebody had scored.

The last time they'd spoken on the telephone, Chief Inspector Steve MacDonald had had his leg in a cast after an obligatory Sunday match for his pub team in Kent. Come over for a few days whenever you feel like it, he'd said. You're not so important, but I'd like to see Angela. Again.

They had met Steve briefly in Gothenburg just over three years ago, but they hadn't met his wife. Or the twins. Perhaps they should wait until there were three youngsters. At the beginning of April. Three.

"What do you think of Elias?" asked Angela as he marched into the kitchen. Tears were rolling down her cheeks.

"Should I do it?"

"Yes, please." She handed over the knife and Winter started chopping the onions. Half of them were still waiting to be done.

"What do you think? Elias? Or Isak? Emanuel?"

"Why not Esau?"

"Be serious now."

"Well . . . a bit biblical . . . but I suppose there's nothing wrong with that."

"You believe in God."

"Occasionally."

"You've always said that we have to have something to give us strength."

"Yes."

"Isabella."

"An excellent name."

"Olivia."

"Also excellent."

"Leo."

Winter blinked away the tears as the onions were chopped.

"Hmm . . . maybe. You seem to have stopped feeling sick now."

"It normally stops after twelve weeks or so, and we're well past that point. Now comes a quiet, peaceful period. For the mother, at least."

"How's your stomach? How's Elias?"

"Feel for yourself," she said, getting up from the chair she'd only just sat down on. "Come with me."

She went to the bedroom and Winter put down the knife and followed her. Angela lay down and exposed her stomach, which had grown bigger still. Winter sat down on the bed. It could be the first time. He hadn't felt anything so far. Everything was so hard to grasp. Was it real? She'd been feeling fetal movements for weeks now, maybe five. Kicks. Winter thought about football again, could picture the guys at Heden.

"Put your hand there."

He did as he was told. He could feel something moving. It was real.

25

Morelius and Bartram stopped at a red light. Morelius saw a movement in a car way over to his right out of the corner of his eye. He turned his head and saw an elderly man fastening his seat belt. Bartram had seen him as well. Morelius gave the man a friendly nod.

Bartram grinned. "If he'd kept still we wouldn't have noticed."

"No."

"One thing this job gives you is split vision," Bartram said.

"What else does it give you?" said Morelius, moving away as the lights changed.

"Eh?"

"What else does this job give you, apart from split vision?"

Bartram didn't answer. He was busy watching the Christmas decorations going up in the streets and at the entrances to the arcades.

"Here we go again," he said.

"What?"

"The hell that is Christmas is once more upon us."

Morelius stopped at a pedestrian crossing. A young woman was wheeling a wide stroller with two children in it. She waved in acknowledgment, and Morelius raised his hand in return.

"Poor her, having to push those two around when she goes Christmas shopping," Bartram said.

"Poor you, when you have to go Christmas shopping," Morelius said.

Bartram didn't answer.

"You don't seem to hear what I say today, Greger."

"I hear."

"But you don't answer."

"I don't go Christmas shopping. I never wander around the center of town when I'm not on duty. Especially in this seasonal hysteria."

"Really?"

"Don't you get annoyed by all the drunks and other scum drifting around? Don't you think: there's somebody who's sure as hell wanted? Don't you think: there goes the bastard, and where are the damn police?"

Morelius agreed. It wasn't only when he was on duty. Whenever he walked down the Avenue he noticed the staff entrances where they'd been to pick up shoplifters. He saw the entrance to a pub or outside the post office where everybody peed after dark. That's where somebody had his shoulder broken. That's where that woman ran amok. That's where that guy was shot. That's where the fight took place . . .

"I don't like Christmas," Bartram said.

"Is there anything you do like?"

Bartram didn't answer. He was staring straight ahead. Morelius turned into Götaplatsen. The sun was strong, the sky blue. The high pressure was persisting, which was unusual. There were little drifts of snow in corners on the steps. Gangs of youngsters were standing around outside the library. People streamed into the Park Avenue Hotel for lunch. A line of twenty taxis were outside. Some of the idiots had left their engines running for half an hour. The exhaust fumes hung in clouds around the cars. Morelius was tempted to stop and make them switch off.

"What was it like inside there?" Bartram said.

"Eh?" Morelius turned right after the hotel and found himself behind a bus in Engelbrektsgatan. "Inside where?"

"What was it like inside the apartment? Aschebergsgatan. The double murder."

"You're asking me now?" They'd hardly spoken about it at all since it happened. It was like that sometimes. He hadn't said anything. Bartram had stayed outside on the landing. "What do you want to know?"

"What did it look like?"

"What do you mean, look like?" He glanced toward Bartram on his right, but Bartram didn't turn to look at him. They'd gone as far as the Scandinavium. No calls were coming over the radio. A gang of ice-hockey supporters were parading around with banners before that night's match. "What did *they* look like, do you mean?"

Bartram nodded without looking at him. Morelius didn't say any more. They were negotiating the roundabout at Korsvägen. I've been around this thing eighteen million times, he thought. Over there I was in another squad car once. I lugged teenage drunks from the Liseberg pleasure gardens, and then their friends hauled them back again. I've bought newspapers and Snickers bars at the newsstand over there. Now we're driving up Eklandabacken. I'm at the wheel. The car's going straight ahead like it's on rails.

"What's the matter, Simon?" Bartram had turned to look at him, then looked ahead again. "Look out, for CHRIST'S SAKE!" They were about to ram a taxi outside Panorama. Morelius stamped on the brakes. They stopped a few inches short. The cabdriver stared at them. His passenger, who'd been getting out, did the same. "Did you fall asleep?"

Morelius reversed, overtook the taxi, and continued. Everything was the same as before. The street was still there. The car was going straight ahead. Bartram looked at him. Morelius turned down toward Mossen. The radio crackled into life, but the call was not for them.

"The heads had been exchanged," said Morelius.

"What?"

"Their heads had been exchanged. Didn't you know that? It's not public knowledge, but surely every cop in town knows about it."

"Not me. Nobody's told me."

"He had her head, and she, his."

"Jesus."

"They were holding hands."

Morelius came to another roundabout. He checked carefully this time before proceeding.

Patrik acknowledged that he would have to do something. He'd phoned the police and been put through to somebody called Möller, or something. He'd been asked for his own name.

"It's about that . . . murder," he said.

"I thought we'd spoken to all the newspaper boys," Möller said when he'd explained who he was.

Now Patrik was sitting in front of a large, short-haired police officer who didn't seem all that old, and another who did. He felt a bit like a celebrity. Important. But it wasn't fun. When he'd arrived, the younger man had looked at him as if he were made of glass, all the way through.

This was the guy Ria had been going on about. The one he'd seen on the tram. The skirt he was with was a babe. He seemed to be a hard case. Expensive shirt. He looked like somebody from a gangster film. They'd rented *L.A. Confidential* because Ria liked the cover, and he could easily have been in that. The right style.

"So you saw somebody leaving the elevator?" Winter asked.

"Yes."

"A man?"

"Definitely."

"How can you be so sure?"

"I caught a glimpse of him from the side as he left the building. His profile."

"How much of the profile?"

"Er . . . at an angle from behind. But enough to see that it was a guy."

"How old, would you say?" Ringmar asked.

"Well, about your age," said Patrik, looking at Winter.

"All right. What happened? Start from when you entered the building."

Patrik told them his story. It was the same as he'd told Maria. They asked about dates, days, times.

"What about his clothes?" asked Winter. "The overcoat. Long, short?"

"Longer than short. Er . . ."

"Below the knee?"

"I think so."

"What else?"

"Eh?"

"What else did you see besides the overcoat?"

"That's just it. There was something else . . . but I can't remember. I've been thinking about it a lot. Something else."

"What do you mean, something else?"

"Not connected with the overcoat."

"His hair?"

"I can't say anything about his hair, as I said before. When I sort of got to his hair he was, like, in the shadow in the entrance hall. I can't say anything about his hair. Not the color or anything."

"Would you have noticed if it had been long?" Winter asked.

"Hmm . . . maybe." He scratched his cheek. "Yes, I think I would."

"Was he tall?"

"Normal."

"Normal?"

"Like, he wasn't a dwarf. Not a seven-footer either. But I was a few steps up, and the light was bad." He looked up at the ceiling. It had been a different ceiling. He could see the lamp in front of him. It was weak . . . "That's a point! The light wasn't as bright as usual. I noticed it at the time, and I remember now. There must be several bulbs in it and one must have been a dud, because when I came the next day it was good again."

"Good again? You mean the light was brighter?"

"Yes. The caretaker guy must have replaced the bulb. Fixed it."

"When can he have done that?" Ringmar asked.

"That day. The same day. I'm quite sure that the light was crappy on only one morning."

"You're quite sure?"

"Yes. Quite sure. Sort of sure."

"Okay."

"You'd better talk with the caretaker guy," Patrik said.

"We'll do that," Winter said. He could see a trace of a smile on Ringmar's face. "Thank you. But let's get back to the clothes. If it wasn't the overcoat, was it his trousers? Was there something about his trousers that you recognized?"

"I can't remember what it was now. It was, sort of, something I re-acted to. I don't really know how to put it."

"Take your time, Patrik."

"I don't think I'm going to remember right now."

"You can keep on thinking about it when you get home as well, of course."

"Of course."

"Where do you live, Patrik?" Winter asked.

"Eh?"

"If you deliver newspapers in the Vasaplatsen area, you must live near there as well."

"Kastellgatan. I live with my dad in Kastellgatan. That's on the other side of Haga."

"All right. Do you think you'd recognize this man if you saw him again?"

Patrik shrugged. "I mean, the light was a bit odd. And I saw him from behind. I'm not sure."

"But it wasn't somebody you'd seen before?"

"What do you mean? Somebody I'd seen before. On the stairs?"

"We can start with that. Somebody you've seen on the stairs when you've been delivering papers."

"Not that I can remember. Thing is, I hardly ever see anyone there."

"Hmm. Maybe we'll ask you to help us to check everybody who lives there. So that we'll know if it was one of them."

"All right . . ."

"Then there is the question of whether you might have seen him before," Winter said. "Somewhere else, that is. Not in the building or on the stairs. Some other place, some other occasion."

"Yes, I'm with you."

"Think about that."

Patrik was already thinking. Thinking, thinking. He looked at the police officers who were asking all the questions. The older one seemed as if he were asleep, but he'd suddenly turn his head and look out of the window at the bare branches and blue sky outside. The guy had a profile . . . holy . . . was it the pro—

"It might be the profile," Patrik said.

"What do you mean?"

"The profile. That business about something being familiar. It might have been the profile that I might have recognized. That I'd seen before. The head."

"You're making progress all the time, Patrik." The younger cop smiled. "You've remembered quite a few things while we've been sitting here."

"Brick wall time now, though, I think."

"Maybe for now," said Winter. "But keep thinking when you get home, as we discussed."

"Of course."

"One more thing," Ringmar said. "Didn't you hear the music coming from the apartment when you pushed the newspaper through the letter box?"

"Of course. As I told the caretaker."

"Say that again?!" Winter said.

"It was me who told him about it. About the metal."

Winter looked at Ringmar, who made a resigned gesture. They hadn't had a report about that. Hadn't anybody checked with the newspaper boy?

"Had you been hearing it for a long time?" asked Winter. "When you were delivering the papers?"

"A few days. I can't remember exactly how many." He turned to Winter. "I'll have to think about that."

"Did you recognize it?" asked Winter. "The music?"

"Not really. I mean, it sounds a bit different when it's been traveling through the hall and the mail slot and all that shit. Sort of."

"You said 'Not really.' What do you mean by that?"

"Well, it's obviously death metal, or black. But it's not my thing."

"We think it might be a Canadian group called Sacrament," Winter said. "Are you familiar with them?"

"Sacrament? Never heard of 'em."

"*Daughter of Habakkuk*. That's what the disc is called. Does that sound familiar?"

"No. But I have a few friends who are, like, metal nerds. Or were, at junior school. Last year. They go to another school now and, well . . ."

"But this is their . . . thing?"

"Could be. I don't know about this particular disc, but black metal is what they do. One of them plays, in fact. Drums." For the first time Patrik took a sip of water from the glass in front of him. He suddenly felt extremely thirsty. He was talking too much. Didn't understand why. It was as if he had to. "Should I check with them? What did you say the band was called? Sacrament?"

26

"Why would the caretaker keep quiet about that?" Winter said.

"Is it true?" Ringmar said.

"That the kid heard the music first? I think so."

"Some people like to claim all the glory. Perhaps the caretaker thought there would be a reward."

"Is there anything else he's seen that he hasn't mentioned?"

"You mean that he's keeping something from us?"

"Yes."

"That's a good point."

"We'd better talk to him again."

"The kid seems sharp," Ringmar said.

"He knows something important."

"You think so?"

"I'm sure of it. When he remembers what it is it will be a real help to us." Winter lit a Corps and squinted at the smoke. He took another drag, exhaled, and squinted again. "I've been thinking about the writing on the wall," he said. "And about the expression, 'The writing's on the wall.' Meaning something like, you can't avoid seeing what is obvious, that it's there for anybody to understand. The writing's on the wall. Is this some kind of double message we've been sent? Or a sort of subtext? Is the writing trying to tell us that we might have the answer under our very noses? Part of the answer, at least? I don't know. But maybe the word 'wall' is just that: it's saying that the writing's on the wall. That the word in itself isn't significant. More like an arrow point-ing in another direction. Do you follow me, Bertil?"

"I'm not sure. Go on."

"In other words, that we don't need to worry about the message it-self, but rather the fact that it's there."

"That the solution is closer to hand than we think?"

"Yes. That there's something close at hand that we can't see."

Ringmar rubbed his eyes and ran his hand over his forehead. He pic-tured the wall in the flat, red letters on a white background. Like a headline. A rubric.

"I've been thinking of it as a sort of rubric as well," he said, putting his hand down again. "Rubric in the sense of a heading. So the most important thing is, what follows?"

"Hmm."

"Did you know that the word 'rubric' comes originally from the Latin *'rubrica,'* meaning red?"

"No. Is that so?"

"Jonas told me that over the weekend. He asked me if I knew what a rubric actually was, and he explained it to me."

"He's studying journalism, isn't he?"

"In his first term at the College of Journalism," Ringmar said, sounding almost proud of his son.

"Not exactly a chip off the old block, eh?" said Winter. "What else did he say about the origin of the word?"

"Rubrica, you mean? Decisions made by the Roman senate started being publicized in 59 B.C. by messages on plaster tablets being nailed up in public places," said Ringmar, as if delivering a lecture. "The tablets were called *Acta Senatus* and had rubrics in red."

"Are you suggesting there might be a connection?"

Ringmar threw out his arms.

"It was just a thought."

"So the murderer knows about Latin rubrics? Should we go looking for him at the College of Journalism? Or is he in fact a journalist? That's all right with me."

"It was just a thought, as I said."

"Interesting," Winter said. He took another drag at his Corps, studied the smoke again. Maybe this was one of his last cigarillos. There was every reason for him to give up now, before the first of April, and get the blissful but strong aromas out of the apartment and his clothes. "But we're getting nowhere with this. Yet. And, of course, it could be that it means nothing at all."

"What?"

"That he just wrote whatever came into his head. The first thing he thought of. Just to confuse us."

"Intentional misinformation? Yes, that would be the worst possible answer. There'd be nothing at all to go on then. That could mean we were dealing with somebody who enjoyed doing it."

"Could be. Rather than someone looking for help."

"Do you believe that as well?"

"That the message is a cry for help? Yes. Otherwise we're lost."

"We're not going to clear this up on our own," Ringmar said.

"When did we ever?" said Winter.

"Will it happen again?"

"No."

"Why not?"

"This isn't a serial murderer. He might be a psychopath, but I doubt that. Presumably not a psychopath. Crazy in a different way. And not a serial murderer."

"So it's something personal."

"I don't know, of course. But I suspect the answer is somewhere in the victims' past. In the past of both, or hers, or his. Yes. Personal in that sense."

Ringmar sighed audibly.

"We can't go through every bit of paper, every memory, in Västerås and Kungsbacka."

"We're not on our own. We have colleagues."

"It takes years to trace a person's past. All the relationships he's had since birth. Any one could be crucial. Any single person he's come up against could be the one we're looking for. Anybody at all."

"We'll have to start eliminating."

"That work has already started," Ringmar said without a smile.

"Perhaps it's personal in the sense that the two victims are representatives for somebody else," Winter said. "Symbols. Possibly stand-ins. They stand for something. A lifestyle. Or something as banal as their appearance. Both of them, or just him or her."

"Are you thinking of the heads?"

"No, not in this context. But, of course, that is also an outrageous message. Perhaps. A symbol of something. I don't dare speculate about that. We need help, as I said."

Patrik was sitting in his room with earphones on and didn't hear his father come in behind him to pull them off. The music was hissing out of the earphones like a snake, wriggling its way over the floor among the cables.

"I've been calling you for hours!"

"I didn't hear you."

"Well of course you didn't, when you're listening to that crap."

Patrik could smell the alcohol, and saw his father stumble as he stepped back from the bed, then sit down awkwardly.

"What do you want?" said Patrik, trying to reach the earphones from the bed. They were too far away. He stood up and was about to pick them up when his father grabbed him by the arm.

"Leave them where they are. I want to talk to you."

"What about?"

"Just a minute, there's something I have to do."

His father got up and left the room. Patrik could hear him unscrewing the bottle top. He came back. The smell of liquor was even stronger than before. He sat down on the bed.

"She's moving in," he said.

"Eh?"

His father looked at him. Several blood vessels had burst in one of his eyes. You could see it clearly when he looked to one side.

"Ulla. You know. Her I've been . . . keeping company with for a while."

Patrik knew who Ulla was. He'd seen her twice, and that was two times too many. The first time his father had dragged her in over the threshold, and the second time it was the other way around, although it wasn't easy to see who was dragging whom. Ulla. She had leaned over him when she was there the second time, when the old man was snoring like a pig on the living room sofa where she'd dumped him, and he thought he was going to be sick when she bent down. She'd mumbled something, but he'd wriggled out from underneath her and she'd collapsed into his bed.

Now she was going to move in. Fucking great. *Fucking great.* He had his father to put up with, and now it was going to be twice as cozy.

"She's moving in here? But she can't."

"She can't? Did my ears deceive me?" His father had raised himself up. His body was swaying backward and forward. "Why can't my fi- ancée move in here?"

"We've only got two rooms. We live here. I live here."

"There are bigger apartments."

Oh, sure. Who would have them as tenants?

"But we've only got one sofa."

His father slept in the sofabed in the living room.

"You'll have that."

"What?"

"We need your room. Fuck it, it's not your damn room. We need this room. You're never at home anyway so you can manage with the sofa."

Patrik could feel the sweat on his brow. He looked at his CD collec- tion, his magazines. Posters.

"You mean I have to move out of my room?"

"She's coming tomorrow." His father stood up. "That's that." He left the room, and Patrik heard him unscrewing the bottle top again.

The party had started before he'd even closed the door behind him. Where could Patrik go now when he needed to be at home?

Then again, he didn't need to be at home. He didn't know where he would go, but he didn't need to be at home. He looked at his CDs again. Could Ria keep them? Could he rent a room there, sort of for the time being? He laughed so as not to burst into tears.

· · · · · ·

Angela kicked off her boots and put on some water for tea. The sun was blazing down on the buildings across the street. The light out there was so bright, brighter than in any winter she could recall. It was winter, all right. The year had decided that it was winter long before it should really have started for real.

She felt a movement in her stomach, then another. She sat on a kitchen chair. She looked around: everything in this room had become hers. That felt good. She'd brought her things with her, but nothing looked the same in this bachelor apartment. Not that it could be called that any longer. It was a part of her life now.

We'll repaper the place and change a few things, she thought. Or we'll move to that house by the sea. Parties in the garden, under sun umbrellas. The sound of children's voices, toys strewn all over the lawn.

Erik at the barbecue wearing his chef's hat. A smile as broad as the sun is hot.

The telephone rang. She stood up with difficulty and went to answer it.

"Hello?" No answer. She looked at the clock over the door: five-fifteen. "Hello?" A wrong number, she thought.

DECEMBER

27

It was like when he was a child. The sun in his eyes. All the smells inside his nose, where they stayed until well into the evening. You could smell all the scents in your clothes even when you were indoors. A little smoke and a lot of snow. What did snow smell like?

He bent down and scooped up a handful of snow. The sun transformed it into brightly sparkling powder, and he sniffed at it. What was it like? It smelled like a memory he had, but couldn't pin down. That's exactly what it was like. A memory of something special.

He threw the memory away and it disappeared into thin air. He moved into the shadow of the buildings and the sun was gone.

The snow was piled up like a wall and he could see it nearly all the way to the crossroads. The shop was on the corner. A minimarket, as they're called. It had changed its name, but he knew what it used to be called. Had he described it, perhaps? He had mentioned what it used to be called. Not directly, but he couldn't tell everything, could he? Not now.

He was well known in there. He thought he was, at least. He had done his duty there. His d-u-t-y. He was her friend and he had seen her looking at him in a special way, but he didn't think it was *that* way. He was only a friend.

Once he had been on the point of saying it. I'm only a friend.

I'm just somebody who is here. Just somebody who was here. In the right place at the right time. But that wasn't true. He'd been there at the wrong time. Or, rather, that applied to *the other person,* to be absolutely correct. To be correct. A-b-s-o-l-u-t-e-l-y c-o-r-r-e-c-t.

Some children were running around in the playground between the building where he used to live and the road. A lot of children. Now there was snow to play in. It wasn't wet snow, because there was no sign of any snowmen or snow lanterns. He scooped up another handful and tried to pack it into a ball, but he couldn't. Children knew when it was possible to use it for making things.

They'd sprayed water and made a skating rink as well. He almost wished that he still had his ice skates. But what would that look like? His feet were twice as big now as they were then, weren't they?

The road had been cleared, but it could have been done more efficiently. The apartment buildings didn't look up to much. It was like a depopulated area in the middle of the city. Depopulation in the middle of the city! There was less and less on the minimarket shelves every day. They boasted that they still had an assistant serving at the meat counter, but he'd never seen anybody there. Never. He hadn't been there all that often, but still.

A car drove past and he had to stand on the piled-up snow. It was dirty here. He didn't want to touch it. He stepped down again. Soon it would be time to go home and get something to eat and then go to work for a long evening shift, and he'd go home again and not be able to go to sleep, and he'd sit in front of the TV, watching videos.

Suddenly the shop was there without him noticing that he'd gone into it. He had the films under his arm. Two posters outside advertised films. One of the actors looked familiar, but he didn't waste time there because he knew what kind of videos he wanted.

There was somebody else behind the counter, somebody he hadn't seen before. He didn't say anything when he paid for the videos. Now he was crossing the street. He looked at the tall buildings that looked like a row of huge building blocks.

Later this evening he would drive past the tall buildings in the center of town.

One morning he'd been waiting outside and watched her get onto the tram. He'd followed behind, although he knew where she was going. Nevertheless, he wanted to see her get off the tram and then disappear among all the thousands of others who were going in and out of the hospital doors.

28

Winter turned off the main road. He drove past the seven-story buildings on the right, turned into the parking area, and found a place directly opposite the huge apartment buildings marked with a housing association sign.

They seemed to be in good condition. The entrance had a sort of superstructure, and stone paving slabs on the floor.

Bengt Martell answered the intercom and Winter was let in. The entrance hall was attractive, painted in soft pastel colors not yet disfigured by graffiti. Perhaps there weren't any young people here. Winter hadn't seen a soul outside.

The man opened the apartment door. There was a smell of coffee in the hall. The sun shone right through the apartment, which presumably had windows facing in different directions. The man was a little shorter than Winter, about the same age, dressed in gray trousers and a cardigan that might have been green. He held out his hand.

"Martell."

"Winter."

"My wife's popped out to get something for us to eat with the coffee."

He showed Winter into the apartment. Through the window Winter could see the hill and the streets down below. Several clouds had appeared during the few minutes since he'd entered the building and taken the elevator.

"Please sit down," Martell said. He blew his nose. That was the second time. He didn't sound as though it was necessary. Perhaps he needed to do something with his hands. The apartment didn't smell of smoke. He ought to do something else with his hands, thought Winter.

The door opened in the hall.

"It's my wife," said Martell, as if he were keen to reassure his guest.

A woman came into the room. She was tall, possibly as tall as her husband. Her hair was cut short and she seemed to have a tan. She was wearing a long, brown skirt and a tight-fitting polo shirt. She had a paper bag in her right hand, but transferred it to her left and shook hands with Winter before going into the kitchen, which Winter could see into through the half-open door.

"Well," said the man, who had stood up when his wife arrived but had now sat down again. "What a terrible business."

Winter nodded, and sat down as well. The woman returned carrying a tray with coffee cups, a pot, and some Danish pastries. She set out the cups and asked Winter if he wanted milk or cream in his coffee. He told her neither, and waited while she filled his cup. The man blew his nose again. The woman raised her cup and her hand was shaking. She took hold of it with both hands and put it down again, without drinking.

"When did you last see the Valkers?" Winter asked.

The Martells looked at each other.

"Didn't we tell the other officers who were here?" Bengt Martell said.

Winter looked down at the notebook that he'd taken out of his inside pocket.

"It wasn't quite clear. I might have mixed up some of the information."

"It was several months ago," Siv Martell said. "They were here for . . . a cup of coffee." She looked down at the table and the coffee things as if to confirm the truth of what she had just said.

"Two months ago." Winter was reading from his notebook. "Is that right?"

"If that's what we said, then no doubt it is," Bengt Martell said. He looked at Winter. "Such things are not easy to recall precisely." He blew his nose again and then tried to find somewhere to put his handkerchief.

Uncomfortable, Winter thought. They seemed to be uncomfortable in their own home, Halders had said. Scared shitless, he'd also said. But they didn't seem like that now. Under the surface, perhaps.

"We didn't note it down in a diary or anything," Siv Martell said. She had started her coffee now, a quick sip. "We rarely do."

"But you've never been around to their place, is that right?" asked Winter.

"Never," Bengt replied.

"Why not?"

He looked at his wife, who looked out the window.

"What do you mean? Why we never went to their place?" He looked at Winter again. "Does it matter?"

"All facts are important to us," Winter said. "Details. Things people notice." He leaned forward, picked up his cup and drank some of his coffee, which was getting lukewarm. "We haven't yet had the opportunity of talking to anybody who's been to the Valkers' place."

He didn't mention the Elfvegrens. Per and Erika.

"Anyway, we haven't."

"It was never in the cards?"

"Er . . . you must understand that we didn't know them all that well." Bengt Martell leaned forward. "We only saw them once or twice."

"But you phoned them." Winter looked up. "You left a message on their answering machine."

"Yes . . . That's why the police know about us."

"We were going to suggest a meal out," Siv Martell said.

"I gather you first met at a restaurant."

"Yes. A dance restaurant. I don't know if we mentioned this before, when the other officers were here. It was at King Creole."

"Do you often go there?"

"Hardly ever," Bengt Martell said.

So you met at a place you never go to, Winter thought, but even so you wanted to keep the acquaintance going.

"Did you ever meet them together with other people?" he asked.

"What do you mean?"

"At a party, or a gathering with several people present."

"What do you mean by several? More than us four?"

"Yes."

"Never."

"You didn't know any of the Valkers' friends?"

"None at all."

"You didn't meet any of them at that dance restaurant?"

"No."

"More coffee?" Siv Martell offered.

"No, thank you." Winter checked his notebook again. He was getting nowhere with this pair. Was there any point in staying? Perhaps the Martells were lonely people who had a fleeting acquaintance with the Valkers that might have developed into something more.

They might be scared, but at the same time uninterested. It was as if they were doing their best not to think about the Valkers. They were polite but uncooperative. It could be some sort of delayed shock. Or it could be something else, something lurking in the background. A shared experience. An incident. Something.

"What actually happened?" asked Bengt Martell out of the blue. His wife stood up and went to the kitchen.

"I beg your pardon?"

"What actually happened to them?" Martell asked again. "To Christian and Louise. There's been a lot about it in the press, but nothing about how . . . how they died." He seemed to be listening to his wife, who was running water in the kitchen. "How did he do it?"

"I can't tell you everything for legal reasons," Winter said, "but I was just coming to that." He flipped to another page in his notebook and asked some questions about music.

It was overcast when he left the building. There was a wind from the northwest. Winter shuddered, and felt a stab in his throat when he swallowed. A slight headache these last two days might be the sign of an infection coming on. He'd have to rely on his immune defenses. The headache was a sign that they were assembling to repel boarders. There's a battle taking place inside your body, Angela had said.

His car felt cold, and there was a smell of damp.

He took the letter out of his inside pocket and opened it for the first time. The letter paper bore the logo of the Spanish police, just like the envelope.

The letter was handwritten and in English, straightforward and purposeful. Just a few sentences greeting him, and thanking him for his hospitality. He read it several times. It was a part of the dream. There was no need to reply to this letter. Not even to read it. He could close his eyes and then look, and the letter would have disappeared, just like the dream.

Why do I think about it? he asked himself, and then he thought of Angela.

Angela, there's something I have to tell you.

No. There was nothing he had to tell her because nothing had happened. Angela: I had a very strange dream last night. You don't say? Do you want to tell me about it? I've forgotten it. Almost completely. Was I in it?

She'd been in it. And only a few hours later he'd picked her up at the terminal in Málaga. Not long afterward they'd stood side by side in the cemetery by the mountain. His father.

Winter rolled down the window, felt the wind blowing into his face, and now his thoughts were filled by his father.

He closed the window again and got out of the car. There was a minimarket only a few yards ahead, and he wanted to buy some throat lozenges. There was a sign over the entrance. It looked new. Krokens Livs was its name.

The wind was making the posters at the entrance to the shop sway back and forth. *City of Angels,* one of them said, the other was advertising *The Avengers.*

A local bus shuddered to a halt a few yards away and disgorged a couple of elderly people. Winter went into Krokens Livs, which seemed to have the usual assortment of dairy products, chips, confectionery, videos, dish-washing brushes, and newspapers. He bought a pack of Fisherman's Friend from a woman who looked Arabic or Turkish.

When he came out, the wind was blowing even stronger. Winter felt a few drops of rain. The yellow buildings on the other side of Hagåkersgatan lost their color in the rainy wind.

Morelius was eating the usual deep-fried prawns from Ming. Why could they never think of anything else to order?

Somebody from the Gothenburg council was on television, explaining what the millennium celebrations would entail. If you believed him, they would be more impressive than anything on offer in London and Sydney and New York.

In fact Gothenburg would be subjected to the same old uproar, the same old crowds of staggering revelers. Tears, shrieks, guffaws, fireworks projected at eye height by lunatic antiaircraft gunners in the center of town. The same old uproar as usual.

"I've changed my mind," Bartram said.

"Eh?" said Morelius, getting up to throw away half of the prawns and the sickly salad. As usual.

"I'm going to work on New Year's Eve after all. In the thick of the revelry."

"Welcome to the club," Morelius said. "But you'd already changed your mind. First you were going to work, but you decided not to."

"Yes. But just like you"—Bartram scraped the last bit of sauce from the foil container—"I've decided to work after all."

"Why not do a good deed," Morelius said. "Others need time off more than we do."

"Speak for yourself."

"What's your reason, then?"

"I have nothing better to do," said Bartram, going to switch off the television that was now showing the weather forecast for western Sweden. It was going to be fine but cold again. "And I'll get time off later instead."

"When?"

"In summer, maybe. How the hell should I know now?"

"What will you do?"

"In summer? No idea. It's a long way off."

"We have the revelry to cope with first," said Morelius.

He went to his locker and opened it. His overcoat smelled of the cold that hadn't completely gone away when the rain came.

Tomorrow he would see Hanne again, and it would be the last time. She couldn't help him anymore, and he didn't need any help. It had happened, but now it was more like a dream. He couldn't say any more than that. Maybe he wouldn't know what he'd said when he said it. He'd forgotten all the questions he'd asked himself during the night with the videos playing on the TV screen, and he never did know what they were about anyway.

He put on the earphones of his Walkman and pressed PLAY. Just a few minutes. He saw Bartram moving his lips and switched the music off again.

"What?"

"I can hear it plain as day."

"Really."

"Sounds awful."

Patrik had asked to speak to the short-haired younger policeman, and Winter took the call immediately after he had come back to his office from Mölndal.

"Hello?"

"Er . . . hello . . . Patrik Strömblad here . . ."

Winter hadn't recognized his voice. There was something gravelly about it.

"Hello, Patrik."

"Well . . . that CD. Sacrament."

"Yes?"

"Jimmo has it. My friend Jimmo . . ."

Bergenhem had searched the attic at Desdemona in vain. But in the end they were receiving help from another quarter.

"He has that exact disc? *Daughter of Habu* . . . whatever."

"That exact one, yes," Patrik said. "He could go straight to it. You can buy it chea . . . There are bett . . ."

His voice had become inaudible.

"What?"

"You can buy it cheap."

Winter couldn't help giving a little laugh.

"Okay! Where is it?"

"I have it here." Patrik seemed to snort into the receiver. "An ugly cover." His voice was unclear again, as if he were chewing something.

"Can you come here with it?" Winter asked. "Now?"

"Just the cover?"

"Don't joke with me, Patrik."

"I wasn't joking." It didn't sound as if he was joking.

"Can you be here in half an hour?" Winter checked the time. "Aren't you at school?"

"No . . ."

"Can you come here to the police station? Or we can meet in town."

"Can't we do it tomorrow?"

"Why?"

"I'm . . . I don't know if I . . ."

"What's the matter, Patrik?"

"Er . . . all right, I'll come."

Winter put down the phone and looked at the anonymous cassette in one of the pigeonholes on his desk. He put it into the stereo and played the first tune at high volume, took out the photographs again but only looked at the first two. He picked up the phone and rang Beier, but his colleague in forensics was out. Winter examined one of the photographs again, and made a note.

29

It was Halders, of all people, who found the connection. He hadn't said anything at the meeting. He found it later, during the afternoon, and marched in to Winter without even knocking on the door. He was carrying a black book.

"About that Habakkuk," he said. "The guy who's the father of the daughter."

"Yes, I know who you mean," Winter said, looking up from his latest notes.

"He was a prophet. He has his own book in the Bible." Halders held up the Bible. "A short one."

The Old Testament, Winter thought. The canonical books. Of course. They ought to have thought of that sooner. They were too profane.

"Well done, Fredrik."

"There was something in the back of my mind. When I realized what it was, I dashed down to the library, and there was his name. The prophet Habakkuk, in between Nahum and Zephaniah." Halders held up the Bible again. "I know what made me think of it. I haven't managed to dig out the old Bible I got when I was confirmed, but I'm sure the vicar wrote some reference or other on the flyleaf to Habakkuk."

"How could you remember that?"

"And then forget it?"

"Remember, I said."

"I suppose it was the name, because it was so unusual. A friend said it was a misprint for 'Haveacock,'" Halders looked at the book in his hand. "That was pretty irreverent." He looked at Winter again. "I must have looked up the text because I was curious. The same as now."

Winter took the book from Halders. It was the 1995 version. Winter looked up the Book of Habakkuk and started reading. The clergyman who prepared Halders for confirmation must have been a bit of a prophet himself. The text was about the work of the crime squad. The first chapter went:

"I am Habakkuk the prophet. And this is the message that the LORD gave me.

"Our LORD, how long must I beg for your help before you listen? How long before you save us from all this violence?

"Why do you make me watch such terrible injustice? Why do you allow violence, lawlessness, crime, and cruelty to spread everywhere?

"Laws cannot be enforced; justice is always the loser; criminals crowd out honest people and twist the laws around."

"Therefore the law is paralyzed, and justice never prevails. The wicked hem in the righteous, so that justice is perverted.

"'Criminals twist the laws around.' 'Why do you make me watch such terrible injustice?'" Winter read the beginning of the first chapter again. He had spent a lot of time dealing with injustice and evil, but he had started to think differently—or perhaps he'd thought this way from the very beginning: evil was not some kind of creature in the underworld. Evil was people, actions. Evil was injustice. It arose from cruelty. It was caused by violence.

"'Laws cannot be enforced.'"

Like hell they can't! He closed the holy book with a bang and put it on his desk. It could be a coincidence, but he didn't believe in coincidences. If the murderer chose that particular music and a CD with that particular title, there was a reason. They would soon have the disc with its cover, and the Bible, and they would read it all.

Why? Did the murderer want to tell us that the world is evil? That he had seen the writing on the wall? Did he want to tell us that *his* world was evil? The murderer's world? Or Winter's world? The human world. Were they the same?

The text. He was waiting for Patrik. More reading to come. The men in black at Desdemona had said that black metal was meaningless without the words, but they were words that nobody could pick up just by listening.

Halders had left the door open, and Winter saw Patrik outside accompanied by Möllerström, who ushered him into Winter's office and left. Winter stood up. Patrik came to his desk.

"What's happened to you?"

"What do you mean?" Patrik said. "It's nothing."

"That's very nasty bruising you've got."

Patrik felt his cheekbone with his right hand, under his right ear.

"It's nothing. I slipped as I was getting off the bus."

"Slipped when you were getting off the bus? Don't talk such crap," said Winter, walking around his desk and peering at Patrik's face. "Have you been to the hospital with that?"

"No."

"You might have broken your zygomatic bone." Winter resisted a temptation to touch the boy's cheek. "Will you let me feel it?"

"Are you a doctor as well?"

"Let me feel it." He had hardly touched it before Patrik flinched in pain. "Does it hurt as much as that?"

Patrik said something he couldn't understand. The boy was hanging his head.

"What did you say? I couldn't hear.

"It was . . . the bus."

"No," Winter said. "Somebody's been hitting you." Patrik looked up at him. The bruise was beginning to look like an irregular birthmark. His face seemed to be lopsided. "This happened recently."

Patrik didn't respond. He looked as if he wanted to leave. He had a bag in his left hand.

"Who was it?" Winter asked. "Somebody at school?"

Patrik shook his head. Winter could see his shoulders starting to twitch. I shouldn't scare him. He has tears in his eyes. Now he's crying. He's only a kid.

Patrik looked down and sobbed silently. Winter held his shoulders, which had started to shake. Patrik was standing with his back to the open door and Ringmar appeared in the doorway. Winter signaled with his head and Ringmar backed out.

"It's all right, Patrik, all right."

The boy sniffled, then pulled himself away. He looked vulnerable, as if on the run.

"Sit down, Patrik."

He flopped down onto the chair. Winter squatted down a couple of feet away.

"It happened at home, didn't it?"

Patrik didn't answer, didn't nod, sniffed, looked anywhere but at Winter.

"We won't worry about that now, but you should have this looked at," Winter said. He went to Ringmar's office. "Can you arrange for a squad car to get the kid to the hospital?"

"When?"

"As soon as you can."

When Winter went back Patrik was just a little head barely visible over the chair back. Winter sat down at his desk. Patrik's face was twitching, and Winter could see that it hurt to cry. Winter fetched him a glass of water and Patrik took a sip. He sniffled again, put down the glass, and gestured to the bag he'd put on Winter's desk.

"Don't you want it?"

"Of course," Winter said, pulling it toward him and taking out the CD. "You've done a great job, Patrik."

"Sacrament," Patrik said, his voice steadier now. He ran his hand over his eyes. "There you have it. The *Daughter* disc."

"What's the name of your friend?"

"Jimmo."

"How did he get ahold of it?"

"Secondhand in Haga, I think it was. I can't remember which shop it was. He—"

"Never mind, we'll look into that later. Now let's . . ."

Winter's desk phone rang.

"There are a couple of officers waiting outside," Ringmar said.

"Okay, thanks." Winter looked at Patrik. "I want you to get this looked at. It's very important, as I think you realize. We'll give you a lift to the hospital, then we can chat a bit more. All right?"

"I don't know . . ."

"You don't need to say who hit you. I just want you to have it seen to." Winter stood up. "We need the people working on this case to be in top condition, and you're one of them. All right?" He held out his hand to Patrik, as if to give him support. "Okay?"

"Okay," said Patrik, getting to his feet.

"I'll take good care of the disc," said Winter, putting it in the inside pocket of his jacket. It was wide, Italian. The Italians made voluminous inside pockets in some of their jackets.

They took the elevator down. It was snowing again by the time they came to the entrance, and the squad car that had been waiting for them drove up. The driver got out and walked around the car. Winter raised his hand in greeting.

"Hello, Simon."

"Hi, Erik."

"Haven't seen you. How are things at Lorensberg?"

"The usual. We keep an eye on where you live."

"I think I saw you there the other day. In Vasagatan."

"That's on our patrol route."

Winter looked down. Morelius's colleague rolled down his window and introduced himself: "Bartram." Winter nodded.

"Bartram hasn't been in Gothenburg long," Morelius said.

"I've seen him around," Winter said. "With you, in fact." He turned to Morelius. "I'd be grateful if you could take this kid to the ER."

"Bertil Ringmar told us about it," said Morelius. He turned to Patrik, who looked as if he were ready to run.

"Hi, Patrik."

"Do you know each other?" Winter asked.

"Only in passing," said Bartram "But we've never seen him without Maria." He turned awkwardly in the passenger seat and looked up at Patrik. "Where is she now?"

"Maria?" Winter asked.

"Hanne's daughter. The vicar," Morelius said.

"Hanne Östergaard?"

"Yes."

"Can we go now?" Patrik asked.

Winter nodded without asking any more questions. The boy needed to see a doctor.

Patrik got into the back and the car drove off. Winter had his home number. He wondered briefly what must be going on there. Then he thought of Hanne Östergaard for the first time in ages, and he felt the CD hitting against his rib and he thought about the music.

Patrik closed his eyes. His cheek and eye were pounding, more now than before. The cops didn't say a word. It had grown darker, and was nearly black outside. The pair in the front seats became lighter and darker as they passed the streetlights. Lighter. Darker. They seemed to be sitting diagonally opposite one another. What he could see most of was the backs of their heads. They weren't wearing hats. It got lighter again as they passed Slottsskogen. He closed his eyes, then looked again. He could still see the profiles of the men in front of him, and still nobody spoke. He closed his eyes, looked. He was back on the stairs that morning. He was here. On the stairs. And here. His cheek started hurting. He was sweating, he felt as if he were running up the stairs, carrying the newspapers. Stopped, looked. Somebody went out through the front door, into the darkness out of the light. The profile.

Morelius stopped outside the ER and turned around.

"Here we are, Patrik."

The boy said nothing. Didn't move. Bartram turned around to look at him.

"Patrik?"

"He's dozed off," Morelius said.

Winter listened to the CD on his portable Panasonic, which was on the floor in front of the window. First track, second track. He changed to the cassette, then back again. They were the same so far. He listened to the whole thing and compared them. A challenge.

The text was a fold-out rather than a booklet. The cover itself was brown and black, a clumsy drawing of a brown sea and black cliffs and a horizon that melted into the night and a black sky, with bright, tiny stars. It said "Sacrament" at the bottom, in a Gothic typeface that Winter recognized from the magazines and catalogs he'd leafed through.

There was also a logo in the top left-hand corner, maybe a silver bat, or a prehistoric bird.

The leaflet was made up of four pages, three of the pictures depicted men who could be members of the band. Or they could be any metal fan who happened to be passing, he thought. The three people could be Nordberg and Sverker and any of the other staff at Desdemona: black sweaters and trousers, bright yellow patterns, studs like the bright stars in the black sky, black waist-length hair, extremely pale faces. But there were some extra features here: bare tree trunks, weapons such as swords and maces. Every character had a different sky: orange, green or dark blue.

He couldn't see any sign of a daughter, nor a prophet. Nor a cross, unless the mace one of the men was holding could be interpreted as a cross together with one of the trees.

The last page comprised white text on a black background. A lot of text, most of it very small and densely packed. As if it had intentionally been made unreadable, Winter thought.

But he was going to read it. He had his reading glasses with him. He'd had to face up to that reality this last year.

The disc was recorded in the Machine Room, Edmonton. The winter of 1995. All the songs had been written by the Masters of Horrid Nuclear Hate-filled Blackness.

He started reading the piece in the top left, the first song. The narrator was walking through a forest that could have been the one he'd seen on page two of the leaflet.

He played the first track again, and tried to follow. He listened as he read. *Blood trickles to the floor. This woman has broken a sacred bond. The black angel. This woman has deserted me and I must take revenge.*

Winter switched off the music and continued reading. He found himself sinking into a sea of blood. Black galaxies of hatred. Stars that exploded in the underworld and created demons who wandered through demilitarized zones on the hunt for victims. Perhaps it contained some kind of humor, but it was difficult to see that after what had happened in that room.

30

Dusk was approaching again. The buildings on the other side of the river were yellow and red in the beams of winter sun. The sun goes away just when it's at its best, thought Winter, and left his office, walked along empty corridors and staircases to forensics.

Beier was at his desk, waiting for him. He was wearing a tie and a white shirt. He was generally smartly dressed. Winter sat down.

"The sperm is Valker's," Beier said.

Winter nodded. They had found traces of sperm on the sofa the couple had been sitting on.

"But not exclusively," said Beier. "There was sperm from two or three other men as well. Two, I think." He tapped a folder on his desk. "It's all in here. Several stains from several occasions. From at least five months ago, and at various times later." He picked up the folder and handed it to Winter. "But the latest is Valker's own."

"Could it have been from the night of the murder?"

"Yes."

"But nothing from anybody else? At that time?"

"No."

"There could have been several people in the apartment on that night," Winter said.

"Obviously," Beier said. "We have about ten fingerprints from various people that are not in any of our registers. But there again, fingerprints are not unusual in an apartment or a house. People come and go."

"But not all of them leave sperm behind."

"No." Beier stood up when the coffee arrived. He always gave Winter coffee whenever he visited his office. Beier took the tray from the secretary, put it on his desk, and handed a cup to Winter.

Winter wondered briefly how Beier could persuade the girl to come in with a tray of coffee. Perhaps they had an agreement. Next time it would be Beier's turn to go around with the tray. Beier added milk and sugar and looked up. "All the secretions we've found were on that sofa. Or adjacent to it."

"What does that mean?"

"What does it mean? That things happened on the sofa and adjacent to it."

"Nothing from the woman?"

"Oh yes."

"Hers? And two others?"

Beier nodded.

"Three men and three women," Winter said.

"Three couples."

"We have three couples in the investigation," Winter said.

"I know."

"So all we need is more sperm and secretions that we can compare."

"Good luck," said Beier.

"Am I letting my imagination run away with me?"

"I don't know."

"They know something," said Winter.

"What do you mean?"

"I spoke to the Martells. Djanali and Halders spoke to the others. The Elfvegrens. There was something behind what they said, something implied but not spelled out. With both couples."

"It's called the subtext," Beier said. "But it doesn't necessarily have anything to do with what happened at the Valkers' place."

"No. I don't know if the Martells are mixed up in the murder in any way. I don't think anything. But we need to put more pressure on them. And the Elfvegrens. I'll drive out to Järnbrott tomorrow." Winter stood up, folder in hand. "There's one other thing, by the way. I haven't seen the complete list of objects in the room."

"You haven't? That's also in the folder, of course." Beier looked at Winter. "There might be a few other things to add."

"Were there any newspapers or magazines?"

"You must be joking. The hall was full of old copies of *Göteborgs Posten*."

"I mean in addition to those."

"Not many. Is there anything specific you have in mind?"

"I don't know," Winter said.

He was reading Sacrament's texts. The hero in song number three flew into space imprisoned in his own hatred. There was a lot about hatred, of oneself and others.

This is the most idiotic load of old crap I've ever read, thought Winter.

They're teasing us.

Here is the dream I live with, this is my plan. To kill mankind and destroy the universe.

A big task that others have tried before.

Most of the text was in the first person. Whoever it was rarely stayed on earth. Just a short visit to Manhattan. A voyage on the Red Sea. A voyage on the Black Sea. Otherwise it was alien worlds.

This could keep a dozen psychologists going for years, Winter thought. But it's not much good to us. I can ask the guys at Desdemona if this is any different from other lyrics in the genre.

He noticed several references to walls, a few in every song. Wall of Hate. Wall of Blood. Wall of Corpses. Wall of Horrors. It became tedious after a while, worn, like flaking wallpaper.

He took off his reading glasses and examined them. The lenses seemed to have been dirtied by the words, covered by a thin layer of translucent soot.

His mobile phone rang in the inside pocket of his jacket. The display showed his mother's number in Nueva Andalucía. Winter felt a sudden shooting pain in his chest.

"Hello, Mom."

"Hello, Erik. I can never get used to the idea that the person I'm calling can see my number."

"Makes you wonder why some people never answer, eh?"

"You always answer, Erik."

"Of course! How are things?"

"I'm taking it a day at a time, as they say. But it's going . . . quite well. I visit the grave almost every day. It's a sort of outing. You can see the sea from there."

"It's an attractive place for a grave."

"It's so lovely with the mountain and the sea. He's gone to a beautiful place, at least."

"Yes."

"And now Christmas is approaching. I suppose serious Christmas shopping is getting under way now?"

"I don't honestly know. Not for me it isn't, at least."

"I can understand that. Another murder. It's terrible. And just when you got back home from here." There was a pause and Winter could hear the sound of ice cubes in a cocktail glass of Tanqueray and tonic.

"I read about it in *GP*. Awful. And only a few doors away from where you live."

"Where I live isn't a crime-free zone, Mother."

"I was thinking mainly about Angela. She must be wondering what kind of a place she's landed in."

"She is."

"No, that was a silly thing for me to say. How's she doing?"

"Everything's fine."

"Have you felt any kicks yet?"

"Yes."

"What was it like? Tell me!"

"It was . . . fantastic. A very special experience."

"I remember when you . . . when I . . ." and Winter heard her voice break and the sound of ice cubes rattling next to the receiver. "I'm sorry, Erik. I was thinking about when you . . . and Dad . . ." and her voice broke again, more rattling, and then she was back. "It was like you say. A . . . very special experience. When we felt Lotta and when we felt your . . . kicks."

"You can feel for yourself when you come."

"Yes, well . . ."

"What's the matter?"

"Well, er . . ."

"Don't say you're not coming home."

"I seem to feel more unsure the closer it gets . . ."

"It's nothing to hesitate about. We're looking forward to seeing you. Think about Lotta and Bim and Kristina. And Angela. And me. But maybe most of all think about yourself."

"It might be better for me to stay here. I mean, you have your own life to lead."

This is really what you might call a role reversal, Winter thought. Before, she was the one urging *us* to come to Spain, and now it's us urging *her* to come to Sweden.

"Everything's ready," he said. We've bought the Tanqueray, he thought. "You have to come."

"Yes, well . . . I want to."

"I'm expecting you at the airport on December 23."

"As long as it's not snowing."

"The snows will have thawed or been washed away by rain before then."

"Give my love to Angela."

"Of course."

"To both of them."

"Naturally."

"Have you got a name? For the baby?"

"Lots of them."

It was thawing the next morning. The air looked heavy, as if it had been hung up like a curtain as the night drew to a close. Winter stood in his boxer shorts, cup in hand, listening to Angela's Springsteen while she was in the bathroom. *Happy, happy in your arms.*

He was seldom at home as late in the morning as this. There was less traffic now than at the time he usually drove to work.

Angela emerged from the bathroom and headed for the hall.

"We have to be there in half an hour," she shouted.

"I'm ready," Winter said.

"What?"

"I'm nearly ready," he yelled, and took his empty cup to the kitchen before heading for the bathroom.

It wasn't raining, but the air was just as damp as it had appeared to be from the window.

"Let's walk," Angela had said on the way down in the elevator.

"It's wet."

"I need a walk."

It was the first time for him. He felt nervous.

It was only a ten-minute walk to the Social Services Clinic. Thin sheets of ice were floating down the canal. A car passed and splashed slush onto Angela's coat. Winter memorized the license plate number.

"Do you want us to find the driver?" he asked.

"Yes," Angela said, who was trying to brush off the dirty liquid. "Put him behind bars."

They hung up their coats and waited in a room with two other women. Winter was the only man. He leafed through a women's magazine he'd never heard of before while Angela went off with the nurse to have samples taken. Winter read about why women in Stockholm preferred to stay single. That's not the case in Gothenburg, he thought. This isn't a place for singles anymore.

Angela came back.

"What samples did they take?" he asked.

"Blood tests. Hemoglobin, blood group, blood sugar."

"Couldn't you have done that yourself? At home?"

"Stop it now."

"I'm serious."

"So am I. They did HIV and rubella, in the tenth week. When I first registered."

"What's rubella?"

"German measles."

Winter wondered what it had to do with the Germans. The Berlin Wall. The writing on the wall . . .

"Are you nervous, Erik?"

"What do you mean?"

"You sound as if you are." A woman opened a door and beckoned to them. "It's our turn now."

They followed the woman through the door. She ushered them into a smallish room with a desk and two comfortable-looking chairs.

The woman was normally dressed. No white coat, no uniform, Winter thought. He shook the hand she offered him.

"My name's Elise Bergdorff. I'm a midwife, as I'm sure you know. Welcome! I'm glad you could come."

Winter introduced himself and sat down.

Angela and the midwife talked about the previous couple of weeks.

It only took Winter a few seconds to realize that there was an understanding between the two women. Angela felt secure. He relaxed, listened, made the occasional contribution.

Time for the ultrasound. Angela lay down on a hospital bed, the midwife applied a translucent gel to her stomach, and held up a microphone connected to a machine.

"What's that?" Winter asked. Does it matter? he wondered. I'm just so used to asking questions.

"It's a Sonicaid. For measuring ultrasound waves." She held the microphone against Angela's blue stomach with its slightly convex mound.

Winter could hear the sound of a heart beating. Actually hear it! It was beating fast, twice the speed of an adult's. It filled the whole room, all around him. Angela took hold of his hand. He shut every other thought out of his mind, simply listened.

31

Patrik closed the refrigerator door, but it was opened again immediately by one of his father's friends who had brought with him from the living room an acrid smell of smoke and liquor.

"I had a bottle of Marinella here that should be cold and tasty by now," he said, looking at Patrik. "Have you stolen it?" He burst out laughing. His eyes were porcelain: frigid, gleaming. Before long they'll sink back into his skull and he'll end up on the floor, thought Patrik. Maybe the old man will end up on top of him.

Pelle Plutt slammed the fridge door shut. "WHERE'S MY 'NELLA?!" he screamed into the living room, where the party was going with a bang. They'd been struggling to get to where they were now, but from here on in it was downhill all the way. Pelle Plutt looked at Patrik. He was only twenty-five, but could have been the old man's brother. He still had all his hair, but that was all he still had.

"What have you done there?" he said, screwing up his eyes and pointing at Patrik's face. "That was a king-size wallop if ever I saw one."

"It's nothing."

"You had it seen to?"

"Yes."

"It'll go away, but it'll be black and blue for a while," said Pelle Plutt, opening the fridge door again and rummaging around inside. A tub of margarine fell out onto the floor. "Here's the fucking nectar!" He held up the bottle, half full of the yellowish-red liquid.

One of these days I'll dilute it with piss. Fifty percent piss and he won't notice a thing. Patrik smiled at Pelle Plutt. Piss, you bastard.

"This looks like your face," said Pelle Plutt, gaping at the blue label. He looked at Patrik. "Only joking." He looked at the bottle again, then back at Patrik. "Would you like a drop?"

"No, thanks." Patrik went into the hall and put on his jacket and his shoes, which were very wet inside. You could put newspaper in them when you took them off, to dry them, but it was a long time since he'd done that. He had a vague memory of it. Maybe it was his mum, when he was very young.

Some woman started singing in the living room. His father laughed, and Patrik closed the door quietly behind him.

Maria was sitting with a cup of hot chocolate on the table in front of her when he arrived at Java.

"It's getting worse," she said.

"It'll get better eventually."

"Was anything broken?"

"No."

"You ought to turn in that bastard."

"That's what the police say as well," he said, taking off his jacket and hanging it on the back of his chair. "Your mom's pal, Winter."

"He's not exactly her pal."

"Well, him, anyway." He eyed her cup.

"Would you like one?"

"Chocolate? No, thanks. I had enough at your place."

"Four cups." She smiled. "Mom figured you'd get into the *Guinness Book of Records*."

"I'll order a coffee," he said, getting up.

"You haven't gotten any further with what you saw on the stairs?" she asked when he came back.

"I'm not sure."

He said hello to somebody walking past. The café was full of young kids smoking and drinking coffee or tea or hot chocolate. There were books everywhere. Patrik himself used to come here with his school-books when he really should have been at school with them on his desk.

"You look half dead," she said. "And it's not just your swelling."

"Thanks very much."

"I'd never be able to start delivering papers at four in the morning."

"Five. I get up at four."

"Damn early."

"You get used to it."

"You can borrow from me if you're short of cash."

"From you? Hasn't your mom cut off the supply?"

"I have a bit."

"So do I," he said. "I don't need anybody to help me."

Winter had asked Hanne Östergaard to call in the next time she came to the "police palace" at Ernst Fontell's Square. That was today. She knocked on his door and went in.

"Hello, Erik."

"Hi, Hanne. Thanks for coming."

"I was in the building, after all."

"Please sit down. Would you like a cup of coffee?"

"No, thank you." She sat down on the visitor's chair. Winter was in a short-sleeved shirt and suspenders. He'd draped his tie over his jacket, which was on a coat hanger by the side of the sink. His hair was shorter than when she'd last seen him. He was slimmer. His face was narrower than she remembered it, more sharply outlined. It was softened somewhat by the thin-framed glasses he was wearing. If she knew Erik Winter they wouldn't be Giorgio Armani spectacles. Nothing as simple as that.

"I see you're wearing glasses."

"Reading glasses. We're all getting older."

"Nice. They're not Armani, are they?"

"Er . . . no, they're . . ." He took them off and peered at the inside of one of the earpieces. "Air Titanium." He looked at her. "Is that one of your special interests?"

"Spectacle frames?" She gave a little laugh. "No. I don't have time for hobbies like that."

He put his glasses on the desk. She waited for him to say something.

"How are things otherwise?"

"Otherwise? What do you mean? When I'm not in this building?" She crossed her legs. "That's a good question."

"Well . . ."

"Come to the point. You want to know about me and my daughter."

"What makes you think that?"

"You know perfectly well."

"Know what, Hanne?"

"Stop it, Erik. Everybody here in the police station must know that my daughter was taken into custody by some of your colleagues when she was drunk. Drunk and disorderly is what the crime is called, if I'm not mistaken?"

"Give it up, Hanne. Yes, I know about it. No, that wasn't why I wanted to talk to you."

"You're welcome to do so."

"What?"

"You're welcome to ask me how things are . . . after that incident."

"How are things?"

"Better now," she said, and smiled. "Maria has been behaving herself since then." It sounded as if she let out a sigh. "As far as I know, that is."

"No doubt it taught her a lesson, for want of a better way of putting it." He put on his glasses again. "It's only human, after all."

"Yes. We are poor, sinful humans. That's what I try to tell the Social Services," she said.

"Social Services?"

"There's always an inquiry when something like that happens."

"Regard it as a formality."

"You don't have any children, I can tell that."

"Not yet."

"Yes, I've heard. Terrific. Congratulations. And pass them on to Angela."

"Thank you. But you really must regard all that business as a formality."

"As long as it doesn't happen again."

Winter didn't know what to say.

"There's no guarantee that it won't happen again, is there?" she said.

"Er . . ."

"It would be me, in that case. I'd be the guarantee. But I've obviously failed."

"That's a lot of crap, if you'll pardon the expression, Hanne." He repeated the comment but not the apology: "A lot of crap."

"I hope so."

"But there are cases."

"What do you mean?"

"Maria has a friend by the name of Patrik."

"Yes . . . how do you know that?"

"I was told by my colleagues who met Maria. It's nothing special. They spend a lot of time wandering around the center of town and all that. But what I'm interested in is Patrik, who we've been speaking to because he delivers newspapers in the building where those murders took place. You've no doubt read about it in the papers."

She nodded.

"Was Patrik a witness to something?"

"I don't know yet."

"But he was there?"

"He delivered newspapers, yes. But what I wanted to say is that he's got into a bit of a mess, in a different way. He was here, and he'd clearly been beaten. His cheek was black and blue. I sent him off to the hospital to get it treated."

"What had happened?"

"I think he was beaten up at home."

"That could well be," she said, her face becoming serious.

"Have you seen anything like that before?" he asked.

"Not really, but he has looked a bit tousled on some of the few occasions he's been to see us. To see Maria. Which isn't very often."

"Has he said anything to you?"

"No. Not directly, but I have had thoughts."

"His father is maltreating him. We can't prove it, but that's the way it is."

"What are you going to do about it?"

"We'll have to see. Patrik will have to sort out what he wants to do about it."

"That's terrible."

"I must do something to help."

Winter went to the CD player. "I'd like you to listen to this." He started the Sacrament disc. He was familiar with the music by now. For a brief moment he even thought he might be able to hear a tune, like a vague sort of message inside the cement mixer. Like Coltrane's meditations.

Hanne Östegaard listened with her eyes closed. She has a teenager at home. This is nothing so unusual to her. He switched it off after a minute.

"Not exactly what I like listening to," she said. "What is it?"

He filled her in and gave her the text that came with the CD.

"Patrik has played metal for us at home."

She scrutinized the cover, the black line tracing the coast, the sky, the silvery gleam. Winter had written out the text from the leaflet in a readable form.

He asked her to read the words for the first of the songs. She seemed almost to smile, despite the seriousness of it all.

"A large dollop of imagination," she said.

"You can say that again."

"A wide scope. All the way, from bottom to top, as it were."

"From hell to heaven."

"And then they make a little corner available for one of the prophets."

"And that brings us to the real reason why I wanted to talk to you, Hanne." He gestured toward the first page of the leaflet that had accompanied the CD.

"Habakkuk? You want to know about Habakkuk?"

"Yes."

"Erik, I'm not that kind of theological expert. He was an honest professional prophet, but that's just about all I know. Have you read what he wrote? In the Bible?"

"Yes. Did he have a daughter?"

"I've no idea. I don't think anything is known about his life. You'll have to look at the theological literature. Exegesis. The exegetic reference works."

"Okay. I'd thought of turning to the university. Religious studies."

"Yes. There's something called an *Interpreter's Bible.* And similar stuff. That's where you'll find whatever is known about Habakkuk." She looked at the cover. "How on earth could he get involved in something like this? Habakkuk?"

"The murders, you mean?"

"Or just this CD cover. That's enough." She looked at Winter. "What are you going to make of this?"

"For starters, we will try to avoid making anything of anything, and concentrate on establishing some facts."

"Heaven and hell."

"That's what it looks like right now."

"But perhaps it's just a game. This band, Sacrament—are they really trying to say something serious with all this trash?"

"That may not be important. But somebody is using it to mean something."

"I read an article in one of the Sunday papers last week," Hanne said. "It was about the spirit of the age. It went on about there being only a couple of weeks left until the new millennium, when all concepts would have to be redefined."

"*Fin de siècle.*"

"Yes. The end of the century, in spades: the end of the millennium. We're a bit lost about where we go from here."

"Whether we're on our way up or down, you mean?"

"Yes. Heaven or hell."

"And we finish up with a remarkable mixture of both," Winter said. "The world is being pulled in different directions."

"Not my world," said Hanne, and smiled again. "In my world we spend all our energy on fighting against evil."

"But does it produce results?" Winter closed his eyes, then looked again at Hanne. "'Our Lord, how long must I call for your help before you listen? How long before you save us from all this violence?'"

"That sounds like the Old Testament. I'd guess Habakkuk."

"Right the first time."

"Are there any quotations here? From the Bible?" she asked, holding up the printouts of the text.

"Not as far as I can see. Not literal quotations."

She put down the leaflet.

"More and more people are looking for some kind of guidance in life, some kind of comfort or consolation," she said. "In their different ways."

"Everybody wants a box of chocolates and a red rose," Winter said.

"Isn't that reasonable?"

"I suppose so."

"Or a bowl of soup," she said. "Our parish runs a pretty good soup kitchen."

"So I've heard."

"Isn't that awful?"

"The soup kitchen? I don't know about that. If you didn't do it people would starve out there in the darkness."

As he said that she turned and looked out the window.

"Light will soon be back," she said.

32

Morelius stopped at a red light. The town theater was attractively illuminated. The same applied to the whole city. One week to go to Christmas, and the light was intense when it grew dark.

A Santa Claus went past, and bowed in the direction of the police car.

"Do Santas bow?" Bartram asked.

Morelius didn't answer. The light changed to green.

The Avenue was full of people carrying packages.

"Have you bought any Christmas presents?" Bartram asked.

"Not yet."

"Are you staying in Gothenburg for Christmas?"

"Why do you want to know?"

"I was only asking."

Morelius turned into Södra Vägen. The council workers were busy on Heden, building a stage that would be used for the New Year celebrations. Gothenburg would enter 2000 with bright lights and a fanfare of trumpets. That applied to the whole city. Everybody would be on their feet, apart from those who had already fallen over before the clock struck midnight, thought Morelius. And he would be standing in the midst of them.

"All right. I'm going to spend Christmas with my mom."

"Kungälv?"

"Kungsbacka."

"Oh, yes, that's right. You're from Kungsbacka. I don't suppose you knew the woman who was murdered? Louise?"

"No."

"I guess the town isn't all that small."

"No."

"Are they talking much about it? In Kungsbacka, I mean?"

"Mom phoned but she hadn't heard anything." Morelius waited

while several people carrying parcels walked over the pedestrian crossing. "She didn't know her, either, this . . . Louise." He set off again. The city center was packed, and driving was a nightmare.

"What are you doing?" he asked.

"For Christmas, you mean?"

"Hmm."

"Working."

"What? You're going to be working over Christmas as well?"

"Christmas Eve and Christmas Day." Bartram shifted his position. "All the more free time for next summer." He looked out at the people, the packages, the lights. "I don't like all this stuff anyway." He turned to Morelius. "I've never liked Christmas."

"I bet you'll like it even less if you're working in the middle of it," Morelius said. "It's not much fun having to sort out families when Mom and Dad have been overdoing the celebrations."

Bartram didn't respond, seemed to be lost in thought.

"I'd be happy to skip it," Morelius said. "It feels pointless sometimes."

"'Our Lord, how long must I beg for your help before you listen? How long before you save us from all this violence?'" Bartram said.

"That sounds like a quotation."

"It's from the Bible."

"You don't say."

"Don't ask me which part. It's the sort of thing that sticks in the memory, but you don't know why. Useless knowledge."

"I wasn't going to ask."

Winter met the caretaker in the latter's cramped office. He'd considered summoning him to the station for questioning, but decided to take the softly, softly approach. The man had given the impression of being nervous from the start, and that could be disastrous for his memory.

The office smelled of tools and tobacco. Shabby files were stacked on a desk that also seemed to serve as a chopping block. There was nothing of the century-old elegance of the rest of the building down here.

The man looked down at his desk as if he were searching for something.

It occurred to Winter that this might be the caretaker of his own building as well. He asked.

"What's the address?"

Winter told him.

"Yep, that's me. That's part of my job as well. I look after three buildings in all, from here down to Storgatan."

"You do?"

"Yep." He lit a cigarette and inhaled deeply. "That's what they've saddled me with this last year." He looked at Winter and tapped ash into an old soda bottle that was half full of cigarette butts and dark brown tobacco juice. "Nowadays you have to be thankful that you've got a job."

"Sounds like a lot of work."

"Too much."

"Still, I'm glad that you discovered that there was something wrong in that apartment."

"In the end, yes."

"You didn't speak to anybody else about it?"

"What do you mean, anybody else?"

"Anybody else who also thought the same thing."

"No."

All right, Winter thought. We'll leave it at that for now. He might get wary, on his guard for anything and everything.

The man flicked off more ash, half of which missed the neck of the bottle. A fire risk? Winter thought. There again, the caretaker was sitting in his own basement room. His own office. If this could be called an office.

"Do you have an office in my building as well?"

"Of course. There are three, from here down to the crossroads." He inhaled again, and squinted through the smoke hanging in a cloud around him. "The second crossroads, that is."

"Of course." Winter could feel the irritation in his throat. No point in a discreet cough here. The old bastard lit another cigarette. Winter coughed even so. "Er . . . the Valkers . . . how often do you think you met them?"

The caretaker didn't remove the cigarette from his mouth. He wiped his hands along his trousers to get rid of the oil on them. He examined his palms, which had been clean at the start. Then he turned to Winter, with a new furrow between his eyebrows.

"Not very often, I must say."

"Were you working here when they moved in?"

"I've always worked here," he said, and succumbed to a combined cough and laugh that turned into a nasty smoker's hack and reminded Winter of the man at the next table when he'd breakfasted at Gaspar's in Marbella.

The caretaker finished coughing and dropped the cigarette end into the bottle, where it hissed away and went out. He lit another one, and waited for the next question.

"But you did meet the Valkers sometimes?" We'll take them separately later, Winter thought.

"I don't know about *meet,* but I've come across them, obviously. I've never been in their apartment, though."

"Never?"

"I suppose he managed to change washers himself." The man took another drag on his cigarette, flicked ash in the direction of the bottle. "It's the same with you. I look after the building you live in but I've never spoken to you. I've seen you, but that's not the same thing." He looked up at the ceiling and then back at Winter. "On the other hand, I've only been in charge of your building for the last few months."

"Have you ever spoken to him? Christian?"

"No."

"To her? Louise?"

"Yes. Once . . . ," he said, and a new furrow returned between his eyebrows. "She once asked me about . . . hmm, it might have been the heating. I can't remember now."

"Is there anything about them that made you wonder? Or about one of them?"

"Such as what?"

"Their visitors." Winter coughed again, turned away. "Did they have visitors, for instance?"

"People come and go in this building just as in any other. Who knows who visits who? And I don't go running up and down stairs unless I have to, you could say."

Winter could see his point.

"But they did have the occasional party now and again," said the caretaker.

"Really?"

"Things got a bit lively there at times."

"In what way?" Winter tried to encourage him.

"People coming and going, sort of thing. I sometimes had to change a bulb or something on the stairs in the evening, so I might have heard something then." He reached for the cigarette packet again, but it was empty. "Could have been somebody else, of course."

Winter nodded again.

"No, I can't remember if it was them or not," the man said. "Have you finished with me yet? I'll have to go out to the newsstand to buy some cigarettes." He waved the empty packet. "None left in here."

Winter asked about dud bulbs on the stairs, about dates.

"Good Lord, you stink!" Angela said when she came to greet him in the hall.

"A witness chain-smoking like a chimney."

"Do you normally allow that?"

"We were in his office. He's our caretaker as well, incidentally."

"What was he a witness to?"

"Nothing here. But he looks after that other property as well," said Winter, nodding his head in the direction of "that" apartment.

"But what was he a witness to?"

"Nothing more than he's told us so far, it seems."

"But you can call him a witness even so?"

He is that type, thought Winter. Takes all the credit for himself.

"Get those clothes off and have a shower," Angela said.

Winter put his pigskin briefcase on the floor, beside the shoe rack, took off his overcoat and jacket and hung them up. He started unbuttoning his shirt, went into the bathroom, and put all his clothes except for his trousers in the big wash basket Angela had brought with her.

He closed the door, got into the shower, and was just going to turn on the water when Angela shouted something. He shouted back that he couldn't hear a word, and she opened the door.

"I'm looking for a form from the maternity clinic," she said. "I think you put it in your briefcase. That was a while ago, but I need to check something."

"It's probably still in my briefcase," he said. "In the hall." She went out, he drew the shower curtain again, and turned on the water. The pungent smell of tobacco smoke started to fade away and eventually disappeared altogether as he rubbed the shampoo into his hair. He tried to clear his mind, and was rinsing away the lather when he heard a shout from the hall. He turned off the water.

"What?"

No reply. He shouted again. Still no reply.

"Angela?"

He opened the curtain, took the bath towel from its hook, and quickly rubbed his hair, shoulders, and stomach. He dried his feet and fastened the bath towel around his waist, then opened the door. He could see his briefcase standing open on the floor outside the bathroom.

"Angela? Did you shout?"

No answer. He hurried into the kitchen and then into the living room. Angela was on the sofa, staring at him with a piece of paper in her hand. She held it up and Winter could see the return address of the Spanish national police force in the top-left-hand corner.

Oh shit! He'd been carrying that damned letter around instead of throwing it away as he'd meant to.

"I had to look through the pile you had in your case, and this letter was lying face up," she said. "So don't think I'm in the habit of snooping through your private papers." She waved the letter in the air again. "But now I'd like an explanation of what the HELL this is, Erik."

Winter could feel the water dripping from his hair. Or was it cold sweat? Despite the fact that it was nothing. The letter was nothing. There was nothing to explain.

"It's nothing," he said. He took a step toward her. There was water on the floor.

"But I've read it, I'm afraid. It wasn't very long. But long enough."

"Absolutely nothing happened," he said.

"She seems to have a different idea about that." Angela looked at the letter. "Alicia. Do you have a photograph of her as well? Maybe it's hanging on the wall of your office?"

Winter went up to Angela and tried to touch her. She knocked his hand aside.

"I promise you, Angela. Nothing happened."

"Oh, shut up!" She punched the air. "You're talking to a witness who's seen it all." She burst into tears, quietly, with a soft, constant whimper he'd never heard before. "How could you, Erik? How could you?"

He sat down on the sofa beside her. It felt as if all his blood had rushed to his head. Damn it. He should have told her right at the start, but there was nothing to say. Why say something that could cause pain when there was nothing to discuss? It would be pointless. Destructive.

He started to say something but she stood up and headed for the hall.

"Where are you going?"

"Out."

"But I must . . . we must . . ."

She turned and threw the letter at him, it soared like a swallow for a couple of yards, then flopped down on the polished wooden floor, and he watched one corner sucking up the water that had dripped off him. She just stood there.

"I haven't said anything because there's nothing to say," he said holding out his hands so that she could see how pure and guiltless they were.

"Your conscience is clear?" she said, and maybe that was a laugh he could hear. "Do you take me for an idiot?" She looked down at the letter, which was wet through by now.

"No."

33

Bergenhem woke up with a headache. He seemed to have been resigned to it even in his sleep, and made himself ready.

He heard a little cry from the foot of the bed and saw Ada trying to climb onto their double bed. He could hear her struggling. He could also hear Martina working in the kitchen, and the screech of a lone seagull flying past the window.

Martina came into the bedroom and gave Ada a little shove so that the girl did a forward roll onto the bed and squealed in delight.

"Is it the usual again?" Martina asked.

"Yes."

"You have to go to the doctor." She reached out to prevent Ada from falling off the bed. "You said you would if it kept coming back." She put Ada in the middle of the bed and Bergenhem sat up, took the girl's hands, and lifted her up. It was like lifting a pillow.

"I know, I know."

"Is it still behind one of your eyes?" She reached out to touch him. "The left one?"

"Stop it," he said, pushing her hand away, perhaps too brusquely. He looked at her and took hold of her hand. "I'm sorry. But I seem to get so damned edgy with this."

"You've been . . . edgy for a long time."

"I know, I KNOW."

"Is there anything else?"

"Meaning what?"

"Is there something wrong between us?" she said, and he could see that she was trying to avoid looking at Ada.

"No, no."

"Can't you go to the doctor's? You'll have time tomorrow before nine."

"All right. I'll go."

He reached for Ada and lifted her up, and again she squealed in delight. When he looked up at her everything turned black for a tenth of a second and he put her down again, fumbling almost like a blind man.

"What's the matter, Lars?"

"I suddenly felt dizzy."

"Good grief, you really must go to the doctor's."

"I bet it's just migraine."

"You've never had migraine before."

"What sort of a comment is that? Say that to somebody who's getting MS."

"That wasn't funny."

"Well, stop nagging me."

He got out of bed and strode from the room.

"Coffee's ready," she called after him, but he didn't answer.

Angela had put on her overcoat, pulled on her leather boots, and left the apartment, and he wouldn't have been able to hold her back by force.

He picked up the letter. It felt like a wet leaf. The letter heading was a disaster. Just as the conversation had been a disaster. The quarrel.

She came back after seven minutes, but she wasn't carrying a bag of Danish pastries. She kicked off her boots and went to the living room, where he was still standing with the letter in his hand. She hadn't taken her coat off, as if to signal that this was going to go on all evening. Backward and forward.

"Rereading it, are you?"

"No . . ."

"You'd damn well better have a good explanation." She ripped off her coat and threw it on the floor. "A true explanation." She took a couple of paces toward him. "Do you understand, Erik? I want to know the truth. No spin and no goddamn lies."

"You don't need to swear like that."

"I'll swear as much as I damn well want."

"All right, ALL RIGHT." He looked around the room, then put the letter on the coffee table. "Should we keep standing, or should we sit down?"

She went to the sofa and sat down. He followed her.

"Listen now," he said to her profile. She was staring out at the electric-blue sky. It was fine weather, like most evenings. She'd only been out a few minutes, but her cheeks were flushed. "This woman was an interpreter at the police station. I met her when I reported the theft of my wallet."

"Terrific."

"I beg your pardon?"

"A great way to meet."

"Do you want me to explain this, Angela?"

"Yes, please." She was still staring straight ahead.

"Anyway, I met her again when I got the money from the bank. It was pure coincidence. We just bumped into each other outside the bank."

"Maybe she was following you? Shadowing you?"

"Angela, don't get paranoid."

"Paranoid? Is that the chief inspector's diagnosis?" She moved her head for the first time and looked at the letter on the coffee table: it had started to dry out and was curling up. A papyrus roll, Winter thought. The Dead Sea Scrolls. You can read about the past there. It can be true or false, depending on how you interpret it.

"And then you never left each other's side until I arrived," she said.

"Angela, that's not true and you know it."

"What is true, then? I'm still waiting." She nodded at the letter again. "That wasn't about a chance meeting outside a bank."

Winter closed his eyes, then looked out the window and saw only the evening, the night.

"That evening . . . that night . . . after my dad died. And afterward as well. I felt so . . . disconsolate. Sad. I went back to my room quite late. It was the night before you arrived. I sat on my bed and it felt so . . . so hard in a way, as if I'd made a mistake that I couldn't put right. Or as if we'd all made a mistake. Or both of us." He looked at her and saw that she was listening. "I don't really know what I thought. But it felt impossible just to sit there on the bed staring at the picture of the Madonna on the wall and emptying the whisky bottle. If there'd been a television set . . . I don't know. Spanish football or some stupid talk show. I don't know. But I couldn't just sit there. I went out for a walk, up to the Old Town."

"And she was sitting there, waiting for you?"

"It wasn't like that at all. It was another coincidence." She turned to look at him and he continued, quickly. "It WAS a coincidence. She was sitting in a little square with some friends." It had been a coincidence, he told himself. When he'd seen her in the square that first time, it had been a coincidence. Then something twitched in his legs and he went back there. The sorrow, his thoughts. Perhaps the shame. "I said hello, and joined them, and had a drop of wine."

"And that was all?"

"That was it, really."

"REALLY?"

"Yes. I went back home with her and drank a drop more wine and that was all. Mainly lots of taxi rides and an early sunrise over Torre-molinos."

"Torremolinos?"

"That's where she lives."

"And you went back there with her to watch the sun rise? You really are a pushy tourist, Erik. Forcing your way into a stranger's apartment or whatever you did in order to watch a new sunrise."

"Angela . . . I know. I should never have gone back with her and I . . . didn't want to. It wasn't ME . . . but all those other things. But I swear to you that nothing happened."

"You said a few minutes ago that one shouldn't swear."

"Angela . . ."

"Can you give me one good reason why I should believe all this?"

"Because it's true."

"Ha." She stared out of the window again. "Ha, ha."

"I don't know what I can do to get you to . . . We can contact her if you like."

"Don't be stupid."

"I really am telling you the truth. I promise. We got to her place and drank a glass of wine and I slept for a while in the living room. She didn't make any passes and neither did I."

"Real gentlemen, both of you."

He stood up and could feel the sweat pouring down his back. He didn't know what to do now, or what to say.

"It was just my . . . restlessness," he said.

"I think it was more than that."

"What do you mean?"

"This, among other things," she said, pointing to her stomach.

"For Christ's sake, Angela!"

"Now you're swearing again."

"You mustn't say things like that."

"It could well be true. We're supposed to be telling the truth, aren't we? Perhaps you're not the kind of man who should have a family."

"You're wrong. You're so wrong." He sat down again, tried to take her hand, but she wouldn't let him. "I'm so pleased about it. I'm so pleased about everything." He was holding her hand now. "You've got to believe me, Angela."

"Everything, you say?"

"Yes."

"Why didn't you simply throw that letter away, then?"

"That's a good question. I meant to. I don't know. Maybe because I find it difficult to throw any papers away. Everything is documentary evidence as far as I'm concerned. Evidence. Reports. Well, you know."

"Have you reported back?"

"Eh?"

"Have you replied to the letter?"

"No. Of course not."

"And you expect me to believe that as well?"

"It's the absolute truth."

He was getting into the part. No, not the part, the situation. It was an interrogation. She was the opposition and he was the suspect. He was the suspect and she was conducting the interrogation, and she was good. She's better than me, he thought.

So this is what it was like. Searching for the truth in the gaps between the words of what the suspect said. There might be fragments of
the truth in those gaps. But he was telling the truth. It *was* the truth. In
all important and essential points it was the truth, and he was forced to
convince a skeptical interrogator of that. He wouldn't be able to do it
yet. It would take a long time.

Aneta Djanali could feel the sun in her eyes. Beams were targeting the
highway and dazzling the drivers. Before long there'll be a massive
crash and we'll be in the middle of it, she thought. She could smell the
familiar aroma of newly baked bread when they passed Pååls. Halders
was staring forward, into the white glow, as if to guide her along the
right path.

She turned off at the Järnbrott exit and it was like getting her sight
back.

"So, here we go again," Halders said, pointing at the snow piled up
three feet high by the side of the road. "Snow," he said, turning to
Djanali. "It's called snow."

Here we go again, she thought.

Halders liked to remind Djanali of her African origins. I was born in
the East Gothenburg Hospital, but that doesn't seem to be good
enough for Fredrik, she thought as she turned west.

"Christmas tree," Halders said, pointing at a dressed Christmas tree
at the entrance to a garage. "There are lots of them around," he said,
pointing to lots of them. "It's a Nordic symbol for light and the celebration of joy."

"You don't say."

They drove past all the little detached houses and parked in front of
the Elfvegrens' hedge. The houses had been built in the 1950s, when
people used to live in cramped homes but had large gardens.

There was snow everywhere, but no sign of footprints. Djanali noticed tracks made by rabbits and cats.

"Lynx tracks," she said, indicating the track to her left.

"Lion," Halders said. "They've moved a long way north this year."

"This one was born at the Borås zoo."

"How can you tell?"

"Its claws are pointing inward," she said, ringing the Elfvegrens' doorbell.

The phone rang. Angela didn't want to answer, although she was nearer.

"Erik here."

It was Lotta Winter.

"Have you spoken to Mom?"

"I'll pick her up from Landvetter."

"That's the day after tomorrow."

"Yes."

"Only three days until Christmas. Time flies."

"Hmm."

"I'm expecting you and Angela here on Christmas Eve."

"Of course."

"Have you gotten around to buying Christmas presents yet?"

"Only Mother's gin."

"Stop joking now."

Winter looked at Angela's profile. Always Angela's profile. He wasn't joking.

"It'll be last-minute. Apart from a few things," he said.

"You got Bim's and Kristina's lists, I assume?"

"By e-mail. They were big."

"Just like they are now."

"No doubt they've grown an inch or two since I last saw them."

A sudden wind had eliminated some of the lion tracks outside the Elfvegrens' house by the time Halders and Djanali left again. It looked as if the animal had backed away and taken its paw marks with it.

"We'd better watch our step," Halders said once they were outside.

Erika Elfvegren closed the door behind them. Djanali felt the cold sinking down inside her fur collar.

They got into the car and drove off.

"They had two copies of *Aktuell Rapport* under the sofa," Halders said as they negotiated the roundabout.

"Aktuell what?"

"*Aktuell Rapport.* The men's magazine bought by more people than any other in Sweden. Or maybe I should say, it sells more."

"Really?"

"I wonder why." He said it again. "I wonder why."

"So you recognized the magazines, did you?"

"I recognized the spine. Half an inch of red at the top. And I could see a bit of the logo."

"You have a skill for recognizing men's magazines."

"True. But if you think I buy crap like that, you have another think coming."

"I don't think anything."

"Is it usual for people to have pornographic trash in their homes?" wondered Halders, mainly to himself.

"I've no idea," Djanali said.

"I think it's getting more common. The spirit of the times. The collapse of the old order. People read pornographic magazines and watch pornographic films on Channel Plus and TV One Thousand."

"You may be right."

"They're advertising sex toys now every evening on one of the major channels. Every night. Every damn night. And they've been doing it for over a year."

"How do you know?"

"Eh?" Halders looked at Djanali as if he'd just woken up from a dream.

"How can you be so sure about that?" Djanali asked with a smile.

"Because I keep a check on it, of course. Always keep a check on things, that's the way to go about it, isn't it? I check for two seconds and I get so annoyed and that makes my day."

"Make my day."

"I'd have loved to ask them," Halders said.

"What?"

"That ever-so-nice couple, the Elfvegrens. I'd have loved to ask them what their favorite reading was."

"You might get a few more opportunities."

34

Lareda Veitz studied the photographs and listened to Winter. She had read parts of the investigation report. This was the second time they'd met in the last two weeks. They were in Winter's office. The forensic psychologist had made it clear that she couldn't produce a clear profile of the killer, but she could discuss it with the officer in charge. It was not the first time they had worked together, nor was it the first time Winter had turned to forensic psychology for help.

"It's obvious that it's a message," she said, looking up again. "Then again, everything is a message, but in different ways."

"So there's enough there for it to be taken seriously?"

"Very much so. What did you think?"

"I don't actually know. In situations like this you think about . . . all the things at the side of the tracks as well. Whether this might be a sort of diversion."

"I don't think so."

"Are you sure?"

"Of course not. You've asked that before, and I have to give you the same answer."

"Okay. It's just that one has so many questions."

She looked at one of the photographs between them on the desk, held it up, and ran her finger over the necks of the two dead bodies on the sofa.

"One of the answers could be this," she said. "The swapping of heads. It could also be interpreted as an exchange of bodies."

Winter nodded. Veitz's tone was neutral, concentrated. It was the only possibility when the unspeakable was being examined in close-up. Winter had issued instructions that no calls were to be put through to his office. His mobile was on forward to Ringmar, in his office a dozen yards away. Ringmar was there should something urgent crop up.

Veitz put the photograph back on the desk.

"Let me think out loud," she said. "Let's have a good think about it, okay? From various different angles. Then we can dissect what we come up with." She indicated the tape recorder next to the stack of papers and pictures. "Then you can edit the tape."

"Of course." Winter checked that the tape was running.

"He . . . we'll say he . . . has changed the sex and identity of his victims. One of the answers lies in that action. The swapping."

"Why?"

"I'm not sure he knows that himself, Erik. We might have to search for unconscious motives that led him to commit the crime in this way."

"Something else was directing him?"

"*Somebody* else. Somebody other than himself."

Winter nodded again, picked up one of the photographs and examined it closely. He'd done this so often that they had acquired an absurdly mundane quality. It was like looking at the patterns on the wallpaper at home, or the framed photographs on the bedside table. Aneta Djanali had talked about the violently themed advertising posters hanging on the walls of the hairdressing salon where Louise Valker had worked. Murder as a sales pitch. He thought about that now. He looked at Louise Valker's contorted face; it had lost all human expression. It occurred to him that he hadn't seen that poster for himself. What had it looked like?

How carefully had he read the case notes on the interviews with all the people working at the salon?

"One moment," he said, reaching for his black notebook. He scribbled a note, then looked up at Lareda, who was deep in thought. "Keep going, Lareda."

"I'm improvising a bit," she said. "He's put down a marker . . . or several that might be interlinked. Somehow or other the text and the music and the action are interlinked." She looked up at Winter.

"They're not disparate markers." She looked down at the desktop again, with a glance at the tape recorder. "And what they're saying is that he wants to be stopped."

"Yes."

"You'd come to that conclusion as well?"

"Yes. He wants us to liberate him from his misery."

"The action itself is an anxiety reduction or conversion. When anxiety gets sufficiently strong it deforms the normal. Eventually he's forced to act and that brings him some calm. Temporary calm because the anxiety starts building up again and he's back to square one."

"Back to square one? You mean it will happen again?" Winter looked at the tape recorder and spoke to it. "Unless we stop him, that is." He turned to the psychologist. "Unless we help him?"

"I think we're dealing with a person who's been on the way to becoming psychotic for a long time, and his ego has been increasingly fragmented. Visions, dreams . . . in the end he has to act them out."

"He acts out his visions? Is that what you mean?"

"He might have had an experience earlier in life that's at the bottom of all this. Or an important part of it. Perhaps a long time ago. Perhaps fairly recently. But it was too horrific for him to forget. Though at the same time it hasn't been possible for him to remember it. Do you see what I mean?"

"I think so."

"And then it all comes back to him." She looked at the photographs highlighted in the sunlight from the window, seemingly split in two by sunshine and shadow. "And what he finally does is to act out his drama. It's a force that drives him to turn the drama into reality. Do you follow me? An inner vision becomes external reality."

"What exactly happened, then?" Winter suddenly walked over to the window and adjusted the venetian blinds. The sun had been in his eyes. The conversation had pained him. Lareda's sober voice intensified his feeling that they were now sinking into an abyss. This is what life's like. Abysses lurking in the human condition—memories and feelings of isolation and alienation and a lack of contact.

He turned around to face the room. Lareda's glasses looked black in the shadow inside his office. "What kind of an experience was it? Do you dare make a guess?"

She didn't answer right away. She took off her glasses and squinted at Winter, who was still by the window.

"He's been greatly outraged at some point. Perhaps several times, but not necessarily so."

"Outraged? Greatly outraged? How?"

"I think it has to do with the woman. Women." She held up one of the photographs again, and Winter went to stand beside her.

"The wounds on their bodies are different, and that can't be a coincidence. I've read the pathologist's report and studied the pictures on the basis of that. The man here is 'only' killed; but it's different with the woman. She's more than killed. She's more than dead." Veitz ran her finger over the woman's naked body. "There and there. There. There. None of the injuries were fatal in themselves." She looked up at Winter. "It's different with the man."

"I know. But not how, or why."

"He's been greatly offended by women. Perhaps one, perhaps several. Maybe not this woman. Maybe another. She could be a substitute."

"Substitute? She could be anybody at all as long as she's a woman?"

"That could be the case. Don't push me into saying anything more than that."

"What if I do push you, even so?" Winter remained where he was and she put on her glasses again, then looked up at him. "Can't you sit down?" she said. "My neck hurts if I have to look up at you like this."

Winter sat down.

"I'm pushing you," he said.

"Well, I think that this woman, Louise, wasn't the one in his dreams or visions. But I can't be sure."

"No, I understand that. But he's been outraged. Was it something to do with sexuality? Do you think his outrage was triggered by something sexual?"

It often is, he thought. Something to do with loneliness and a person's secrets.

"That's possible," Veitz said. "The outrage could be linked with a sexual act, or a sexual conception. He might have been made to feel ridiculous in a sexual context. It could well have been something like that. There are many examples of that nature in forensic psychology."

"Made to look ridiculous?" I'm repeating everything she says, Winter thought.

"In one way or another. A more risky interpretation is that he's been spiritually castrated. By a woman. And that it happened in somebody else's presence. A man."

"Castrated?"

"He's felt castrated. He couldn't put it into words when it happened, but now it's dawned on him. It might have happened with another man looking on. But it's the woman who's the guilty one. Who's done that to him."

"Who is therefore guilty of making him what he's become," Winter said.

"Yes. Who is responsible for his being driven to subject her in this way. And it could be that the 'her' is a substitute. His imagination has finally become so strong that he has to turn it into reality. The other reality that he still has a foothold in. The *real* reality."

"He can act normally, then? Still?"

"I think so."

"So he could be any of us?"

"I suppose he could, really," she said, and Winter thought of Angela for a tenth of a second. "But probably not for much longer. It depends on how he handles the fantasy that on one occasion he's now turned into reality."

She fell silent, deep in thought. She cleared her throat.

"Could you get me a glass of water, please, Erik? Tap water would be fine."

He went over to the cupboard where several clean glasses were kept and filled one with water for her.

She drank deeply, then went on.

"I can also see an element of domination here—as a consequence of what might have happened. It has to do with the change of identities. It exposes a conflict to do with a desire to dominate."

"Dominate? Dominate the woman?"

"Domination. The reason for his torture. That's the woman. And at the same time, the desire to be somebody else. He wants to be two different people, and acts on that basis. Afterward. After the murder."

"I don't get that last part."

"He wants to dominate as a man, but he also wants to escape from himself and become somebody else. The swapping of heads, or bodies, is a metaphor for that. A way of making it real."

"So to some extent at least, we're talking about revenge here? A twisted act of revenge? Frustrated love? Could it be as simple as that?"

"On one level I think it could be."

"And the people involved don't need to be the actual people who are the targets for revenge? For hatred?" The people in the photographs, Winter thought.

"No."

"But they could be *reminiscent* of them? In other words, in one way or another he or she, or both of them, are reminiscent of the real person. Or persons?"

"That could be the case."

"Does this mean that he—I'm talking about the murderer—could be somebody who's always thought of himself as inferior? Sexually, for instance. Who's felt himself to be castrated, ridiculed, without actually having been subjected to a direct . . . er, public humiliation?"

"A good question."

"And?"

"It's possible."

"That would mean in turn that we might not have any one specific incident involving him that could provide us with any answers."

"Yes."

Winter suddenly realized how thirsty he was. He got himself a glass of water and refilled Lareda's glass. Then he sat down.

The woman who had been killed. Louise. Who was she? Was she part of a history, or just a symbol for somebody else? In which case, who was the *real* woman? Was there somebody out there who could supply them with an answer? Who'd been in contact? But what if it *was* Louise? Had they dug sufficiently deeply into her past? Of course not. How far had they gotten?

He would take it upon himself to pay a visit to Kungsbacka. Her mother still lived there. She had answered the questions his colleagues had put to her, but he had some more to ask.

"Keep going," he said.

"What about?"

"About power, domination." He looked at the tape recorder again. "I'll listen to it all later. Edit it, as you suggested."

"Yes . . . power . . . that's a new word. But, all right, if we say that he wants to be in command. . . . What happened to him once upon a time—his humiliation—might have led to a life devoted to recovering the foothold he'd lost."

"A life searching for domination?"

"Yes. But more or less unconsciously. We talked about the conscious and unconscious before." She looked at the tape recorder, as if expecting to receive confirmation of what she'd just said. "But he was searching for some sort of status."

"Status? In life? In which life?"

"In which life? Well . . . I think his private life is in ruins. Perhaps that's how it's always been. We're dealing with somebody who doesn't have many contacts. Few friends."

"Lives on his own?" Winter asked.

"Yes." She looked at the tape recorder again, as if it were a short-hand secretary. "Let's say that, for argument's sake."

"What about his job?"

"Hard to say, of course. But it's not impossible that this person has a job that gives him a degree of domination."

"But you can dominate in a variety of ways."

"It has to be obvious." She looked at Winter, having removed her glasses. "I think that's the point."

"Obvious? You mean that people have to realize that this man has a bit more power than the rest of us?"

"You could put it like that. A man is judged by the power he exerts."
She was silent for a while, thinking. "If we take the sexual thing a bit
further, we can talk in terms of penis extension."

"As opposed to castration," Winter said.

"Yes. But still on a subconscious level."

"He becomes aware of it later? Is that what you're saying?"

"We were discussing this before, weren't we? Murder is caused by
an imagination that has grown too powerful. There are no smoke
screens any longer."

"But what triggers the actual murder?" Winter asked. "What evokes
sufficient evil to make him kill them?"

"That's a very good question," Veitz said.

"The murderer must have gotten into the apartment, and he must
have had a reason for being in that particular place, at that particular
time, with those particular people."

"Maybe not 'those particular people.'"

"All right. But you know what I mean."

"Yes. It's still a very good question."

Winter stood up. His head felt feverish, overheated by the headlong
rush of thoughts through his mind. He tried to concentrate, closed his
eyes, walked over to the window, opened the venetian blinds and
looked out at the blue sky and the white ground. Cars were passing
silently on the other side of the river. The façades of the buildings were
illuminated. The trees were weighed down with snow that had frozen
onto the branches. It was the day before the day before the day.

He turned around.

"Let's think about what you said about his job. You said he wanted
to be seen."

"Yes. It's important for him to be noticed."

"He has to be noticed when he walks along the street?"

"Yes. Could be."

"People walking along the Avenue who happen to be brain surgeons or Nobel Prize winners in medicine can't prove that, right? You
can't tell by looking at them, is that right?"

"That's right, assuming they're not wearing their stethoscopes. But you don't do that when you're walking around Gothenburg, do you?"

"Brain surgeons don't use stethoscopes anyway."

"Knives, then," Veitz said, and Winter started laughing uncontrollably. It was as if the lid were being forced off a pressure cooker. He had to hold on to the window frame for support, and when he saw the disapproving look on the psychologist's face, he burst out laughing again and the lid blew off.

"Oh, dear . . ." she said, and Winter tried to put the lid back on. Not knives, he thought. That might make them mistaken for chefs, especially along the Avenue. He felt the pressure building up on the lid again.

"Are you thinking about something funny, Erik?"

"No . . . no, I'm sorry, Lareda. It's just the tension." That's true, he thought. The tension, the private, the professional tension. His private life wasn't in ruins, as Lareda had said about the murderer's, but it was not exactly idyllic at the moment either. His professional life: you couldn't see by looking at him that he was a chief inspector. He didn't have a uni—

"Take yourself as an example," she said. "You can walk down the Avenue, but nobody would know that you are a detective chief inspector."

"No, but . . ."

"You dress as—"

"Uniform," Winter said. "A uniform. What's the easiest way of telling that someone has power or authority?"

"A uniform," Veitz said.

Winter sat back down. Rubbed his eyes, put on his reading glasses, then took them off again. He could feel a film of sweat on his brow. It felt warm in his office, almost hot.

"Let's take it easy now," he said. "Uniform. How did we get there?"

"You'd better listen to the tape," she said. Winter lifted it up carefully. The tape was still running.

"What is this?" he said. "Are we looking for a man in uniform?" He looked at her, as if expecting her to nod in agreement. But she didn't respond.

"What do you think?" he asked.

"We said at the start that we'd have a good think about this, from various angles. That's what we've done, and one such angle is this one." She breathed in audibly. "But when you listen to the tape you'll hear what it is—hypotheses, rambling thoughts. We've touched on this and that. A man in uniform? Well, yes, if we still think we're looking for a lonely man who's trying to impose some sort of order and status on his external life. But we don't know if that's true."

"But I've got all the words on record," Winter said, tapping the tape recorder. "Brainstorming is never wrong. Nor are words."

"You mean you call this conversation brainstorming?"

Winter didn't reply. He was looking at the photographs, which had acquired the same nuances as his desktop, now that the sun was on its way to somewhere else.

A word can say more than a thousand pictures.

35

Winter went to the coffee room, stood by the window, and smoked a Corps. The snow lay undisturbed on the other side of the car park. Police officers in uniform were talking to one another down below, their breath forming speech balloons between them.

Visitors came and went. He could see his own bicycle in the stand outside the main entrance. Eight inches of snow on the handlebars, frame, and saddle, like icing on a gingerbread bike.

A laugh floated up from one of the speech balloons. One of the policemen had put on a Santa hat.

He poured out some coffee and took it back to his office, two cups. Lareda Veitz looked up from her notepad.

"Could it be that he wants to look for new challenges?" Winter asked as he gave her the cup. "Take it by the handle. It's hot."

"Thank you. Challenges? Well, what do you think yourself?"

"I thought of that while I was getting the coffee. That he might be growing. *Feels* that he's growing. This business of it possibly happening again."

"But the desire to be found out is always there," she said, taking a sip of coffee. She started to say something, then stopped.

"What were you going to say?" Winter asked.

"Power. We spoke about power before, and dominance. I don't quite know how to put it . . ."

"You've done pretty well so far," Winter said, taking a drink from his own cup, which had cooled down a little.

"It's not all that unusual in cases like this for the murderer to try and get power over the person who exposes him. His unmasker."

"His unmasker? But there is no unmasker. Has he already defined his unmasker?"

"His *future* unmasker. He's left messages, hasn't he? They're aimed at somebody."

"At whom?" Winter asked, but he knew the answer already.

"At you, Erik." She was sitting in the shadow and her spectacles were black again. "You are the hunter. The detective. The one who will presumably unmask him."

"So he wants to dominate me? Erik Winter?"

"You in your role as hunter. Detective Chief Inspector Erik Winter."

"It's nothing personal, then," Winter said, but he wasn't smiling. Nor was Veitz. He looked at her. "Can it *become* personal?"

"How do you mean?"

"That he actually focuses on . . . me? Me personally, because I'm the hunter?"

"No."

"Are you sure?"

"No."

"He has something I don't have in this case. He knows why it happened. And who did it. That gives him the upper hand, doesn't it?"

"In a way, yes. Go on."

"In that way he already has power over me." He stood up again, thought, took two steps. "Is there more, Lareda? Is that enough, or not?"

She stood up as well, went to the window, and looked out with her arms folded. She turned around.

"I don't know if we're getting anywhere, continuing along these lines. But all right . . . It could be that you have something that he doesn't. In order to dominate you, he must get some of it for himself. In order to have power over you."

"What do I have?"

"Compared with him? Everything. You have everything."

"What, for instance?"

"A proper life. His life is ruined, may have been in ruins for a very long time. You have a life."

Winter breathed out. It was still very hot in the room. No empty speech balloons. He didn't want to go any further in the direction the conversation had taken. Later, but not now.

He went to the Panasonic and switched on the music. Lareda had listened to it at home, and her husband had gone to the cinema to avoid it.

"I prefer Carreras," she said when the song started.

"For me the borderline comes with The Clash," Winter said.

"You're familiar with The Clash?"

"I'm an expert on them." He motioned with his head toward the CD player on the floor. "But how can anybody analyze this stuff? Has it given you any ideas?"

"Well, speculation mostly . . . All right. I won't go on about the 'intensity' of the music. You can be misled by that, perhaps look in the wrong direction."

"The tempo's not the important thing, is that what you mean?"

"Yes. It can be misleading. Everything gets so much more ghastly with this in both the foreground and the background. Do you follow me? If you come to the scene of a murder and find Carreras singing, the impression you get is different."

"But, Lareda, we try to be professional here. Carreras, Sacrament . . .

Mysto's Hot Lips . . . Tom Jones . . . it's not important in that way. I'm not influenced by the music when I'm standing there."

"You can say whatever you like, but you're missing the point. I'm saying that the ghastliness of it all is made more intense by the choice of music, and that must influence you when you are searching for answers."

"How does it influence us?"

"Let me ask you a counterquestion. Do you see a particular type of person when you envisage somebody listening to this? Listening by choice, that is."

"I try to avoid doing that."

"That wasn't what I asked you."

"I take your point," Winter said.

"There's something in the music that might conjure up what has happened. It's latent. This isn't background music. This doesn't invite you to relax with smooth classics at seven."

"Who does listen to it, then?"

"It could be somebody who's always listened to this kind of music, but I don't think so."

"Why choose it now, then?"

"That's another good question."

"I don't think either that the murderer is necessarily an out-and-out metal type, with long hair and black leather. We're not setting out to put away the types who dig black metal."

"Maybe he doesn't listen at all," Veitz said.

"That had occurred to me as well."

"The message—if it really is a message—might be in the words. Maybe we should concentrate on the words. When you lent me the cassette, you said that this music is impossible without the words. Without the booklet with the lyrics that comes with the CD. Didn't you?"

"Yes."

"Well, I've tried to think about the words. And the cover. The pictures. We can't forget them. In other words, all the things that are not the music itself, or whatever we should call it. I haven't got a word for it," she said, gesturing toward the CD player. The room was still filled with Sacrament, but Winter turned the volume down now. "Apart from the words describing the genre, that is. Black metal."

Winter agreed. He didn't have a word for it either. It was more physics than music.

"There are lots of symbols here, but the pattern indicates just one thing," she said. "The choice of title, the words, even the pictures. It's all about a sort of tug-of-war between good and evil. Represented by heaven and hell."

"I'm with you so far."

"But their relative strengths are not spelled out, as it were. Who will win? Where is the power based?"

"The words don't provide an answer to that, is that what you mean?"

"They express a wish, rather, but against a background of darkness. Hopelessness. And that's the world that is part of the key to all this. Perhaps."

"The world? What world?"

"The world that predominates." She looked up at him, and he noticed that her facial color had changed slightly. She was getting excited. She was thinking aloud, thinking clearly. "That could be the key question. And the paradox. There's an enormous difference between committing sin in a world ruled by God, and in a world ruled by the Devil."

"There's no hope in a world ruled over by the Devil? A world made up exclusively of evil can offer no hope. Is that what you mean?" Winter said.

"Yes. And that could be the way he sees things. He's a part of the evil world. But he might still have some idea of the other world."

"He wants to go there again? Go back to it?"

"He wants to get away from everything he's having to put up with," she said. "And he wants to make up for a deficiency by committing a crime: castration. A deficiency and a longing. The crime takes him back to his experience of humiliation, and he also wants to show us that 'This is where I fall short.' He wants to tell us."

"He wants to be found out?"

"He wants to be helped. And this is where we find the biggest paradox of all. He's longing to be helped, and he's saying that his crime shows you where his deficiency is, and that it is a cry for help." She looked at Winter, stared hard at him. "In that way he demonstrates that there is still hope."

"So there is still some hope? Both for him and for me?"

"And all the time there is a longing," she said. "His dreams are an imagined world that he has now made real." She looked at the CD player. "And, so, we're more or less back where we started, don't you think?"

A dream, Winter thought, gazing out the window again at the snow that was starting to glisten in blue. A dream in a winter land.

It was quiet in the apartment. Patrik could hear his father snoring in the bedroom. He was trying to read, but his mind was elsewhere. He had bought a Christmas present, but he hadn't decided on anything for Ulla. He didn't want to buy her a Christmas present.

Maybe they'd be spending Christmas Eve somewhere else. And Ria had said that he didn't need to be at home anyway. He could be with her family at Örgryte. That would be wicked. Celebrate Christmas in a posh house. Wicked.

His father was up now. The whole room seemed to be grunting. Ulla was out buying booze, and he knew that his father wasn't feeling too well at the moment.

"Patrik!"

His father stood in the doorway, rubbing his eyes. He could smell him even at this distance. The same as usual—but not really, because he always used to be in his own room, where he could be at peace.

"Was it you what woke me up?"

"No."

"Something did," his father said, rubbing his eyes again. He went through the living room and into the kitchen. There was a bang and something fell down and broke. Glass. "For fuck—" yelled his father, coming back into the living room. "There's glass on the floor. Pick it up, will you, I haven't got the strength."

"I'm going out."

"What did you say?"

"I'm on my way out."

"I told you to clear up that glass out there. Ulla will be back soon and she doesn't know about the glass on the floor."

"Yes, all right. I'll do it."

He went into the kitchen and tried to clear up the biggest pieces first. He ought to have put something on his feet, but he didn't cut himself. Then he swept up the rest of the shards, wrapped them in a plastic bag, and put the bag into the trash under the sink. Ulla came back, he could hear her in the hall.

"What are you doing?" she asked when she came into the kitchen.

"Nothing."

She put her shopping bag on the table. His father appeared and took down some new glasses.

Patrik went into the hall and put on his coat and shoes. It was dark outside now, but light everywhere. People were carrying Christmas trees wherever you looked. They cost 150 kronor, but he didn't want one.

There was no sign of his mom's things anyway. Some colorful baubles. They'd disappeared, just like her.

There was a police car parked at the newsstand when he passed. He thought he recognized the two officers. Then it drove off. The sign over the newsstand was reflected in the car's polished side. He thought about something he'd seen on the stairs. That reflection made him think about it. Was there some connection?

36

"I've read the door-to-door reports and what is striking is that nobody pays any attention to anybody else," Winter said. "'Hear no evil, see no evil, speak no evil.'"

"What's it like in your building, then?" Ringmar was trying to straighten out a paper clip. "What kind of a check do you have on your neighbors?"

Winter thought of Mrs. Malmer. Angela had made insinuations about Mrs. Malmer's midnight masses. But Angela didn't make insinuations anymore. Angela wasn't even there. No, it wasn't as bad as that. Angela doesn't live here anymore. It wasn't as bad as that. He had told the truth and nothing but the truth that had any significance for them both and their future.

"Not much," Winter said. "Not much at all."

Ringmar held up the now straight paper clip.

"Well done, Bertil. You can start picking a few locks now."

"Was that how he got in?"

"We haven't found a single scratch. Either he had a key or they let him in. He was known to them."

"We've interviewed all their friends and acquaintances that we know about."

"He was a secret acquaintance."

"What are you thinking about?"

"Secrets. People's secrets."

"Hmm."

"He was a part of the secret. Something was going to take place there and he was going to be involved. But they never got that far. It didn't happen. Not that last time."

"He had other intentions."

"Yes."

"Did he have other intentions from the moment he arrived?" asked Ringmar, now trying to restore the paper clip to its original shape.

"That's an important question. Had he made up his mind when he went there, or did it . . . did something happen that led to the murders?"

"Or to what happened *after* the murders?"

"Yes. Was he a stranger when he was invited, or was he somebody who'd known them for a long time?" For a long time, Winter thought. His job had become a sort of criminal archaeology. He was digging backward in time in order to find answers. Climbing down into the shadows of the past. He was tired of it. He had enough to do with the present. "Had he known them for a long time," he said again.

"Did he know her? Him? Both of them?"

"Hmm. Her. I think it has to do with the woman. Louise. I think so even more now, after my conversation with Lareda."

"Lareda gets carried away sometimes," Ringmar said.

"But it makes sense, even so," Winter said.

"If we assume that he was let in, the next question is how they made contact," Ringmar said. "If they were acquaintances from some time in the past, or not known to one another at all but had arranged to meet in the Valkers' apartment, how did they get into contact?"

"An advertisement."

"Do you think so?"

"Lonely hearts."

"Do you know how many lonely hearts ads appear in the daily papers every day? Or even just on the weekend?"

"No, I don't. Do you?"

"No sir. But you only need to take one glance to know that there are lots of them. Lonely hearts."

"Do you read them, Bertil?"

"They are very entertaining. But to start searching through them all would be like searching for a needle in a haystack," Ringmar said, studying the paper clip that had turned into two steel needles.

"Pornographic contacts," said Winter. "Contact ads in the porno magazines."

"More needles, more haystacks."

"Hmm."

"Are you thinking of the sperm? Are you wondering if it was *that* kind of acquaintance?"

"Yes."

"Well, it's one theory. They got in touch via an advertisement."

"It's not impossible. It evidently happens more and more often."

"People need tenderness and affection," Ringmar said. "It's a growing need."

"And they find new ways of getting it."

"We haven't found any pornography in the Valkers' apartment," Ringmar said.

"Films," said Winter. "We could start there. Talk to the local video stores."

"And then what? Even if they did rent a porn flick now and then, I don't see how that would help us. I suspect we'd be surprised by the statistics on the renting of porno."

"What do you mean?"

"Practically everybody rents one at some point. Chairmen of the local council. Clergymen. Sture Birgersson." Winter couldn't help smiling when he thought of the crime unit boss. Birgersson had performed his annual disappearing trick and Winter had no intention of talking to him.

"Or they buy one on the Net," Ringmar said. "Nice and discreet."

"Yes, no doubt."

"Have you ever thought about doing it?"

"Renting a pornographic film? I haven't, in fact. It wouldn't be . . . me."

"Not your style?"

"No style at all."

37

When Angela closed the door and he heard her boots dropping onto the floor, he opened the oven and took out the two small stuffed woodcocks that needed a short time to rest. It was nine-thirty.

"What's that?" asked Angela, going straight to the kitchen, perhaps tempted by the smells. "Doves of peace?"

"Just a bit to eat."

"Yeah, right."

Winter was busy with the salad dressing, whipping a teaspoonful of French mustard into some olive oil and three drops of honey vinegar.

"I suspect there's a hidden meaning here," Angela said. "A subtext."

"You could have a guess," he said, tearing up salad leaves of various types; he nodded toward the woodcocks as if everything depended on them.

She went over to the work surface and sniffed. The birds certainly looked tasty.

"Guinea fowl?"

"No."

"I give up."

"Already?"

"I'm tired."

She sat down and massaged the toes on her left foot. Her stomach was quite a mound now. There was a little hole in the heel of her tights. In the light from the stove lamp and the two candles on the table, he could see that she had dark circles under her eyes, but that her face was still flushed from the wintry climate outside. Her hair seemed to be flattened, as if dried out after an afternoon and evening at the clinic, where the air-conditioning left much to be desired.

She looked up, her hair fell away to the sides and the shadows had gone. Her face looked young again. "It's nothing new. Tired. The nurses probably feel much worse." She held her hand cautiously over the nearest candle flame. "We had a scandal at the clinic today. A king-size one." She continued waving her hand to and fro over the flame, without looking at him. "The boss resigned. Made a hullabaloo about it." She looked at him again. "Just left his desk and cleared off." She smiled. "Our beloved chief executive was in with Olsén discussing the latest cutback proposals . . . no, decisions. I was with a patient and didn't hear anything of it, but they said there was a sort of bellowing from inside Olsén's room and then Olsén emerged without his coat and Boersma followed him, looking embarrassed."

"About time."

"Meaning what?"

"About time the director was embarrassed."

"To him that's like water off a du—" she said, looking hard at the little bird nearest to her, which was still giving off a bit of steam and smelling delicious. "Surely these aren't ducks?"

She seemed to have forgotten her question, took her hand away from the candle, and massaged her right foot.

"Olsén didn't come back. He phoned half an hour later and said he wouldn't be coming back today. Or ever. He'd quit."

"So there'll be even fewer of you doing what has to be done."

"Yes. But some good may come of it."

"I've brought something good home with me," Winter said, indicating the woodcocks as he opened the oven door to check the potatoes.

"Doctors can command a bit of respect," Angela said, following her train of thought. "If they shout loudly enough, they can shake the foundations a bit."

I've noticed that, he thought, but he didn't say anything.

"They can stir up the administration, I mean," she said, and walked over to the counter again. He embraced her, and noticed the smell of winter that was still clinging to her hair and clothes. He held her tightly, and felt her stomach. She moved closer.

"Have you burned the letter?" she asked, barely audibly, addressing his neck, or the birds on the work surface.

"It's all gone," he said. "Everything that never existed is no more."

"All right," she said, pulling away. "All right, all right." She looked at the table, which still wasn't set.

"Do you think I might have time for a shower before dinner?"

"You have five minutes," he said. "Max. I'll put some foil around these beauties, and the sauce will be ready in a couple of minutes."

"But what are they? Could they be woodcocks? They're in season now, aren't they?"

She recalled the French word for them as she turned on the taps in the shower. *Bécasse.* She knew that because she'd worked in a French vineyard a couple of late summers and one autumn when she was a student—although she wasn't studying at the time—and the vintner hunted woodcock. One or two would often be hanging on the porch as she set out to tend the vines in the morning.

．　．　．　．　．

They'd been in the office that Hanne generally used at the police station. It was a quiet room, well lit.

She always put freshly cut flowers on the little table by the chairs that had to serve as armchairs. They were just like she was, she'd often thought: inadequate, a bit different from what they would be like on other occasions, under different circumstances.

"I can't shake off those dreams," Morelius had said. "Like last night again."

"Do you want to tell me about it?"

"It was the same as the night before last, and the one before that. Somebody laughing as I stood there, but I didn't know . . . which one of them."

"Was it during that traffic accident?"

"It's always then," he said. "Now it crops up as a sort of flash when I'm in the car, for instance. Working."

"What's it like then?"

"A sort of memory. It just crops up, then disappears."

"What does the image look like?" she asked.

"The same image. From the accident."

"Go on."

"It's as if it's haunting me," he said. "And not only when I'm working." She was listening. Waiting.

"I think about it even when I'm not on duty."

"I understand."

"And then there's going to sleep." He was twisting his head from side to side, as if to avoid getting a stiff neck. "That's the worst, I suppose." He twisted his head again. "You need to get some sleep. If you don't, you can't work properly." Then he said something that Hanne didn't really understand, and that would give her food for thought later. Much later. "I mean, you have to show people who you are," Morelius said.

Patrik and Maria were in the center of town, wandering around the shops that were open late, browsing the CDs in music stores, rummaging through shelves of books, touching the clothes hanging on long racks. Street musicians were wearing Santa Claus hats and singing songs about Christmas in English and in Swedish.

In the southeast corner of Femman was a Peruvian band: small, dark men, ponchos in earth colors, songs that smelled of sorrow and high winds. Patrik and Maria joined the semicircle of twenty or so listeners, swaying in time to the rhythm. In front of the musicians was a battered suitcase full of CDs.

"Maybe I should buy one for Mom," Maria said. "I haven't found a good Christmas present for her yet." She gestured toward the CDs. "One of those, and something else as well."

"A bit of black metal," Patrik suggested.

"No, thank you." She looked at him. "You haven't found anything yourself yet, have you?"

"For Dad, you mean? No."

"Aren't you going to get anything for . . . her?"

"Ulla? No."

"I think I saw her on the tram near Haga Church the day before yesterday."

"Was she drunk?"

"If it was her. No, not as far as I could tell. But she had a shopping bag with some bottles."

"She'd been to the booze shop, no doubt. Too heavy for her to walk home with, I suppose."

"I never want to get drunk like that again," Maria said.

"Like what? Like Ulla?"

"You know what I mean, Patrik."

"All right."

"Don't you think?"

"Straight edge," he said. "That's the thing from now on." He was watching the musicians, all of whom seemed to be playing panpipes at the same time as they strummed open chords on their guitars. They sounded like birds circling over mountain peaks. Get away from all this. "Well, are you going to buy some music from the Andes?"

"I need a bit more time to think."

"It's Christmas Eve the day after tomorrow."

"Don't remind me."

"It's all right for you."

"You can spend Christmas with us."

Patrik made no reply. He turned and saw Winter approaching from Brunnsparken, at the edge of the mass of people making their way to the shops. He hadn't noticed them. Christmas shopping. No parcels yet, but he seemed to know where he was going, unless he was just being carried along by the tide of people.

Patrik looked away, but it was too late. Gothenburg was a small place.

"How are things?"

He was standing close, but not too close. Maria looked up.

"All right, I suppose."

Winter eyed the band. The song had finished, and some of the onlookers applauded. He turned to the youngsters again. Patrik's cheek was almost back to normal now. Winter didn't know whether the investigation had started and he didn't want to ask, but the boy had been beaten up for the last time.

"Nothing new from your memory bank?" he asked, and felt immediately that it sounded idiotic. Corny.

"No."

"You still have my phone numbers, I hope?"

"Of course."

"Okay. I'd better get moving. Last-minute Christmas presents, as usual." He looked around. "Most people seem to be in the same boat."

"Us, too," Maria said.

"So long," Winter said and started walking away, but after a few feet he looked around and smiled, as if at the hustle and bustle all around him, and something jogged in Patrik's memory. He caught sight of the dark gray trousers that Winter had on under his overcoat. They could be . . . could be the same kind of trousers that . . . that he'd seen when he was on the stairs and *he* came down in the elevator and went out through the front door. Was that it? Was it the trousers he'd been searching for in his memory bank, as the detective had called it?

Maria said something, but he wasn't listening.

He was standing on the stairs now. He'd seen half the man's face, or a bit less, and the overcoat rode up and there was something about the trousers. And there was something else as well, higher up. Something higher than the trousers that sort of gleamed. There was a gleam on the trousers as well, like reflector tape. It could be reflector tape, or just a reflection of the light. And he had a sort of belt over his chest, diagonally.

Patrik could still see the detective, but only the head now, bobbing up and down a bit higher than most of the others.

The man who'd left the apartment building had been wearing a uniform or something of the sort underneath an ordinary overcoat. Patrik turned to Maria, who said something again.

"What?" he said.

"Are you asleep or something?"

"Let's move on," Patrik said.

Bartram went home with two videotapes. It was starting to snow again, but the sun was still shining. Perhaps it was so localized that it was only snowing on him and this part of the street. He hadn't gotten to know it yet. At first it had just seemed long, but now it was divided up by recognizable things. The advertising agency that was unable to do much in the way of advertising even for themselves, judging by their own display card.

The playground.

Ladies' clothing—or was it just hats?

The buildings that changed color block after block, but didn't have much color left after all the rain and wind and sun. It was very windy here. Perhaps that had to do with the hill. The wind came from below, was stopped by the hill and sent back to create a circle of wind. When it was at its worst it became a vicious circle.

Now the snow had stopped, as if he'd walked right through it. Just as the wind could turn back when it hit the hill, the haze of the sun had come back and grown stronger.

He was inside now. There was a faint smell of hyacinths. That's what Christmas ought to smell like. He'd bought ready-made meatballs, and they might add to the Christmassy aroma. He had a bottle of spiced wine to mull, a new brand. That didn't really matter. He didn't have a Christmas ham, and had hardly given it a thought.

He put the videos on the chair in the hall. The crispbread was still out in the kitchen. He'd forgotten to put the tub of margarine back into the fridge, and it had acquired various yellow streaks that reminded him of piss. Piss. The tub was more than three-quarters full. He held it at arm's length and threw it into the sink. Right on target at the first attempt. He raised his fist and lapped up the applause. Anybody who is bang on target raises his fist. As far as he could see, he was the only one doing so.

That night he held Angela in his arms. She moved slowly in time with his movements, her back toward him. His body was a part of her. After a few minutes he abandoned his caution. He lifted her up and it was as if she were floating on air. She shouted something in a different voice, but he didn't hear as he was on his way to the same powerful feeling as she was, simultaneously. It was filled with light.

Afterward, as they listened to her CD, *the boatman calls from the lake, a lone loon dives upon the water,* and they were lying still and silent, he thought about a name for their child, but didn't dare to be too bold. Angela had also grown more careful.

It was to do with the fact that the time was coming. January, February, March, April. Perhaps before then. Less than three months, perhaps. Had he really grasped that? Had he, hell! Had she? Of course not. Who could?

There will always be suffering, it flows through life like water. It was dark, self-evident music, beautiful, suitable for bright afternoon light, but here, on the way into the small hours, it was floating on air, just as they had floated into each other a few minutes before.

Ringmar had said that there's an Arab proverb: "You're not a man until you've written a book, planted a tree, and fathered a child."

He's done the biggest of those. Almost there now. Angela hadn't said anything more about houses, but he knew. A plot with a hole he'd dug, a tree, a hundred trees.

He could write a book, or think one, keep it in a drawer within a drawer, pages full of thoughts. Was his life over already? In that sense? Retirement after working for thirty years and then the quiet life that always followed. Had he ever set foot in life?

Or did he have anything else in him? Good Lord! Imagine writing a book that wasn't a handbook on interrogation techniques or about the significance of intuition in criminal investigations.

To write well you needed to think well, it seemed to him. Did he think well? He'd always had faith in himself in that respect, relied on his thoughts sooner or later moving things forward. Now he knew. So much was happening in his life this winter, and had happened that autumn. Who he was, who he was becoming. His father, and the baby, everything part of an enormous progression that was bigger than anything else he could conceive of.

His wavering concentration on the case, on the murders. Yes. Wavering concentration. He had to admit that to himself. He was still being professional, but his mind could wander off in the wrong direction. That hadn't happened before, not like this. It had wandered off in various directions, but never very far. Was something happening to him? Was it only the child, and his father's death? . . . and Angela, their new, more serious relationship?

"I can hear that you're thinking," she said, making the effort to turn and face him. "I hope it's about us."

"Yes."

"I hope you're not bringing your work to bed with you."

"Not in that way."

"Meaning what?"

"I don't know. I feel as if it's becoming . . . becoming more difficult to keep my eyes fixed on what I'm doing. This case. I don't know . . ." He kissed her.

Maybe he knew what it was. He'd barely had the courage to allow the thought to enter his head. Maybe he was afraid. Afraid for them. There was something making him afraid.

She sat up and was about to get out of bed and go to the bathroom. He felt thirsty, and at that very moment she asked him if he wanted something to drink.

"Yes."

"Wine for you."

"Sounds like an excellent idea." He reached out for her before she'd had time to leave the bed.

"Angela."

"Yes?"

"Have you had any more silent calls?"

"Wrong numbers, you mean? Isn't that what you called them?"

"Have there been any more?"

She could see from his face that he was serious. Why was he reminding her? Was he afraid, in spite of everything?

She had moved on. She wasn't scared now. *They* weren't scared. It was one time then, another time now. Everything was bright and she'd been feeling optimistic at last, happy. That damn business of the letter *was* a misunderstanding. No more misunderstandings.

"No," she lied.

The flight from Málaga landed in the Nordic twilight. Winter saw it touch down as he pulled into the little parking area to the east of the international terminal.

His mother was one of the first out through customs. She hugged him tight. She smelled of sand and a different kind of sun. No gin. Her trolley was fully loaded, in danger of tipping over from the weight.

"I didn't realize that you'd decided to move back to Sweden."

"It's just a few Christmas presents, Erik."

In the car she huddled up, then stretched out again, blew into her hands.

"It's colder than I expected."

"We're having one of the coldest winters of the twentieth century."

"And tomorrow it's Christmas Eve."

"Exactly."

"When are you going to Lotta's?"

"I gather we're eating at half past one."

"I'm looking forward to that." She looked out into the dark night and the white snow lighting up the landscape.

"How's Angela?"

"Never felt better."

"She's growing as she should?"

"Everything's going according to plan."

"You're taking Christmas off I hope, Erik?"

"Of course."

38

Two burning torches flanked the front door. There was a hissing noise as drops of sleet fell into the flames, but they didn't go out. Lotta's house in Hagen was ablaze with light in the murk of the afternoon. The sunshine had gone, and it now felt as if it had been a casual visitor. The sky was acting backward this winter. Winter paused on the slippery stone path and looked up at the first floor. As an eleven-year-old he used to gaze out of that window, at the Hagen chapel and Berglärkan on the other side of the valley.

Angela slipped and held on to him. There was a rustling noise from the packages in the paper shopping bags they had brought with them from the Mercedes he'd parked in the street.

Bim and Kristina opened the front door before they'd even started walking up the steps. Lotta's daughters were well on their way into the adult world, but not today. Today was *the* day. Winter tried to hug the two teenagers as best he could with his arms full of Christmas presents.

There was a smell of Christmas the moment they entered the hall: fried spare ribs, spices, the thin, salty smell of anchovies. Hyacinths. A special glow from the candles, and from the Christmas tree that they could just glimpse in the living room; the unusual radiance of festivities in the early afternoon when it was dark outside. Winter noticed the slightly sharp smell of needles from the fir tree as he took off his outer clothes in the hall, and his mind went to the pine grove above his father's grave in Nueva Andalucía. He could see it even more clearly when his mother emerged from the kitchen with a tray of steaming mulled wine.

"Welcome, my dears," she said.

"When you're carrying that, Siv, I can't give you a hug," Angela said.

"Give it to me," Lotta said, following her mother out of the kitchen, drying her hands on a towel. She took the tray.

Ferdinand the Bull was wheeled back home to the cork oak. The Andalusian landscape recovered its air of tranquillity.

"Have you ever seen a bullfight, Grandma?" asked Bim from the floor, where she was half-lying on a beanbag.

"Oh no." She turned from the television screen to the young girl. "There's a little arena down in Puerto Banús and your granddad went once or twice, but it's not for me."

They had spoken about Granddad earlier. Not much, but the girls had asked a few questions. Winter hadn't said much, but he'd been *there*. He wasn't left out.

"It seems pretty nasty," Kristina said. "And why do they have to kill the bull? Surely you can still have a bullfight without killing it?"

"Yes," Winter said. "That's how they do it in Portugal, I think. And the South of France."

"What did Granddad say?" Bim asked. "When he'd been to the fights?"

"He said it was a kind of theatrical performance," Siv answered. "Above all else, it was drama. The arena was a sort of theater, with various different sections where you could sit, depending on how much you wanted to see." She reached for the nutcracker and a walnut. "Sitting in the sun all afternoon's hard work." She cracked the shell and extracted the brain-shaped kernel. "But some of the seats were in the shade."

Winter was Santa Claus, and all went well despite the fact that nobody in the house believed in Santa Claus. As he got changed, he thought about his mother's words describing death as a theatrical performance with the spectators sometimes hidden both from one another and from whoever died or lived down below in the red sand.

He wore a mask that was at least thirty years old. Maybe he should do this more often. He marched into the living room asking if there were any well-behaved children there, just like every other Santa in every other Swedish living room on Christmas Eve.

Of course, he wasn't actually there when Santa came with all the presents. Bim explained that he'd gone out to buy an evening paper, and so Santa put all the presents for Winter in a little pile under the Christmas tree.

The teenagers insisted that everybody should open their parcels in order, one at a time. Everybody had admired their presents by the time Winter returned from the newsstand.

"Oh, has Santa been already?" he asked.

"Your presents are under the tree," Angela said. "Where have you been?"

"I went to buy a newspaper."

"Where is it, then?"

Everybody burst out laughing and Winter went over to his pile, and when he opened his first parcel it was something that felt hard but turned out to be soft. A fur hat, the sort that men in Russia wear.

"That's to keep your head warm," Lotta said.

His father had fallen asleep by the time Donald Duck started on the television. Ulla had left in a huff an hour earlier, as something had annoyed her. She'd slammed the door so hard that some flakes of paint fell off.

Mickey Mouse was dressing the Christmas tree. You don't need a Christmas tree. Look what happened to that one. Patrik could hear the snores coming from what used to be his room. He raised the volume of the television. Ferdinand was under the oak tree, smelling the flowers. Patrik could smell the hyacinth he'd bought the previous day, from a stall at Linnéplatsen. His father didn't say anything when he saw it, and Ulla wasn't there.

His mom always used to buy a hyacinth at Christmastime. It was *the* Christmas smell, it seemed to him, and he went to close the door so that he could hear the squeaking of the wheelbarrow when Ferdinand was taken back from the bullring.

That brought the cartoons to an end. He went to the refrigerator and took out the party sausages and meatballs he'd bought. They were all right. He didn't like the traditional marinated herring, so it didn't matter that there wasn't any. He could whip an egg and make an omelet. An omelet was good with thick mushroom sauce, but mushrooms were expensive and so was cream and there were other ingredients and he didn't really know how to make it.

He fried a few sausages. They smelled good. He looked for some mustard, then realized he'd forgotten to buy any. There was ketchup. His father had bought a tin of red cabbage. Christmas isn't Christmas without red cabbage, he'd said—but he seemed to be managing all right without it, fast asleep in *his* room. Dad will manage all right without any Christmas at all. So will I.

Christmas is for amateurs. Just like New Year's Eve.

He heard somebody laughing on the landing, then the front door opened and Ulla shouted something, then marched into the kitchen, still in her overcoat and boots and followed by a couple of winos. Abruptly he walked away from the cooker and the frying pan and into the hall. As for the party sausages, they could turn to charcoal for all he cared, so that those bastards couldn't eat them, but they'd eat them even so, not now, but some time later tonight.

He pulled on his boots and was halfway down the stairs before he put on his jacket.

Once in the street he noticed that the snow he'd watched dancing past the kitchen window had turned into sleet. He pulled up his hood and set off toward the center of town. When he got to Haga Church he saw they'd erected spotlights to shine on the walls: what was the point of that?

It was nearly dark now, and a car came down the Allé, followed by another. One was a taxi and the other jumped a red light. His head felt wet, even through his hood. It was more rain now than snow.

He walked down the Allé as far as the Avenue, which was deserted and quiet. Another taxi drove past, and he saw a police car turn around at Götaplatsen and head back toward him. He crossed over the Avenue when the police car had gone past, and he thought about *that* again. There'd been a flash, as if from a reflector or something of the sort.

There were two police officers in the car. It continued in the direction of Kopparmärra. A number-five tram was approaching, and he noticed that he was more or less at the Valand stop. When the tram came to a halt he got on. He'd meant to pay, but the inspectors weren't going to ruin their Christmas celebrations by chasing fare dodgers on Christmas Eve.

He got off at Saint Sigfrids Plan and before he knew where he was, he found himself standing outside Maria's house. Light shone from most windows, but he couldn't see anybody inside. Then he saw Maria's mom walking from one room to another with something in her hands. Now he could see an old lady: that must be Maria's grandma.

Lights were on in all the houses but one. Either they were away, or they were in bed, snoring, he thought. Quite a few were in bed snoring tonight, but that was okay. He hadn't given his father his Christmas present yet, but it didn't have to be today, did it? Christmas would carry on for ages yet.

Once again his legs started moving without his being in control. He found himself standing on the steps leading up to her front door, and he had to hold himself back from going closer still and ringing the bell. He turned away, then back again. Then he turned away once more and started to walk off.

"Patrik."

He turned back yet again. Hanne was standing in the doorway.

"Why don't you come in, Patrik?"

"Nooo . . . I'd better be off . . ."

He set off down the steps with the open door behind him, and then he noticed Maria standing there.

"Come on in, Patrik." She came up and almost touched him. "Have you eaten?"

"Er . . . yes, of course."

"Do you think you could force down a bit more? We haven't started our Christmas dinner yet."

"Er . . . I mean, it's your . . ."

"Don't be silly! Come on in now, the cold wind's blowing into the house."

Bartram was driving, for a change.

"Rain, for once," Ivarsson said.

"The farmers could do with a bit," said Bartram, turning off when he came to Götaplatsen.

"We used to block off this square in the evenings," Ivarsson said.

"Block it off?"

"It's not all that long since the public order police used to come here every evening and block off the whole of Götaplatsen with chains, and then we'd open it up again the next morning. Weren't you here then?"

"No, I was working somewhere else."

"I see."

"Why did you block it off?"

"Teenage hell-raisers in their cars."

"Eh?"

"The hell-raisers. The bosses didn't want them congregating here every night."

They were heading northward, toward Kopparmärra.

"Look at that poor bastard. Left to his own devices on Christmas Eve," Ivarsson said, pointing at the boy plodding along the Avenue, his woollen hat clamped down on his head as he leaned forward into the driving rain.

"Yes."

"Or maybe he's on his way from one party to another."

"Could be."

"Just like we are."

"It's pretty quiet so far."

"The partying hasn't really gotten under way yet," said Ivarsson. "And when it does, we'll turn up and gate-crash."

"Is that how you see it? That we gate-crash?"

"I'm only making conversation."

"I suppose we have to do that when we're going around and around here on Christmas Eve." Ivarsson looked at Bartram. "Back home they're all celebrating Christmas, but not us. Sad."

"We'll have to make up for that later."

"You can say that again."

Kungsbacka looked as if a neutron bomb had hit it. The buildings were still there, and the streets, but there was no sign of any people. Morelius drove through the town before it was dark enough to be able to see if the windows were lit up.

"Couldn't you have come yesterday?" was the first thing his mother said to him.

"You know what it's like. Work."

"Haven't you nailed whoever it was that did such awful things to Louise who came from here?" asked his mother. He hadn't even taken his overcoat off.

"No. Not yet."

"She came from here, though, poor thing."

"Yes."

"Perhaps he's from here as well. The one who did it." She went to the kitchen, and he followed her. The ham was on the work surface, and there was a smell of anchovies and spices. The lutefisk was still soaking in an enormous cauldron. "Have they thought of that possibility?" She opened the oven door to check what was inside. Ah! Jansson's Temptation—the traditional sliced herring, potatoes, and onion, baked in cream. Best of all, the anchovy topping. "They must have thought of that," she said, addressing the Jansson's.

"When are we due to eat?" he asked.

"In an hour or so. It sounds as if you can't wait."

"I was just wondering if I could do anything to help."

"Nothing, thanks."

"I'll go for a little walk, then."

"Now?"

"I think I need some fresh air before we start eating. There wasn't any in the car."

He went out, but after a hundred yards turned off in the other direction and was soon standing outside the school, which was the same color as it used to be.

They used to go through the pedestrian underpass that was still there, but the graffiti at the entrance was different now. From where he was standing, the tunnel was just a black hole.

Run. They'd sometimes run. The shouts and laughter had been magnified by a thousand decibels inside the tunnel, bounced around from wall to rock wall.

"Did you see any people out there?" she asked when he got back.

"Just one," he said.

39

Sture Birgersson had returned from his excursion into the blue. It was Boxing Day. Birgersson was not tanned, but, then, he never was when he came back from his mysterious holidays.

Maybe he stays in Gothenburg, thought Winter, who was sitting opposite the head of the crime unit.

Birgersson squinted at his second in command through a thick cloud of smoke.

"Did you have a good Christmas?"

"Excellent."

"Mind you, it's not over yet. Technically speaking." Birgersson flicked ash into the ashtray, cleared his throat tentatively, and held up some documents.

"Interesting."

"What's that?" Winter asked, lighting a Corps. He didn't like cigarette smoke, never had.

Birgersson put the papers back on the desk.

"Lots of possible leads shooting off in all directions. But interesting." He was holding one of the papers in his hand now, a transcript of a tape recording. "I liked your chat with Lareda. Smart girl." Birgersson used the ashtray again. "Perhaps a bit too smart."

"What do you mean by that, Sture?" Winter drew at his cigarillo and looked hard at him. "She came up with ideas, hypotheses. We're the ones who make the judgments."

"Have you made any, then?" Birgersson waved the documents. "On the basis of this stuff?"

"Not yet. There's a lot to take in."

"Like I said, lots of possible leads shooting off in all directions. That business of uniforms, for instance. That sounds interesting, but we'll have to be careful, I suppose." Birgersson stubbed out his cigarette and eyed Winter's cigarillo. "Is there any risk that somebody might leak stuff to the press, do you think?"

"Who would do that, Sture?"

"The press would love it," Birgersson said, without answering Winter's question. "Love it." He looked at the papers spread out on his desk. Birgersson's desk was usually empty. It was a peculiarity of his, possibly something more serious than that. He would read things by the window, on a chair, keep everything away from his desk. But not now. Maybe something had happened while he was out in the blue, Winter thought. Birgersson looked up. "Just as much as some people evidently love this so-called music. That's just as odd." He seemed to be smiling. "They're similar to each other in that respect. The press and the death rockers."

"Is that what you call them, death rockers?"

"Or black rockers or whatever their goddamn name is. I know it's really called black metal, but here, in front of you, I'll call it what the hell I like." He stroked his chin, then rummaged among the papers again. "I was a bit curious about this prophet, Habakkuk. Have you got anything more about him that isn't in this paper?"

"Not really. What it says there is taken from a biblical encyclopedia."

"The thing that seems to be the biggest distinguishing feature of this prophet is that there was evidently nothing of interest about him as a person," Birgersson said.

"Yes. He was apparently very reticent about his private life," Winter said.

"That's a good quality," said Birgersson. "We know next to nothing about Habby and even less about his daughter." Birgersson looked at Winter. "Did he have a daughter?"

"I've just sent Halders back to the seventh century B.C. to investigate that very thing."

"Excellent. Halders needs to get out more." Birgersson looked at the document again, and read an extract out loud. " 'So, Habakkuk was a professional prophet at the temple in Jerusalem, he was a Levite, and an angel took him by the hair and flew with him to Daniel in the lion's den with some food.' " He looked up again. "The information has no historical value."

"That's where Halders comes in."

"On second thought, I don't think the seventh century B.C. is up to coping with Halders," Birgersson said. "He could cause a lot of trouble." Birgersson gave a short, hoarse laugh. "Perhaps we wouldn't be sitting here now if Halders had been on the loose twenty-six hundred years ago." He put down the paper and turned to Winter again. "That reminds me of another thing, in parentheses, as it were, before we go on." Birgersson stood up and seemed to be stretching his long legs. He towered over Winter, shutting out the Boxing Day light. He was a gigantic, shadowy figure and Winter could imagine his body in a long silken robe, with long hair and a beard, brandishing newly written documents on parchment rolls. Or stone tablets. Habakkuk had received a message from the good Lord: " 'Then the Lord told me: I will give you my message in the form of a vision. Write it on tablets clearly enough to be read at a glance.' "

The Book of Habakkuk. Winter thought about Ringmar and what he'd said about the word "rubric." It was all connected.

Evil will be conquered in the end, even if it always seems to win, was what the prophet meant. The story always had a meaning for those with eyes to see and the ability to put it into the perspective of their faith.

Habakkuk could mean "dwarf."

Birgersson said something.

"I beg your pardon?"

"There'll be nine of us on duty in the control room on New Year's Eve and I'll be one of them. I've known that for some time, but it won't have any effect on your work."

"No."

"I admit that I did think about sending you, for a moment." Birgersson had sat down again, and the robe, shoulder-length hair, and beard down to his chest had disappeared. "To make it clear that you are as important as I am. An equal deputy. But I don't think it would have been a good idea, with this case on the go."

"Things shooting off in all possible directions, is that what you mean?"

"You think well when you're at home, Erik. I've no doubt you'll be doing that while Gothenburg celebrates the party of the century."

"Of the millennium."

"Yes. I can hardly wait to celebrate it along with the chief constable of the province, that very dear lady."

"You won't be on your own," Winter said. He could see them now in his mind's eye, the nine senior officers from the various units with the task of supporting the communications HQ on this exceptional night that was drawing ever closer. It was a sacrifice by those in high places, proof that the top brass put duty before partying.

"It'll be interesting," said Birgersson. "I'll be able to say afterward that I was there."

"I'll think about you when midnight comes," said Winter. "I hope all the electronics can cope."

"That's why we'll be there."

Winter laughed.

"What will you be doing at the magical moment? Any special plans?"

"Yes . . . we'll be eating at home. My mother's visiting us. Angela and Mom and me. Nice and quiet."

"I suppose a bit of peace and quiet is what's called for, in view of the coming addition to the family. And all's well with Angela?"

"She's working away and getting more annoyed about the goings on in the hospital than ever. So, yes, all is well."

"Anyway. Now you know where to find me when the carnival explodes in a riotous crescendo."

"Let's hope that everybody can handle their jubilation," Winter said.

"To be honest, I think it's going to be a hard night for the boys on the ground," said Birgersson.

"There are quite a few gals in the cars as well," Winter said. "And in the street patrols."

"Yes, yes, but you know what I mean." Birgersson lit his second cigarette since Winter had come to his office. Winter was reminded of the chain-smoking caretaker. Perhaps Birgersson was cutting down? He looked up: "We've said it a thousand times before, but it's still true that what holds us back in this job is a lack of imagination. But, in a way, the reverse is true with regard to this case. Are you with me? There's so much imagination floating around that we have to make an effort to keep it in check. The material is somehow . . . so comprehensive. All these trails that could be leading us in the same direction but don't necessarily do so." Birgersson's face suddenly looked heavier, older. "This is an imaginative sonofabitch we're dealing with here. The bastard. He's building up a façade that takes up more space than the deed itself. Are you with me?"

"I'm with you. It sounds interesting." It was interesting. This was Sture Birgersson the detective speaking.

"Just for a second you think it hasn't happened. That feeling. You have to go back to an earlier feeling in order to proceed. Try to think under and over these tracks. Messages."

"I'm with you."

"Do you think he's making fun of us, Erik? In the sense that all those messages are really fakes?"

"Fakes?"

"That they are fantasies and nothing to do with the deed. Something that happened afterward . . . consciously. Intentional misinformation."

"No."

"Nor do I really. But what we've got is not enough." Birgersson looked down at the pile of papers again. "There are marks and stains and fingerprints but nothing to compare them with. Beier's team found some sperm stains, but that's not enough."

"I'm afraid I can't present you with a suspect yet."

"I'd be happy with somebody to interrogate."

"Not even that."

"Perhaps AFIS could be of help," Birgersson said.

Yes. That had helped in the past. The automated fingerprint identification systems contained the prints of everybody who had been arrested for any crime or misdemeanor, so they could insert the prints they had and see if there were matches. The case could be solved.

"What does the team say?" asked Birgersson. "Is anybody complaining about how long it's taking you to get anywhere?"

"Not that I know of."

"I don't suppose we're landed with a serial murderer, or . . . ?"

"We'll know that if we have a series."

"We don't have serial murderers in Sweden anymore."

"If you say so."

"I do say so. And I'm prepared to repeat it."

"Hmm."

"Get somebody linked with the scene," said Birgersson. "That's where we have to start. Those other couples. Can't you bring 'em in and shine a light into their eyes? There are several things that aren't clear."

"It's more like vagueness in the way they act," said Winter. "That can be due to all kinds of things. General uncertainty when it comes to facing the police, for instance. Fear, simply."

"Exploit it."

"I am, in my own way."

"They seemed to have a pretty vague past. The Valkers."

"Well . . ."

"A few semi-indecent possibilities, but there's nothing substantial to work on."

"We shall see."

"You said you were going to pay her mother a visit yourself. Louise. In Kungsbacka. You're not satisfied with the interviews the team's had with her so far."

"I'm going there on Thursday."

Bergenhem was building a snow lantern in the garden. He was building it, and Ada was demolishing it.

"We have to leave an opening to put the candle through," he said. More snow had fallen during the night, and it was workable. One more night, though, and it would freeze. The snow lantern might survive.

Martina came out with hot juice.

"Ooce!" Ada said.

Bergenhem stroked his hair back.

"Has the headache gone?" she asked.

"I didn't feel anything last night."

"What about now?"

"Only a little bit when I bend down."

She didn't say any more, but he knew she wanted him to go to a doctor. No. It would get better of its own accord. It's just that he was . . . under stress. Now it was almost New Year's Eve. The mother of all celebrations. He was on emergency call. Just as well. He would stay sober and watch the biggest fireworks display in the history of Gothenburg. They'd all be standing near the bridge, watching the display on the other side of the river, and he'd be among them. Unless he was needed somewhere else.

Ada was tired, and they went indoors. Darkness fell quickly. Ada went to sleep.

When she woke up he went out and lit the lantern and they sat by the window. There was a breeze, but it didn't blow out the candle. Then came a stronger gust and he had to go out and relight it. It had grown noticeably colder during the last hour.

That night he dreamed about faces whirling around him in a circle. He recognized two of them. There was music he'd never heard before. He was angry with somebody, and the antagonism wouldn't go away. Somebody was approaching his head.

He woke up, and it was worse than ever. He went to the bathroom and took three painkillers in half a glass of water, then went back to bed and waited for them to work.

The lights were out and there was nobody to blame. He'd have to go down to the cellar and test his way through the fuses.

As he went in, the police officer came out. He nodded. Looked as if he was going out to dinner. Elegant. He smiled and inhaled deeply. Did crooks work over the Christmas and New Year holidays? Surely your normal criminal had a break like everybody else? Maybe it wasn't an attractive idea to plan something when you'd rather be at home having a good time. He'd had a good time, when he eventually got there.

Now the light was on in his cubbyhole. It was no more than a cubbyhole, even though he called it his office. The fact that his light was on meant that at least a third of the floors up above also had lights working. He checked the staircase but there was no light there. He kept on testing. Now his light went out, but it came right back on again.

He detected a funny smell.

He went further into his cubbyhole, which was big enough for him to be able to see into the shadows. The light had never been good in this office. Then again, he wasn't there all that often. It didn't really feel like his apartment building. It was in his own building that it was all at, as you might say.

This block was where the detective lived, so nothing could happen here.

On a bench, behind a few clamps, was a box from McDonald's and an empty soda bottle. He poked at the hamburger carton and saw a few lettuce leaves, some ketchup stains, and some of that disgusting mayonnaise stuff. There was, in fact, a bit of soda left in the bottle, but no-thank-you.

Who the hell had been down here for a meal? It was a pleasant-enough cubbyhole, but not exactly a restaurant.

He'd never experienced this before, not anywhere. To start with, the door was locked. He checked the door, but there were no marks. Somebody had got in using either a key or a damn good pick, or a piece of steel wire. That was possible, of course.

Some youngster? Why the hell should some youngster come down here to eat a hamburger? Was it more fun than the school cafeteria? School dinners weren't much fun, but even so. This was odd.

He poured the remains of the soda down the sink and put the bottle underneath. You didn't throw bottles away where there was a deposit on them, but you threw away empty hamburger boxes, and he dropped it into the half-full bin next to the door.

40

It started snowing again as she waited at the tram stop. The piles of snow in the park were ten feet high, and it seemed they would never melt away.

She felt a movement, then another. Three months to go. They still didn't have a nursery in the apartment. No clothes, no crib. Nothing that could tempt fate. There was such a thing as fate. Why did she think so? What fate was that? How could it be tempted?

It wasn't something she wanted to talk to Erik about. He had a different attitude to life, but she wasn't sure that you could direct everything yourself.

The tram was late. It was a means of transportation that relied heavily on dry weather, without much precipitation. Trams are made for southern California, she thought, and read the electronic screen in the shelter, red letters on a black background: NOW had been changed to 15 MINUTES.

The baby kicked again. The movements had become a part of her body, of course. It would feel strange to be one again. Or suddenly two. That was a better way of putting it. Becoming two.

She was going to be late and there was no excuse. Sensible people took into account the fact that trams would be running late when it was snowing. She left the shelter and looked for a taxi, but they were never around when you needed them. That's simply how it was. When you needed to arrive on time, public transportation wasn't working, and when you turned to Plan B, there was no taxi in sight.

She walked to the road junction, but there were no trams approaching and no sign of a taxi. She looked around. This is what people look like when they need a taxi, she thought. The others still have faith and are waiting in the shelter. If a tram comes, it comes. That's fate.

A police car stopped on the other side of the street next to the bakery just as she was crossing the road. The driver's door opened and a police officer got out and raised his arm in greeting. His colleague remained in the passenger seat, behind the windshield wipers. The officer shouted something and she paused when she reached the pavement. He was shouting to her. She approached him.

"We're heading for Wavrinskys Plats," he said. "Excuse my asking, but could we offer you a lift?"

She didn't know what to say. He was around her own age, fair-haired, maybe a bit on the small side for a public order officer. Open face. He seemed familiar.

"I recognized you, that's why." He looked slightly embarrassed. "I know Erik a little, so . . ." he said, gesturing as if to indicate the weather and the lack of public transport. "You work up at the Sahlgren Hospital, don't you? We noticed you at the tram stop before, so if you'd like a lift, then . . ."

She glanced at her watch.

"All right," she said with a smile. The other officer got out and opened the rear door for her, and she looked around before getting in. Caught red-handed outside her own front door. What would people say?

The other officer was more heavily built and older. He said his name, but she didn't catch it.

Neither of them was the type to indulge in small talk, and she appreciated that. A couple of messages over the radio sounded almost like advertisements. It was warm inside the car, pleasant. They dropped her outside the main entrance to the hospital.

"Give our greetings to Erik," said the driver as she was closing the car door. "And a happy New Year."

Winter hesitated halfway to Kungsbacka, but continued even so. The road ought to be still passable when he drove back home as well. He'd seen two snow plows with lines of traffic behind them.

It was Thursday, December 30, 1999. Tomorrow all hell would break loose. He'd barely given it a thought. He felt that he needed to get out, leave his office, his desk, the investigation reports that he'd read from beginning to end three times, as one of the contributors. Get out into the world, the wide world. It was around about him, everywhere.

He turned off the E6 and found his way into Västra Villastaden. Traffic grew denser as he approached the town center and people were walking through the snow like faintly drawn cartoon figures.

He passed the Fyran House of Culture and stopped to look at the map. He turned southward, passed a school, didn't see the street sign until it was too late, and had to stop and reverse when the road was free.

The run-through of police plans took somewhat longer than usual. This was going to be the biggest party ever, and Chief of Police Söderskog and his support services had been working hard on the preparations for a whole year. The Millennium Celebration was a very special event. On the scale from catching a petty thief to war, the Millennium Celebration was closer to war, or at least civil war.

"Nevertheless, we're trying to cope with the normal level of public holiday staffing," their colleague from Support Services had said a long time ago. That meant restrictions on leave, more standby duty, more cover for mealtimes and other breaks. Everybody was well prepared, and there would be no panic if panic were to erupt.

"But why should it?" the officer from the administration unit had asked. Yes indeed, why?

Bartram and Morelius were sitting by their lockers with Ivarsson.

"That damn procession is going to bring Gothenburg to a standstill," Ivarsson said.

"The Goddess of Light leading us into a new millennium," said Bartram. "Just think about that."

"I suppose that's all right for people who can't see beyond the end of their noses, but I can manage on my own, thank you very much," said Ivarsson. "The center of town will be constipated. Much worse than when the damn students are mucking things up on rag day." He adjusted his holster and his SIG-Sauer gleamed. "Söderskog's merry men were going on about panic when they were here. What'll happen if there *is* panic? It's obvious some people won't be able to cope with the pressure from the crowds, and there could be panic when we carry them away." He adjusted his belt. "Nobody will be able to move an inch."

"But where should it go, to make it safer?" Bartram asked. "The procession, I mean? Should they stick to the park out at Upper Hisingen?"

Iversson snorted with laughter: "That would be great as far as I'm concerned. But that's where the problem lies. This long procession with the Goddess of Light leading the way." He looked at Morelius. "I mean, we've already had the Lucia procession earlier this month, welcoming the light. What more do they want?"

"More than that," Morelius said.

"Where are you allocated to?"

"I'll be at Heden to start with, until they've finished building the Tower of Babel."

"What a damned crazy idea that is!"

"At least it'll be standing still."

"The hell it will," Ivarsson said. "It'll be moving upward!"

"Speaking of moving upward," Bartram said, "who's going to look after all the wounded after the fireworks display?"

"Let's not get too negative now," said Ivarsson.

"Look who's talking."

"I'll be making my way to Skansen Kronan as midnight approaches," Ivarsson said.

"I'll see you there, then," said Bartram.

"I thought at first that we ought to think special thoughts when the clock strikes twelve, but I don't think we'll have time for that," Ivarsson said. "We'll be too busy calming down the youngsters."

"Not only the youngsters, I'll bet," Bartram said.

Louise Valker's mother was alone in the house, which was lit up on the outside but dark inside.

"She didn't have an enemy in the world," she said as soon as Winter had introduced himself.

No. Perhaps what had happened to her wasn't personal. He could see her in his mind's eye. Her face. Her body. The writing on the wall, which looked fainter at the bottom where the blood had dribbled. The light from Vasaplatsen was not far away. The same light as in his own apartment.

Louise's mother was tall, powerfully built, leaned forward when she walked—back trouble? She might have been around sixty-five, seventy at most. She showed him into a living room that was mainly in shadow. There were two framed photographs on the low coffee table. Louise when she was about twenty, and when she was some ten years older.

"She should have stayed here," her mother said. "But I suppose that wouldn't have worked." She looked at one of the photographs, spoke to it. "She was good at her job, and there aren't so many ladies' hairdressers in Kungsbacka."

"Did she have a lot of friends?"

"Well . . . she had quite a few when she was a teenager, I suppose."

"Did she have a best friend?"

"I've answered that before, surely? I told the man who was here . . . after it had happened."

"Yes, I've read what you said then. But I was thinking more specifically about the idea of a best friend. You didn't seem to have discussed that."

"Really? Oh. Maybe because I couldn't recall one then." She was looking Winter in the eye, but the room was so dark that he couldn't make out her features. Just the shape of her head.

"My husband died five years ago," she said. "Louise's dad."

Winter said nothing.

"He was her best—best friend," she said, and Winter could hear from her voice that she was crying. "She missed him so much."

"They were pretty close, were they?"

"Very close."

Winter waited a few seconds.

"But she had quite a few other friends?"

"They came and went. It's not easy to remember them all."

"And then Christian came along."

"Yes, then he came."

Winter noticed an altered tone of voice now.

"Did you see them often?"

"No."

"What did you think of Christian Valker?"

She didn't answer. Winter could see part of her face, now that he'd become used to the gloom.

"Christian Valker. What did you think of him?"

"They hardly ever came here. I don't think he wanted to come here, and Louise did whatever he said." She looked at the photographs again. "She listened to him more than she did to me." Winter heard a deep sigh, as if she were gulping for breath.

"I never liked him." Now she was looking straight at Winter, and he could see her eyes. "I don't think Louise liked him much either." She shifted on her chair. "She might never have."

"Did she tell you that?"

"More or less."

"Meaning what?"

"I don't think he treated her well."

"Did she tell you that?"

"She was thinking of leaving him."

"Did she say that?"

"It was only a question of time."

Winter repeated his question yet again, but didn't get an answer. In the end she said that a mother knows things like that.

Winter continued questioning her about Louise's life. He received vague answers regarding her boyfriends, evasive answers, just as when he'd asked about her friends, and best friend.

He stayed for an hour. When he returned to his car he switched on his mobile phone and found that he had several messages. The first was from Ringmar. The boy had been trying to contact him, Patrik. He didn't want to say what it was about. Ringmar had the kid's phone number, in case Winter didn't have it handy. Ringmar didn't know if he'd been phoning from home, as he'd hung up so abruptly.

Winter rang Ringmar, but there was no reply. In the bathroom, perhaps. Winter found the road home not too bad. It was still snowing, but more gently now. Traffic was moving faster than it had been when he'd driven south earlier. It was starting to get dark. The day was giving up the ghost, and he sympathized.

The piled-up snow at the side of the road was sometimes high, but in places the wind had blown it into the fields. It was like a wall, a hundred yards long. The Wall. Wall. His mind was wandering as he drove back toward the metropolis. Wall. He'd thought about it briefly, for the first time in days, while in the dark house at Kungsbacka. Wall. Vall. Vallgatan. Desdemona wasn't in Vallgatan, but it wasn't far away. Those middle-aged men dressed in black, among all those piles of CDs and all those computers, posters. Wasn't there a shop selling CDs in Vallgatan? Had it closed down? There was nothing in the case notes about a record shop in Vallgatan. It must have closed down. He remembered passing by a shop selling music in Vallgatan, years ago. He thought of Patrik, and his friend who'd had the Sacrament CD. Where had he bought it? Didn't he say Haga? But that wasn't certain. Had Winter been too excited to ask the right questions? Did he have any more questions?

He came to the industrial district and turned off toward the docks. He phoned Ringmar and was given Patrik's address.

"Is he going to call back?"

"He didn't say."

"What did he sound like?"

"Hard to say. It was so funn—"

"Did he sound upset? Scared? Calm?"

"A bit . . . upset. Maybe."

"Surely he could have told you what it was about."

"Don't think I didn't try."

"This isn't my personal case."

"The kid didn't say anything. He hung up the moment I said you were out. He didn't ask for your mobile number, and I didn't have a chance to say anything else before he slammed the receiver down."

"All right, all right."

"What are you going to do now? Call in on him?"

"I'm already on my way. I'm at Linnéplatsen now."

Ringmar mumbled a good-bye and Winter continued driving northward. Ringmar was the last person he wanted to fall out with. It was Winter's own fault if Patrik was not keen to talk to anybody else. He must have given off the wrong signals, given the impression that this was Winter's case and nobody else's . . . that it was essential for him, Winter, to be the one contacted first. This sort of thing could cause problems, delays.

He parked illegally on the other side of the road and walked up the three flights of stairs. There was an aroma of cooking. The walls were painted, but a long time ago. Somebody somewhere was playing music, and the bass echoed around the stairwell. There was a bicycle on the second floor, and a plastic shopping bag full of empty bottles outside one of the doors on the third. Winter rang the bell, but could hear nothing from inside. He rang again. Still no response. He knocked on the door several times. There was a scraping noise from inside. Somebody opened the door slightly. The man was between fifty and sixty and looked like an alcoholic. Winter could smell the telltale old wine plus some more recent fuel. The man was drunk, possibly dead drunk.

"Who ish it?" A woman's voice could be heard from inside the apartment. "Ish it Perrer?" The voice was slurred. "Ish it the quack?"

"Who are you?" the man snarled. "Wodduyawant?"

"I'm looking for Patrik," Winter said.

"What the fu—Wotsie done?" the man asked, glaring at Winter and his ID.

"He's been trying to get in touch with us," said Winter.

"He'sh not well," the man said.

"I beg your pardon?"

"He'sh got nothing to shay," the man said.

"Is Patrik at home?" Winter said, raising his voice. He could see the woman now, in the hall. As she staggered toward the door, he could see the fear in her eyes, perhaps something else.

"He'sh got nothing to shay," said the man again. Winter decided to act, entered the apartment, pushed the man out of his way and against the wall, and continued into the hall.

41

Patrik's father collapsed in a heap behind Winter, and the woman had fallen into a doorway on the left. Winter went quickly through the long, narrow apartment. He could find no sign of the boy, so went back into the hall and looked down at the man, who didn't raise his head.

"Where's Patrik?" Winter asked. "Where's the boy?"

"Eesh . . . out." Saliva was hanging from the side of his mouth. He seemed to be more drunk than ever and on the verge of passing out. "Eesh out." He waved his hand in the direction of the door.

"What's the matter with him? Is he injured?" Winter took hold of his arm, but could feel only bone under the coarse shirt. "What have you done to him, you bastard?" Winter squeezed harder, had the feeling he was in danger of losing control. He let go of the arm, sank down on one knee, and tried to make eye contact with Patrik's father, but it was no longer possible.

The woman had reappeared, leaning against the wall, gaping at the intruder.

Winter stood up.

"When did Patrik leave here?"

She shook her head, refused to answer such an obnoxious jerk who had broken into their lovely apartment. People couldn't just burst into . . .

"I'll be back," Winter said, dashing down the stairs and into the street, at the same time dialing on his mobile phone the number he'd looked up in his address book.

"Is that Hanne? Erik Winter here. Have you seen Patrik? In the last couple of hours or so?"

"No. I can ask Maria. She's just come home."

"I'll wait."

He could hear the conversation in the background. Hanne returned to the phone.

"No," she said. "She was out with another friend. But they're supposed to meet tomorrow afternoon." There was a pause. "Here, I hope."

"Can I have a word with her?" Winter said, and waited until Hanne had handed over the receiver.

"Hello?"

"Hello, Maria. This is Erik Winter, from the police."

But she didn't know what Patrik had wanted to say, didn't know where he was at the moment. He might be at Java or one of the other cafés in Vasagatan. Or round at Jimmo's. She had Jimmo's number. Yes, she'd tell him to get in touch with Winter the moment she heard from him. And a happy New Year to you as well.

Winter ended the call and tried the number he'd been given, but there was no reply.

He drove home, parked in the garage, and went to Java. All the tables were occupied, but none by Patrik. The air was heavy with cigarette smoke. There was a strong smell of coffee and hot chocolate, damp clothes, and perhaps perfume. The average age was eighteen at most. There were handbags or shoulder bags on every table. Young men even carry handbags nowadays, Winter thought. Practical, no doubt, but not for him. He'd suggest to Halders that he should get one.

He walked among the tables and felt like an alien.

It was similar in some of the other places along the street, and still no sign of Patrik.

He would call again but Winter was worried, and it was not primarily because of the investigation. He tried Patrik's home number one last time, but nobody answered. The boy would phone again.

The procession flowed through the center of town. The Goddess of Light was at the front, on a float. It's like a catafalque, thought Winter, observing from his living room window. Habakkuk's daughter. The procession wriggled like a glowworm down below in the early evening, continued eastward over the crossroads. The mass of spectators was a black sea, filling all the streets and choking all the buildings.

Not everybody has booked into the Empire State Building, not everybody is flying back and forth over the lines of longitude in order to fool time. We are having a nice, peaceful time here and we can smell the flowers, he thought as one of the floats passed by under his window: a gigantic bouquet of flowers made of wood, or whatever it was, chipboard, surrounded by living flowers.

He felt Angela's hand on his shoulder.

"Are you sure you don't want to go out?" he asked.

"Absolutely certain," she said, sniffing at the long-stemmed rose he'd given her a few minutes before. "We're having a nice, peaceful time here and we can smell the flowers."

"All the rest of Gothenburg is down there," he said.

The phone rang. His mother answered in the hall.

"Erik, it's for you," she shouted.

Angela looked at him.

He took the couple of strides necessary to get to the living room phone.

"Hello . . . er . . . It's Patrik."

"Hello, Patrik. How are things?"

"Er . . . all right, I guess."

"Where are you?"

"I'm around at Ria's place. What do you want?"

"You were trying to get hold of me yesterday."

"Oh, it was nothing. I had an idea, that's all."

"Tell me what it was, then."

"Well . . . er . . . that guy who came down in the elevator. You know, in that building where the mur—"

"I'm with you, Patrik."

"I think he was wearing a uniform."

"Why do you think that?"

"Under his overcoat, I mean."

"Why do you think he was wearing a uniform?"

"I dunno, it just looked like that."

"What kind of a uniform?"

"Well, it was sort of . . . with things on. Dark blue . . . with things on, maybe his shirt was light blue, and his overcoat sort of opened up a bit . . . when he went out of the door and there was a flash of something sort of gold on his shirt. In front of it."

"You sound as if you're describing a police uniform, Patrik."

"Yes, well."

"Did you think of a police uniform?"

"Not then."

"Now, though?"

"Maybe."

"Anything else?"

"What?"

"Did you see anything else that could be part of a uniform?"

"Well . . . it could have been a belt or a strap, but I'm not sure if I saw that."

"What about his head? Now that you've had time to think. Did he have anything on his head?"

Winter watched the tail end of the procession wriggling away toward the Avenue. A snake. It looked like a snake now, thinner at the tail end, wriggling from side to side and followed by the black mass filling the street and the park.

Angela was still standing at the window, rose in hand. It sounded as if his mother was filling the shaker with ice in the kitchen. Charlie Haden and Pat Metheny were playing "Message to a Friend" at low volume.

"He didn't have anything on his head," Patrik said.

"All right."

"There is one thing . . . I've thought about it a lot."

Winter waited, said nothing. His mother looked into the room. Angela gave her a smile.

"I think I've seen him somewhere else," Patrik said.

Bartram followed the procession at a distance, taking parallel streets and giving way to the crowds of people who seemed to be getting forced back from the center of activities.

He waited at the corner. The Goddess had turned left and was coming toward him. There were twice as many people as usually turn out for special festivities.

Some people near him were singing. Others were hugging one another with sudden, jerky movements. Everything was so tremendously big. The newspapers had almost killed themselves in their efforts to outdo each other in hyping the millennium. The television was even worse.

Nobody thought any longer that all things electronic would break down. Everything would work just as badly as usual, he thought. The trams would continue not running. People would still get furious. People would still spit at him.

He continued northward. The procession began to close up as it approached its destination at Lilla Bommen. There were still a few idiots who hadn't caught on to what was happening, standing by their cars on the road, ringed in for the evening, and indeed the night, by the cheering crowds.

People were keeping an eye on the sky over the river, waiting. It had grown cold again, and people's breath formed clouds that slowly rose and grew denser. That could start it raining, thought Bartram, but the mist dispersed higher up and suddenly the sky over Hisingen exploded.

Two thousand years of pyrotechnical skills came to a climax. It started with a fan of gold that covered the whole province.

Winter was in the kitchen preparing the New Year's dinner. He could hear his mother's and Angela's voices in the living room. He took a sip of the champagne he'd served earlier. Dry and light. The best champagne should be served early in the evening. Angela had sniffed at it, then drunk a little of the best table water on the market. Patrik was an observant boy and he was always strolling around town. Half a million people lived in Gothenburg, and that wasn't all that many. You kept seeing faces. Once, twice, three times.

They could talk to him after the holiday. It was an opening, possibly a beam of light.

He decided to concentrate on the first course. The fish stock was ready and strained. It had been simmering for four hours the previous night, and had been made with fish bones, a leek, shallots, fresh ginger, white peppercorns, and water.

He mixed the dressing and put it to one side: the stock, fresh lime juice, grated horseradish, sea salt, and a little freshly ground black pepper.

He carefully stirred a teaspoon of freshly ground, unrefined sugar and half a teaspoon of sesame oil into three eggs, then fried thin omelets in a little rapeseed oil before letting them cool on top of one another. Then he rolled each of the omelets and cut the rolls into thin slices and put them on one side.

He had just finished opening the oysters, two and a half dozen. He checked them again, then cut twenty-five rinsed sugar snap pea pods diagonally and blanched them in boiling water for thirty seconds before cooling them with cold water. Having drained them, he mixed them in a large bowl with finely chopped red onion, a little watercress, and some leaves of a lettuce known as upland cress that had a delicate, slightly hot, peppery taste. Finally he added the thin slices of omelet.

He heated up some more oil in a deep frying pan and sautéed the oysters very quickly on both sides at a high heat. He repeated this several times, then placed them on top of the salad, one by one. When he had finished, he drizzled over the dressing. He carefully tossed the oyster salad, divided it onto three plates, endeavoring to be as fair as possible in distributing the oysters.

He thought that should keep them going until the more substantial course, which was rack of veal with mashed garlic potato and pesto. The meat had started to turn brown and interesting smells were coming from the oven. It was spiced with coarsely chopped cloves of garlic, newly ground black pepper, and olive oil—he'd put the ingredients into the mixer and turned them into a paste, then rubbed it into the veal and allowed it to marinate for five hours.

For Morelius, Gothenburg was like a sea of fire. No. It was the sky that was a sea of fire, constantly shifting shades of red, never still. The official fireworks display had been followed by the unofficial ones, everybody competing with everybody else. He'd heard that five or six people had had accidents with rockets already, and it wasn't midnight yet. You could hear ambulance sirens occasionally, but as far as he knew, nobody had died so far.

The slopes leading up to Skansen were full of people, mainly youngsters. The police were in position. Many of them were in uniform. He saw a girl hanging around Ivarsson's neck, trying to give him a kiss. Ivarsson allowed it to happen, then bowed graciously by way of thanks. All was calm. No panic. It was just after eleven. Skanstorget, below where he was standing, was starting to fill up, like a semiarctic Times Square. Morelius had never been to New York, but he'd seen pictures.

He was a bit to one side of the worst crush when the couple emerged from the crowd. They recognize me, of course, he thought. This is a small town, really. They seem to be sober enough. Now they're coming to me.

"A happy New Year," Maria said.

Morelius nodded in acknowledgment.

"You're keeping calm, I see," Morelius said.

"Straight edge."

"Eh?"

"We're not getting carried away," she said. "We're taking nothing, drinking nothing."

"Very sensible."

"You enjoy everything all the more," the boy said.

"Exactly."

"Are you busy tonight?" she asked. "Is there a lot to do?"

"It's all been very quiet so far."

"But the fun will be starting soon."

"Yes."

"Will you be working all night?"

"Until four in the morning."

"All over town?"

"In the town center. But they might call out the circus to somewhere else, of course."

"This is amazingly good," Siv Winter said.

"It was hard to find decent calamari," explained Winter.

"Just as well," said Angela.

"Oysters are even better when they're cooked," Winter's mother said.

"I agree."

"Anyway . . ." Winter said. He raised his glass of Sancerre. "Cheers."

"Cheers," said Angela and his mother, raising their glasses.

They drank and put their glasses down again.

"I think it's going to be a lovely year," his mother said. She looked at them. Winter hadn't noticed any difference in her voice or movements. She had drunk two glasses of champagne earlier and said no to a Tanqueray and tonic, which was a good thing, good for the taste buds apart from anything else. Anybody who drinks liquor before a gourmet meal should have it injected intravenously. "Is it awful of me to say that? After what's happened . . . your father and the . . ."

"It's good that you can say that, Mom." He could still taste the trace of dry earthiness after the wine. "It is going to be a lovely year."

"It hasn't even started yet," Angela said, looking at the clock and thinking about fate again. She took a sip of bottled water. The baby was calm just at the moment. She ate a little more and thought about all the things that were going to happen in the next few months. Nothing would be the same as before. It's going to be a new life. I'm not sentimental, but there's something special about New Year this year. The millennium coincides with us.

The new millennium boomed its way over Gothenburg, the churches sang. Two thousand people stood arm in arm in Skanstorget and sang "Auld Lang Syne" in exactly the same way as they were doing in Aberdeen, in a straight line westward over the North Sea.

Twenty jet planes appeared as the clocks struck. One for every century after Christ. Two thousand people held their hands over their ears and screamed in delight. The jets crisscrossed the sky in a series of highly dangerous maneuvers, then headed off back to the south.

Patrik and Maria were holding hands, and some of the people around them burst into tears. One girl threw up into a snowdrift. Two men fell backward into the snow and made snow angels. That tempted several more to start a sort of wave of snow angels. After three minutes there was a long line of people making angels in the snow. The fireworks display seemed never-ending. The angels shone red and gold.

"Do you feel anything special?" Patrik yelled.

"I feel a bit older," Maria yelled back.

"We're a thousand years older," Patrik yelled, and a gang of revelers who had set up a meal on some stones started cheering.

"A happy New Year, Angela," he said, kissing her. She tasted of the four drops of Lanson champagne she'd allowed to moisten her tongue. "A happy New Year, Mother," he said and bent down over his mother, who had lain down and was crying.

The twelfth chime from the radio died away. The apartment seemed to change its proportions as the red sky was shattered by all the shooting stars from the fireworks display. They heard the jet planes.

Then they heard an ambulance in the street below, the first of the night.

Angela kissed him.

"A happy New Year, Erik."

"It will be the best yet, I can promise you that."

When the door opened he said what he'd intended to say and the man smiled, or gave a laugh. Then he kicked the door in and hit the man twice in the stomach and the chest with his baton. He put on the mask.

She shouted something from inside and he walked through the hall that was striped from the explosions outside, the wall was changing all the time, new patterns were appearing. He heard the man groaning on the floor behind him. Hard to breathe.

She was getting up from the sofa but he was there before she could stand up and he did the same to her. She made the same kinds of noise after half a minute, groaning, gasping for breath. A wheezing sound from somewhere farther down.

He was panting so much himself that he thought he'd be forced to take the mask off in order to get some oxygen to his brain. He turned to the window, pulled his mask halfway up, and gulped in air. The world out there was a glittering slit through his almost-closed eyes. His headache was getting worse.

 JANUARY

42

He was driving southward. There were thousands of people in the streets, staggering from pub to pub. Singing to one another. Last night I dreamed something I've never dreamed before. He braked suddenly when a group of revelers ignored a red light and reeled across the road ahead. Waved two fingers at him. They had become immortal.

The dashboard clock said four-thirty as he navigated the round-about at Korsvägen. Liseberg amusement park was ablaze with light, as if it were another time of year. The first buses were stopping for people who had decided to go home.

As he turned off Bifrostgatan it looked as if thousands of people were standing outside the apartment building. The flashing lights of the police cars had taken over from the fireworks. Reality had returned. Police officers were dealing with the crowds, sealing off the road. An ambulance drove off with a roar, hurtling out of the side street into the main road.

He parked carelessly in Häradsgatan and walked over the patio again, in through the front door. He'd been here recently. It seemed like only yesterday, but it was in another millennium.

The newspaper boy was outside the door with one of the public order officers from Mölndal.

"How many are there inside?" Winter asked.

"Only the pathologist."

"Don't let anybody else in. When the other crime unit officers arrive, ask them to wait here."

"Okay."

"Keep the boy here as well," Winter said, nodding at the boy who was cowering against a wall, shaking. Pale face, seventeen, maybe sixteen. He could be Patrik's cousin. Same thin body, same staring eyes.

It was quiet inside the apartment. No metal music, and Winter wasn't sure whether he'd expected any. Perhaps the silence was worse.

A ceiling light was on. There were streaks on the walls in the hall, lines, patches, specks; a pattern that reminded him of the sky that night, as if somebody had tried to re-create the last big sky before the world renewed itself.

"It's blood," said Pia Fröberg, who was standing in a doorway at the other end of the hall. She was an outline in the same way that the police officer had been in the apartment in Aschebergsgatan.

"I saw an ambulance."

"She was still alive when they left here."

"Good God!"

"I give her little hope," Fröberg said. "Very little." Winter had moved closer. The experienced pathologist looked scared, her face was as if sculpted in marble. Not scared. Tense, on guard.

She backed up a couple of paces and Winter went into the room and looked around. "It's the same," she said. "It must be the same murderer."

Bengt Martell was sitting on the sofa. His clothes were in a heap on the floor in front of him.

"He was holding her hand," the doctor said.

"Yes."

"The paper boy had a mobile phone. I don't understand how he could have acted so quickly. That he had the presence of mind." She gestured toward the hall. "The door was standing open when he arrived."

"Did she say anything?" Winter asked, turning to Fröberg. "Was she able to say anything?"

She looked at him as if she didn't know how to formulate her reply. She looked again at the sofa. Winter had sat there. Bengt Martell had sat there and Siv Martell had sat in the armchair, which was still where it had been the last time.

"She'll have difficulty ever speaking again," Fröberg said. "Irrespective of how it goes."

He looked at the body on the sofa. The same position as Christian Valker had been in.

"Where is his . . . where is his . . ." asked Winter, but couldn't bring himself to say the word. "Maybe it isn't . . . him sitting there. Martell. Is it him sitting there?"

"Yes," she said.

"But where the hell *is* it then?" Winter said, his voice getting louder and louder.

"With . . . her," said the doctor. Winter watched her face changing, growing whiter.

"What? What the hell . . . what do you mean?"

"It was with her. When we took her to hospital. We weren't . . ."

"Holy Moses," Winter said.

He paused in front of the sofa. Perhaps it was his imagination, but he thought he could see the exact outline of the woman's body. It wasn't only the blood.

Every second was like a millennium. Fröberg had left him now and he refused entry to everyone else.

There was no cassette player there. There hadn't been one there *then,* and nobody had brought a stereo system since he, Winter, had been there.

There's always a first time for everything, he thought. I've never been to visit people in their home and then returned later to find . . . this. To find them in this state.

The writing on the wall was clear in the light from the streetlamps outside.

Capital letters. Six of them.

STREET

Nothing else. STREET. The letters seemed to be pressed into the wall, but even so had started to trickle down from the bottom, to dissolve away. STREET. As in WALL STREET.

Winter could feel a shudder coming, but fended it off. "Street" was the English for the Swedish "gatan," and since *V* and *W* are the same letter in Swedish, did it mean Vallgatan? Was Wall Street Vallgatan? Were you leading my thoughts in the right direction, God, yesterday or the day before or whenever it was? Is it Vallgatan we're looking for? Is that where the answer is? Don't lead me astray here.

Fröberg had come back. He could hear her behind him, but he didn't turn around.

"She's still alive," she said. "They just phoned."

Winter nodded.

"But she's not awake, if you were thinking of that."

"I wasn't thinking of that."

43

"Go through the place with a fine-tooth comb three times over," Winter said to Beier when the forensic officers had begun their work.

"Don't insult me, Erik."

The deputy head of the technical squad looked focused, sober. Beier had celebrated the New Year in moderation.

"I suppose the new millennium has to begin somehow or other," he'd said when they first arrived, and it was not meant as a joke. There was nothing to joke about here.

The forensic officers were moving carefully around the man on the sofa with his right hand extended, as if in greeting.

Beier came back from the kitchen.

"There seems to have been three of them around the table."

"The same as at the Valkers'," Winter said.

Beier nodded, then nodded again at Ringmar, who came in from the hall with snow in his hair. Winter could see that there was a heavy snowfall outside in the dawn.

"She's still alive," Ringmar said, "but not exactly thanks to her own efforts."

"No more detailed prognosis?" Winter asked.

Ringmar shook his head.

"I saw him there," Ringmar said, looking at the man on the sofa. "At the hospital."

Nobody wanted to comment on that.

"I'd like to have him now if I may," said Fröberg, who had been waiting patiently to take the body away for the postmortem.

"Okay," Winter said.

"If she survives, we've got the bastard," Ringmar said.

They assembled at eight-thirty. The room smelled of damp and perhaps also day-after breath. The whole of Gothenburg had a hangover, but in that conference room they all needed to be alert.

"Is Bergenhem ill again?" Halders asked as he came into the room.

Winter nodded.

"That's some goddam headache he's got."

Everybody sat down apart from Winter.

"I don't need to remind you how important the next few hours are," he said.

The photographs were passed round. Here we are again, Djanali thought, sitting here like Peeping Toms.

"It's the same bastard," Halders said. He was red in the face and smelled of spirits when he leaned over Djanali, and took one of the pictures with his right hand. He had phoned her at about one-thirty, but didn't seem to remember. Or maybe he's just pretending, she thought. "Of course it's the same bastard, isn't it?"

"We don't know yet," Winter said.

"Oh, come off it." Halders looked at Winter. Halders's eyes were clear from a distance, as wide open as they'd go. A sure sign of a man trying hard to be sober. "You surely don't think it's a copycat?" Halders said.

"This isn't an exact copy, is it?" Sara Helander said.

"No," Winter said. "Beier's looking more closely at the writing as we speak, but obviously it's very reminiscent of the previous murders."

"How much detail has there been in the press, in fact?" Djanali asked.

"We've managed to keep the writing quiet," said Möllerström, the registrar, rising to his feet. "And the music, too. I haven't seen that mentioned anywhere in the newspapers. Nor on the radio or television." He wasn't looking at anybody in particular. "It's actually a bit odd."

Winter thought about the men in black at Desdemona. They didn't appear to be chatterboxes. On the other hand, it might not have been flattering for the genre if the murderer's choice of music had become public knowledge.

"No music this time, then," Halders said. "If we can call it that."

"No."

"No music while you work."

Djanali groaned.

"One thing I do know," Halders said, waving the photograph in his hand. "About reactions to this." He looked around the room. "When it becomes known that another couple has been in the wars, if you can put it like that."

"What do you know?" Ringmar asked.

"When this comes out there'll be a mad dash for the divorce courts," Halders said, looking around the room again. It sounded as though somebody sniggered, but Djanali saw Winter stiffen. "Who wants to be married or living with some . . ."

"That's enough, Fredrik," Winter said.

Djanli thought about Winter. He used to live alone but now he had a partner and would soon be a father. On the other hand, Fredrik was already a parent, but lived alone. When had he last seen his son? He'd tried to talk about that last night, but had had trouble finding the words.

"So they didn't have a very big party," Helander said.

"Three people, it seems."

"The same as last time."

"Yes."

"So we're waiting for Siv Martell to tell us. They must have been planning to dine with the murderer."

Winter said nothing.

"How is she?" Djanali asked.

"Still unconscious," Ringmar said. "Or perhaps they're keeping her anesthetized."

"Exactly what happened to her?" Halders asked.

Winter told him. Several of those present breathed in sharply, there was a sort of whisper all around the room.

"Oh, hell," Halders said. "And they think she's going to be able to give evidence?"

"Meanwhile, we have a job to do," Winter said.

"Wall Street," Halders said.

"Yes?"

"Vallgatan. That's where the record shop is. It's still there, I suppose?"

"Yes."

"Didn't that kid buy the CD there?"

"That's right," Winter said. "He was there. We've checked."

"Did they have several copies?"

"We're checking that now," Ringmar said. "Again, I should add. The question's been asked before."

"He must have bought the crap somewhere," Halders said. He turned to Ringmar. "But it doesn't have to have been there."

"No. But what are you getting at exactly?"

"It could have been bought in the USA. That's where the CD comes from, isn't it?"

"Canada."

"Canada. All right. That's not far from the USA. What's in the USA? Wall Street's in the USA. New York, to be exact. Manhattan, to be even more exact."

"Are you saying we should start looking in Manhattan?" asked Börjesson, one of the younger detectives.

"Manhattan," Winter said.

"Yes . . ." said Halders.

"Manhattan . . ." Winter said again. "Janne, could you get a copy of the words for the Sacrament CD, please?"

Möllerström hurried off to his office, but was soon back. Winter took the paper and started reading.

It had been somewhere toward the end—there. He looked up, then down again. There it was. In two places.

He read the lines out loud, two lines from each location in order to make the connection clear. They were about Manhattan. Short visits to the earth.

"Sonofabitch," Halders said. "I was right."

"But it could be a coincidence," Winter said. "We must keep reminding ourselves that all these clues, or whatever they are, might be pure misinformation."

"But we shouldn't take any risks," Halders said. "I hereby volunteer to go and check on the spot."

You're already on your way to the seventh century B.C., Winter thought, and read the lines again. Manhattan was there, albeit as a place deep down in the Valley of the Shadow of Death.

"This only makes matters worse," Djanali said. She looked at Winter. "How could we check if it's relevant? Are you really going to send Fredrik to Manhattan?"

Everybody burst out laughing. Winter cleared his throat.

"This is only one part of a bigger picture," he said. "Manhattan or not."

"There are Manhattans all over the world," Djanali said. "A newsstand could call itself Manhattan. Or a pizzeria."

"What does it mean?" Möllerström said. "The word must mean something."

"It's Indian," Ringmar said. "We'll check up on that."

"Why did he let her live?" Djanali asked out of the blue.

"A good question," Halders said.

"What does it mean? The fact that she's still alive?" Djanali looked at Winter. "Have you spoken to Lareda about that?"

"Not yet."

"Something disturbed him," Halders said.

"Any ideas?" asked Winter.

"The newspaper boy."

"It's incredible," said Möllerström. "For the first time ever *Göteborgs*

Posten is published on New Year's Day, and just see what the poor newspaper boy finds."

"No national holidays for newspapers anymore," Halders said. "Talk about a successful premiere."

"It happened before then," Winter said. "The murder."

"The telephone," Halders said.

"We're checking calls."

"A second person involved?"

Ringmar shrugged.

I'm fed up with speculation, Winter thought.

Just then Beier came in without knocking and stood beside Winter.

"I thought you'd want to hear this." He paused for effect. "The man's fingerprints . . . Bengt Martell's. They match several we found in the Valkers' flat."

"Sonofabitch," Halders said.

No more speculation, thought Winter.

"They've always sworn blind they'd never been there," Halders said. "Both when Aneta and I were there, and when Erik paid them a visit."

"So they were lying," Ringmar said.

"He was, at least," said Winter.

"The sperm," said Halders. "When you've taken the blood samples you'll find the DNA test shows that the guy's sperm was on the Valkers' sofa."

If there's enough blood left for that, thought Djanali, who had passed on the photographs, one at a time.

"You think there was something fishy about that relationship, then?" Helander said to Halders.

"I think their mutual interest was sex," he said. He stood up. Beier was still there. "You can never tell about such things by looking at people, you can't even suspect it, really. But more and more people are trying to make new contacts . . . and they want to have sex with one another. Wife-swapping parties. Group sex. God only knows what else." He paused for breath. "Swinger parties. I think they're called swinger parties."

"You seem to know all about them," said Möllerström.

"Shut your trap." Halders remained on his feet. He turned to Winter. "It's a way of meeting people. We've been wondering about how they got to know each other, haven't we? They didn't seem to have anything in common. No past history or anything like that."

Winter recognized his own train of thought.

"Good thinking, Fredrik," he said.

"Now that you mention it," Beier said, "we did find a few pornographic things at the Martells'. Magazines."

"Which magazines?"

"I can't remember. Just a minute." Beier went to the telephone on a table in the corner, and dialed the direct number to his team at the scene of the crime. He asked his question, listened for a moment, then replaced the receiver. "Right. They were *Aktuell Rapport*."

"Bingo," shouted Halders, who was still standing. "Bingo."

"Would you mind explaining?" asked Winter.

"I noticed a few copies of *Aktuell Rapport* hidden away at the Elfvegrens' place. Under the table." Halders looked at Aneta Djanali. "Isn't that right, Aneta. I mentioned it to you at the time."

"Yes."

"*Aktuell Rapport*," Halders said. "And the good news is that the Elfvegrens are still alive and kicking." He turned to Beier. "When do we get the DNA results?"

Is that the lowest common denominator? Winter thought, sex contacts?

"You're saying that they run ads for sex contacts?" he said. "In those magazines?"

Halders looked at him as if he were a child.

"Just a few little ones," he said.

Ads for sex contacts, Winter thought again. It could well be that the Valkers and the Martells met in that way and got to know each other. Or are we jumping to conclusions? They'd have to come down hard on the Elfvegrens again. And if that really is how the couples met . . .

"That could be how the murderer came into contact with his victims," Ringmar said, thus voicing Winter's thoughts.

44

He had no memory of any words, no screams. Everything had been an enormous weight bearing down on him like a mountain.

Over the threshold and into the room and then he'd gotten him.

There was a noise . . . and the light outside had become stronger and stronger and he could no longer see. It seemed like hours. Somebody was waiting.

Somebody was running up or down the stairs, shouting. The light was still as strong as ever.

Was it the light that put a stop to it?

It had been like the last time. They'd eyed him up and down. This time she didn't laugh. He was the one who'd laughed. Laughed away any chance of mercy.

There was a whistling noise in his eardrums.

In the elevator on the way down he kept his face averted. The light outside had become normal. He slipped as he walked over the street. There wasn't far to go.

He had saved something. He knew now. It grew lighter again, looked different.

Ringmar was loitering by the window. His face was marked by lack of sleep. He looked out. The afternoon emitted an air of calm. It had never been as quiet as this.

"A happy New Year, Erik."

"And to you."

Winter rubbed his face, over his eyes. He'd phoned home. Angela sounded worried. His world had become hers in a much more straightforward way now. Maybe that was a good thing, for their future together. His absence wasn't only his. It wasn't just *him* who shot off into the night like a lost soul. A year or so ago Angela had said that he seemed to prefer living among the dead than the living. That was at the end of a discussion that had grown more and more desultory as the night wore on, and they hadn't referred to it the next morning. But he'd never forgotten her phrase: a life among the dead.

She'd witnessed his life at close quarters now, the brutality it involved. The cruel telephone call in the early hours. Rarely did they come at any other time. Fumbling for his underpants as the adrenaline started to flow.

"Börjesson hadn't found anything called Manhattan here in Gothenburg when I visited him."

Winter scraped his hand over his chin and reached for his cigarillos. He rubbed his eyes again. He had a burning sensation in his eyes.

"Our man could well be wearing a uniform," he said. "I was sitting here before you came, thinking about that."

"Really?"

"Two neighbors said they thought they saw somebody in uniform not long after midnight. A bit vague about when. And a bit vague about how sober they were by that time."

"Was there any trouble in the area?"

"A bit of a disturbance. The Mölndal police had sent a car to somewhere just a few blocks away."

"Could they be the ones the neighbors saw?"

"I don't know. As I said, they were a few blocks away. Why should they leave their car and go there? I don't know. I haven't had time to talk to the guys yet."

Winter stood up without lighting his Corps and started pacing up and down.

"Where can you get hold of a uniform? We'll assume that we're talking about police uniforms."

"Why?"

"Let's just assume that, Bertil."

Winter struck a match.

"But you're not assuming that it's a police officer?"

"If it is, I'll resign on the spot."

"Hmm."

"Do we have to start investigating two thousand police officers?"

"No, no. The whole business is diffuse enough already."

"What do you mean?"

"Uniforms. The boy's just making assumptions."

"A bit more than that. It's a bit more than that. Patrik had spent ages thinking about this. Waiting for insight to strike him." Winter drew on his cigarillo and looked at Ringmar. "And we spoke a moment ago about the neighbors in Mölndal."

"Okay. Uniforms. Some idiot or other could have thrown his old one in the trash can instead of sending it off to be burned."

"Hmm. Or somebody could have had one made. Police uniforms are not copyrighted."

"Had one made? Privately, you mean?"

"Yes."

"But they're not made in Sweden anymore, surely?"

Winter didn't answer. He had an idea.

"Doesn't the City Theatre keep uniforms? For the plays they put on?"

"If they're police plays," Ringmar said.

"And films. Police films certainly exist, no doubt about that." The smoke from his cigarillo was invisible in the thin winter light coming in through the window. "Didn't I read something about some film or other being shot in Gothenburg? A thriller? I seem to remember reading that. In *GP*."

"I've no idea what you read," Ringmar said.

"Haven't you seen anything about that?"

"Certainly not." He turned to look at Winter. "But if you think we might have loaned police uniforms to some film company, you can forget it. Our madam police chief has said no to anything of the sort."

"I know."

"A good thing, too, I think," Ringmar said.

"I'll follow up all this, but first there's something else I need to see to," Winter said, putting his cigarillo in the ashtray and going to get his overcoat.

Not many people were out and about. He drove past Ullevi Stadium, which cast a shadow over the canal covered in gray-black ice. The sun glinted on Lunden Hill.

He parked in the quiet street. A dog started barking in the distance. It sounded as if somebody was shoveling snow, and when he walked around to the back of the house he saw it was Benny Vennerhag.

The gangster was wearing a red woolly hat and a black suit. He was shoveling away some icy lumps of snow with considerable skill.

"You're always working when I come to see you," Winter said. "If it's not pruning roses, it's shoveling snow."

Vennerhag was panting heavily and leaned on his shovel.

"I thought I'd make the place look good, ready for your arrival." Vennerhag stood the shovel against the wall, took off his woolly hat, and slicked back his thin blond hair with the aid of some sweat from his brow. "It was a big surprise when you called."

"For me too when you answered. I thought you'd chartered a yacht in the West Indies."

Vennerhag eyed Winter up and down.

"You thought almost right." He opened the back door. "Something cropped up and got in the way."

"What was that, Benny?"

"Business. You know. How's Lotta, by the way?"

"Enough of that."

Benny Vennerhag had once been married to Winter's sister, but it had lasted only a few days. The memory lingered with Lotta Winter as a vague nightmare.

Vennerhag led the way into a big room facing the garden. The picture windows stretched almost from floor to ceiling.

"I'm afraid the swimming pool is snowed over," Vennerhag said. "But you can have a sauna if you like."

There were bottles on the tables, and glasses. The room smelled of smoke.

"I haven't gotten around to cleaning up, only snow shoveling." He picked up a bottle and held it to the light. The whisky glinted like amber. "It tasted good last night, but I don't know about now." He looked at Winter. "Would you like a coffee or something?"

Winter shook his head.

"You look a bit under the weather, if I can put it like that."

"I had to get up early this morning."

"I heard something on the lunchtime news."

"What did you hear?"

"Something about a murder, in Mölndal. That's about all they said."
He looked at Winter again, more closely this time. "You don't think
that I—"

"No. But I need some information."

"What about?"

Winter thought for a moment.

"This business," he said. "The murder. Or murders. There've been
several."

"Really?"

"How are things on the stolen goods front nowadays?"

"I beg your pardon?"

"Have you got tabs on what's being passed around?"

"No." He asked Winter again if he wanted something to drink, and
Winter said no. Vennerhag excused himself and went to the kitchen to
get a bottle of mineral water. "Where were we? Trafficking in stolen
goods? That's not a nice thing to do."

"Uniforms."

"Uniforms? What kind of uniforms?"

"Do you know anything about trafficking in uniforms? A batch
that's been stolen . . . or borrowed, for some reason? Or just individual
uniforms that have been in circulation. Maybe for . . . copying."

"I don't go in for terrorism, Erik."

"I'd like you to look into it."

"I've never heard of anything of that sort."

"Look into it."

"Yes, yes. All right."

Winter lit a Corps.

"Has there been any talk about anybody in your circle of friends
who's been acting oddly?" he asked. "Or outside it, come to that?"

"Now you've lost me."

"Do you have tabs on all the madmen?"

"Don't you?"

It was a long shot. Winter was asking about Vennerhag's acquaintances in the criminal world. He wasn't getting any answers he could use.

He thought for a moment about how much he ought to reveal. He gave Vennerhag a brief outline of what had happened.

"That's a loner," Vennerhag said. "He doesn't belong to our . . . business circle." He fetched the coffee he'd made anyway. "Somebody like that always works on his own. Mad. No contacts."

"There's another thing . . ."

Vennerhag poured out some coffee for Winter and himself.

"Do you move in any circles that . . . well, that play sex games?"

Vennerhag gave a start and very nearly dropped his cup of coffee into his lap.

"What the hell was that you said?"

"That's one of the lines we're following. We have grounds for suspicion. All right. You are as pure as the snow on the pool out there, but you're not ignorant."

"About what?"

"Sex parties. Swinger parties. Wife swapping. That kind of thing."

"You're talking about other people's private lives here, Erik. How should I know anything like that?"

"Is it common?"

"No idea. Are you suggesting that me and my . . . business contacts are likely to be involved in that kind of thing? I'm starting to get angry."

"That's not what I said."

"Back off."

"I'd like you to do something for me. If you know anybody who acts as a contact for these kinds of goings-on, I'd like to hear about them."

"How do you mean? A sort of spider in a web?"

"Yes, something like that. Somebody who knows others who know others."

"As I said, I have no idea."

"But you know others who know others," Winter said.

"Will you leave if I nod my head?"

"Yes."

Vennerhag nodded his head and Winter stood up.

"I heard you were expecting a new member of the family," Vennerhag said.

"How did you hear that?"

"Come on, Chief Inspector. The private lives of celebrities are simply not private. And in the circles I move in, you're a celebrity."

The Elfvegrens were politely asked to come to the station to be asked some questions in connection with the investigation.

"No more Mister Nice Guy," Halders said to Djanali.

"No. I mean, you're widely known as a kind, friendly man."

"No more."

Winter had decided that Halders should do the talking when the Elfvegrens came. Winter sat in the background.

"Why do you have pornographic magazines in your apartment?" Halders asked.

Erika Elfvegren's face turned as red as a beetroot. Per Elfvegren was nonplussed.

"*Aktuell Rapport*," Halders said. "I saw a few copies when we came to talk to you."

"What . . . what's this all about?" Per Elfvegren said.

"It's about murder," Halders said. "People you knew have been murdered. That's what this is about."

Good, Fredrik, Winter thought, making himself invisible in the corner diagonally behind Halders. The woman had looked at him, as if seeking support. Winter hadn't moved a muscle. No more good cop, bad cop.

"What does that have to do with the . . . magazines?"

"That's what we're wondering as well. That's why we're asking."

"I don't understand," Erika Elfvegren said. Her face was still red and she kept pulling her skirt down over her knees. Halders had touched a nerve. Winter could see that her husband was taking it better. He was starting to get angry in the midst of his humiliation.

"What the fuck is all this?" Per Elfvegren said. "It's ridiculous." He looked at Winter, but Winter was busy with his notebook. This was an important moment in the investigation. Perhaps we're closing in now, he thought. Perhaps this is where it starts getting serious. "Are we being accused of anything?" Elfvegren said. "And we damn well don't have any copies of that magazine you're talking about. *Fib Aktuellt,* did you say?"

"*Aktuell Rapport,*" Halders said. He turned to the woman. His profile softened. Winter saw it happen. "All we want is some help from you. This is nothing to get worked up about. I know lots of people who regularly buy *Aktuell Rapport.*"

"I'm damned if *I* do," said Per Elfvegren. "And I never buy it myself."

"But you did know people who bought it," said Halders. "The Valkers. The Martells."

Halders glanced at Winter. They hadn't found any copies of the magazine in the Valkers' apartment. But Winter had a brainwave and made a note.

"What does that mean?" the woman said, in a tiny voice. "You said yourself it's not unusual." She looked at her husband. "If that's the case."

"I'm not sitting here and asking you questions for fun," Halders said. "There have been some grisly murders in Gothenburg this winter, and you knew all the victims." He eyed them up and down, one after the other. "We're looking for the common denominator, you must understand that."

"I had no idea they had magazines like that," Per Elfvegren said.

You're lying, Winter thought.

"Neither of the couples?"

"No."

"Not the Martells?"

"Eh? . . . What?"

"You didn't know that the Martells bought *Aktuell Rapport*?"

"No."

"You didn't know the Martells at all, in fact?"

"Eh? . . . No."

It's not easy to lie, Winter thought. You have to be consistent.

"You didn't react a minute ago."

"What?"

"You've never said that you knew the Martells, but a minute ago you didn't react when I referred to them as people you knew."

"I must have misunderstood you," Per Elfvegren said.

"So you didn't know them, in fact?"

"No."

"I'll ask you one more time," Halders said, looking at Winter, who was sitting, pen poised, ready to make a note of the lie. Per Elfvegren knew that they knew. He looked at his wife. It occurred to Winter that perhaps one of them was in this on their own. "I'll ask you one more time: did you know, or did either of you know, the Martells, or one or other of them?"

Erika Elfvegren seemed to have made a decision. She looked at her husband, and then at Halders.

"Yes," she said. "We knew them both."

"Them both? What do you mean by that?"

"We knew both couples. The Martells too."

"So, that's established," Halders said. "The next question is: how?"

"What do you mean?"

Halders turned to look her in the eye.

"What kind of a relationship did you have with them? Dinner parties? Barbecues? Sporting events? Hiking? Sexual intercourse?"

The end justifies the means, Winter thought. Before long Per Elfvegren will get up and thump Halders. If he's innocent he will. I would have.

"I still don't understand what this has to do with it," Erika Elfvegren said.

"Tell us again how you got into contact with them," Halders said.

45

Morelius turned right at the roundabout. The traffic had intensified during the afternoon. Somebody flashed his lights in greeting. Perhaps there was a general feeling of benevolence toward the police.

"It wasn't much worse than any other street party," Bartram said. They were talking about the millennium celebrations.

"A few more people."

"A lot more people. But reasonably well behaved, even so."

"Did you go off duty early?" Morelius asked.

"What do you mean?" Bartram turned to face his colleague.

"I didn't see you at three."

"There was a bit of trouble outside the Park Hotel."

"I never got that far."

"You didn't miss much."

"There was a bit of trouble with unlicensed taxis as well."

"So I heard. The Africans had overstepped their bounds."

Most drivers of unlicensed taxis in Gothenburg were foreign and were far from integrated into Swedish society. They'd divided the center of town among themselves. Iranians, Iraqis, and former Yugoslavs operated in the Avenue, as far as the moat. The Africans ruled the roost in Östra Nordstan. The borderline between them was strictly imposed.

The radio crackled into life. Bartram responded. A drunk on a number-three tram at Vasa/Viktoria. Possibly two. The driver had tried to offload him for causing serious disruption.

"Roger," Bartram said. "We'll take it."

The tram was standing in Vasagatan just where it was due to turn right. Cars were able to pass normally. The passengers had disembarked and were dotted around outside. The drunk was clinging on to the rail at the entrance.

A woman was beside him, presumably they were together. Bartram and Morelius parked on the cycle track and approached the tram. The man was brandishing a broken bottle. The woman was trying to take the bottle from him, but melted away as the police came closer.

"Put that down," Bartram said.

The drunk gurgled some kind of response and swung the bottle at Bartram, but lost his balance and fell out of the tram, doing a half-forward roll and collapsing in the slush. He made no attempt to move. The woman screamed and stared at the police officers. She was drunk, but more mobile than he. The man was now grasping at fresh air, hoping to find something to hold on to to help him to sit up. Morelius couldn't see any blood. The man managed to get onto all fours, then stand up unsteadily.

"I'd like to get going again," said the tram driver, who was standing next to Bartram.

"That's fine," Bartram said. "We'll take it from here."

Angela had started to waddle, really waddle. It was a nice feeling. Both of them were visible now, she and the child. They waddled out of the elevator and unlocked the front door.

If it was a girl, she'd be called Elsa. Perhaps. They weren't sure about boys' names. Erik had suggested Sture, Göte, or Sune. Why not all three? she'd said. Or if we call him Göte he can change his surname and become Göte Borg. Sounds like a great idea, he'd said, then gone back to his repulsive murder investigation.

She tried to avoid thinking about the apartment building up the street. The caretaker there also looked after their building. He'd given her a knowing smile when they'd met in the entrance the other day, as if they shared a secret.

The telephone rang. She took the call with her overcoat still on. She was sweating after coming from the wet snow outside into the higher temperature of the elevator.

"Hello?"

No reply, and she shuddered, felt suddenly cold, as if the sweat had turned to ice.

"Hello?"

She'd almost forgotten, it was months ago.

She could hear somebody breathing, somebody was listening. Her hand had started to tremble. She felt a movement in her stomach, then another. There was a click and the line was free again.

There was a scraping noise outside the door and then it opened. She gave a start.

"Angela!"

Siv Winter was standing in the doorway, key in hand.

"I didn't think there was anybody in."

Angela replaced the receiver.

"What's the matter?" asked Siv. "Are you sick?"

"Yes."

"Come on, take off your coat and sit down." She helped Angela with her coat and boots. "Would you like a glass of water?"

"Yes, please."

Siv went to the kitchen and returned with a glass.

"You should take things easier. Do you have to keep working until the last minute?"

"It's not that."

"What is it, then?"

"Some bastard keeps phoning this number. But never says anything."

"Really? Nuisance calls?"

"I wouldn't call them that." She took a drink and kept the glass in her hand. "It's horrible. The last one was some time ago, but this—"

"Did you get one of those calls just now?" Siv asked, interrupting her.

"Yes."

"What does Erik say about it?"

Angela took another drink. Well, what did he say? They'd agreed that the calls had stopped, but they'd have to do something about them now.

"That we should wait, but now I'm not so sure about that."

"You have to tell him."

Bergenhem's head was burning as if the sky were on fire. All the fireworks seemed to have eased the pain, but now it was much worse. Far worse.

He'd screamed out loud during the night, talked in his sleep, rambled. Then he'd dozed off and when he woke the pain was still there, but more like a muffled swishing noise.

His vision had started to blur. That happened in fits and starts.

Martina came back from next door. Ada had simply laughed and waved. He was all dressed and ready, sitting in the hall, fastening his shoes.

"I'll drive," she said.

He closed one eye as they drove over the bridge. A ferry was just leaving. The roofs were weighed down with snow. White caps, Ada had said the other day, pointing up at them.

He started to feel terrible. Martina was driving like an ambulance driver.

They were attended to immediately. X-rays, cold light, lamps shining into his eyes. He knew what it was, had known for some days. That's perhaps what had been dictating his mood all year, his restless worry. He thought he could hear them talking about the operation. The words were bouncing and thudding all around him.

"I want to keep my sight."

Everybody was dressed in white. White caps. He tried to get through to them. Please spare my eyesight.

The Elfvegrens had eventually wriggled off the hook, got away from Halders. They hadn't admitted anything, but they had left their fingerprints.

"I refuse," Per Elfvegren had said. "You have no right to do this."

"When we are conducting an investigation we have the right to take fingerprints for purposes of comparison," Winter said. "For specific purposes."

"Who decides that? Who makes the decision?"

"The person in charge of the investigation."

"And who's that?"

"Me."

They were waiting for answers. Beier's team was just as eager.

"Sensitive stuff, this," Halders said.

"What stuff? Their leisure activities?" Winter asked.

"Nobody wants to talk to a few cops about their screwing activities."

"No, obviously not."

"They should have thought of that before they went in for it," said Halders.

"You'll have to hold your horses for a while," Winter said. "It's possible that they've never been there. At the Valkers' place."

Elfvegren had said, during the very first interview a long time ago, that they'd been around at the Valkers' once, but he claimed later that his memory had let him down. He'd changed his mind. They had never set foot in the Valkers' apartment.

"A load of crap," Halders said. "I'll bet on it."

"What's the prize?"

"A year's subscription to *The Beano*."

Beier phoned.

"They match," he said. "They've been in the apartment."

"What about the Martells?"

"Nothing there."

Winter winked at Halders and replaced the receiver.

"Did you take the bet?"

"We'll bring them in again," Winter said.

"Blood tests," Halders said. "Don't forget the sperm stains."

"We can't do that yet."

"Are you sure?"

Winter was sure. The prosecutor would never agree to blood tests. That needed convincingly specific evidence, and all they had was a couple of witnesses, sort of witnesses.

"Copulating witnesses," Halders said. "Two-backed monsters."

"Don't get ahead of yourself, Fredrik. Maybe they only had coffee."

It was the last time. She'd spent more time on him than he was worth. That's the way he saw it.

"I'm sorry I'm late," he said.

"No problem."

"We had to take a drunk to the cells."

"Was it difficult?"

"He fell asleep in the car." He sat down. "We knew him, incidentally. Indirectly, at least."

"Meaning what?"

"It was Patrik Strömblad's father. I've come across Patrik once or twice and it was—"

"Don't remind me," Hanne said.

"I didn't mean it like that," Morelius said.

He didn't need to remind her. Maria seemed to be a changed character now, but the memory was crystal-clear and so were the aftereffects. The investigation by the Social Services. "Whatsoever a man soweth, that shall he also reap."

They left the subject of Patrik and his father and spoke about Morelius himself.

He told her about his visions again.

"I can't stop thinking back to that . . . accident," he said.

Hanne nodded. Morelius looked down at the table. He wasn't looking at her now, he was avoiding her eyes.

"She's haunting me. That poor—"

"What do you mean?"

"What do *you* mean?"

"You said she was haunting you."

"Did I?" He looked out the window. "Sometimes I don't know what I'm saying. I mean that the experience I went through that day is haunting me, and maybe not only that. Other things that have happened."

Later he said that he felt there was no point in continuing as a police officer.

The caretaker sat in his usual office, waiting for Winter.

"Newspapers? Magazines? I don't have anything to do with newspapers and magazines."

"You mean people take them to the trash room themselves?"

"Always."

"Okay."

"I want to make a little report, incidentally."

"Go on."

"Somebody keeps getting into my little . . . cubbyhole in your building, and he sits there eating or drinking soda."

"Your cubbyhole? You mean your office down in the basement?"

"Somebody keeps getting in there."

"Breaking in?"

"It's happened several times lately, in fact. I've never seen anything like it."

"Is the door damaged?"

"No. It must be somebody with a key. Unless he picks the lock."

"Has anything been stolen?"

"Not as far as I can see." The man seemed to be keen that Winter didn't downplay the crime. "It's not very nice, is it? You can't go around doing things like that, can you?"

"No. You should make an official complaint."

"I'm doing that now."

"Okay. But you should contact the police station in Chalmersgatan as well, so that the formalities can be completed."

Winter said good-night and walked the few yards home. He took a deep breath. January would soon give way to February, and there'd be a whiff of something else in the air.

They'll be well on the way to spring already in London, he thought. A few years ago he'd worked on a distressing case there. He didn't want to think about it now. Instead he thought about the fact that the old guy hadn't smoked a single cigarette while Winter was with him.

His mother shouted something from the kitchen as he entered the hall.

"Angela's gone out to buy some bread," she said when he came into the kitchen.

Winter went to meet Angela when she came back.

"There's been another phone call," she said.

"What do you mean? Who called?"

"Whoever it is that rings and breathes and doesn't put the phone down again."

"Shit!"

"What should we do?"

"It's probably best to get a new number. Unlisted."

"Good."

"I've thought about doing that before."

"Just do it now."

That should put a stop to it, at least. But what's going on? Should I speak to Birgersson and ask for an official bug? For what? It's part of the investigation, Sture. He suddenly thought of what Lareda Veitz had said. He saw Angela's profile in the door. Convex. He thought about the cellar.

He checked his notebook and rang the number of the office he'd just left. The old man was still there.

"You said that somebody had been in your office, drinking soda."

"Yes."

"How do you know?"

"The bottle was still there. It's happened several times. Several bottles."

"Have you kept them?"

"Kept and kept. I've put three to one side. I was going to take them away tomorrow."

46

Winter put on his gloves and took the elevator down. It was the first time he'd collected proof material in his own building. The world was getting closer.

He had to wait a few minutes until the man arrived.

"I didn't realize it was so important," he said. "Good thing I mentioned it."

He unlocked the door.

"Look. No scrape marks around the lock as far as I can see."

Winter agreed.

"This is a rapid response by the police, I must say." He opened the door. "You evidently take everything seriously."

"Yes," Winter said. No, he thought. This was a response he didn't really understand himself. Angela's worries. Some silent telephone calls. Somebody who shouldn't be there sitting in the cubbyhole drinking soda. A case for Detective Chief Inspector Winter.

They were Zingo bottles.

"I'll take them," said Winter, picking up all three in his gloved left hand.

"I can see you've worked as a waiter," the caretaker said.

Bergenhem regained consciousness and looked around the room. If this was paradise, it looked remarkably like the world he'd just left.

He could focus his gaze. There wasn't the same burning sensation in his head. Martina's face was distinct, close. She said something, but he couldn't hear what. He tried to sit up. She said it again.

"Lie still, Lars. You have to be careful."

Somebody in white was hovering behind her. It could be an angel, and in a way that's what it was. He recognized her face first, then her voice.

"I just called in on my way past," Angela said.

Same here, he thought.

"You look better."

I have nothing to compare with, he thought.

"Where am I?"

"In a ward at the Sahlgren Hospital."

Now I remember. Now I can ask the big question.

"Has the tumor gone?"

"The tumor?"

"The brain tumor. Did you take it out?"

Perhaps he detected a little smile in the midst of all the solemnity. She turned to another angel in white, who seemed to nod.

"We suspected encephalitis at first, but it turned out to be the nastiest attack of migraine imaginable."

"Migraine? But I've never suffered from migraine."

Beier had the bottles. I didn't know they still sold Zingo, he'd said. Is this another message for us, do you think? he'd asked. Winter had waved a hand dismissively: end of messages.

He listened to Sacrament again and read the text. The singer was wading through blood in Lower Manhatten, but managed to get away and head for the outer Cosmos. Winter had listened to it so many times by now that he could make out more and more words without the crib sheet. Or perhaps he was just imagining that.

Whenever he was walking through the town he used to listen for black metal, for echoes of roars from predatory animals in the Muzak in department stores or in record shops. He would react whenever anybody passed by listening to a Walkman. A lot of people did. They all sounded the same, a rhythmical buzzing noise, shut in the earphones. They would occasionally remove one of the phones, or the earpiece. Never black metal. But always very loud.

Winter had never listened using earphones. He wanted to move in time with his music, but from a longer distance away. Now that he was looking out for such things he noticed that several colleagues came to work with portable CD players.

He had spoken to Lareda again, briefly. They were in his office.

"Was he interrupted?"

"No."

"What happened, then?"

She didn't answer at first. She was standing by the window. It was lighter than it had been at the same time on the previous occasion. February was approaching, within reach outside the window.

"He's on the way to . . . somewhere else," she said.

"What does that mean?"

"I don't really know myself." She was watching the sun starting to set. "Either he lost interest halfway through, or it was the intention from the start. Wait . . ."

"How can I make progress with this investigation?"

"Think about the words," she said. "The words on the wall."

"Is that a more important clue now? Wall Street?"

"I think so."

"I don't know."

"Try following it."

"Following it?"

"It won't be taking you away from him."

"Will he make another attempt?"

"The same type of crime? No. I don't think so. Not any more."

"Why not?"

"Do you remember what I said about one world governed by God and another world governed by Satan?"

"I will never forget it."

"Something has happened in the world. His world."

"Something has happened? What do you mean 'happened'? Has somebody taken it over?"

"Perhaps."

"Who? God?"

"More likely the other one."

"The Devil? That would mean a world without hope, that's what you said last time."

She nodded and sat down again. Winter had switched on his desk lamp. His desk was clear.

"In a world without hope there's no longer any point fighting on," she said. "That means he can't get any farther. It no longer makes any difference what he does."

"So he'll stop."

"He might."

"So our hope lies in a world without hope, governed by Satan?"

Ringmar had been in touch with Swedish Television. They were making a film in Gothenburg about crime and punishment.

"They've been around for quite a while. Several months in fact, with a break. The interesting thing is that it involves forty police officers in uniform."

"Forty? Forty actors?" Winter asked.

"No. Extras."

"Are they filming at the moment?"

"Yes. I talked to the boss. He's the one in charge."

"Ah," Winter said, with a smile.

"What I mean is, he's the one who arranged for the costumes."

The location was within walking distance, so they walked. The team was busy in the extensive car park outside the Gamla Ullevi stadium. Six-foot walls of snow lined the edge of the car park along the Allé. There were cameras and microphones everywhere, and two women were shouting into megaphones. A group of police officers were leaning against a panda car. Extras, Winter thought.

Ringmar went off and came back accompanied by a tall man with mutton-chop whiskers, wearing a green woolly hat and a brown leather jacket, and carrying a folder.

"We're innocent, honest," he said, and looked at Winter. "Interesting that you want to take a look at what we're doing here."

"What do you mean by that?"

"Well . . . the film's about a DCI in Gothenburg, and his adventures."

"You don't say."

"A guy about your age, in fact."

"There aren't any," Ringmar said. "Erik's the youngest in Sweden."

"This is a film."

"Ah, of course."

"So you're making a film about a detective chief inspector, are you?" Winter said.

"It's a series for television about stark reality in Gothenburg and Sweden in general. STV drama."

"When will it be shown?"

"Probably in a year or so."

Winter looked around at the actors and technicians.

"What's happening here just now?"

"At the moment we're recording a scene in which the DCI visits a television team to ask some questions in connection with a case he's working on."

"All right," Winter said, and went to peer into a nearby camera. "Let's get started." He pointed at the squad car and the group of extras wandering around close to it. "Are you the one who procured those uniforms?"

"Yes. But not from you."

"No, I'd gathered that."

"The Gothenburg police are hopeless when it comes to that kind of thing."

"Quite right too," Ringmar said.

"Where did you get them from?"

"Swed Int, the supply depot in Södertälje."

"How many did you order from there?"

"Forty-one, to be precise. One in reserve."

"Can you account for them all?"

"How do you mean?"

"Could any of them be stolen?"

"Anything can be stolen. It's possible to break into the costumes store. But, obviously, when we've finished, I'll check that they're all there before we send them back to Södertälje." He looked at the squad car. "I've already done that once. This is the second round of recordings we're into."

"How much longer will you be doing this?"

"Until we've finished." He turned to Winter. They were more or less the same height, but he was about ten years younger than Winter. "Could be another month. Maybe longer. You can ask the director."

Winter nodded.

"So you always know where your props and costumes are?" Ringmar asked.

"Well . . . I won't pretend I'm a hundred percent certain while we're actually shooting. Not every second."

"So somebody could take a costume home in between takes, or whatever they're called?" Winter asked.

"Well . . . I suppose it's possible."

"Has it happened?"

"I expect so. If we're working late and have to start early the next morning . . . well . . . it could be that not all the uniforms spend the night in the costumes store. I don't actually know, now that you mention it."

"All right."

"I do know one thing, though." He tucked the folder under his arm and rubbed his hands to warm them up. "These scenes we're shooting . . . some of them . . . take place in the suburbs and involve immigrants, ethnic groups that are a part of the plot, I mean."

Winter nodded.

"I don't want any more problems than necessary. . . . No more than all the crap that can be flying around when we're shooting, that is. So I mean . . . here we have forty extras running around in police uniforms and sometimes they nearly all appear at the same time . . . out in Hammarkullen or Biskopsgården say, and I don't want to run any risks now, do I? Are you with me? That some bastard says something to an immigrant, or something. Makes the most of his opportunity, if you like."

"You mean that one of the extras might turn out to be a racist?"

"Exactly."

"And?"

"And so I've sent in all the . . . let's call them 'police extras' . . . all their ID numbers in." He held up the file. "We've got all their names and addresses."

"Sent them in? Sent them to the police, do you mean?"

"Yes. For a check, so to speak. To be on the safe side. You've got their details already."

Beier had received the results of the DNA test from the lab in Linköping.

"It was Mr. Martell's sperm."

"Well, I'll be damned," Ringmar said. Whatsoever a man soweth, that shall he also reap, he thought.

"How is his wife?" Beier asked.

"In a bad way," Winter said.

"Still more dead than alive," Ringmar said.

"I don't like that expression," said Beier. "You're either dead or you're alive. There's nothing in between."

"Have you seen her?" asked Ringmar.

"No."

Ringmar said nothing, and it was an eloquent silence.

Winter broke it.

"The Elfvegrens are coming in again tomorrow."

Winter dialed Patrik's home number. The boy's father answered, as if he'd been standing next to the telephone. Winter said who he was.

He had consulted the social services: the family was notorious, but there was no history of abuse.

Winter had been thinking about Patrik. It was his duty to report a suspected case of ill treatment. It was his duty, his obligation. Nevertheless he had hesitated, spoken to the authorities. But now he had filed the report. He didn't say anything to the man.

"I'm looking for Patrik."

"Can't you leave us alone?"

"Is Patrik at home?"

"You're the second damn cop who's phoned today and asked for him."

"I beg your pardon?"

"The third, in fact."

The murder investigation, Winter thought. But three cops?

"Who were they?"

"Can't remember."

"Did Patrik speak to them?"

"He's not at home."

"Can I speak to him now?"

"He's not at home, I keep fucking telling you."

The weather was fine again when they drove to Landvetter. There was not much traffic about as early as this in the afternoon.

"Blue skies both here and there," his mother said. She turned to look at her son. "I'll come back when the baby's arrived."

They drove around the terminal and parked in his usual place. He got a cart and they went into the departure lounge.

"There doesn't seem to be any delay," his mother said, then burst into tears.

He gave her a hug.

"This is the first time . . . the first time I've flown down there on my own," she said in a faint voice. She looked up at him. "I know you want me to stay here, but I need to go. Can you understand that?"

"Yes, I understand."

"I mean, that's where . . . where your father is."

Winter could visualize the grave, the grove, the mountain, the hill, the sea, the soil.

"He's there and he's also . . . here."

"Of course he is, Erik."

Let's not go into it now, he thought, but he is here. Perhaps it's easier this way.

She waved from the escalator up to customs and the departure gates. She was late.

He waited by the car until the plane rose like a heavy migrating bird of silver. It was sucked into the blue five thousand feet up.

 FEBRUARY

47

There were fingerprints on the Zingo bottles, but far too many.

"Give me something to compare them with," Beier had said.

"I can't very well compare them with everybody's," Winter replied.

"Half Gothenburg has held these bottles." Beier looked at Winter, who seemed to be scrutinizing him. "Are they so important?"

Winter didn't reply.

He drove to Häradsgatan and parked in roughly the same place as before. The wind was stronger now, and had brought clouds with it. Sleet was falling. It was afternoon again.

The clouds were scudding swiftly over the sky when he looked up at the windows of the Martells' apartment on the sixth floor. He walked around to the entrance with its glossy tiles. A notice on a door to the right announced that a representative of the property owners would be available to tenants in this office between five-thirty and seven-thirty on the first Monday of every month. That's this evening, he thought. They had spoken to the caretaker, but had failed to get any new information out of him.

So, somebody wearing a police uniform had passed by here in the early hours of New Year's Day. Nobody had seen a police car. But a uniform had been seen. The witnesses all agreed: a police uniform. That had been after the murder, or murders, if Siv Martell didn't survive. What lay in store for her if she did? Winter wondered. Not an enviable life, he supposed.

He walked back to the street and continued for a few yards as far as the crossroads. A woman was maneuvering a stroller into the Cityfast supermarket. Winter approached the shop. It looked run-down in the late winter light. There were streaks of rust in joints and around pipes, and in cracks in the paint. Winter went in. The shelves were half-empty. The only customers were Winter and the woman, who was already waiting at the checkout. At the back of the barren shop was a meat counter, the blue light around it highlighting two faded and soiled posters showing butchered cuts.

He went out again. An advertising poster had blown out of its frame and was fluttering toward the crossroads. It flew over the lawn on the other side and was stopped by the Martells' seven-story apartment building, pressed against the wall level with the windows on the second floor.

The woman with the stroller followed him out. She turned left past a pizzeria and a baker's shop, both of which had closed down. Chairs piled one on top of the other could be seen through the pizzeria's windows. She continued up a hill. Winter could see the church tower. He went down the steps in the opposite direction. The buildings were in a hollow and the clifflike hillside blocked the view. Nobody was coming or going now. Cars were swishing past on the main road ahead. He walked as far as the shop called Krokens Livs, where he'd bought a packet of Fisherman's Friends last time. Two posters advertising films were fluttering in the wind, like the last time. They were the same films, *City of Angels* and *The Avengers*.

Also like last time, a bus stopped ten yards away and several old people got out. Winter went into the shop to buy a box of matches. He stood among the dairy products, packets of chips, film, candy, dishwashing brushes, and newspapers. He could see the wind blowing outside through the glass in the door. The woman at the checkout was foreign, possibly from Turkey or Iran. She smiled. Winter took his matches and paid. Behind the woman was a picture of the building he was standing inside. It had been cropped drastically but showed the minimarket in bright sunshine. There was no doubt that it was the same shop. Then as now there were two frames on either side of the door with posters advertising films. The photograph had been enlarged to about two feet by three and was partly obscured by advertisements for cigarettes. Winter couldn't remember seeing the photograph last time, but surely it must have been there? The colors were faded and pale. The picture could have been three years old, or ten. An old man was standing outside the shop door, holding a pile of newspapers and looking like the proud owner. But it wasn't his appearance that made Winter continue to stare at the picture, forgetting all about his change and not hearing when the woman spoke to him. Over the man's head was a sign that was no longer there. Now the sign projected at right angles from the wall, and on it was written Krokens Livs.

In the photograph the name in red letters was different: Manhattan Livs.

Börjesson had asked again at Powerhouse, the record shop in Vallgatan. The young detective didn't mind going there. He'd been there before, on his own time.

"I've been here before. Privately, if you see what I mean."

"That's nice to hear." The young man behind the counter was chewing away and working through a pile of secondhand CDs. "I haven't seen you." He opened a jewel case and checked the condition of the disc. "But I've been away this last year." He closed the case, looked up at Börjesson and smiled. "New York, L.A., Sydney, Borneo."

"That sounds great," Börjesson said. He took a CD out of his pocket. "Do you recognize this?"

The man took Sacrament and looked at the cover, then at Börjesson.

"If you mean have I sold it, yes, sir."

"You recognize the disc?"

"I recognize most things in the music line." He looked at the gloomy landscape on the cover. "Maybe it was this lousy drawing that made me long to get away to the sun." He opened the lid. "We had two," he said.

"That's exactly what I was going to ask you about," Börjesson said.

"It's not bad stuff if you ignore the production."

"I don't suppose you can remember who you sold them to, can you?"

"You must be joking! In the first place I'm not the only person working here, and anyway, I'm better at album covers than I am at faces." He turned the cover over and looked at the pictures of the men of darkness against the shocking-colored background. "Sometimes I can remember who I bought the disc from. Some people come in with mountains of CDs. Sometimes you come across a find." He looked at Börjesson. "This one's a borderline case." He took out the booklet with the words and leafed through it. "Why is it so interesting?"

"The music is linked to a case we're working on," Börjesson said.

"That murder I read about?"

"Why do you say that?"

"Well . . . it's the obvious thing." He looked at Börjesson. "The songs on this CD are pretty bloody. But fairly innocent, really." He gave a laugh. "It almost reminds you of that song. Blood, blood, glorious blood!"

"Have you any idea of when you bought the CD?"

"I'm afraid not. Maybe it wasn't me. No, it wasn't me. Have you asked the others?"

"Yes. They don't recognize it at all."

"I suppose it might have been me, then . . . I do remember that we had it . . . let me see . . . we had two, one of them was in the shop when I started . . . it's quite an old CD, of course . . ." He left the counter and went over to the hard rock section and scanned the titles. "Nothing here now. But we did have two, not at the same time, though."

Börjesson thought. Somebody had changed the music and now it was Led Zeppelin.

"When I took off there was one copy," the man said, looking at Börjesson. They were about the same age. "When I came back, it had gone."

"All right."

"We sell so much stuff it's simply not possible to keep tabs on every-thing, as you can imagine."

"I can imagine."

"We get all ages here, all races, all sizes."

Börjesson looked around the shop. There were more than twenty customers in the big sales area, all of them men. Most of them were youngsters, but there were some men in their thirties working their way through the racks, and at that very moment in marched a man who must have been about forty-five, with a pile of LPs in his arms. Two young girls followed him in.

"There's a fair amount of turnover among the staff as well. Several have come and gone this last year."

"Business is good, is it?"

"You can say that again." He went back to the counter and the pile of CDs that had now been joined by the pile of LPs. He stopped and turned to face Börjesson again. "As you're from the police you've reminded me that a guy kept stopping in and checking to see what we had in stock. Several times. A cop, that is. That was shortly before I went off on my travels."

"A cop? A police officer? How do you know?"

"I hope I can recognize a police uniform. I wouldn't recognize the man, but the uniform . . ."

"What do you mean by checking to see what you had in stock? As a customer?"

"Yes, obviously."

"Is that unusual?"

"That police officers come in uniform and check our stocks? I suppose he's the only one I've ever seen in here. You should ask the others. Didn't any of them mention him?"

"No."

He looked at Börjesson again. The man with the LPs was being served by another assistant. "Do you men have time to buy a few discs in working hours?"

The woman repeated what she had said. Winter dragged his eyes away from the photograph.

"Have you got anything smaller?" she said. "No small change?"

"I'm afraid not." He looked back up at the picture on the wall behind her.

"Did this shop use to be called Manhattan Livs?" he asked, pointing at the photograph. She turned to look, then spun back around on her chair.

"I don't know," she said. "I only recently started here."

Winter knew that the owner was a man. They had routinely interviewed all the people living in the vicinity and he'd read the transcripts, just as he'd read all the other material connected with the investigation.

"The man who owns it comes in the evening. Bertil Andréasson."

"Could you give me his telephone number, please?"

Bertil Andréasson answered after the second ring. Winter explained who he was and asked about the name of the shop. He had gone back to his office and hung his wet overcoat on a hanger next to the sink.

"I changed it when I bought the place," Andréasson said.

"When was that?"

"Er . . . nearly three years ago."

"And you changed the name right away?"

"More or less, yes. Manhattan . . . I couldn't see the link, to be honest. Mind you, I've never been to New York, but I don't think it looks anything like the area around Hagåkersgatan. Not the Manhattan you see in films, at least."

"Are you often in the shop?" Winter asked.

"I beg your pardon?"

Winter could hear the man's voice sort of stiffen, become more guarded.

"Do you often work in the shop yourself?"

"Why should I? When I have people working for me? You've met Jilna."

"She was only hired recently, I believe—isn't that so?"

"I had two others before her. And I have another job as well."

"Two other employees before her? Have they left?"

"One moved and the other couldn't count," Andréasson said.

"I have a few more questions to ask you," Winter said. "It would be better not to have to use the phone. Could you stop by my office?"

"What's this all about?" Andréasson said. "I've already talked to the police, after that murder. I don't know any more than I did then."

"It's just routine," Winter said. "When we're busy with an investigation we sometimes need to talk to people several times. If new facts turn up."

"What kind of new facts? Ah, yes! The name."

"I saw the photograph," Winter said.

"The picture of Killdén? Behind the counter? I've thought of taking it down at least eighty times, but some old customer or other might ask where the old guy's gone to, so I've left it there for sentimental reasons."

"Killdén? Was that the previous owner?"

"Åke Killdén. He used to own a few shops, but then he sold up and now he spends his time sitting in the sun."

"In the sun?"

"He bought an apartment, or maybe it was a house, in Spain. Costa del Sol, I think."

48

Bertil Andréasson had come to the station. It was obvious that he had been worried about how much they were going to ask about his other activities. Winter had tried to convince him that he wasn't interested in any work he did on the black market, provided he cooperated.

The shop owner gave Winter the latest known address of his two previous employees. Jilna had been working for him for around half a year. Five months, to be exact. She hadn't yet mastered the Swedish language but she could count and checked to make sure no bastard swapped the price labels on goods. She was also good at refusing to sell beer to young brats.

Winter had continued his conversation with Jilna before leaving the shop, but she hadn't seen anything or anybody worthy of note. He said that if she recognized any regular customers, he would take her some photographs or plant some of his officers in the shop to wait until she gave a signal when somebody she recognized came in. There are a few, she said. Okay, we'll put a plainclothes officer there, Winter thought.

Andréasson was unable to help when it came to regular customers.

"I'm not in the shop all that often, you see. I don't even live around there."

"Surely you must remember somebody coming in from time to time?"

"No . . . you'll do better asking Jilna about that."

"I already have."

Halders and Winter met the Elfvegrens again. It was in the same gloomy room. She looked as if she was feeling cold. Winter still couldn't decide if maybe this only concerned him. The husband. She looked to be in a state of shock.

"All right," Per Elfvegren said. "We have been there . . . for coffee. Twice, I think."

"Why did you lie about it?"

"I don't know."

"It's not usual for people to tell lies if they've only been around to have coffee with somebody."

"I suppose we were . . . scared," he said. His wife looked scared to death.

Halders sighed.

"Come on now, tell me the truth," he said.

Elfvegren didn't respond.

"You had a relationship, didn't you?" Halders said.

Elfvegren shook his head.

"We could be forced to give you a blood test," Halders said.

"Why?"

Halders explained, and Erika Elfvegren turned ashen.

Her husband bit his lower lip hard, and looked at Winter. Winter could see that he'd made up his mind, possibly to tell the truth.

"All right," he said. "We met them through an advertisement."

"What kind of advertisement?"

"The personal ads. To make contact."

"What kind of contact?"

Elfvegren looked at his wife and she nodded, although it was barely noticeable.

"It was an ad in . . . er . . . the magazine."

"The magazine? What magazine?"

"The one we talked about before. *Aktuell Rapport.*"

"Have I got this right now: you met them via an ad in *Aktuell Rapport*?"

"Yes."

"Is that true?" Halders asked, turning to Mrs. Elfvegren.

Her "yes" was scarcely audible.

"Did you place the ad?"

"No, we answered it," Per Elfvegren said. "It was an ad . . . their ad . . . that we replied to."

"When was that?"

Elfvegren gave an approximate date.

"It's the only time we've ever done it," she said.

A likely story, Halders thought.

"Did you meet the Martells in the same way?"

"No," Elfvegren said.

"How did you meet them, then?"

"Through the Valkers. But we . . . but we . . ."

"Well?"

"We never had a . . . relationship."

Halders said nothing.

"There were only the Valkers."

"Did the Valkers meet anybody else?" Halders asked.

"What do you mean?"

"When you had . . . a relationship. Were there other people present as well?"

"Never."

"Never?"

"Never. I swear to it," said Per Elfvegren. He looked as if he'd decided to tell the truth and nothing but the truth, but faces can lie.

"Did you hear about any other relationships?"

"No."

"The Valkers didn't say anything about other meetings? If they got together . . . in that way with anybody else?"

Winter admired Halders's tact now. Halders was growing into the role of occasional interrogator in chief.

"No."

The woman cleared her throat. She looked at her husband and cleared her throat again. She was about to say something. Halders waited. Winter was barely visible from the table in the center of the room, was not much more than a shadow on the wall.

"There was a . . . man," she said. Per Elfvegren looked genuinely astonished. "Louise once told me . . . about a man they'd met a few times."

Patrik was trying to read. It was evening. He had spent some time looking at the sky. There was something stirring inside him. Spring is on its way now, he thought. I have to get out more.

He was on the sofa and Ulla sounded in high spirits in the hall as she closed the apartment door behind her and kicked off her shoes. Patrik went to switch off the stereo in the middle of a song, then sat down again.

Ulla came into the room, taking two steps back in order to manage one forward.

"Where's Dad?" he asked.

"I dunno," she said, flopping down on the sofa some three feet away from him. He moved. "I left." She shook her head, slowly, from side to side. "He was making such an awful scene." She turned to look at Patrik, trying to focus. "You're a nice boy, Patrik. You're not like him."

Not like you either, he thought. Patrik stood up and she grabbed hold of his arm, hanging on to it.

"Can't you sit here for a bit and talk?" she said.

"I have to go."

"Just sit here for a bit." She was holding harder now. She started humming a tune, then suddenly burst out laughing. Oh no, the bitch was as drunk as a skunk. "Come and sit here next to Auntie Ulla and we can have a little chat." She tugged at his arm, pulling really hard now.

The sleeve of his sweater grew a foot and a half longer. He could smell the familiar stench of stale liquor topped up with fresh stuff.

She gave another heave and he lost his balance, falling on top of her.

The apartment door was flung open. As he fell he could hear the sound of his father staggering through the hall.

"What the hell . . ." He heard his father's voice and felt him grab hold of his arm and pull him up. It was his arm now and not his sleeve. It hurt and he screamed. He felt like his head would explode.

Maria was baking a sponge cake. It felt like two thousand years ago. Hanne watched the girl spraying flour all around her in the kitchen. A few years ago it was the only thing she did for a while. Sponge cakes. All right by me. Two thousand, one after another.

She went back to the living room, sat down on the sofa, and picked up her book again. The sky had turned dark blue, almost black, but the promise of spring was still in the air outside. Or is it just my imagination? she wondered. Or a dream about the light. We start hoping before winter has even started to go away.

There was a clattering in the kitchen. She loved that sound. A siren was howling from the direction of Saint Sigfrids Plan. A long, rising note that could well be from a police car. She'd learned to distinguish between sirens since starting work at the police station. She heard the sound once more, then it was cut off abruptly. Somebody breaking the speed limit, or maybe a crash. She thought of Simon Morelius and his awful road accident. He couldn't shake it off. The memory was too strong for him, painful. It could lead to him leaving the force. She didn't know of anybody else who'd made such a decision for reasons like that.

He kept repeating the horrific details, as if by describing them often enough he could make them go away. But the result was the opposite. She could recite them herself by now. But she hadn't been there, hadn't seen it all. The last time, he'd said . . .

The doorbell rang.

"I'll get it," she shouted, getting to her feet.

Patrik was standing outside. He had blood all over his face, a dried-up rivulet under one eye.

"Patrik!" screamed Maria, from behind her mother.

"A man!?" Halders said. "Louise Valker told you about a man?" Why have you kept this to yourself? he thought. It could have cost *lives!*

"Once . . ." she said, then fell silent.

"Go on."

Winter could feel the tension in his body, could see it in Halders. Per Elfvegren seemed to be paralyzed. His wife appeared to be calmer now. She'd been working her way toward this.

"She . . . she said they'd met a man a few times. That's all, really . . ."

Halders stared at her. The penny dropped.

"It never occurred to me that it could have anything to do with . . ."

"Tell me exactly what she said."

"I've already told you . . ."

"In what connection did it crop up?"

"I can't really remember." She looked at her husband. "But it was when we were alone."

"What did she say?"

"That they'd been visited . . . a few times . . . by a man."

"And?"

"I had the impression that he was . . . exciting."

"How did they meet?"

"I don't know . . ."

"Through an ad?"

"Yes, perhaps she did say that." She seemed to be thinking. "Something about them having been lucky . . . yes, that they'd been lucky with their advertisements."

"Had that man answered an ad?"

"I don't know."

"Had the man placed an ad?"

"I really don't know."

"Did you know him?"

"Certainly not."

"Did Louise Valker say what he looked like?"

"No."

"Nothing . . . personal about him?"

"Not a thing."

"Nothing at all?"

"No."

"His clothes?"

"No. Nothing about that."

"She just mentioned him, and that was all?"

"Yes . . ."

Winter heard a slight hesitation. Halders had heard it as well, waited.

49

Winter phoned Möllerström. The registrar answered after the first ring.

"Could you please get me the latest issue of *Aktuell Rapport,* Janne."

"You mean the men's magazine?"

"That's what I said."

Winter hung up and turned to the list of forty extras who were wearing police uniforms in the film based on the adventures of a detective chief inspector in Gothenburg. Why not an inspector's? Halders wanted to know. You'll be in it as well, Ringmar assured him. We'll all be in it.

"Should we do that, then?" asked Ringmar, who was sitting opposite Winter. "Have you spoken to Sture?"

"He says we should go ahead if we think it's worth the effort."

"Forty people," Ringmar said. "That means ten to fifteen officers tied up for perhaps a week. How long will we need per extra? An hour and a half? An hour? We'll have to track them down, check their addresses, arrange a meeting, interrogate them."

"And compare," Winter said.

"That's your job."

"I can get ten officers," Winter said. He lit a Corps. It was still reasonably light outside. The snow was still there. He looked Ringmar in the eye.

"Are we heading in the right direction here . . . the police trail? The uniform trail?"

"I'm damned if I know, Erik."

"Say what you think."

Ringmar screwed up his eyes, rubbed his forehead, and produced a noise like sandpaper on rough timber. His features became more marked in the twilight, his wrinkles seemed deeper when the sun was reflected into the room from the buildings on the other side of the river. There wasn't going to be any leave for Ringmar this February either. Perhaps when the grandchildren came. But the best time for skiing was already past.

"There has been talk of police officers—or police uniforms—a bit too often for us to simply ignore it," he said in the end.

"I agree."

"What Börjesson had to say about the record shop was most interesting."

"I agree."

"We've checked places where there are uniforms, but nobody has reported any missing."

"No."

"None at all."

"No."

"That only leaves the filmmakers."

"I agree."

"Perhaps it's an omen."

"A good omen?"

"Are there any good ones? I once saw a film called *Omen*. It wasn't exactly teeming with benevolence."

"There were several," Winter said. "Parts one and two, et cetera."

Ringmar rubbed his forehead again.

"I think we ought to get going on that."

"Will you take charge, please?"

Ringmar agreed, took the list, and went to his own office in order to start organizing the work. A messenger arrived with an internal mail envelope and the secretary raised her eyes heavenward. The girl on the front cover was scantily dressed. A big headline in red and yellow explained the best way to get sex at work. Winter turned the pages until he came to the personal column with the subheading "Make It Quick." There were a lot of ads. Several pictures of naked genitalia and faces with thick black censor lines over the eyes. Why not the other way around? he wondered.

At the end was a coupon for the text of an advertisement. The Valkers must have filled in one of these and posted it, he thought. Maybe the Elfvegrens as well. And the Martells.

Maybe somebody else.

What did you have to do?

He read on until he came to information about answers. Telephone replies, postal replies. They hadn't asked the Elfvegrens about which type of ad it was. Or ads. Replies. That was careless and showed lack of knowledge and perhaps it was also creditable. Not even Halders had asked.

They had lists of all their telephone calls, so they could check.

They hadn't found any filled-in ad coupons at the Valkers' nor at the Martells'. No ad texts, no replies.

Winter phoned the editorial office of *Aktuell Rapport*. A woman answered and he explained who he was.

"The coupons with the text for the ads are kept for three months," she said.

"Does that mean that you have the addresses of all the people who've advertised over the last three months?" Winter asked.

"Yes. Generally speaking."

"Generally speaking? What does that mean?"

"Sometimes we don't manage to keep up with the shredding. There are so many of them . . ."

Shredding, he thought. That damn shredding. There should be a law against shredding. In order to assist police investigations into serious crimes.

"How long could they be saved in those circumstances, then?"

"Six months, perhaps. But that would be exceptional."

"How?"

"What do you mean?"

"How are the addresses saved?"

"We keep the coupons people send in. We also have a computer record that we erase when the paper is shredded."

"Are they mainly home addresses?"

"Yes."

"Don't you have anonymous box numbers that a lot of people use?"

"No, we don't allow that. When we did, the ads turned out to be . . . not serious enough."

Winter didn't dig any further into that.

"Can you see who replies?"

"No. The respondent puts the reply into an envelope, seals it, and writes the contact number of the advertisement on it. Then he or she puts that envelope in another envelope and sends it to us at return postage rates that include a handling charge. We then pass the replies on to the advertiser."

"And the respondent has three months in which to react?"

"Yes."

Winter thought that over. With a bit of luck the Valkers' ad coupon might be in the records at the editorial office, or their home address confirming that they'd put in an advertisement. He would phone his colleagues in Stockholm, which was where the magazine's editorial office was based.

They might also find a coupon from the Martells. Or the Elfvegrens. The Martells. He thought about the Martells again. They had been murdered less than three months ago.

If the Martells had advertised, they wouldn't have received their replies yet. There could be replies being kept by the editorial staff. He recalled Erika Elfvegren's story about "a man."

That was how the man got in. Winter had wanted to know how he got into the apartments, and this could be the answer, the solution.

But the ads could have been put in at any time, several years ago. Calm down now.

He asked the woman a few practical questions, hung up, then phoned Stockholm again and talked to a DCI colleague.

No answer from Matilda Josefsson, who had worked at Krokens Livs. Djanali tried the other number, and a man answered by repeating the numbers she had just keyed in.

She said who she was, and why she was ringing.

"That was ages ago."

"What was?"

"When I worked there. The fool was out of his mind."

"The fool?"

"Andréasson. Claimed I couldn't count. So I quit. Of my own free will."

Djanali asked some more questions about regular customers.

"I suppose there were a few who came in quite often. It would have been odd if that hadn't been the case." Pause. "And then there were the shoplifters."

"Excuse me?"

"We used to get a few shoplifters. A few little things kept disappearing. I never noticed anything myself, but there were a few incidents."

"When?"

"I can't remember exactly. I didn't write it down in my diary or anything. But the girl who worked there at the same time as me knows more about it."

"Matilda? Matilda Josefsson?"

"Exactly. That was her name."

"Did she tell you about shoplifters?"

"She said something about shoplifters when she was on shift. You'll have to ask her."

"We will. But she's left as well."

"There you see. And she could count. Ha, ha."

"We're trying to contact her now."

"She was always going on about running off to where the sun is. Try there."

Winter checked up on where the sun is. His mother didn't know anybody called Åke. He probably didn't live in Nueva Andalucía, but that wasn't the only colony. The Swedish consul in Fuengirola answered after the third ring. Winter could picture the town in his mind's eye, the motorway looking like a black wound, the houses that seemed to have been hurled down the mountain at the sea.

"Of course I know Åke," said the consul, who was a Swede. "And your name also sounds familiar."

There was no reply from Killdén in the Elviria colony. That was to the east of the hospital, on the other side from Marbella. He could remember restaurants, hotels, golf courses, little whitewashed houses.

Passing through by taxi one night on the way to Torremolinos. The taste of wine lingering on his palate.

Winter drove out to the Sahlgren Hospital. Siv Martell was still in a merciful coma. He didn't need to drive out there to discover that, but he wanted to escape the confines of his office. Her body was a sort of reminder of something.

He studied her through the glass. Would she be able to provide any answers if she came around? Or was allowed to come around? He felt a cold flush. As if he had a layer of ice underneath his clothes.

He went out. The new and old buildings at the hospital gave the impression of being a stage set. Ambulances and police cars drove backward and forward over the stage. Nurses in white hurried over the stage, doctors. Angels. He was on the stage himself, but there was no limelight.

He had no script. Just the feeling that a catastrophe was on its way.

50

Bartram bought the magazine and rented a war film. The woman gave him a friendly smile. He didn't know if she recognized him from one time to the next. She should. That kind of thing was the same even at the other end of the world, or wherever she came from.

She was pretty new. They'd come and gone. He didn't like the young man. Not suited to work involving service. If you're going to provide a service you have to make an effort to help your customers. Otherwise you're better off doing something else.

He'd seen the old man one evening. Presumably he owned the place. He didn't look like a service type either. Seemed to have a bonfire under his backside when he sat on the chair. Couldn't keep still.

He'd liked the girl. Then one day she'd gone. She could have said something the previous week. But there again, why should she say anything to him? Just because he liked her didn't mean that she had to like him. Perhaps she laughed at him when he'd gone. Or behind his back. He'd spun around quickly and she hadn't been laughing then, but maybe that was because she didn't dare. She knew that he was a police officer sometimes. When he had his uniform on he was a policeman and he would come in here and be a policeman. Now he wasn't a policeman because he was wearing civilian clothes. Now he couldn't go around telling people to put their seat belts on and expect to be taken seriously.

She'd been there when he stood in the way of the boy who stole some videos. He thought it was better to see it like that. He'd stood in the way. The boy had intended to pay, he said. Just forgotten.

He'd made a concession. He'd written down the boy's name and address but that was mainly because the girl was watching. She didn't want to report him. He could give the boy a second chance. Why not? The boy produced his ID card. That meant he'd been identified and could be arrested. Bartram let him sweat a bit, then allowed him to go. Don't do it again. That kind of crap. The boy seemed a bit odd. You almost felt sorry for him. Stared at the uniform as if the man wearing it was a general, as if it were covered in glittering medals. Mumbled something.

He'd asked her if she knew the boy and she'd just shrugged. He didn't ask her what that meant.

Outside, the wind was making the posters flap. Must be goddam terrific films to be popular for so long. He glanced at the apartment building a bit farther on.

He crossed the street and walked through the silence. The cliff-like hill on the left shut out the noise from the city center, and the slope up toward the church muffled the traffic noise from the main road.

It was a long street, but he didn't get tired. There were yellow buildings to look at after all. They were different from the building he lived in, which was red brick.

Two workmen came out of the building with advertisements on the gable end. They were carrying a bathtub that was long past its expiration date. Bartram never took a bath. Didn't have time.

Three children were running around in the playground as he went past. The Dumpsters were blue like yesterday's sky. The wind was making the birch trees sway. Now he could hear the traffic on Göteborgsvägen. The entrance door lock still wasn't working. The walls in the stairwell were the same blue as the sky the day before yesterday. The apartment door was the same brown as this morning's shit. He unlocked it, went in, and shouted that he was home. One of these days somebody might respond.

He sat down at the computer without taking off his jacket and had soon entered the right files. He was following the investigation. Everything was there, he knew all about it, and smiled.

Hanne Östergaard phoned Winter.

"How is he?"

"He's had a nasty bang on the head."

"Does he need to go to the hospital again?"

"I don't know, Erik."

"That bastard. I'll send a car around to the apartment and we'll throw the swine in a cell."

"What will we do with Patrik?"

"What do you think?"

"He's having a rest here. I think somebody has to have a look at him."

"Should I send an ambulance?"

"No, I'll take him in the car."

"All right."

"There's . . ."

"Yes?"

"There was something I was going to ask . . ." she said. "But it can wait. I'll take Patrik to the hospital."

Morelius and Ivarsson went to get Patrik's father. The man was unconscious when they got there. The woman opened the door, then ran away down the stairs with no shoes on. She'd been red under the eyes, blue. There'd been blood on her shirt or whatever it was. Blouse.

They carried him down. Ivarsson put a plastic sheet over the backseat.

The man was still more or less unconscious when they locked him up. "Was that necessary?" Ivarsson wondered. "Yes," Morelius said.

"Was it you who phoned their apartment a week ago?" Winter asked, who was also there. They were walking along the corridor, which smelled old.

"What do you mean?"

"Have you been trying to contact Patrik for some reason?"

"No."

"Somebody from the police phoned. In addition to me, that is."

"It wasn't me."

"You know him pretty well, don't you?"

"You get to know people when you're patrolling the streets all the time."

"Has he calmed down a bit?"

"He's always been pretty calm," Morelius said. "It's . . . her . . . er, the vicar's daughter who's been a bit wild, rather than him."

"Yes, evidently."

"But she seems to have calmed down now as well."

Winter's colleague called from Stockholm.

"We've been up there."

"Well done, Jonas."

"An interesting place."

"Did you find any completed ad coupons?"

"The shredding business hadn't worked as it should have done for the Valkers. Too many advertisements. Too many people trying to make contact. They've got thousands of bloody advertisements in that office. And that's only one of these so-called men's magazines."

"Well?"

"We have the coupon from the Valkers, duly filled in. And we have the coupon from the Martells."

"Just what I was hoping for."

"And they only use letters," DCI Jonas Sjöland said. "No telephone responses. And your hopes were also fulfilled when it came to the replies to the Martells' ad. They'd already sent out the replies to the Valkers, but they still had the ones for the Martells. Hadn't got around to sending them."

"How many answers have you got there, to the Martells?"

"I haven't counted them yet . . ." Winter listened to the pause. "Have you got authorization for this, Erik?"

"Don't worry about that."

"You've got the Code of Judicial Procedure there on your bookshelf, what does it have to say? Are you a hundred percent sure of what you're doing?"

"Don't worry, I said."

"I looked it up, in fact," Sjöland said. "Chapter twenty-seven, paragraph three. Interesting."

"Especially as it's never been tested," Winter said.

"Who's your prosecutor?"

"Molina. Do you know him?"

"Only by name."

Winter had decided to inform the prosecution service immediately after the first murder. Peter Molina had been following the investigation closely all the time so that he would be able to make decisions fast.

"So you are creating new practices, are you? Setting precedents, in fact," Sjöland said. "Sensitive stuff, this. Opening other people's letters."

"If you study the paragraph carefully, you'll see there is scope for the officer in charge of the investigation to make a decision in a criminal case as serious as this."

"Well, I suppose you could interpret it like that."

"But I've asked permission from the public prosecutor, and got it. Positive." In the end it was positive anyway, Winter thought. He owed Molina.

"All right. I give in."

"I'd like the letters by tonight if possible. You can fax me the completed ad coupons."

"We'll fix that." Sjöland paused again. "Has it occurred to you that if you hadn't been so damn quick off the mark, the pile of letters would have turned up at the Martells' place. By post. They gave their home address, no dodgy box number. The girl at the office said they would probably have sent off the pile in a week or so. Just imagine, that would have been interesting. . . . A possible solution suddenly drops in through the mail slot."

"I've been anything but quick off the mark," Winter said.

Winter's reasoning presupposed that somebody who replied to the Martells had also replied to the Valkers.

He was sorry not to have the replies to the Valkers. He needed them more. But somebody who had made contact with the Valkers through the advertisement might also have gotten to know the Martells. Erika Elfvegren had told them about Louise Valker's "man." Had the Martells also heard about this man? Had they also met him?

Or had *he* heard about them? Even before their ad was published? Or in the meantime? Would he prefer to answer an ad rather than simply telephone? Would that have been too indiscreet? Did he want to go about it as he had the previous time?

Be that as it may. They would shortly have names and addresses. They had started interviewing the film extras. More names and addresses. He was waiting for the transcripts.

Winter phoned Åke Killdén in Fuengirola. No reply. When he put the receiver down the picture inside his head changed. From small white-washed houses on a roasting-hot slope to glass and steel monsters shooting up through the clouds from a Manhattan he once had a good view of from a twenty-seater airplane as it circled on hold, waiting to land at La Guardia on the other side of the river.

Perhaps they were on the wrong track altogether. No. It was no coincidence that there had been a shop called Manhattan Livs and that it was still there: 150 yards from the seven-story apartment building where the Martells had lived. Not a skyscraper, but the highest building within a mile or so. Three or four miles from the Gothia skyscraper in the center of Gothenburg. Mölndal's Manhattan: the apartment buildings with their attractive entrances.

There was a key somewhere. But where?

The phone rang.

"It's Matilda Josefsson," Möllerström said. "She used to work in the minimarket."

Winter waited for her to be put through. Here she came.

"Er, hello?"

"Detective Chief Inspector Erik Winter here."

"Yes . . . I've had a message saying that I should get in touch . . ."

"Good. Can you come to see me?"

"I've just this minute gotten home. . . . Will tomorrow do?"

"No, I'm afraid not. I can come around to your place if you'd prefer that."

"I don't know . . ."

"I'll have my ID on prominent display," Winter said.

He heard a giggle.

"What's it about?" she asked.

"We're investigating some very serious crimes, and we'd like to speak to you about when you worked in a minimarket in Mölndal."

"Krokens Livs? What's happened to the old shit-heap?"

"Can I come around in about half an hour?"

"Er . . . all right. You've got my address."

Winter drove over the bridge. The huge oil tanks glinted, as they always do when the sun is shining. There was a clear view to the west, to far beyond Vinga. The sea was calm, like blue oil.

She lived behind Backaplan. Winter drove past roses growing through the asphalt as he pulled up. He closed his eyes and let his memory of the catastrophe linger there.

Matilda Josefsson was brown-haired and blue-eyed, and about twenty-five. Her apartment was full of heaps of clothes. There was a set of golf clubs in the hall, and a smell of sea and sand in all the rooms. Winter recognized the smell immediately.

"Golf on the Costa del Sol," she said, without his needing to ask. "I work now and then as a golfing instructor. The high season down there is coming to an end now."

"Do you know Åke Killdén?" Winter asked, who had sat down on a chair in the kitchen.

"Who?"

"Åke Killdén. He lives down there. Fuengirola. He used to own the shop you worked in. Man—Krokens Livs."

"I don't know him. The owner who employed me was called Andersson."

"Andréasson."

"If you say so. What did you say your name was? Winter?"

"Yes."

"There was a Winter who used to play on the golf course I worked for. Las Brisas. That was last season. I remember a Winter. Tall. Elderly gentleman. Bengt Winter. A Swede, of course."

Winter nodded.

"A relative of yours? Winter isn't that common a name."

"He was my father."

"Really? It's a small world sometimes." Then she looked as if she was thinking about what Winter had just said. He *was* my father.

"When did you finish working at Krokens Livs?"

She was watching him as she replied. She'd noted the rapid change of subject.

"I take any job that's going when I'm at home," she said. "As you can tell—I mean, Krokens Livs!"

Winter explained some of the background to why he was there. Asked a few questions.

She'd seen the photograph of Manhattan Livs. But the only thing she could remember clearly as being of any interest at all was when the policeman caught the shoplifter.

"I beg your pardon?"

"There was a police officer in the shop, in uniform, and he caught a shoplifter who was on his way out with a handful of videos. He said he'd forgotten to pay, and, of course, you always believe that!"

"But he was a petty thief?"

"I think he'd stolen a few things before. I recognized him, or at least I think I did."

"What happened?"

"The police officer asked me if I wanted to make a formal complaint, as he put it. But he looked so wretched . . . I said no."

"So you didn't report him?"

"The officer said he would see to it. The thief had produced his ID card, I saw that."

"Then what happened?"

"He just showed his ID, sort of." She held up her hand as a demonstration. "The officer made some notes and then they left and that's all I know."

"So you didn't make a formal complaint?"

"No, like I said. He was going to see to it."

"Why was he there? This police officer?"

"I can't remember. I suppose he was buying something. Or renting a video. He'd done that before."

"So you recognized the police officer?"

"Yes . . . he'd been in a few times. Sometimes in uniform and sometimes in civvies."

"Did you talk to him?"

"I did when that shoplif—"

"Any other time, I mean?"

"No, I don't think so."

"You don't know his name?"

"No. Is it important?"

I don't know, Winter thought. It could be extremely important, or just an everyday occurrence.

"Is it so important?" she asked again.

"Would you recognize this police officer if you saw him again?"

"I don't know. I'm not very good at faces."

"You recognized the shoplifter."

"Yes . . . because that was different. It was sort of . . . a crime. I looked at him more than I did the policeman."

"Did you see the shoplifter again?"

"Not in the shop."

"But somewhere else?"

"In the street on one occasion, when I was either coming to work or leaving. I suppose he lived nearby. He looked the other way when he saw me."

"You don't remember his name?"

"I never heard what it was. The policeman wrote it down."

"Was there a squad car outside? Did the police officer have a patrol car outside the shop?"

"Good question. No, I can't remember. But I didn't look out of the window just then." She looked Winter in the eye. "Police officers are all the same anyway. Tall, fair-haired. It's hard to distinguish between them."

Morelius was on his way to see his mother. The road was very icy.

The traffic got worse as he came to Söderleden, and came to a standstill at the golf club. Idiots in thick anoraks and woolly hats were waiting to tee off and hit balls into thirty-foot snowdrifts.

"This is a surprise," his mother said.

"I felt like getting away."

"You've lost weight, Simon."

"Not a lot."

He noticed the photograph of his father over the piano in the drawing room. He was looking solemn, as always, an expression made more austere by his clerical collar. White against all the black.

51

He sat in the dark. After last time he thought they might have fitted a new lock, but it was still the same one. Not that it would have mattered.

People passed to and fro. There was a special kind of echo in there. Sounds traveled through the cubbyhole as if along a tunnel, from the noisy stairwell where all hell was let loose when the elevator went up or down and the front door slammed shut. You needed to put your fingers in your ears for that.

Perhaps those were his footsteps out there now. Awkward. Who was in control now, then? Whoever has control now, put your hand up.

He raised his right arm, and as far as he could see, there was nobody else in there holding up their own hand. Control.

It was obvious when he arrived that he was in control. Anybody with eyes to see could see that.

He wept.

He missed her. Her face once when she turned around on her bicycle and laughed.

He repeated the prophet's name as a mantra. Repeated it over and over again. He kept the other god at bay. He kept the faces away and if he continued doing that they would disappear.

He wept.

Where were they? He was sitting here after all.

Perhaps those were his footsteps again out there. Or hers.

He'd gone past when there was a car parked outside the shop that could have been *his*. Then he'd run home. His heart in his mouth.

He stood up now, in the dark. He had nothing to drink with him this time.

Outside in the street the sun felt hot on his face.

Somebody looked at him as if he still had . . . as if he was in charge. You couldn't see it from his clothes now, but you could see it about him even so. Now.

He walked uphill all the way, then down the slope to the hospital. He stood outside, waiting. Saw her. He knew exactly.

It had gotten to 5:00 P.M. There were six couples who had just introduced themselves. The man sitting to Winter's right felt a great need to describe his work.

The group of parents was mixed, some of them already had children. Winter recognized the midwife. It was the same one he'd met before, with Angela. Elise Bergdorff. She gave them ten minutes to write down what they wanted to know, what they hoped to get out of the meetings. There would be five meetings. By the end of March. Just before the event.

"Ask about reducing the pain," Winter said.

"Ask yourself," said Angela, giggling.

"Clothes," Winter said. "What we should buy. How much you have to plan beforehand."

"But we've said we're not going to plan anything."

"No harm in asking." He continued writing.

"What are you writing?" asked Angela, looking happy. Everybody looked happy, except for the man who wanted to go on about his work as if he couldn't wait to get back to it.

I've never longed to get back to work, Winter thought. Not like that. This is more important.

"How do we know when the baby is hungry and when it's full?"

"Good, Erik."

"How much sleep?"

"For whom?"

"For me, of course," he said. He started writing again after a short pause.

"What are you writing now?"

He looked up with a different expression on his face.

"Let me look," Angela said, grabbing his notepad and reading it. She looked at him: "Are my eyes deceiving me? 'Check police force addresses against the pornography replies.' Is that one of the questions you want to ask the midwife?"

"I thought of something."

"Erik . . ."

"Maternity care," he said quickly. "You've talked about maternity care after the reorganization."

"Write it down," she said. He didn't. "I mean it literally," she said.

The midwife offered them coffee, as this was the first time. In future perhaps they might like to take turns in bringing something nice with them, if they felt like it.

I can bake some brownies, he thought.

The midwife talked about relationships, how things change during pregnancy and after the birth. The men and women looked at one another.

"The woman is more busy with the baby," the man said on his right, who had a job to get back to. "The man feels that she's devoting a lot of time to the baby."

"Surely the man is busy with the baby as well?" Winter said. Was that really me speaking? he wondered.

It's a matter of keeping your love alive after the baby's come, Angela thought. What this is all about is meeting others who are in the same boat. It could be of benefit to us.

There was a brief discussion. Perhaps the idea was that they would get help in improving their roles, Winter thought. As parents. Being mothers and fathers. Roles. Could you call it that? Some people never played a role, ever.

They walked home. The smell of winter had started to fade away, together with the smell of the New Year rockets and Bengal lights. The name kept coming back to him: Bengal lights. Pretty.

"What did you think of the group?"

"Hmm . . ."

"We'll meet again when we've all had our babies."

"Do you think the advertising chap will be there then?"

"Will *you* be there then?"

"You shouldn't answer a question with another question."

They waited for a green light before crossing over the Allé.

"He'll be there," she said. "I've heard it's quite usual for the groups to carry on meeting afterward. Celebrate a one-year anniversary, a two-year anniversary, and suddenly we're all great friends."

We must first get through what lies ahead unscathed, he thought.

"Sounds nice," he said.

"Do you really think so?"

"I think I do."

They had reached the entrance. It was a clear evening, like so many others that winter. The Pressbyrå newsstand near the old university building created the atmosphere of a small-town square, Winter had sometimes thought. He didn't know much about small-town squares, but he could recognize the feeling. He'd sometimes felt that when he'd come home alone late in the evening. Perhaps it was a vague yearning deep down.

Angela took a deep breath.

"What terrific air," she said. "For a big town."

"This is a little town," Winter said. People were shopping at Pressbyrå. He could hear music coming from the restaurant on the corner. The buildings on the other side of the park loomed skyward. Trams looked like jerky sparklers shooting off in all directions. A few youngsters walked past and their voices reached them as fragments of words borne along by the breeze. They vanished into the Java café at the crossroads. "So, let's go in and have a *café con leche*," he said.

They couldn't find any report about a shoplifter in Manhattan Livs, also known as Krokens Livs.

"There are circumstances when it's better to give a caution rather than to report somebody," Ringmar said.

"There's something that doesn't add up," Winter said.

"Calm down now, Erik."

"I could have used that report."

"You have other stuff to read."

He had the text of the advertisements in front of him. It wasn't the best piece of writing he'd ever come across:

We are an average couple coming up to middle age in the Gothenburg area who still have a healthy curiosity and appetite for sex. We are looking for a man as she is going to be the main attraction. 100% discretion. We are lovers of soap and water. Completely healthy, of course. If the personal chemistry is right we can have a really juicy time together.

"A really juicy time together," Ringmar said, who could see that Winter had read the whole text.

"Lovers of soap and water!"

"Fucking perverse, that's what it is. Sex with a bar of soap."

Winter smiled, then turned serious.

"I'm beginning to wonder about this line of investigation," he said. "There's nothing to indicate that the man we're after replied to this."

"No."

"The Valkers must have destroyed the replies," Winter said. "Why?"

"Perhaps it was the murderer."

"Yes."

"He—assuming it's the same guy—was looking for something in the Martells' flat."

"Yes."

"What do you think about the replies?"

The pile of responses to the Martells' ad was next to the two ads themselves. The one submitted by the Martells was worded roughly the same as that from the Valkers, possibly a bit more cautiously. A quick read-through might suggest that they were looking for somebody to have coffee with.

"That there are lots of them."

"I was afraid we might find somebody we knew among them," Ringmar said.

"Our chief of police?"

"Or the mayor of Gothenburg."

"The editor in chief of *GP.*"

"I don't recognize any of them."

"Me neither."

"We'd better get started on them."

"Yes."

"But we haven't finished with the film extras yet."

"Well, nearly." Winter looked at the files with transcripts of all the interviews. Nearly forty of them.

"It will be . . . delicate."

"What we're faced with here *is* delicate."

Halders was worried.

"Have you talked to Molina?"

"We can't arrest them, Fredrik."

"I appreciate that. But what does he want? Something concrete?"

"Something clear-cut," Winter said. "We've got to pry out something more."

Concrete rhymes with secrete, thought Halders. Cut is very nearly cu—.

"We'll bring them in again," Winter said.

"Good."

Åke Killdén answered after the third ring. It sounded as if he were on the beach, with a wind blowing.

"Hang on a minute while I close the veranda door," he said. "Someone's cutting my hedge," he said when he came back.

Winter explained what the call was about.

"That's awful." Killdén was breathing fast, as if he'd been the one doing the gardening. "It's the deadest spot in the northern hemisphere usually." He coughed. "I mean . . . the quietest spot. The most boring spot."

Unlike Fuengirola, Winter thought, and asked Killdén about his employees.

"I only had three. All of them part-time."

"Can I have their names?"

"Of course."

"Do you have their addresses?"

"They must be there somewhere in the accounts material."

"Where can we find that?"

"If it's still in existence I suppose it will be in my accountant's archives," Killdén said.

The employees, Winter thought. We haven't given enough thought to the people who worked at Manhattan Livs.

"Did you have many regular customers?"

"They were all regular customers."

"Do you think you could help me by thinking hard about your . . . regular customers? Was there anybody who stood out? Anybody you thought acted a bit oddly some time or other? Anything at all."

"Anything at all," Killdén said.

"Was one of your regular customers a police officer?" Winter asked.

"A police officer? What do you mean? Somebody who came in uniform?"

"Yes, or without."

"Well . . . police officers called in occasionally to buy something, I suppose, but I don't recall anything in particular."

"Think hard about that as well."

"Will do."

Winter thanked him and hung up.

The employees. Matilda. The man who couldn't count. They'd only spoken to him over the phone. Winquist. Kurt Winquist. The others, in the accountant's archives. This was getting bigger by the hour. He was conducting an investigation that could choke him. The Mölndal police. The duty roster for New Year's Eve.

The answers were all in the investigation material. Everything was there, in the papers he had in front of him. How many more times would he need to read them before the penny dropped?

The telephone on his desk rang, as did his mobile. He said, "Be with you in a moment," into the mobile and picked up the receiver on his desk. It was Möllerström.

"That kid Patrik has taken a turn for the worse at the Sahlgren Hospital."

Winter answered his mobile, but whoever had called him had hung up.

52

Hanne Östergaard and her daughter were in the waiting room when Winter returned from the ward.

"They don't really know yet," he said. "It's something to do with his brain."

"Shit, shit, shit," Maria said.

"Perhaps he's had too many blows," Hanne said. "For too long a time."

"He said he'd remembered something else," Maria said.

Winter turned to look at her.

"Something about him recognizing somebody. On the stairs."

"Did he say that?"

"Yesterday."

"Did he say anything else about it?"

"No."

"But he recognized somebody? Somebody he'd seen before?"

"I don't know any more."

Now I have two hospital patients who can help us to make progress, Winter thought. Both of them are unconscious. We must have people here, around the clock. I'd better tell Angela. She'll have to get used to seeing police officers at her place of work.

He met Morelius as he was about to leave.

"I know," said Morelius, adjusting his belt. "It feels almost like being one of the family."

"Are you on your own?"

"Bartram is in the car. I just wanted to see how things were going."
He waved to Hanne and her daughter. "That fucking bastard."

Winter drove through Toltorpsdalen to Krokens Livs. Jilna smiled at
him, but he wasn't convinced that she remembered who he was. He
went outside. The wind was still battering the city, bang, bang. Elderly
folk were getting off buses. He turned around and let his eyes wander.
Somewhere . . .

Should they set up a camera in the shop? Make a video recording
and show it to Killdén and Andréasson and Matilda Josefsson and all the
other employees? If so, for how long?

The possibilities were endless. So was time, of course, but not now.

He had the feeling that time was slipping away. It was on its way to
something that would be a bigger problem than anything that had
gone before. He could feel it.

His mobile called again. It was Angela.

"Was it you who called a few minutes ago?" he asked. There was no
number displayed on the screen, nor in his memory.

"No."

"How are things?"

"I've just got home, and . . . I don't know. I suddenly felt so . . .
scared. Can't you come home, Erik?"

"Has something happened?" He could feel his hand trembling slightly.

"Not really. It's just that it suddenly felt odd when I went in through
the front door. That's all. As if somebody was looking at me. Scrutinizing me."

"You didn't see anybody?"

"No. I looked around, but there was nobody there. It's ridiculous.
Maybe it was that door at the bottom of the stairs, down to the cellar."

"What about it?"

"It was open. It's so dark and horrible in there."

Winter drove home. He called Ringmar from his car.

"I want somebody posted to keep an eye on Angela."

He'd spoken to Ringmar about the telephone calls and the break-in.

"Have you discussed this with Sture?"

"Screw Sture. Can you fix it?"

"From when?"

"Tomorrow morning. Outside. I'll ring you later about times."

Bergenhem kept his head still. Concentrated on following the painting's frame, first with his eyes and then with his head. It went well. Better than yesterday.

"How do you feel?"

"Better than before."

Martina had put Ada to bed. She'd been quieter than usual since he'd come home.

He stood up.

"Do you really feel well enough to go out?"

"I have to keep moving."

"Is it really a good idea to start work again on Friday?"

"No."

"Then don't do it, Lars."

"I can't just stay at home all the time, Martina. All the time."

"But you have to get better."

"I am better. Nearly. I'll be okay by Friday."

Night was falling over Torslanda. It looked as if a searchlight had been aimed at the row of terraced houses. Perhaps the light is only shining on my house, he thought.

"I don't know what to say," Angela said.

"I've learned that almost anything is worth taking seriously," Winter said.

"You feel so stupid," Angela said. She smiled at him. "I'm influenced . . . by your job."

He hadn't said anything to her about his visit to the caretaker's cubbyhole in the cellar. He didn't know himself what he ought to do about that.

"Can't you stop working?" he said.

"Not yet."

"But can't you take it easy . . . until April 1?"

"Isn't it a bit early for April Fool's?"

"No."

"I *want* to work, Erik. It feels good. I don't believe in going home and then sitting waiting for something to happen."

"We're keeping an eye . . ." He wondered about the best way to put it. "We . . . I've asked for a radio car to drive past now and again and to keep an eye on what's happening."

"Keep an eye on what's happening?"

"Yes . . . you know."

"You mean you're giving me a bodyguard?" She was standing by the kitchen window. "Has it gotten that bad?"

"Not a bodyguard. More a bit of . . . observation."

"Whenever I leave the apartment?"

He didn't answer.

"Whenever I go to work?"

"It'll be discreet, don't worry."

"Oh, yes? And who will it be?"

"I don't know. Does it matter?"

"I don't know. It depends on how much effort he has to put into it."

"All right. I'll ask Bergenhem to do it for a few days." He needs to get back into the swing of things, Winter thought. And he's good as a shadow.

"But he's not going to hold my hand?"

"You won't even know he's there."

It was late. He read very carefully the transcripts of the interviews with the film extras. The documentation had only just arrived, the first draft. It was a bit of a hodgepodge. All kinds of jobs, or rather joblessness. Some of the individuals seemed barely sane at first glance, but there was nothing unusual about that. It's the normal ones we have to look twice at, he thought.

The filming went on. They had been hanging around the police station, but weren't allowed in. The chief of police made it as difficult for the team as she could. Whoever sees that film will have to work out for himself if that building has anything to do with the uniforms, he thought.

It could be that the film has a role to play in this investigation. Thanks to the extras. It could be. It helps us to find a solution at the same time as it's a possible indirect cause of what happened.

He was holding several papers in his hand. Names, addresses. He hadn't recognized several of the names. He phoned Möllerström.

"Janne? Can you drop everything and compare the names and addresses of those film extras with the result of the door-to-door operation after the Mölndal murder?" Or murders, he thought. "Ringmar will send you a few more officers to help."

"Okay." There was a rustling noise on the line. "How wide a radius?"

"Make it pretty wide. I'll be with you shortly."

"Okay. Should I wait with Vasaplatsen?"

"Take Mölndal first."

Winter hung up and took the photographs from one of his desk drawers. He scrutinized one of them on his desk, then held it up and studied the necks of the two dead bodies on the sofa.

One of the answers could be here, Lareda had said. It's all down to the swapping of heads. Or bodies.

He was sitting outside the church. Next to him were two statues. He asked the guide, who was Alicia, and she said that it was always the same in Torremolinos. It was the Moors who cut off heads. Off with their heads. They had a different god. Once the heads are off, those people are no more. Their faces are erased. One of the statues was pointing at him now. Angela was sitting next to him. It's pointing at me, she said. The statues were in a row outside the church. No heads, no arms. He could hear the music, the guitars, then the drums.

Winter woke up, his ears throbbing. Angela moved, but didn't wake. He got out of bed and drank some water. It was three-fifteen. The lit-

tle red lamp was shining on his laptop. She'd said good-night, and then
he'd worked on into the early hours.

Neither the Valkers nor the Martells had a computer. That didn't
necessarily mean that they'd never owned one. But there'd been no
sign of them on the Net. Despite millions of souls seeking contacts.
Tens of thousands of sex contacts.

Winter went back to the bedroom and got his dressing gown from
the chair, then went to the living room and sat down in the armchair by
the window.

What should he do about Per Elfvegren? There was something
about him . . . Something he didn't want to let go.

Winter had asked Molina about a DNA check, but there was no
chance of that—yet.

"Put a bit more pressure on him," Molina had said. "Then we can
talk about an arrest."

"More pressure? How?"

"Halders. Give him his head."

"Not possible. I don't dare."

They'd interviewed them. Individually.

"Give me the details," Halders had said to the woman.

"The . . . details?"

"Everything. From the moment you got to their front door."

Per Elfvegren was talking about engaging a solicitor now. About
time, Winter thought.

Then he changed his mind. I have nothing to hide.

They'd searched the Elfvegrens' apartment. Nothing. No computer.
Halders had the men's magazines. They'd read the Valkers' ad. Per
Elfvegren had thrown away his reply. Of course.

Why hadn't they found anything in the Valkers' apartment? Nothing at all. The place was clean. There ought to have been something
there. Why had they cleaned up the apartment? Not cleaned up. Thrown
things away. Got rid of things. No magazines. No notes. Not even a
copy. Did the murderer take those away with him? Maybe. Or maybe
not. Could he have been in a fit-enough state to make a search? Who
else could have done it?

Elfvegren didn't seem to be able to understand that it could happen again. That also made Winter think. Elfvegren was putting on a mask, maintaining a mask. It could fall off.

We can save you, Halders had thought while he was conducting the interrogation; and then he'd said as much outright to Elfvegren. You, and perhaps others.

53

There was a small, flat package on the hall floor among the rest of the mail.

"Why don't you try this tonight?" Steve MacDonald wrote in the letter accompanying the CD. Winter read the title: Tom Waits. *Sword-fishtrombones*. "His real breakthrough in a way," MacDonald wrote, "and there's more to come. It's got some jazz in it too! And: good luck with the baby."

His colleague in Croydon was continuing with his mission to educate Winter in classic rock and other music that was more than an arm's length away from Coltrane.

"Steve's sent another CD," Winter said to Angela, who was lying in the bath with her feet in the air. He ventured a couple of paces into the mist. "Hard day?"

"It's even worse for the patients." She moved, making the water slop about. "This is my famous imitation of a walrus turning over in the bath."

"Imitation?"

"Shut up, you pig. What has Steve sent now?"

"Tom Waits."

"He's good." She sat up and reached for the shampoo. "It would be nice to meet him. And his family."

"Tom Waits?" said Winter, with a smile.

Angela stuck out her tongue.

"We'll head for London just as soon as we can," Winter said. "All three of us."

"I can just see you strutting around in front of Steve and the whole of the south of England," she said, peering through the lather. "The proud paterfamilias."

"With every right," he said as the telephone rang in the hall.

"I hope I'm not calling at an inconvenient moment." It was Benny Vennerhag.

"If you've phoned here it must be something important," Winter said. Vennerhag had been given a new unlisted telephone number.

"I don't know, but there is something. As you can probably imagine, some of my . . . business colleagues are very good at recognizing the police officers in Gothenburg."

"You keep tabs on us just as we keep tags on you."

"Hmm. My acquaintances might go a bit further than that definition. But all right. I asked around a bit and there wasn't a lot of solid resistance, if I can put it like that. What's been happening doesn't do anybody any good. People get worried. Your boys can get a bit inquisitive, if you see what I mean."

"So you did some asking around."

"All right, Erik. Somebody has been seen a couple of times wandering about in a police uniform, but he hasn't been recognized. He might be a cop, of course, but I don't think so."

"Go on."

"That's about it. A couple of times. But it was some time ago now."

"Where and when? Who?"

"You can't ask me to disclose a source of information, Erik. But I'm happy to continue helping. I've asked a lot of questions, in fact."

"Where and when, then?"

"In several places in the center of town."

"Day or night?"

"Night . . . both times."

"When?"

Vennerhag mentioned several dates.

"That was it. I hope it's useful."

"Now I need a face and a name. Or an address."

"Don't we all?"

"You've taken this seriously, Benny. Keep on doing so."

"I can't see what else I can do. Am I supposed to attach a shadow to the fake cop if he's seen again?"

"That would be good."

"Are you joking?"

"No. Tell that to everybody."

It was light in the morning. Nearly March. On March 5 he'd be forty. Less than a month later he'd be a father, and life would really start.

They'd listened to the CD from Steve last night and Winter was going to buy everything else by the same guy, when he found the time. I think he made a new one last year, Angela had said. His first for several years. Last year. Last year was the twentieth century, now they had to remember to say two thousand. The naughties, Halders had said.

"Can I take the car today as well?" Angela asked.

"Of course."

"I can't cope with the tram anymore."

"You ought to stay at home."

"There'll be plenty of time for that later."

She could take a taxi, but she preferred to drive. A bit of freedom. The Mercedes gave her a feeling of security, the smells, the soft, dark colors inside.

The investigation material was growing in breadth and height, with names, addresses, transcripts of interviews.

"We still haven't been able to get hold of some of the people who replied to the advertisement," Ringmar said.

"So I see."

"Several of them didn't give their real names, but we usually discover that when we check the address."

"Some helpful neighbor who lets them use his name or address?"

"Hmm, that's a thought."

"Maybe we should go a step further. Bring in the neighbors as well."

"Huh?" Ringmar said.

Winter was studying the lists on his desk. He was wearing his reading glasses.

Six days to go now, and he'd be forty.

"There's something odd about these two addresses," Winter said. "Call me paranoid, but I requested the home addresses of the entire Gothenburg police force and . . . well, if you compare them there is none among them that matches any of these four ad replies."

"Yes, we'd established that. Good, isn't it?"

"In a way. Möllerström has been working with the addresses of the film extras, and with this lot as well. Sture gave the green light for a few more officers. When he smells something in the air he smells something in the air, as he put it."

"And?"

"It's the uniforms . . ." Winter thought of Vennerhag, but he wasn't a hundred percent convinced that there *was* somebody dressing up as a police officer.

Bartram was tapping away at the computer. It was clicking and swishing. He could see a manual hanging on the notice board and smiled. Some people never learned. Some used to come to him, because he was best. Especially this last year when there was panic as the millennium approached. All the files not properly tucked away, the back ups, security, copies everywhere out there in the electronic night.

He didn't want to show how good he really was. That could cause problems. He would have to answer all the idiotic questions.

If only he'd been in the crime unit, or the new city squad. But he'd never been asked. Never.

Bartram was a hacker. It wasn't difficult for anybody who knew what he was doing. He liked the word. Hacker. Hack into wherever you like, then withdraw, discreetly, with knowledge.

Morelius emerged from the toilet. Pale. Perhaps he was having stomach problems again. The kid should be doing something else. Maybe that's what he was planning.

Bartram continued tapping away.

He changed files and then he was inside his home computer. It was still interesting suddenly to find yourself in your own computer while you were still at work, gliding around all the software.

The lists with the forty film extras flickered on his screen, borrowed from the internal network. Disappeared the moment he saw anybody in the corner of his eye. He'd take a closer look at them tonight. Detective Inspector Greger Bartram. Or Detective Chief Inspector, like Winter, who thought he was somebody. Or his registrar. Greger Bartram was a better registrar. Just wait and see.

Halders stopped at the late-night supermarket.

"This is where I had my car stolen," he said to Djanali in the passenger seat. "I just popped in for a couple of seconds and he got my car."

"I know, Fredrik."

Halders got out.

"I must get some chewing tobacco. Guard the car."

Djanali rolled down the window and breathed in the smell of exhaust fumes and dry, late winter, or early spring. The sun glinted on the Tower of Babel, which was still standing after New Year's Eve, at the north end of Heden, like a symbol of something she didn't understand. Were they going to use it for some other occasion? It was only a hovel on a hill, after all. There probably wasn't enough money to pull the pile of crap down. The hangover always kicks in afterward.

She could see Halders talking to the man at the counter. Halders turned to look at her, as if to make sure that she hadn't let anybody steal the car.

"He was telling me about the problems they've been having with goddamn shoplifters," Halders said as he sat behind the wheel and pulled out into Södra Vägen. "Somebody came in this morning and stole a bag of chips."

"Maybe they shouldn't stock chips," Djanali said.

"Maybe they shouldn't stock anything at all," Halders said. "That's the way things are going."

"Toward empty late-night supermarkets, you mean?"

"Yes. The big void. All those damned minimarkets and so on are signs of the times, they reflect the approaching death of society," Halders said, turning right again at Lorensberg. "Nothing but chips and tobacco and other shit, and videos."

"I gather you're their best customer," Djanali said.

"I'm a victim. Take the films. People do their best to deaden their senses in front of the VCR." They were in the Avenue now. "Harry Martinson was right. Films are temples for those who can't cope with life."

"Harry Martinson?" said Djanali, sounding confused.

"Swedish author. Unknown in Ouagadougou."

"No, I don't remember him from school," she said.

"'Ello, 'ello, 'ello! I spy a police constable," Halders said. "In civvies, but you can tell by the way he walks."

"It's Morelius."

"Do you know him?"

"Not really, but don't you know everybody in the force?"

"I'm afraid I probably do."

Halders pulled up at the taxi rank outside the Park Hotel, as they had business to see to there. Morelius was on his own, staring down at the ground. He was wearing earphones. Halders got out just as Morelius came level with the car.

"Do you patrol here in your free time too?" said Halders. Morelius saw him, but couldn't hear him. He removed the earphones and they could both hear the music.

"God that's loud. Sounds terrible, whatever it is."

Morelius took his Walkman from his pocket and switched off.

"Hello, Halders."

"Don't you get enough of the Avenue when you're on duty?"

"I'm on an errand, unfortunately."

"Same here."

Djanali waved from the car window.

"I'm quitting," Morelius said out of the blue.

"Eh?"

"I'm leaving the force."

. . . . . .

Angela could feel the weariness now. When she described the fate of her latest patient for the cassette recorder, exhaustion hit her like a lump of stone, a large block.

I'm quitting after today, she thought. It was fun as long as it lasted. Now my head can't keep up anymore.

She stood up, went to the sink and splashed some water on her forehead. There was a knock at the door and Hildur peeped around it. The nurse looked worried.

"Another broken bone," she said. "It seems—"

"I'm coming," Angela said.

The new multistory car park was not pretty, but it served its purpose. She took the elevator up to the third floor and studied her pale features in the mirror. But now it was over.

Everybody was full of understanding. I wondered how long you would last, Hildur had said. Until now, she'd replied.

Tomorrow she could attend the parent group meeting as a full-time mom. In her thoughts everything was ready, prepared.

She used the remote control to unlock the car and noticed the uniform. A police officer was walking up the exit ramp, hesitantly, perhaps slightly embarrassed. Okay, she thought. I'll be staying at home in future, without a guard. You can take time off, Constable.

The police officer had almost reached her. She waited, with the ignition key in her hand. A car from the level above was approaching and the officer stood on the other side as it drove past and then disappeared from view down the ramp.

He came up to her, still looking embarrassed. Only doing his duty. Surely she recognized him? He was somebody Erik knew.

"Mrs. Winter?"

She nodded, as it was the easy way out. She wasn't Mrs., not yet at least.

"I'm supposed to make sure you get home safely."

"I'm already on my way," she said, gesturing toward the car. "This was my last day at work. But thanks anyway."

"Let me drive," he said. He wasn't looking her in the eye. Another car drove past. There was an unpleasant smell. She didn't want to stand inhaling these poisonous fumes any longer than necessary. She had responsibilities. "Let me drive you home, Mrs. Winter," he said again, holding out his hand for the keys. She noticed his belt, the gleam from his breast pocket, his cap. Everything was gleaming. It was somehow reassuring. His face was familiar.

"It's really not necessary," she said.

"I know the way," he said. "It's my job to help you."

She was dog-tired. She could feel it now, even more thanks to the foul, fume-filled air. She felt a movement in her stomach. Squeeze her way in behind the wheel? Squeeze *their* way in? No, thank you.

"All right," she said, handing him the keys.

54

Winter was reading the transcripts of the interviews with the film extras. They all had different motives for their exhibitionism. None seemed more interesting than any other. He was short a few.

Five of the addresses were in Mölndal. Three were within reasonable walking distance of Krokens Livs, which was a starting point for a line of thought.

He phoned Möllerström.

"Have you spoken to Bertil about the addresses in Mölndal?"

"Yes."

"I can't track him down at the moment. Do you know if anybody's been there?"

"Hasn't he mentioned it to you?"

"Mentioned what?"

"Two didn't answer."

"The first attempt?"

"Twice at one of the addresses."

"I have them here," Winter said, scanning them from the bottom up. "We'll call around later tonight."

"Perhaps they'll be filming until late," Möllerström said.

"I don't know."

"I suppose you know they'll be finished next week, if they stick to the schedule?"

"So I heard."

He concluded the call, glanced at his watch, then phoned home. No reply. He looked again at his watch.

Ringmar called just after he'd put the phone down.

"The boy seems to be a bit better."

"Who's that?"

"Patrik. The boy in the hospital."

"Ah, yes." His father had been released and was drifting around Skanstorget. *That* case was crawling along at a snail's pace. Winter had driven past the apartment, thought about going in. "I'm pleased to hear it. I must have a word with him, if possible."

"They rang a few minutes ago. Said you were on the phone."

"What did they want?"

"He wanted to speak to you."

Winter arranged a car to take him to the Sahlgren Hospital. He was spending more and more time there. He phoned home again on his mobile, but there was no reply and he left a brief message on the answering machine.

Patrik's face was the same color as his surroundings. A chameleon. His eyes were black, sunken.

"I dreamed that I recognized him," Patrik said.

"Recognized him? The man who went down in the elevator?"

"There was something about his face when he turned round." Patrik looked up at Winter, then at something to the side of him. "If I saw him again, I'd recognize him." Patrik closed his eyes and mumbled something.

"What did you say?" Winter asked.

The boy mumbled again.

"Patrik?" Winter bent down even closer, but couldn't distinguish any words.

Winter phoned home again from outside the ward, but there was still no answer. He made his way to where Angela worked, but they said she'd left hours ago.

He requested a car to take him home.

The apartment was empty and silent. It was clear that she'd not been home. There were always things lying around if she'd come in before going off to do some shopping, or to take a walk. He took the elevator down to the basement garage, but the car wasn't there.

He went out into the street and looked around. The Mercedes was on the other side of the street, one of three in a row. He walked quickly over to it and saw the parking ticket fixed to the windshield. He opened the envelope. Two hours ago. The ticket had been issued two hours ago. He checked his watch again. It was ages since she'd left work. Why had she driven here so late and left the car in the street instead of in the garage? Was she scared of going down there?

Bergenhem had stopped being her bodyguard without Angela ever having noticed him. He was now involved in the investigation again. Winter and Angela had looked at each other and laughed, perhaps shrugged at the thought of worrying about it. Over the top. So much was going on now.

One of the cars from Lorensberg checked up on her now and again, but that was more or less it. Waited outside sometimes when she finished work, but not every day.

He took the elevator back up. Didn't know what to do next. He could feel something in his stomach, rising up like lava.

He phoned his sister. Lotta answered after the second ring.

"Is Angela with you?" Winter asked.

"No . . . why are you . . ."

"She's not here, and her car has been in the street with a parking ticket for a couple of hours."

"Have you phoned the hospital?"

"I've even been there."

Bartram kicked off his shoes and went in to his computer, which was glowing like a face looking forward to his arrival.

Only a couple of minutes, and he was in there. He explored, checked. Printed out. Spread the pages out on his kitchen table, then went to the kitchen to get some water. He wasn't hungry. He hadn't washed up for several days, but nobody would complain. Who will complain if I don't? he asked himself.

He was back. The screen lit up the room softly, combined with the desk lamp that was pointed downward.

He used his finger to follow the column down.

He had his notebook at hand. It was the same one as then, shabbier now, but in decent condition even so. He was a man of few words. Concentration. Concentrate.

Coincidence or not? He'd forced his telephone number out of him, but nobody answered when he called. The shoplifter. His address was still there.

Bartram compared the name and address in his notebook with the film extras on the list. You didn't need to be a genius to see that they were the same. It was enough to be able to read, and to be in the right place at the right time. If he'd been in charge of the investigation, he'd have been able to show them how an investigation ought to be conducted. He knew more than the others.

Winter had searched the car, but found nothing. He didn't touch the wheel. Beier's boys were on their way.

He phoned Ringmar, who answered with his mouth full.

"Hang on a minute. I was just having a bite of supper—"

"Angela's disappeared," Winter said.

"What the hell . . . ?"

"Something's happened."

"Have you raised the alarm?"

"Yes." Winter felt his body going cold, the flow of lava solidifying. He felt sick. "No point in holding back."

Ringmar didn't ask what Winter thought.

Right now he was thinking about the parent group. Him and Angela busy asking about how to minimize the pain. The smell of coffee.

"Where are you?" Ringmar asked.

"Here," Winter said. "At home."

"I'm on my way."

MARCH

55

Ringmar had set off immediately. He was there within half an hour, they'd spoken, quickly and briefly. Winter was like a talking and thinking copy of his alter ego. He'd nodded, made notes, spoken. Ringmar had yelled into the telephone. They'd received a barrage of calls.

He had always been bad at putting work behind him. Going in an entirely different direction once he'd finished for the day, or the night. Always found it difficult to do. Difficult to become hardened. He'd avoided the coldness but not been able to become inured.

God. I've always believed in you. Give me the strength to think now, let me retain that strength. You can take it away from me later, but not now. Divide me up now. Two beings, one heart. No panic now.

"Erik?"

Ringmar was there. Had he been standing there all the time? He was in the doorway, but his voice seemed to be next to Winter's ear.

Winter changed his position and tried to be *there* again, with his own strength and with God's help.

"There's one of your contacts on the phone."

"Who?"

"Benny."

Winter reached for the receiver.

"What the hell's going on?" Vennerhag said.

"I've been trying to get hold of you."

"So I gathered. I've been out of town. But what the hell's going on? Has she—"

"The help I asked you for. It's more important now than ever."

"Is that really you I'm talking to, Winter? Your voice sounds—"

"Make an effort, Benny."

"Is this really connected with—"

"Yes."

"Jesus."

"Make an effort, Benny."

"If only I knew what to do. But I'll do . . . continue to do whatever I can. Find out what people have to say."

"Make an effort," Winter said yet again.

They'd put more officers to work on the interviews with the lonely hearts—better to think of them like that. Halders had more names. Names, names.

Winter wasn't sleeping at all now. If he needed drugs, he'd take some.

He knew that all this was interconnected. Ringmar knew, everybody knew. Angela hadn't just vanished into thin air . . .

He scratched his head. Ringmar was in the doorway again. Was it the third day in hell? The fourth?

Tomorrow he'd be forty. He'd noticed that when he'd gone home to collect the mail and some clean clothes. He wanted to make the journey alone. Nodded to Bergenhem, who was standing guard in the dark in Vasaplatsen. There would be others there as well. If . . .

Forty years old. He'd forgotten all about it. Angela had drawn a red lipstick line around the date on the calendar hanging above the stove. Six inches up from the work surface and some four feet up from the floor. As he stood there looking, he'd thought of getting a tape measure and checking the distances, anything that kept him in touch with everyday things. But total control was bordering on lunacy.

During the night he'd thought about the boy again, in the hospital. The boy had recognized somebody. When had he first come into the picture? There was a parallel story here—but it was linked to himself, with the murders.

Winter had driven back in his own car, where there were no traces at all. He'd phoned Hanne Östergaard and asked her to come in. She looked tortured, as if she'd turned into a mirror. They'd sat in Winter's office, and he'd suddenly told her what had happened to the people who had been murdered. *What had happened.* For three seconds he lost his composure, let his hell rain down upon her.

She answered after the first ring.

"I was awake," she said. There was something urgent about her voice.

"When Maria . . . was taken care of . . ." Winter said, and asked some more questions as she described what had happened, who had been there. The urgency was still in her voice, as if she were waiting for her turn.

Then she said it. Broke her silence, you might say. One duty superseded another. Simon had not poured out his memories while in confession. She knew she wasn't bound to silence.

"I don't know what it signifies," she said, "but when you told me what had happened . . ."

Winter could feel the lava again, on its way upstream, just as cold.

"Has he told you about it several times? The accident? The bodies?"

"Yes."

"Erik?"

Winter looked up. He was alone in his office. Ringmar had appeared in the doorway.

"We ran through the addresses again," Ringmar said, transcripts in hand. "The pornography list. There's something . . ." He came into the room, sat down, and spread out the papers on Winter's desk.

"What?"

"It's not close to Krokens Livs. But this responder has given an address in one of the apartment buildings down in Askim and we compared it like you said and, well, there is a link."

"A link? What did I say?" Just now his mind was a blank, as white and blank as the sky and the ground had been in the middle of January.

"Somebody from the force lives in that area. A police officer."

"Well?"

"It's a very long shot," Ringmar said. "We must keep calm about it."

"Who is it?" Winter asked.

"Morelius. Simon Morelius. He's a pol—"

"I know who he is," Winter said.

"Keep calm now."

He was calm. God was holding his hand.

"Do you know where Morelius comes from?" he asked.

"No."

"Is he on duty at the moment?"

"I checked that. He's free."

"Is he at home?"

"I don't know. I didn't try to phone him. I didn't know what to say."

"Have you got the number there?"

Winter called but there was no reply.

He asked the switchboard to put him through to the Lorensberg police station.

"Hello, Winter here. Yes . . . I know . . . there's somethi . . . yes, exactly . . ."

He asked about Morelius, as Bertil had just done. Back tomorrow. In Ivarsson's group. A bit of extra time off after New Year. Do you need to get hold of him?

"Yes."

"He might be at home."

"No."

"Have you tried Kungsbacka?"

"Eh? No."

"That's where he's from, you see."

"Kungsbacka?"

"Yes. Somebody mentioned it only the other day. I think it was him himself, come to think of it." Winter could hear the sound of conversation in the background at the station in Chalmersgatan, telephones, boots clomping over hard floors. "It came up in connection with that murder. She was from Kungsbacka, wasn't she? The woman who was murdered?"

"Yes," Winter said, and looked at Ringmar, who was listening with bated breath. Winter concluded the call, then took the telephone directory from one of the bookshelves.

There was just one Morelius in Kungsbacka. Elna Morelius. Mrs. She answered after the third ring. No, her son wasn't at home. What was it about? Something to do with work? Of course she would tell him to get in touch, but she hadn't heard from him for a while. He ought to contact her more often. Yes, that's the way it is. When was the last time? Well, not too long ago. He wasn't feeling well. He wasn't too good.

Winter tried to think.

"What does your husband do, Mrs. Morelius?"

"My husband? What kind of question is that? My husband's dead." Silence. Winter waited. "My husband was a vicar," she said eventually.

Morelius. Winter could picture his face, hovering over his uniform. In a squad car on patrol up and down Vasaplatsen.

A real police officer. Patrik. Maria. Always at hand when something happened.

When Winter arrived at the Valkers' apartment Morelius had been standing inside it. The silhouette. Pointing at the wall.

Winter thought about Lareda Veitz, what she'd said. She'd phoned the other day but he didn't have the strength, not just now.

Winter turned to Ringmar.

"Let's go there," Winter said. "Now." He stood up and checked his gun, which was pressing against his ribs.

"To Morelius's place? Askim?"

"Where else, for Christ's sake?"

"Erik . . ."

"You can stay here if you like," Winter said, taking his overcoat from its hanger. He felt like running through the corridors, running like a madman, flying.

Ringmar phoned again, but nobody answered.

"Should we ask them to send a car from Frölunda?"

"Yes, but nobody goes in until we get there."

Winter's hands were shaking, he'd checked his SIG-Sauer again. They were running now, both of them.

"I'll drive," Ringmar said.

It was evening now. Ringmar drove fast through the homebound traffic. Winter put the flashing light on the roof when they were caught in a line of cars near Liseberg and Ringmar switched on the siren as they came to the highway.

Two feet of mist were creeping over the fields on either side of the road. Ringmar turned off before coming to the Järnbrott intersection. Winter thought of the Elfvegrens in their pretty estate on the other side of the junction. They hadn't said anything else about the man Louise Valker had spoken about. Louise Valker from Kungsbacka. He glanced at Ringmar. If there was nobody in, the next stop this evening would be the Elfvegrens' house.

They saw the flashing light on the radio car from the Frölunda station. A group of young boys had already gathered. The light was illuminating their faces.

"Switch it off," Winter said when he reached the car.

"Number seven," said Ringmar behind him, and Winter turned around. Ringmar was pointing at the entrance to 7D. The apartment buildings were in brick, possibly red. Three or four stories, it didn't matter.

"He lives on the second floor," Ringmar said.

The entrance door was open, fastened to the wall by a chain. A man carrying a box emerged from the basement as they went in. He nodded at them, and released the chain.

Nobody answered when they rang the bell. The name MORELIUS was in white letters against a black background on the flap of the mail slot. Winter rang again and heard the sound echoing through the apartment, but he could hear no footsteps, no voices. He shouted through the mail slot, listened. Then he drew his pistol and fired a shot through the wooden door, next to the lock.

56

Winter put his hand through the hole he'd made in the door and unlocked it. He flung the door open. His brain was detached from his body now, everything was animal instinct. The cordite was irritating his nose. He regretted nothing.

There was mail on the hall floor, an envelope, a newspaper.

The apartment was lit up by lights from the main road and the estate. All was silent. No guitars, no drums, no hissing.

No Angela. They went from room to room. Everything was neat and tidy. The sink was clean and glinted in the light from the kitchen window. Nothing on the table.

There were two men's magazines on the bedside table, next to an alarm clock. *Aktuell Rapport.* In the living room was a bookcase filled with stacks of paperbacks, an imitation leather sofa, two armchairs facing a large television set. Neat and tidy. Total control.

"Hmm," said Ringmar, seeming disappointed as he looked, first around the room and then at Winter.

Winter could feel his face starting to twitch, and the shock and tension gradually ebbed away. Ringmar's disappointed face. The empty apartment. The shot. The feeling of confusion, disappointment, and infinite relief. Infinite relief. He was twitching, shaking; he gave vent to a sound that could have been a sob or a laugh and what came first was laughter, loud and abandoned: *You should see your face, Bertil!* He noticed that Ringmar took a step toward him, like a nurse, and he had another attack and then it was over and he held up the hand that wasn't holding his pistol and said, "Let's get out of here, Bertil," and he set off through the hall.

Winter gave instructions to the two police officers from Frölunda, a man and a woman.

"I'll drive this time," Winter said.

"How are you feeling, Erik?"

"Better," he said as he drove through the Järnbrott intersection.

"Where are we going?"

"To the Elfvegrens."

"It's nearly midnight."

Winter didn't reply, but drove through the little streets and Ringmar asked yet again for the address. All small houses looked the same. It was like entering another age, the 1950s. Small houses, big gardens.

The Elfvegrens' house was in darkness. Winter rang the bell. Ringmar stood behind him, waiting to see what happened, as if expecting to draw another blank.

Nobody opened the door, nobody switched on a light. Winter pounded on the door then turned on his heel and went down the stairs.

"She's not here at least," he said, and Ringmar understood who Winter was referring to.

They drove past Radiotorget. Winter's mobile phone rang.

"Hello?"

"You were looking for Morelius . . . at Lorensberg . . ." The reception deteriorated, then improved again.

"Hello?"

"You were look—"

"I'm listening," Winter said. "Have you found him?"

"He's here at the station," said the duty officer at the Lorensberg police station, the man Winter had spoken to before. "He came in with Ivarsson, who'd bumped into him in town. He's not on duty—"

"Make sure he stays there," Winter said.

"That won't be a problem. He says he wants to talk to you."

Morelius was in the television room. He stood up when they came in. He was wearing jeans, a black leather jacket, and black boots.

"I think I might be able to help you," he said. "I don't know." He looked at Winter, who didn't reply. An hour ago Winter had been ready to . . . to . . . Now he could grab hold of him, demand answers. He ought to get started.

"I understand that it's urgent," said Morelius, heading for the sink.

"Where do you think you're going?" Ringmar said.

"What the . . . ?" Morelius said. He stared at them, first at Ringmar, then at Winter. Something gave way in his face. "But, for Christ's sake, surely you don't think I did it?"

"The advertisement," Winter said.

"Eh? What advertisement?"

"We talked to your neighbor. He admitted that he'd been your . . . agent," Ringmar said.

"But, for Christ's sake, that's got nothing to do . . . I haven't even . . ." He turned to Winter. "Nothing came of it."

Winter took a step toward him.

"In that case you have kept from us important information—"

"We can deal with that later," Morelius said. "But is this urgent or not, Winter?"

"What do you mean?"

"There's evidence to suggest a police officer is involved. The uniforms and all that. Even we know that, the public order police. I've thought about it a lot. It has to do with the fact that I've been considering my position in the force. I'm packing it in, but I have a colleague. He wants to become a detective. He's got it into his head that it's a posher job." Morelius looked again at Winter. "I'm talking about Bartram. Greger Bartram."

"And?"

"You haven't heard what he's been saying lately. Haven't listened to him. Seen him. There's something funny about him. I don't know . . . I've thought a lot about it. Walked the streets. Took an extra day's leave. Thought about his right to play—" He turned to Winter again. "But then that business with your woman happened." He turned to Ringmar. "I tried to get hold of him at home, but he wasn't there. That's because he doesn't live there anymore. He moved out over a year ago, but he hasn't submitted his new address." Now he was looking at Ivarsson. "We've had his old address all the time."

"Where does he live now, then?" asked Ivarsson.

"It's called Tolsegårdsgatan. In Mölndal. I haven't been there, but—"

"How do you know?" asked Ringmar. "The new address, I mean?"

"Directory inquiries," Morelius said. "It was as simple as that."

"What is there about Tolsegårdsgatan," Winter said. "I recognize the name."

"It's at the end of Hagåkersgatan," Morelius said. "And that's close to where that couple was murdered. Or him . . . if she survives. Häradsgatan it was."

He didn't mention Kroken, Winter thought. Nor Manhattan Livs. Nobody outside my inner circle knows about Manhattan Livs. If he'd mentioned the shop, we'd have nailed him.

"Where did he live before?" Winter asked.

"Not far away," Morelius said. "Even closer to the building where the couple were killed." He paused. "There's a minimarket on the ground floor of the block, I think."

Before Winter had time to comment, Morelius held up his hand.

"Let me show you his computer."

"His computer?"

"This way," Morelius said. They went down the stairs and into the newly built extension on the other side of the courtyard. Nobody spoke. Morelius sat down in front of a computer and logged in. Waited, then tapped in a few commands. Waited again.

"You know what you're doing," Ivarsson said, who'd tagged along as well.

"Yes," Morelius said. "Computer knowhow isn't linked exclusively with crooked cops."

He keyed in another command, and turned to look at his audience. Then he turned back to the screen.

"What's that?" Winter asked.

"It's the list of names and addresses of those film extras who are making that television series." He looked at Winter, then back at the screen. "They all seem to be there. He's hacked into your files and stolen them."

They all stared at the screen.

"And there's more," Morelius said. "He seems to have access to more or less everything. He's either conducting some kind of investigation of his own, or else . . ."

"Has he never said anything about all this?"

"No." Morelius keyed in another command. "Look at this." Winter moved closer. "We have had his old address, not far from the scene of the crime, but he's hacked into the official files and changed it. According to what it says here, he lives in Hisingen."

Winter thought about all the police addresses they'd had for purposes of comparison. If he'd seen Bartram's address then—

Bartram had changed the official lists.

Always assuming they could trust Morelius.

"Is he off duty?" Winter asked.

"Yes," Ivarsson said.

"I'll drive," Ringmar said.

They drove past Krokens Livs, Manhattan. The film posters were still there. *City of Angels. The Avengers.* Ringmar parked in the street and they were out of the car even before it had stopped moving. Morelius was with them.

Winter had glanced at his watch. Past one. Happy birthday to you.

They passed the children's playground and some Dumpsters. The apartments were some fifty yards away, with the main entrance on the other side. A group of birch trees at the back of the building seemed to have been sprayed with silver. "Thirty-six," Morelius said. There was a light on in a second-floor window.

Winter tried the front door. It opened without his needing to shoot out the lock. Ringmar switched on the light. The stairwell walls were sky blue with a pattern in a darker shade. Lilac, Winter thought. Every detail was clear.

The front door of the apartment seemed to be of mock teak.

A police officer, Winter thought. How can you foresee that? The world has come to an end if police officers defect to the other side.

The stair light went out. They could see a light through the gap under the door. Winter rang the bell. Keep calm, Erik. We'll just ask him a few questions because we want to know. We want to know because there's no time left.

An image of Angela's face hovered in his mind's eye, but he knocked it aside with his knuckles as he pounded on the door.

"Who's that?" said a voice from inside.

Winter looked at Morelius and gave him the go-ahead.

"It's me, Greger, Simon. There's something I need your help with."

"Eh? Now?"

"It's urgent, Greger. Please let me in."

Not a sound from inside. Winter could feel his pistol rubbing against his chest, but left it where it was. He was calmer now, better prepared for what might be in store.

"You might have phoned," said the voice on the other side of the door.

"Why won't you let me in?" Morelius asked.

Winter announced his name. He knew that Bartram knew he was there.

He could hear noises on the other side of the door now. Ringmar looked at Winter. The noise grew louder. Winter could hear the music. Morelius looked confused, in the faint light on the landing. Winter could hear the guitars, the drums, the voice hissing and gurgling though the door. He was incapable of moving now. Ringmar did the shooting. Second time lucky, Winter thought. Morelius and Ringmar kicked in the door, forced their hands through the shattered plywood. Blood was pouring from Ringmar's hands. Morelius shouted something he couldn't make out. Ringmar's yell seemed to come from another planet.

They were in. He could hear the shouts. His body detached itself from the stone floor of the landing. He started running. He flew.

APRIL

57

Angela gave birth to Elsa at 3:15 A.M., two days after her due date. The girl weighed eight pounds, eight ounces and was nearly nineteen inches long. Winter kept dozing off, and handed the camera to the midwife.

He held Elsa close to his chest. She was asleep. Her hair was dark, and he was surprised by how dense it was. They said she had his nose and ears. He wept and hummed "You Leave Me Breathless" into those ears. For the last couple of weeks he had played nothing but Coltrane, and prayed for the future. The interrogation room was for others. He read the transcripts, but never went in there.

Angela leaned over and said something. He looked up when she repeated it. Yes, he agreed, it's a miracle.

Angela was radiant. It really was a miracle. One of these days it would all come back to her, but not now, he thought. Perhaps never. She was strong, stronger than he was.

They'd phoned Spain and he'd quickly handed the receiver to Angela.

The sun was emerging from behind the hills as he left the maternity clinic. He seemed to be entering a new world. The new year smelled different. It was spring. He could envisage the child going to school, playing in the street, throwing something. Did young kids still play marbles?

He got the sun in his eyes and lowered the visor. He drove away from Mölndal, but found it more and more difficult to see because of the tears in his eyes.

.   .   .   .   .

An elderly gentleman he didn't recognize passed him as he was walk-ing up the last flight of stairs. A gentleman visitor for Mrs. Malmer.

There was a different smell inside the flat. Not much different from outside. He opened all the windows. He went to the kitchen and opened a bottle, filled a crystal glass and drank.

Bartram had thanked him. Thanked him personally. Bartram had wanted to be saved, but he'd wanted to make it difficult for them. He'd come as close to Winter as it was possible to get.

Angela had come to no harm physically.

There had been a photograph hanging on the wall in Bartram's bedroom. A young man and a young woman. They were holding hands. Winter had taken a closer look. Their faces had been cut out and exchanged. He was she and she was he. The man's face was Bartram's. Younger.

Winter went to the living room that looked out onto the park, and stood in the window.

He drank away his thoughts. Two more days and there'd be an ex-tra resident in the apartment. He took another sip, the champagne tripped off his tongue. He turned around, and felt a twinge in his left knee. He almost lost his balance, paused for a moment, then went into the kitchen and put his glass on the draining board.